THE HARBINGERS

THE SUNDERING SERIES

BOOK 3

D RAE PRICE

DRaePriceBooks

Book Cover Design &
Illustration © Tom Edwards
TomEdwardsDesign.com

Library of Congress Control Number:2023905157
979-8-985-2043-7-7 (paperback)
979-8-985-2043-8-4 (e-book)

First Edition April 2023
Published by: DRaePriceBooks, Concord CA, USA
Contact: DRaePriceBooks@gmail.com

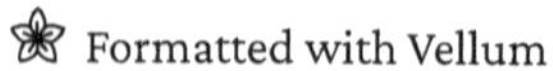 Formatted with Vellum

For my Family

CONTENTS

For printable maps and diagrams:
https://www.draepricebooks.com/maps-diagrams

LAGRANGE POINTS

Not to scale

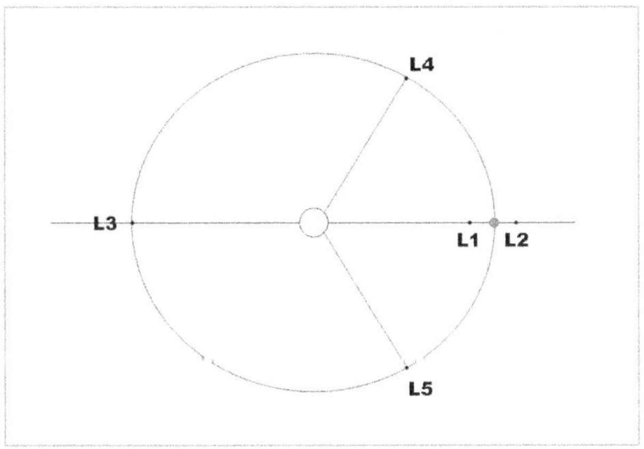

In space, for a planet orbiting its central star, there will be five places, called Lagrange Points, where gravity balances. A small object, such as a space station or asteroid, could be placed in those spots and stay there. This also works for some planet and moon systems. These points were discovered in the late-1700s by the mathematician Joseph-Louis Lagrange.

Three of these points, L1, L2, and L3, are "metastable." It's similar to a ball balancing on top of a hill. A small push will send it down the hill.

However, the L4 and L5 points are stable, as if the ball were inside a bowl. A little push will make the ball roll around in the bowl, but it won't get out. In fact, there are asteroids that ended up in the L4 and L5 points of many planetary orbits, especially the bigger planets like Jupiter. These asteroids are called Trojans.

To see maps and diagrams, go to:
https://www.draepricebooks.com/maps-diagrams

The Bahá'í Faith

The Bahá'í Faith is a real religion, founded by Bahá'u'lláh in the mid-1800s. The quotes used are real quotes from the Bahá'í Faith. For more information: https://www.bahai.us/.

The Badí' Calendar

The Badí' calendar, used by members of the Bahá'í Faith, is also a real calendar. New Year's Day is set on the spring equinox on Earth. It has 19 months of 19 days and 4-5 intercalary days, known as Ayyám-i-Há, so the calendar will match the solar year. The day begins and ends at sunset.

Names of the Months

(On Earth, dates vary slightly with the equinox, but these "set" dates are used in the sectors.)

- Splendor: Mar 21 - Apr 8
- Glory: Apr 9 - Apr 27
- Beauty: Apr 28 - May 16
- Grandeur: May 17 - June 4
- Light: June 5 - June 23
- Mercy: June 24 - July 12
- Words: July 13 - July 31
- Perfection: Aug 1 - Aug 19
- Names: Aug 20 - Sept 7
- Might: Sept 8 - Sept 26
- Will: Sept 27 - Oct 15
- Knowledge: Oct 16 - Nov 3
- Power: Nov 4 - Nov 22
- Speech: Nov 23 - Dec 11
- Questions: Dec 12 - Dec 30
- Honor: Dec 31 - Jan 18
- Sovereignty: Jan 19 - Feb 6
- Dominion: Feb 7 - Feb 25
- Ayyám-i-Há: Feb 26 - Mar 1
- Loftiness: Mar 2 - Mar 20

<u>Heading back to Earth:</u>
Oatah—Special Agent of Sector 1 Council, in charge of Project Restore and Project Contact
Reeder—Oatah's assistant

<u>On the *Drumheller*, stranded at the rogue planet after discovering the *81-Petals*</u>
Beezan—Captain of the *Drumheller*
Jarvie—Youth, Beezan's son, pilot in training
Iricana—Deputy of Oatah, relaying his orders to Captain Beezan
Katie—Doctor
Thunder—Mechanic, husband of Iricana
Kelson—Professor of botany, counselor, founder of the One Tree movement
Sequoia—Kelson's daughter, long jump pilot
Terina—Youth, Sequoia's daughter, journalist and historian
Sky—Beezan's black podpup, sister of Star
Star—Jarvie's white podpup, brother of Sky
Rocket—Terina's coffee and cream podpup

<u>On the *Cheetah*, just after escaping from the pocket universe</u>
Zahar—Youth, acting captain, former special monitor
Thayne—Former captain
Melawn—Thayne's data hunter
Nkiroo—Thayne's engineer
Tenshi—Thayne's doctor
Evan—Jump pilot, spouse of Caspia
Caspia—Crew doctor, spouse of Evan
Kiwi—Zahar's pastel green Ramian podpup
Quay and Family—Ramians rescued from the pocket universe

<u>On the shuttle *Enkindler*, in the a-rings at Friendship, trying to escape the system</u>
Lanezi—Long jump pilot
Euro—Youth, *Enkindler* crew, brother of Io
Io—Youth, *Enkindler* crew, brother of Euro
Whisper—Lanezi's silver mist podpup
Summer—Io and Euro's pastel yellow Ramian podpup
Dusty—Io and Euro's pastel pink Ramian podpup
Blueberry—Io and Euro's pastel blue Ramian podpup

Sector Map

Sector 1
San
Sector 2
Indigo
Sector 3
Malachite
Sector 4
Tropica
Azure
Athabasca
Sector 5
Cove
5, 15
Jump Days
Firelight
Friendship
Luminesse
—Down—
A-ring failure
1, 11
4, 14
Coralia
Sector 6
Canyon
3
8, 18
2, 12
Petrichor
Sector 7
7D
(abandoned)
Windswept
6
1, 11
Mirage
9
Atikameq
Terrace
Tektite
Harbor
2, 12
4, 14
Redrock
Tanuki
7, 17
3, 13
Tundra
Sandune
5, 15
4, 14
6, 16
Tetra
5, 15
Hamada
8, 18
Tyee
7, 17
Radium
Junction
Sector 8
(abandoned)

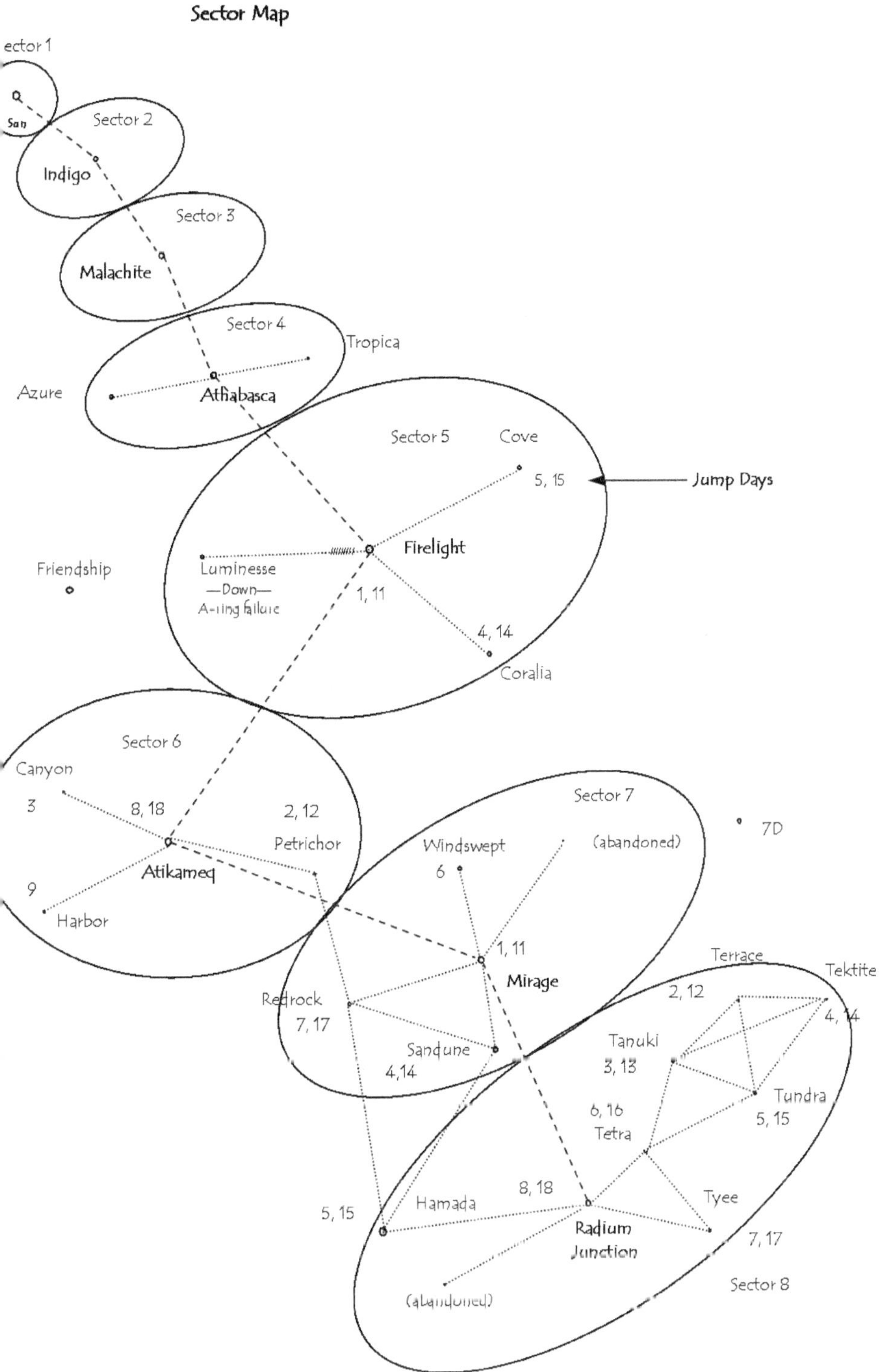

1 / COMING APART

Date: 3-Light-1084

Enkindler, outbound from Friendship

Aboard the shuttle *Enkindler*, in their suits, Lanezi and the twins, Io and Euro, gripped the arms of their chairs as Lanezi slipped into the one clear thread leading away from Friendship System.

The shock of learning at the last moment that the *Cheetah* had survived turned to despair as he realized that Friendship system was coming apart. The *Cheetah* may not have time to jump to safety.

The thread, the elusive jump path between the stars that they were riding, to whatever desperate destination Lanezi had sensed, was just about to drop them into normal space, when something catastrophic happened behind them, at Friendship. The thread snapped up, away from their destination, threatening to whiplash the *Enkindler* into oblivion. Vulnerable in their makeshift jump chairs, with tremendous gees crushing them and the shuttle, Lanezi hung on to the thread as it rebounded back down near the star. With his last conscious effort he tipped the *Enkindler* into normal space, praying for a rescue that they would surely need now.

"**Venting alert!**"

"**Auto stabilize complete.**"

"**Medical alert: Lanezi.**"

"**Medical alert: Euro.**"

"**Medical alert: Io.**"

"**Suit alert: Io.**"

"**Suit alert: Euro.**"

"**A-rings located. Course optimized.**"

The calm voice of the *Enkindler* contrasting with the terrifying venting alarm, the cries of Euro, and the silence of Io dragged Lanezi back to consciousness. Pain. Panic. His ribs were burning. *No. No. It's not supposed to be like this.*

"**Venting damage temporarily repaired. Command Bay doors sealed. Venting alarm canceled.**"

Lanezi gasped for air. "Pain meds, non-drowsy," he whispered. A sting hit his arm, but it gave no immediate relief. *The ship is working. Trust the ship. Trust the suits.* He just hung there in his restraints, trying to slow his heart and partition the panic. Looking through his helmet visor, he realized that debris was drifting around the Command Bay. He flicked through the screens on his helmet. *Still working, thank God. Air in the Command Bay. The computer is working. We jumped in a shuttle and we're still alive. Thank you. Thank you,* Lanezi prayed. *And if it's not too soon for another request, please help us stay alive.* But the shuttle was badly damaged. Despite the pain and confusion, he summoned some primitive parental strength to save the twins.

"Euro," Lanezi whispered, knowing Euro wouldn't speak first.

"Lanezi! Lanezi—Io, I can't see—my helmet is broken."

"Euro, Io is okay. His suit has been punctured, but repaired and he has air. He's breathing, but unconscious. He has lost some blood, but that's stopped. His light is yellow."

"Can I open my helmet? It's dark. I want to see." His voice was so scared and plaintive, Lanezi almost said yes. But his good sense was coming back.

"No. Not yet. I'm sorry. A few minutes. Close your eyes and I'll tell you everything." Lanezi slowly, carefully, got out of his chair, and holding one arm against his apparently-broken ribs, he started snagging the bigger debris while continuing, in gasps, to let Euro know what was happening. "Pups all have green lights. *Enkindler*, where are we?"

"System unknown. Multiple beacons. Ramian and other unknown signals."

"Engage Ramian translator. Send mayday in Ramian."

A schematic of the system appeared on Lanezi's helmet screen. Multiple planets, a-rings. "Ships! There are all kinds of ships, Euro. They're heading for the a-rings, like . . . like they're running away."

"From us?"

The Enkindler answered. **"Ramian ships are all proceeding to the a-rings at high speed. Ships from the third planet appear to be chasing them. Human beacon detected."**

"Attention Human vessel. You have entered Seven system. This is a restricted system in Ramian space. Send messages only during blackout periods for the third planet. Instructions follow. Cooperate with Ramian command."

Well, the *Enkindler* had been blasting their mayday for all to hear. Lanezi scowled. And didn't turn it off. *What have we stumbled into? "Enkindler*, view of the third planet."

The main screen was broken, but a popup slowly emerged from the panel showing a view of the third planet. Lanezi gasped, unable to put it into words. "Euro, open your helmet."

"It looks like Earth," Lanezi whispered in his confusion.

"No," Euro said, sensibly. Lanezi shook himself. "There's no moon," Euro explained. Of course not Earth. But some planet so much like it. Lanezi opened his helmet. He could see tears on Euro's face. He got vapor masks for the three of them and helped Euro out of the chair so he could go to Io, who was waking up.

"*Enkindler*, how much air, counting tanks?"

"**35 hours.**" *Oh my God. That's not much.*

"Time to a-rings?"

"**64 hours, 12 minutes.**" He stopped. Repeated the numbers to make sure he heard them right. *After all this? We can't make it? Stay calm. Think of it as a math problem.*

"Time for two people? No podpups."

"NO!" Euro cried, turning to Lanezi in shock.

There was no answer. "*Enkindler!*"

"**52.5 hours.**" *Okay. I won't have to make that decision, thank God.*

"*Enkindler*, add to mayday and focus broadcast to the Ramian ships. 'Human shuttle requesting rescue. Damaged. Not enough air to make it to a-rings. We need a pickup. Please. Two children aboard. Please.'"

"**Sent. 1.3 minutes lag time.**"

There were extreme spikes of radiation coming from the vicinity of the third planet. "**Explosion near Ramian ship,**" *Enkindler* reported.

"Another one!" Euro pointed with his suit finger.

"**Old records indicate this type of explosion is caused by weaponry.**"

"No," Lanezi whispered. A war is what they had stumbled into. Humans believed that any species advanced enough for space travel would have overcome its warring stage. They had always trusted that the universe, aside from being deadly in itself, was a fairly friendly place. But here was the contradictory evidence. And, he realized with a final bleakness, if the Ramians were running, no one would come back for them.

Drumheller, in orbit around the rogue planet

Beezan was with Sky in the Observation Bay where they'd been doing their social arts lately, forcing themselves to carry on, despite being stranded by the rogue planet. He had picked out music to represent their new situation, something that would take a lot of work, something hopeful. But now, he stared out the window at the rogue planet, the object that had derailed his life.

A gas 'giant' that wasn't even giant, Beezan couldn't believe it had yanked them out of a path and dumped them years from the nearest star. Cold, just one gray homogenous haze, with no bands or storms. No moons, no rings. Ejected from its birth system billions of years ago, its only distinction in creation was that it had captured *two* Human ships.

The first ship, the *81-Petals*, the ship designed and marketed to be the rejuvenator of humanity, orbited the gray planet in eerie silence. Besides the mayday beacon, there was no other contact, even after six days. The crew's initial excitement over discovering the long-lost ship was diminished by the silence. If anyone had survived, they were not answering—and the AI itself, despite Iricana's classified override codes, refused to respond.

Beezan let his mind wander down previously forbidden paths. Could he jump without a-rings? Or a gravity ball? Or even a gravity assist? Could he just find some slower magic jump velocity and drag the ship into a path? Was there some other way to reach jump velocity, even if it took a few years? Was there anything he could steal a gravity assist from? He still hoped that his instinct to sacrifice their speed for the *81-Petals* would be revealed as the right decision, but for now, they could only wait and worry.

Sky hopped from chair to chair behind him as he set out the music "Olympus Mons Ascent." Then he got his violin and stared out at the planet as he absentmindedly tuned up. He could feel the tension in his whole body stretch out along the bow, as if it would never be long enough to let it escape. He sighed and took a breath. He was just about to try again when he felt a tiny electrical snap in his implants.

What was that? He'd never felt anything like it.

Carefully, he set his violin down on a chair. Sky was looking away from the window, eyes unfocused, as if she were staring across the galaxy. The door opened and Sequoia stormed in, closely followed by a pale Jarvie. "Did you feel that?" Sequoia demanded.

"Yes. You did too?" He asked Jarvie, who nodded.

"I saw a thread, blue," she whispered, quickly adding, "just for a second."

"Don't worry. I'm not going to send you to counseling." Which was generally what happened to pilots who reported strange things. "Have you ever felt that before?" he asked.

"No."

"No," Jarvie answered, "but I didn't see anything."

"Me neither," Beezan added.

"It's especially strange as we're out here in the middle of nowhere," Sequoia said.

"Maybe it's something normal for the middle of nowhere," Jarvie speculated. But he only got a scowl from Sequoia. As

Katie, Thunder, Iricana, Kelson, and Terina came in, Beezan explained their incident.

"Hmmm," Kelson said, and offered an actual quote rather than an old saying, ***"Far be it from His glory that human tongue should adequately recount His praise, or that human heart comprehend His fathomless mystery."***[1]

As there was nothing to do about it, the crew took out their instruments and settled in, expressing with varying degrees of humor their appreciation for the difficulty of the music. There were parts with nice long chords that Beezan thought would create some unity.

They were lucky to have a well-matched group, with Beezan, Iricana, and Terina on violin, Sequoia on cello, Thunder on percussion, Katie on horn, and Kelson, who played everything, currently on string bass. Thunder had brought aboard a keyboard for Jarvie, who was doing well relearning the more difficult music.

They started playing, but every time they got the chords, Beezan winced, as if that little snap of electricity was hovering on the edge of the vibration. Sky whined and left, off to play with Star and Rocket rather than deal with it. Finally Sequoia stopped, leaning her head on the cello and closing her eyes.

"Mom, what's wrong?" Terina asked.

"I still feel something."

"What could possibly have such far-reaching resonance?" Thunder asked.

"Black hole merger?" Katie asked, but they shook their heads.

"Black hole explosion." Thunder suggested, wildly.

"We don't even know if that's possible," Iricana objected.

"Gravity ball," Jarvie said with a frown. He'd blamed other things on gravity balls, and he'd been right.

"The one at Daydream didn't cause anything like it," Beezan reminded him.

"You weren't there. Maybe we didn't notice. Or maybe it was a bigger gravity ball. Or maybe two of them."

The speculation was too much for Iricana. "Maybe we could just try a piece in a different key."

Cheetah, in the rings at Friendship

Finally, finally, they were in the rings. *Thank God*, Zahar breathed. *Cheetah* had held together long enough, and they were halfway to jump velocity. Three hours more; that's all they needed.

In the few frantic hours they had had to prepare the Ramians for the jump, the *Cheetah* crew had learned a most astonishing thing. The *Friend Quest*, the Ramian ship, had been sucked into the gravity ball vortex along with the *Cheetah*, and exited with the *Cheetah* three months later. But in the Ramian frame of reference, it had not been months. It had been years.

Almost nine years!

Both the Ramians and Humans were stunned. Even Thayne's genius was stumped, although he muttered something about gravity and time to Nkiroo. To Zahar's relief, the Friendship beacon confirmed that the *Cheetah* had suffered minimal timeslip.

Somehow, most of the Ramians had survived. They had collected energy from their strange environment to power their ship. But they were running out of things they couldn't replace. They were thin, stressed, and battling hopelessness. They were sustained by a mysterious young leader, Quay.

Dr. Tenshi managed to feed the Ramians, and Zahar found everyone a jump chair, medical bed, or emergency restraint. But that meant that many frightened Ramians were alone in *Cheetah* cabins. Quay sat with Caspia, monitoring the passengers. There was no time to make jump drugs for them, and Zahar had no intention of taking hers.

Friendship system was now Enemy system. They were detecting explosions farther out. Thayne and Nkiroo speculated that they were other gravity balls, self-destructing in some kind of mass malfunction. Evan and Nkiroo were constantly correcting navigation anomalies.

Something beyond human experience was happening. The outer planets were changing orbits, comets were coming in and asteroids were spiraling in towards the star. *Cheetah* was ahead of it all, but the whole system seemed to be in slow motion collapse.

The poor Ramians. Plucked from death twice in the last day, they now faced it again aboard an alien ship. The Ramian captain, Getti Fasandar, was seated next to Zahar. She glanced at Quay, on her other side. His white halo-like headband could not outshine the brightness of his eyes. They seemed to reach beyond the walls of the ship, to the literal and spiritual heavens. But Zahar met his eyes and found no calm or comfort there.

Zahar sent up her own prayer for the safety of the crew and Ramians. Every bump in the a-rings was one step closer to their escape from this nightmare. And if there was one thing in their favor—it was Evan. The wandering, hazy, distracted pilot of the past was still as sweet as ever, but focused and steady, as if he now stood on solid deck after years of aimless drifting on a tether.

Zahar had authorized everyone to see and hear the Command Bay feed, linking in the Ramian translator. Today was their shared destiny, dark as it might be. She caught words like *flux*, *roll*, *z-up* and *z-down*, words you never heard in the a-rings.

Evan's voice: steely, determined. Nkiroo: steady, but baffled. Thayne: controlled anger at the universe, but reporting on the deteriorating condition of the system and offering occasional suggestions. Melawn: tense, confirming Evan's navigation, a repetitive lifeline of human-calculated "On target," sometimes only seconds before they entered an a-ring segment.

"On target." They spent a few seconds in each a-ring segment at this point in the jump. Then the Path Adjustment Thrust bump, the surge, and the anxious waiting for the next "On target."

Another segment, the PAT bump, surge, and suddenly, a stray bump.

"Correcting!" From Evan.

"On target."

"Fuel?" Again from Evan.

"Good, even if we have to adjust every time," Nkiroo answered.

Segment. PAT bump. Surge.

"On—"

Another bump—big this time. Exclamations of alarm from the Command Bay. And then it was as if the *Cheetah* was snapped off the end of a giant whip. The forward view slewed into streaks of white star paths. Zahar's head jerked painfully inside her helmet.

"Abort!"

No! She cried to herself, and bit her lip to stay silent. But she knew there was no way to correct for such a thing.

"Segment hazard!"

Metal was screeching and they were pulling hard to the right. Zahar felt guilty for the relative safety of her cocoon. They had distributed as many cocoons and pressure suits as they could find, including one to the Ramian Getti, but Quay had refused.

"Segments continue to move!" Nkiroo said in alarm. "No way to predict course."

"Aborting!" Evan was flying by hand, she was sure. "Calc the go around!" It would take days to try again, Zahar despaired.

Before anyone could answer Evan, there was another huge fling. "Avoid!" She could see it on the screen this time, a segment spinning towards them, faster than they could move away. The ship strained and rolled, but they were too close. They would not miss it.

This is it then. A high-speed collision. We're done, Zahar thought, with heart-rending regret for her family. *We did everything we could.* She was heartbroken that it would end like this, especially for the Ramians, who had waited nine years for a rescue that was not to be. She glanced at Quay. Somehow fighting the gees they were pulling, he raised his hands from the chair in supplication, bright eyes raised to heaven. Zahar strained to raise her hands to join him. We'll be saved by a miracle, or we'll go with joy. There were murmurs of prayers and love over the com system. And then they slammed into the edge of the a-ring segment.

Cheetah, in the destroyed a-rings at Friendship System

Zahar blacked out from the impact, but only for a few seconds. The sickening spinning triggered her stomach meds and again, she felt bad for the unsuited Ramians. She expected to see the ship peel apart and wondered how long they would live. "Engine hit!" Nkiroo shouted after a few seconds of spinning, jolting, and alarms.

"Thrusters," Evan ordered. Evan. Battling the chaos. Bringing the ship to stability. "Course?"

"Anywhere," Nkiroo said tensely. "The a-rings are gone."

"Radiation alarm. The engine casing is breeched," Melawn added quietly. "*Cheetah*, advise on repairs."

Images of the damage crossed her helmet screen. Zahar was astonished that their systems were still working. The main body of the ship had not been hit. The cargo cylinder and engine were severely damaged and partially detached. Evan had somehow stopped their spinning completely. They hung in nogee, gasping. There was no possible way to repair it—and highly dangerous radiation was spewing out by the second.

"Radiation levels increasing," the *Cheetah* warned.

Zahar's captaining instinct kicked back in. "Decouple it!"

Thayne's tight angry voice chimed in, "We have no other means to escape this system."

"It'll kill us!"

"It might be repairable," Thayne insisted, against all reason. They didn't decouple.

Furious, Zahar reached for her restraints. But Getti Fasandar stretched his arm out to stop her.

"Good God," Melawn whispered. "The star." The screen switched to the star. They could now see major stellar flares. "The whole system is coming apart."

"*Cheetah*," Evan asked, "Calculate a gravity assist with the speed we have."

"Too many variables."

"Melawn, can you?" Evan was asking the near impossible, but before Melawn could answer, they were whiplashed again. Zahar must have blacked out, because the ship was already stabilizing when she was able to focus again.

"The a-ring gravity ball exploded," Thayne reported through gritted teeth, as if all this was a personal affront.

"Ship detected." *Cheetah* reported. There was a beat of silence in the Command Bay. All the screens switched to a seemingly blank part of space. **"Unknown beacon. Strong signal. Approaching fast. Not Human. Not Ramian."**

"Send a mayday!" Zahar ordered. *Any port in a storm.*

The ship became visible, approaching at amazing speed.

"They're veering off," Nkiroo explained. "Stopping."

"It's the radiation from the engine!" Zahar practically shouted. "They won't get near it."

Reluctantly Thayne agreed. "Yes, emergency decouple."

Apparently, he'd taken command again and the others had let him. But at least he was doing the right thing now.

Miraculously, nothing hung them up during the decoupling. Once they were detached, Evan wasted no time, angling the *Cheetah* toward the alien ship. The main engine was left behind, but it felt like the thrusters were all still working.

"They're coming!" Melawn announced, as the alien ship started toward them again. Zahar breathed a sigh of hope.

As the ship came closer her hope was tinged with fear. *What is that?* A huge, dark, viperhead ship looked like it was towing a small gravity ball.

"That little gravity ball is pushing them!" she heard Nkiroo say. *Alien.* The Ramian ships hadn't created the same unease. She scolded herself for doubts. *It's our only chance.* Immediately, she went to planning mode. She flicked through her life support screens. They had lost a few Ramians. *So sorry. Go in peace.* She'd have to say formal prayers later. They would have to transfer over in the shuttle as quickly as possible. Food. Who knows what they were going into. *What about air? What if they don't breathe the same air?* Then there would be no hope.

But the aliens had different ideas.

"They're coming too close," Evan fretted.

"Trust them. Don't deviate," Thayne insisted.

"I think they'll pass over us," Nkiroo whispered. "Just barely."

"Top view," Nkiroo said, but the ship was already so close, it filled the whole screen. And then the *Cheetah* jolted. Metal screeched and alarms went off. "Towing clamp of some sort!" Nkiroo shouted.

Oh, no. We have to survive in the Cheetah? Zahar started looking through her screens for life support figures. How much air is even left in the ship?

"Nav still operational. We are speeding up," Melawn said as Zahar was pressed back in her seat.

"Stress on the ship?" Evan asked.

"We're holding together, for now," Nkiroo answered.

The camera switched to the rear view. "We're going to jump!" Evan warned.

How can we jump in this condition? Zahar worried. And then they did jump—for just a second. And then again, and again, stuttering in and out of jumpspace like a light passing by a grill. They were getting farther from the a-rings.

"Star," Melawn managed to say and the camera changed. Something bizarre was happening to the Friendship star. It was elongating, and for just a moment, it was as if they could see the rim of another star beneath it.

The jumping flashed faster and faster, quicker than a person could capture. Were they in jumpspace or normal space? Some sort of malfunction?

And then the star went nova. Zahar turned her face away. "Radiation shields already maxed!" Nkiroo reported.

And then they jumped for real, deep into the path. Even Zahar could feel it. Zahar tried to hang on, to know what would happen next, but against her will, she dropped into oblivion.

4-Light

Enkindler, incoming to a-rings at Seven System

Would I come back? Lanezi wondered, as he watched the Ramian ships in the a-rings, trying to escape the fighting at the third planet. *If I were a Ramian captain, running for my life, would I risk everything to rescue an alien shuttle? With no promise of success?* Already tested, he knew the answer. He remembered with shame that he had walked away from Whisper and would have abandoned the wrecked

Ramian ship at Harbor. He could not pretend to be more valiant than he was. *But the twins.* They had insisted on the rescue. And they would go back, even for a stray old podpup. If there was any karma to leverage their fate, it balanced on the selflessness of Euro and Io. For him, there was no hope anyway. He would die today, or after a painful, ugly death from radiation poisoning.

When the Ramian ships did not respond, Lanezi was forced to face the fact that they only had a day to live. He got them out of their suits, and with false optimism, prepped the suits for another use. He checked the injury on Io's leg. "That must hurt," Lanezi commented. Io looked down.

"It is nothing," he said quietly. They washed and said prayers together, reading some of their favorite passages. Lanezi made them drink a little. The pups were deeply hibernating, but they took them out of their box and held them.

When the Ramian ships in the a-rings reached .5JV, Lanezi asked the twins to record their final messages. They sent joint messages, one quick message to the *Cheetah* crew and a long one of love to their family. Io quoted from memory: ***"Set all thy hope in God, and cleave tenaciously to His unfailing mercy."***[1]

Euro followed with ***"If the heart turns away from the blessings God offers how can it hope for happiness? If it does not put its hope and trust in God's Mercy, where can it find rest?"***[2] And then they sang a prayer together, reducing Lanezi to gutwrenching sobs that made his ribs hurt even more. But they patted him on the back, absolved him of any responsibility for their situation, and in their innocent way, professed their devotion to him.

Lanezi would have just rested there in nogee until the end, even though it was yet hours away, but he had to report on Friendship's condition, the explosion of the Ramian ship, and the possible loss of the *Cheetah*. He attached details of Seven system and pictures of the fighting. He didn't know if the Ramians would send it through to Human space, but he asked them anyway, especially about the destruction at Friendship. He sent it through the Ramian translator too, in case they had any ideas of going that way.

Afterwards, they napped a bit, even though they tried not to. Then Io asked, "Do you think the *Cheetah* is okay?"

"I don't know" Lanezi said sadly. "Something violent happened at Friendship, something bad enough to snap the thread between the stars, to change the resonance, maybe even break the path."

"You mean the *Cheetah* has no way out of there?" Euro asked.

"I don't know," Lanezi whispered. "The star might be a supernova now, or some strange new kind of nova."

"But they have Evan," Io reminded them. And the twins bowed their heads in silent prayer.

After a moment, Lanezi said, "*Enkindler*, show Friendship system."

Of course, it looked fine. The view was lightyears old. "I fear they are lost. No one can risk jumping in there with the a-rings down."

"But on the threads," Euro asked, "everything is in real time?"

"Yes."

"If we jump again, do you think you could see what happened?"

Dangerous talk. "I only ever see the threads," he insisted. "And I never look for anything else." *But if I'm dying anyway? And we do get to the a-rings? Maybe one quick look . . .*

And then a blip appeared on the ship tracker. **"New ship detected."**

Lanezi suffered a sickening surge of hope and despair. **"Unknown origin."**

"From the third planet?" He asked.

"No. It is not Human, not Ramian, not of the third planet. It appeared in normal space near the third planet."

"Wow," Euro said, excited in spite of their situation. Without hesitation, as soon as the ship got near the third planet, the planetary people unleashed their exploding weapons. But the new ship blinked out of normal space and appeared farther out, unscathed.

"They are more advanced than we are," Euro whispered.

"Way more," Io agreed.

A foggy barrier suddenly surrounded the third planet and the explosions stopped.

Way way way more, Lanezi agreed. *Could they have destroyed Friendship?* Then their one unbroken screen went white. A strange logo flashed on the screen and disappeared before they could take it in. The face of a creature, lizard-like and frightening, appeared. Ziz jaw was moving, but not in a Human way. The voice must have been translated by the aliens themselves.

"Listen / Comprehend / HARKEN to the GenTwo:

"This backward / defective / PRIMITIVE system is declared outlaw / reckless / UNWORTHY. It is declared GenSix!" Even the translated voice was filled with distaste.

"It is now barred / cordoned / QUARANTINED from the people / mature generations / CIVILIZATION for safety / propriety / ORDER."

Lanezi stopped breathing. "Aliens!" Io gasped. Euro watched, wide-eyed.

"The Chike are merciful / benevolent / INDULGENT. The Grand Announcement is granted / gifted / APPLIED."

It got even louder. "Hear this! / Hark! / ATTENTION! Produce your herald / forerunner / HARBINGER or any beholder / onlooker / WITNESS, before your system is disabled / closed / SEALED. You eluding / fugitive / FLEEING ships will be pursued / followed / CHASED! The harbingers will be collected / found / HUNTED. The Chike will know by signs / portents / MIRA-CLES!" The screen went off and the word miracles reverberated through their crippled shuttle.

Lanezi sucked in a breath of air. "The Chike? Is this really happening?" With one incredible incident after another, he was beginning to doubt his sanity. He studied Euro and Io. Still wearing the masks, shiny, dark faces strained from the last few hours, and gaunt from the rationing, they looked as shocked as he felt. And would it be ungrateful to wish to live long enough to see what happened? He checked his pain meds to make sure he hadn't had an overdose. No. "What next?" he whispered and then kicked himself for hexing them when he heard a beep. *"Enkindler?"*

"Incoming message. Tight beam, nav data, sent from a Ramian vessel."

Two trajectories appeared on the screen. One showed a ship coming out of the a-rings and circling around to meet a ship that was obviously meant to be the *Enkindler*. "It's an intercept path. They're using the speed they got from the a-rings to get out here," Lanezi gasped, about to force down another surge of hope. But the twins looked at him with wild expectation, and hope swelled in his heart. He grabbed one of their precious protein bars and broke it in three pieces. "Eat!" They'd said their last prayers properly. "We're going to *struggle / persevere / FIGHT* to the end!"

. . .

Io had only seven minutes of air left in his suit. So *Enkindler* calculated when Euro, Lanezi, and the podpup box would have to go back on the tanks so they would all come down to seven minutes together. Io now had the broken helmet on, since he wasn't sure he could walk, if there were gravity. The podpup box was strapped to Io and he had his arms around it. They tried to be ready for anything.

"Three hours to intercept. Three hours, 12 minutes of air remaining." One Ramian ship had boosted out of the a-rings at .8JV, unchallenged by the Chike ship, which remained parked over the third planet. It had allowed all the other Ramian ships to jump, but had sent a small ship after them, keeping the mini-gravity ball with the parentship. *Who are we dealing with?*

Lanezi sent a message to the Ramian ship saying they had no jet packs and could not dock. He feared they would not get aboard in time. And yet they were so close.

The Ramian ship became a silvery ball when it was only an hour away. "Human ship, prepare to enter our hangar." Lanezi could see nothing but fuzz and had no idea what to do. *CALM,* he told himself. *Patience. Don't breathe hard. Don't talk. Don't look at the clock.*

"Ramian transmission. No translator needed:"

"Greetings Human ship. This is Neah, aboard the *Watcher*, commanded by Getti Drann. We will reach you in seven minutes." *I sure hope their seven minutes is the same as ours.*

"Euro, do you want to be monitor?"

Euro straightened in nogee and answered in his most eloquent voice. "God is Most Glorious. This is *Enkindler* under command of Captain Lanezi. I am Europa, and I will be your monitor. We greatly appreciate your assistance." Lanezi couldn't help smiling at the proper message.

The silvery shield vanished. Beneath it, a spectacular spherical ship was revealed, and most beautiful of all, a huge hangar door was opening. "Follow the guide signal."

"*Enkindler*, can you do it?" Lanezi didn't trust himself. His hands were shaking and he was getting dizzy.

"Targeting guide beam."

"Euro, tell them our status."

"*Watcher, Enkindler*. We have 12 minutes of air."

The Ramian Neah dropped the formalities. "You will make it. A team is standing by."

Euro and Lanezi already had their helmets on. Lanezi checked the time. "Seven minutes. Io, secure your helmet." When Io's helmet was secure, Lanezi gave the command to blow the hatch, before they got inside the hangar.

At last, they carefully flew past the hangar door. Inside, the high walls were not the bare metal of Human construction, but material that glistened with paintings of huge trees. It was like landing in a forest.

The *Enkindler* was compensating for damaged thrusters, so the entry was somewhat uneven and the last blip of adjustment left them drifting slightly within the hangar. But two big grappling arms swooped down and nearly crushed them to the hangar deck, jolting Lanezi's already painful ribs. *Four minutes.*

Euro had an exterior camera on, and gave a cry of delight as suited figures stormed toward them, throwing protective covers over the hatch. Lanezi got out of his straps. "There's gravity. Euro, help Io."

"I've got him."

Lanezi had planned to stand back and make sure the twins got out first, but he was grabbed, pulled out the hatch and across the short deck. His ribs screamed in pain, but it was his hope and relief that left him breathless. *We're going to make it!* They were stuffed in an airlock, painted like clouds and sky.

The interior airlock doors opened. Lanezi was pulled into the ship. There were blue and purple Ramians with no helmets. Their headbands of light blazed in white, red, tan, and bright blue. Euro and Io were right behind him. He reached for his helmet visor and unsealed it. AIR. Sweet, amazing, *warm* air. He'd been cold for so long, he'd forgotten about it. Euro had unsealed his own visor and was pulling off Io's helmet. Both twins gasped with pleasure. The first words that came out of their mouths were praises to God.

The Ramians had taken the box and opened it, pulling out the pups. And wonder of podpups, they were awake. The Ramian holding Blue pulled off his helmet, revealing his pink color with a blazing purple stripe. Blue looked up at him and declared "Happy!" and everyone broke into laughter.

"I am Neah," he said, smiling—and speaking in Alkulu. "Getti Drann welcomes you aboard. We are delighted to see our Human friends again."

Again?

"Thank you," Lanezi panted. And having no cultural knowledge, he reached for Neah's arm and gripped it. "We owe you our lives." And then his laughter turned to tears of relief.

A Ramian next to Neah reported to their Getti, "Three Humans, four podpups alive. They send their greetings and thanks."

"Good," answered a stern and harassed voice, this time over Lanezi's translator. "Get to Med. We need to move."

3 / HELL AND HEAVEN

5-Light

Chike ship, leaving Friendship System

For a moment, when she awoke, Zahar thought she was in hell. Surrounded by black and red striped membranes, with heat that left her dripping and parched, and a low-level vibration that set her teeth on edge, it fit her hazy recollection of ancient stories about the underworld.

"Chike ship," Caspia's stressed voice whispered.

"We've been drugged," Tenshi added disapprovingly.

Zahar tried to swallow, but it took several attempts. She struggled to sit, but the room, disorienting with its red and black lines fanning every which way, just made her reel. "Easy," Tenshi said, taking her arm and helping her sit propped against what was apparently, a wall. They were all still in their suit underwear and socks, without shoes. Zahar looked around in growing alarm. "Where are the others?"

"We were separated, soon after they took us," Caspia answered.

Zahar tried to remember, but shook her head—and winced —in confusion.

"You were still unconscious," Tenshi explained. "They latched onto our ARC 1 hatch and came aboard."

"They are lizard-like creatures. This room is only a meter tall." Caspia reached up and poked the ceiling right above her head. "They had translators. They said we had to come with them. Quay encouraged calmness, but Thayne went crazy," Caspia continued. "He refused to go. Melawn and Nkiroo tried to convince him, but it was futile. The Chike just made him unconscious somehow. It didn't seem to hurt him."

"I fear Thayne has truly gone over the edge," Tenshi mused.

Zahar's mind was fuzzy and claustrophobic. But she worried that Tenshi must not be thinking clearly either, if Thayne's mental state was her biggest concern. And Caspia wasn't as focused or concerned as she normally would be.

"The Ramians? Quay? Their Getti?"

"All taken. We made sure," Caspia assured her. "We made them count. The *Cheetah* was lost. They did seem to have a sense of responsibility. Three bodies were taken too."

"Kiwi?" Zahar asked.

Caspia grasped her arm and squeezed it. "They brought him. We hope he's with the others."

Zahar tried to clear her mind, but it just wasn't working. "So we've been, umm, abducted by aliens who live inside the wormguts of hell, been drugged, and we have no idea what's happening, where we're going, or if the others are okay."

"Right," Tenshi confirmed. "We've jumped multiple times. Friendship System is far away now." Tenshi felt around for a shiny faucet. "Here. It fills a little depression and you can drink it."

"What is it?"

"Water," Tenshi said. "Didn't kill us."

Zahar turned it on and scooped it up with her hands, many times, to get enough to drink. "Food?"

"Nothing yet," Caspia answered. "We don't have our p'links, but we think it's been a day or so."

"Oh," Zahar sighed as she realized. "The drugs are in the water." But Caspia and Tenshi were already nodding off.

"The drugs are wearing off," Nkiroo whispered to Melawn. Melawn frowned and nodded. He scooped up the water with two handkerchiefs, so that Thayne could have a long drink. And the more Thayne drank, the more he slept, mercifully for the three of them. Except it wasn't working anymore. Melawn and Nkiroo had been drinking and sleeping fitfully in turns, but it was unnecessary now. The drugs had kept the fear down, but with the rise of fear was also the rise of hope.

There must have been something in the water to reduce hunger too, but as that wore off, Melawn began to think of food more than anything else. When a slot in the wall opened and a food tray finally appeared, he quickly reached for it, not wanting to lose their chance. Three plates with equal food were on the tray. "We need a proper table and chairs!" Thayne demanded to the air, as Nkiroo and Melawn were already scooping the food up with their hands.

Astonishingly, the room buzzed a bit and then a small table and three chairs grew out of the deck. If they'd sat in the chairs, they would have smashed their heads on the low ceiling, so it was pointless. But Nkiroo was thrilled. "On demand engineering!" He put his hand on the table and said, "Shorter." It began to lower. "Stop." It stopped. "No chairs," and they went away. "Amazing!" he said with approval.

"Do not let our captors win you over," Thayne hissed.

Despite the uncertainty, Melawn was hopeful. So far, no harm had come to them, and considering the condition of the *Cheetah*, the Chike lizards had probably saved their lives. He set the food tray on the table and they sat cross-legged around it. "Utensils. Napkins." Thayne demanded, and they appeared. Nkiroo and Melawn looked at each other sheepishly. They were half done. But they switched over to civilized eating.

"It looks like Earth food," Thayne said. "Like farm food."

"It's good," Nkiroo assured him.

When they were done, Melawn put the tray back by the slot. "Exit, please," he requested, but nothing happened. There didn't seem to be any sedative in the food, but just eating made them drowsy again. "Beds," Melawn whispered, and three small foam pads appeared. He collapsed on one, sleeping soundly, the food having banished his fear for the moment.

Zahar set her hand next to the water faucet and sighed, "We really need a cup." A cup formed, seemingly out of the deck. She jumped back. "Did you see?"

Caspia and Tenshi crawled over to look, nodding their heads. Zahar filled the cup and handed it to Tenshi, who drank and handed it to Caspia. "The drug is gone," Tenshi said. "Or we've adapted to it." Caspia nodded.

"Maybe," Zahar said, and then addressed the ceiling. "Paint the walls white." There was a flicker and the whole room became blinding white. "Whoa! Too much. Make the deck brown." She tapped the deck. "Make the four walls cream." She pointed. "And the ceiling blue." In a moment it was as she directed.

"Oh my God," Tenshi said, "Zahar, you're a genius."

"Temperature, decrease five degrees Celsius." Caspia patted her on the back, smiling. And strangely, a table appeared with utensils and napkins on it. They jumped when a slot opened and a food tray slid in.

"Thank heavens," Tenshi whispered. "They don't mean to starve us." They sat at the table, eating ravenously, whispering what else they should ask for, but not wanting to press their luck.

When they were done eating, they agreed on one thing to request. "The other Humans," Zahar said. "We want to see them." But nothing happened.

Watcher, Seven System

Delirious with joy and overwhelmed with recent events, Lanezi allowed himself to be swept along to the Ramian med center. Maybe he was imagining things, but he thought he saw birds. Birds of happiness maybe. Whisper, awake and excited, was demanding food from the Ramians. Lanezi tried to stay in charge of the twins, but it was futile, and unnecessary. A big hard knot in his stomach started to unwind as he realized his long, stressful captaincy was over.

The Ramian med center was like a high-tech art museum. Lanezi couldn't even take it in. Io was up on what must have been an exam bed, with several Ramians surrounding him. Other Ramians led Lanezi to a different exam bed, and gently pulled off his suit.

The bed was a reclined chair, like a luxury version of the

jump chair. "Neah, I'm Neah," the Ramian reminded Lanezi, as the chair rose up to eye-level. "I'll help you. Here. The podpup doctors have arrived," and he gently slid Whisper away from Lanezi.

"Be back," she said easily, as if it was a regular day and she was going for a snack break.

The doctors admired Whisper's color and puzzled over the others. "How do you have Ramian podpups?" Neah asked.

"An accident."

Neah frowned. "Where?"

"Well, we call it Harbor."

"Harbor. Yes. We know of that one." He hesitated. "Any Ramian survivors?"

"Two. Babies. They're probably still at Harbor. And six pups. One is with my parentship, the *Cheetah*, and the other two are with the babies at Harbor." Neah nodded. "How can you speak Alkulu?" Lanezi asked.

Neah touched his chest and bowed slightly. "I am life-friend with Beezan, Captain of the *Drumheller*. Do you know him?"

Drumheller. KATIE! Lanezi grabbed Neah's arm. "Katie! Do you know her? Did you meet her? Is she okay?" And Neah's colors changed to a lively pink as he grasped Lanezi's hand. "Yes! Yes! Katie was quite well. You are that same Lanezi then? I wondered when I heard your name. Small galaxy." They laughed. "To be married soon?"

"God willing." And then Lanezi sobered. "When we're united." *Which might be too late now.* Lanezi didn't know how long he would live. Or even if he wanted to subject Katie to a short marriage.

Neah tilted Lanezi back into the chair as the doctor came. A colorful box was set to buzzing on his chest. The doctor frowned at the box, while Neah attached a small translator to Lanezi's ear. "Captain," the doctor said gravely to Lanezi, and Neah froze in alarm, colors going dark gray with an orange stripe. "What have you done?"

Lanezi met the doctor's eyes. The radiation must have been worse than he thought. "The twins?" he asked.

"They show signs of mild radiation exposure. Nothing we can't easily treat. I suspect they are naturally resistant."

"Yes. I was counting on it."

"Your situation is . . . serious. Extreme treatment must start immediately. You've cut it close."

"You have a treatment?" Lanezi held his breath. The doctor looked at him again, colors unreadable under a hood. "You allowed yourself to be poisoned thinking there was no treatment?"

"I hoped to save the twins," he whispered. "They don't know."

The doctor brushed off his hood, revealing a strong yellow. "You did." He called a couple of assistants. "Neah, explain he must appoint. He'll be regenerating."

"Regenerating?" He must have looked frightened, but really, it was better than being dead. It was just so . . . sudden.

Neah put his hand on Lanezi's head, where his colors would be if he had any. *What exactly were they going to do?* "Do you freely submit to this procedure?"

"It will help?"

"It will save you."

Lanezi heard himself agree. "Bring the pup back," Neah said.

It *was all too good to be true. Even the part that Neah spoke Alkulu. And he knew Katie. Small galaxy. Too small.* And then Lanezi realized with desolation that he was dreaming. It was too much of a coincidence. *It's all a delusion. We've run out of oxygen in the shuttle. This is all just wishful thinking.*

But such a persistent vision. Neah put his hand on Lanezi's forehead again. "Have no fear. We have Human medical records. And we've pulled data from your shuttle. We'll see you in a couple of weeks."

"Weeks?" Lanezi murmured. *I'm dreaming. I'm dying. But why am I going to Ramian heaven?*

4 / THE FIRST HARBINGER

13-Light

Chike ship, location unknown

Melawn stretched out on the deck of the Chike room, reaching over his head with his arms, closing his eyes and trying to forget he was imprisoned on a ship that was a claustrophobic meter tall. *I'm on the Cheetah. No, I'm on Harbor station. I'm on Earth and I can reach up to the clouds.* But he wasn't sure that was how it worked. Probably you had to stand on a mountain to reach the clouds. And then he was embarrassed that an educated Human wouldn't know basic things about the home planet.

I'm going to go there, he determined. *When we escape the Chike. When we get back to the sectors. When we fix the Firelight a-rings. If Thayne lets—*

Melawn curled into a little ball as his dreams deflated. Thayne's constant anger was wearing him down. There was no escape from it in this small space. Their room was exquisite now: painted in the most delicate colors, decorated with shimmering art, temperature perfect, facilities elegant, with a small privacy screen. But that was the only screen allowed. Once, when Nkiroo and Thayne were sleeping, Melawn had begged for a wall, a private spot. He was past fear of being separated. He only wanted peace.

Melawn's clothes were back to the usual white and gold that Thayne insisted on, and he had a blanket that looked like the expensive wool that Lanezi wore. He had a pang of worry, wondering what happened to the *Enkindler,* and feeling like, somehow, he'd let everyone down. *I'll never get to Earth.* Thayne was right of course. As fancy as their room got, they were still prisoners.

Nkiroo had ordered a small lap desk. He couldn't get a pad, but he got old-fashioned pens and notebooks out of the Chike. He sat, designing ships. Melawn crawled over to Nkiroo and sat next to him, trying to calm himself in Nkiroo's familiar presence. Melawn watched Nkiroo sketching a spaceship. Drawing was a mystery to Melawn, and he was amazed how Nkiroo could create a 3D object without a computer. The ship Nkiroo was drawing was sleek and beautiful, nothing like the wheel and canister reality of current ships. Nkiroo started explaining his design, tapping on the page several times, louder each time. Finally, Melawn turned on his brain and focused.

Scanning the line of the ship, following Nkiroo's finger, he noticed little decorative areas with intricate swirls. *Letters!* Hidden on the page. And if he found a set of letters in one area, they made a word.

Find. Others. Cooperate.

"Yes, nice design," Melawn said.

But how to find the others? The Chike were clearly invincibly powerful. Nkiroo tapped again. Cooperate. Melawn shrugged. There was nothing to cooperate with at this point. Patience. Nkiroo tapped. Code.

Knock code? *Too easy.* The Chike would get that in a minute. It had to be hard. And Human specific. But easy enough for the others to understand. If they ever found each other. Something medical? Something with colors, for the Ramians? Melawn frowned and started to think. Something from *The Hidden Words*? They'd all memorized the numbered passages.

The food slot slid open. "Wrong time," Nkiroo whispered. Thayne's eyes popped open but he didn't move. There was a rustling, some breathing, and a man crawled slowly into their room.

Melawn's heart leaped. "Evan?"

A half-relieved, half-terrified gasp escaped the man. "Yes."

Melawn and Nkiroo scrambled across the deck. Evan was pale and shaking. He was dressed in a fuzzy one-piece suit. He grabbed them both. "Evan! Thank God!" Nkiroo said. The three of them hugged awkwardly, balancing on their knees, while Evan clutched them and sobbed.

"I thought I was alone," he choked out. "I haven't seen anyone. Is Caspia here?" They shook their heads no.

"Bring him over," Thayne said mildly, with more compassion than Melawn had heard in a long while. They made a spot for him at their little table and Thayne gave him his uneaten food. Evan looked around desperately.

"We haven't seen the others—Ramians or Humans," Nkiroo explained. "But we've no reason to believe they mean us any harm."

Evan held his chest, sipped some water and tried to find his voice. "Med. Hospital." He pointed to his head. "They fixed my implants."

Thayne's dark eyes flashed. "Aliens did brain surgery on you?"

Nkiroo was feeling Evan's head and looking puzzled. "No cutting," Evan explained. "Like a computer game. One nano at a time, they fixed them."

"Why?" Melawn asked.

"They didn't say. But I think it was for my own good. I had so much pain. Those last three jumps. When we jumped out of Friendship. I kept seeing something, like an exploding supernova." He frowned at them. "Either my implants were malfunctioning, or something horrible happened at Friendship. Or both." Melawn scowled. *A lot horrible happened at Friendship.*

"Are you in pain now?" Nkiroo asked.

"No."

"But you were awake during the procedure?" Thayne asked.

"Yes. No pain but scary. They're so scary. They don't like us. We're unclean or something."

"The sticks?" Nkiroo asked. "Like the ones they had when they took us off the ship?"

"The prods, yes. They make me move. They never touch me, except with the prod, or some other equipment. They look away when they deal with me. If I talk to them they poke harder. Twice, I got a little shock."

Thayne sank into his dark brooding mode. "Okay, Evan," Melawn reassured him. "Try to eat. You're safe now."

"No. You don't understand. None of us are safe."

15-Light

Watcher

Lanezi's warm, soft drifting was occasionally disturbed by

unwelcome clanging, poking, or unintelligible voices. Some-where in his deep being he knew they were the sounds of the outside world, where his body lived. But for now, however long that was, he ignored it.

Floating in his universe wasn't boring. It just was. He was free of the ticking mental clock, free to be a spirit unbounded. So many scenes to paint. Stars, threads, planets with amazing lighting. But slowly, he became more aware of the exterior world. He realized that he was breathing; part of the outer world was coming inside him. And after that, it was harder to go back to the drifting.

Then a strange thing happened. A little thing crossed his mind, like a shooting star. A worry. *Where are the twins?* And then, once he focused on that, fireworks of worries followed. *Where am I? What's happening?* Overwhelmed by the brightness of the worries, he retreated again into his soft universe.

16-Light

Chike ship

Zahar, Caspia, and Tenshi sat in contemplation after their morning prayers and singing. Zahar wasn't able to entirely quiet her mind from the constant, but useless, fretting. She updated their calendar with the Chike-provided crayon. Twelve days since their arrival, give or take a couple. It really wasn't that long. It only seemed long when you wondered if it would be the rest of your life.

They had sent notes out with their food and received no response. They had lectured, pleaded, and ranted at the walls. Nothing. They had requested outrageous items, like laser cannons or axes. Nothing. They considered hunger strikes and escape, but discarded such crazy thoughts. The Chike were clearly in control. They were trapped, like rats.

"I used to play the pipa," Tenshi said as they started breakfast.

"Why didn't you have social arts on the *Cheetah*?" Caspia asked.

"Thayne didn't like it," she replied.

"It's required," Caspia pressed.

"I know. But Lanezi, Nkiroo, Thayne, and Melawn didn't play."

"They don't do anything they're not the best at," Zahar complained.

Tenshi scowled, but didn't deny it. "It seemed pointless to force the issue." She sighed. "But I miss playing. And now I'll probably never have another chance. I should have insisted. Maybe it would have held the crew together better."

Caspia shook her head sadly, probably thinking the same as Zahar, that nothing could hold together a crew with Thayne in it. "I wish I had—" Zahar stopped and redirected her comment to the ceiling, source of all material good. "Please make me a Human guitar, six-string, modern acoustic." They waited a few moments, but nothing happened.

Caspia sat up. "Human classical flute, key of C, modern." Nothing. Tenshi shrugged and ordered a pipa. "Maybe it just takes longer," Caspia added.

"Notice! / Attention!"

They all jerked in alarm.

"Attend / roost in 30 minutes / 5 doks."

Zahar froze in alarm, but neither Caspia nor Tenshi looked afraid, so she chided herself. "Sounds like a fancy way to call a meeting," Tenshi declared.

"About time," Caspia agreed. "Countdown clock please," and one appeared.

Zahar forced herself to say "good," relax, and continue eating. They might need their strength. It didn't sound exactly friendly. "We need *proper* clothes," she announced, looking at their suit underwear. Before she could specify what was proper, three matching sets of clothes appeared. Gold and white.

They gasped in unison. "Melawn's uniform!" Tenshi said.

"He didn't have it on when we left. He doesn't wear it under his suit," Caspia added.

"That means he asked for it here, or described it," Zahar agreed. "Or Thayne did."

"Which means that at least Melawn is alive somewhere," Caspia concluded.

Zahar popped up to her knees with a surge of confidence and reached for the outfit. "Let's hope we're about to find out."

"You can't go!" Thayne shouted at all of them, but saved his angry glare for Melawn.

"We must cooperate," Nkiroo said mildly, but then moved away from their arguing.

"We must resist!"

"It would be futile," Evan argued.

"If they told you to kill each other, would you cooperate?"

"Of course not," Evan answered. "But none of their requests—

"—demands!"

"—have been unreasonable."

"Except imprisonment? Forced brain surgery?"

Melawn hung his head while they argued. He'd learned years ago not to match verbal wits with Thayne.

"Well, I'm going," Evan said.

"I'm your captain and I say you're not going!" Thayne insisted.

Evan took a brave breath. "You are no longer our captain."

"That child you called your captain is not here! And I am senior!"

But Evan shook his head. "Actually, I am." They all turned to stare, or glare, in Thayne's case. Melawn could see Thayne doing the calculations. Even subtracting his years in "retirement," Evan probably did have more command experience. And he wasn't wandering anymore.

"I am in command of this mission," Thayne said in a steely voice.

"The mission is over, clearly. We are now in survival mode. I am going," Evan continued, "and I want Nkiroo and Melawn to come. You may stay if you like." *Evan?* Melawn couldn't believe the person too scared to be in the Command Bay with Thayne was talking back to him. Maybe being captured by the Chike had put other fears in perspective.

Melawn thought Thayne might hit Evan, but he controlled himself. "Fine! Go grovel to the lizards, but Melawn stays with me."

Evan shook his head. "Melawn is not yours to command. And he has the best memory. He can help observe while you cool off." Evan turned and crawled to the slot to wait, while Thayne grabbed his cup and threw it at the wall, where it dissolved.

Dressing in Melawn's uniform was like masquerading as a superhero. Although Zahar felt a bit silly, it gave her a little surge of confidence, which quickly disappeared. She was suddenly scared and overwhelmed. She turned to Caspia. "I can't pretend to be the captain for this," and then was ashamed for being cowardly.

Caspia gripped her shoulder, but, surprisingly, it was Tenshi that answered. "You've been a good captain. You got us this far and you're going to get us home."

Zahar just felt more unworthy. And deep down, she wasn't sure anyone could get them home. Or if home would ever be the same now that the Chike were on the move.

A panel larger than the food slot slid open and a blast of heat hit them. A gender-unknown Chike was standing in the rimway. "Come." The Chike had a decorative mask and a prod slung over ziz back. Ze stood to one side, turning ziz face away. The hideous red and black fan stripes covered the walls, ceiling, and deck. Zahar froze.

"She hasn't seen them before," Caspia whispered to Tenshi.

"I'll go first," Tenshi said and slowly crawled into the rimway.

Caspia pressed Zahar's arm. "Go in the middle. I'll stay right behind you." It took another nudge from Caspia to get Zahar moving. The rimway was a little taller than their cell, but being taller than the Chike, they still couldn't stand upright, so Zahar crept along between them, appreciating the calm bravery of the older women.

They hunched along for about eight minutes, long enough to get tired, before coming to a large door that opened into an auditorium. They entered at the bottom and could now stand. It was an amazingly empowering feeling. They stopped to take it all in.

Flat terraced steps, like wide stairs, followed the half-octagon contours of the walls, with ramps up the middle and both sides. Rows and rows of tired Ramians sat quietly on the steps, like spectators in the bleachers of an alien sporting event. Some sat in clumps, with their arms around each other. *They must have just been reunited with each other.* Zahar was immensely glad to see them.

"Cas!" Zahar's head swiveled to see three Humans at the far side of the room, on the lowest step: Evan, Melawn, and Nkiroo. Evan was on his feet, running toward them. Caspia dodged the guard and met Evan at the bottom of the central ramp, right in front of the Chike podium. In tears, they threw their arms around each other. As Zahar hurried to them and the rest of the crew, she couldn't help but notice the stirring among the Ramians and their lights changing to a soft pink.

Zahar clasped hands quickly with Melawn and Nkiroo, as the Chike herded them back to the bottom row of steps, together, thank heavens. "Thayne is in our room," Nkiroo whispered to her. She nodded, sitting down, and then, surprise of surprises, he handed Kiwi to her. "He was in the box." Nkiroo pointed to the side, where an empty box sat. And next to it, an EEHAB full of rats. *They saved the rats.*

Zahar held the subdued and whining Kiwi to her chest, so happy to have him back, and so glad he was alive and unharmed. "It's okay," she whispered to him. Caspia and Evan sat together with all four hands clasped. It was a nice moment, but they could be separated again. Zahar smiled to herself. By then, Caspia would have collected a full report from Evan.

Two hammer-wielding guards rang gongs with dangling bells that rattled discordantly after the main clang. Kiwi tried to burrow under her shirt, but this fake uniform did not have a podpup flap. She held him tight and shushed him. A row of masked Chike guards, holding tall flags, entered the room, split into two groups and lined up on each side of the podium, faces turned ceremonially away from the audience.

"Attention! / Attend! Lesser ones. You are aboard the Chike ship *Sandstorm / Dust Devil*."

How fitting, Zahar thought.

Part of the wall lit up behind the podium, with the words printed in Alkulu and Ramian. The main audio was in Ramian, but around them, they could hear in Alkulu. Zahar scowled at being called lesser ones. Out of the corner of her eye, she searched for the Ramian Getti, but without turning her head, she couldn't find him.

"Now understand / be informed. This offshoot / leaf of stars / galaxy is protected / administered by the benevolent, the generous, the wise GenOne." At the mention of the GenOne, all the Chike ducked their heads in respect. "This leaf is named / called Kingdom Leaf. For eons, the great GenOne (more nodding heads) have cherished / preserved peace and watched over / protected the development / growth of the lesser ones.

"Eight species of the capable / reliable GenTwo arose to assist / serve in the stewardship of this leaf. The Chike, loyal / striving servants of the revered GenOne (by this time the audience was nodding along) have lived only to increase the beauty of the material leaf, to make it worthy / efficient.

"Across the stars, the Chike built a glorious system of transport, supported by a brilliant safety net of stabilization. Lesser ones know us as The 'Builders.'"

Gasps and murmuring broke out among the Ramians and Humans as they took in this astonishing news. Generations of speculation, of junk news, and academic pondering about the builders was not turning out the way they expected. But the Chike guards stamped their flagpoles in unison and there was silence.

"For centuries, lesser ones have been blundering / trespassing into GenTwo space. Despite repeated clear / obvious warnings, lesser ones continue. As mixing / socializing is forbidden / taboo, all lesser ones have been relocated / settled on a colony / planet. In 26 days / 24 petters, these lesser ones will join them."

Colony? Zahar's heart sank. They weren't going home. She'd never see her family again. Her parents and three little sisters would never know what happened to her. She'd never see the sectors again. She'd led her crew to permanent exile. And God help them if it was a red and black striped planet. She dropped her head into her hands. "I'm sorry," she told the others. "I'm so, so sorry."

Tenshi squeezed her shoulder. "It's not your doing. We're alive. And I'm not giving up yet."

There was a rustling of people and Zahar turned to see Quay walking down the middle ramp. "Stay seated," the unseen narrator warned. The guards stamped their flagpoles. But Quay did not stop.

He approached the central podium until the guards actually held the tips of the flagpoles to his chest. "I can't go to your colony." His voice was anxious and thin, not at all the leader voice from before. "I have to go somewhere. Somewhere else." He was confused.

"Where?" the voice asked.

"Somewhere . . ." Quay closed his eyes and turned slowly. "That way," he said, pointing off to the left past the rat cage. There were several moments of silence. He stood there, trembling, while the guards held the poles a mere handbreadth away. His people's colors turned a unanimous steady blinding white, while his turned bright blazing blue.

Then again, in perfect unison, the guards stood down, stepping back and placing their poles quietly on the ground. And then they turned and *looked* at him. Quay's eyes were closed and it looked like he, and all the Ramians, were praying. Zahar quickly added a prayer of her own, even though she had no idea what was happening. She wondered if she should stand and support him, as captain of the Humans. But two Ramians marched down the ramp and stood next to him. Siblings . . . like his own guard.

Seeming to gain strength, Quay looked up again, eyes shining as they had in the passthrough. "I am called. I must go. I claim passage to the meeting point."

What is he talking about? What don't we know? Ramians have a meet up point with the Chike? Somehow Zahar didn't think so.

The voice came back. "One who claims to be a harbinger must present a sign / miracle."

"Here," Quay raised his arm and turned, sweeping it across the auditorium to indicate his people. "I have brought them through space and time, through the realm of collapsed dimensions, and all are witnesses."

Proof, Zahar thought. Proof was in the *Cheetah* records, if the Chike could scan them. She looked up. The Ramians were standing. *Yes, they are witnesses, and so are we.* Zahar stood as well, and the other Humans jumped to their feet.

Zahar didn't know how long they stood there. The screen had gone off. Quay had lowered his arm. But everyone stood, determined. Kiwi, who had been very still in her arms, suddenly looked at the door, which opened. The guards stamped and filed out.

A new guard came in, bigger and fancier. They escorted a Chike who carried no flag. Ze had a gold vest and fancy green cloak, and was unmasked. Ze came to attention in the center of the stage and looked at Quay. A great breath of relief or hope went through the audience.

"This one," the new Chike humbly indicated zirself, but

continued in ziz haughty voice, "will serve as your Exempt. You may address this one as *The Exempt Pascal*." Ze nodded formally to Quay. "This Exempt may speak to lesser beings without the stain of contamination. This Exempt is here to help." Ze rose to ziz full height. "This one is a warrior for the downtrodden." Ze paused dramatically, looked out over the crowd, and then back to Quay. "The Chike accept the claim of the Harbinger Quay."

5 / THE 81-PETALS

17-Light

The Chike ship *Sandstorm*, location unknown

Melawn crawled back along the horrid Chike rimway on his lonely mission. Quay, with his new highly-respected status, had negotiated that everyone could stay together in the big room. He'd even provided a Ramian "designer" to help reengineer it. But it was Melawn's task to go back for Thayne.

"Thayne?" he called, before crawling through the slot. "It's me." Just in case Thayne had some bizarre attack plan. But Thayne was propped against the wall, looking at Nkiroo's designs.

"So. You're alive. What about the others?"

Mclawn crawled over to him. "Great news. Everyone is alive. Even Kiwi. Even the rats." Thayne tried to look unflappable, but a fleeting look of relief did cross his face. "I've come to get you."

Thayne didn't budge. Melawn had braced himself for drama. He sat calmly as if ready to discuss at length. "So, Melawn, tell me. Who is your captain now?"

"Quay."

Real confusion. "What?"

"Quay speaks for us all now."

"That kid?"

"*That kid* brought his people through God-knows-what to survive in that gravity ball pocket thing, and then he somehow transferred them to the *Cheetah*. That's not normal. That's not even genius. The Chike were *looking* for him. They call him the Harbinger. He's some kind of visionary."

"I'll judge that for myself," Thayne said, and shouldered past Melawn into the rimway, turning his face pointedly away from the Chike guard.

18-Light

Drumheller, at the rogue planet

Terina's cabin was right next to her mom's and she usually left the adjoining door open. Although her mom was in an especially bleak mood, Terina had no fear of Rocket bothering her. For all his craziness, he was very well-behaved around long jumpers. Like they were the only people who got respect. The captain got some respect, but maybe that was because Sky kept Rocket in line.

Still, Terina was working hard on her *81-Petals* backstory and Rocket was just a big distraction. "Rocket! Hey, Rocket! Go play with Star and Sky. Somewhere else." Rocket just whirled by. He was one of the least verbal pups ever, although Terina suspected he understood just fine.

"Play Sky and Star. Play Jarvie. Kitchen!" Terina floated up the stairs and opened the door to the rimway. But instead of Rocket going out, Star came careening in. *Great.* "I have work. You pups need to settle down!"

"Play!" Rocket declared.

Arggg. That Jarvie. "Where's Sky?"

"Sky busy," Star said, rolling toward her head like a fuzzy volleyball. Terina ducked. "Big busy."

"Fine," Terina sighed, and got them some soft colorful balls to chase around.

Terina contemplated the *81-Petals* story. She wondered how much was necessary. Everyone knew it. But as an exercise in completeness, she wrote it out.

The original story, "The Ship Called *81 Petals*" was written near the end of the 100-year period between when the a-rings were discovered at Saturn's L4 and when they were successfully used. It was written in Japanese, an original Earth language. The author, Mirai Yota, was a science visionary, one of the people who worked on how to use the a-rings, as humanity believed they were clearly meant for travel.

At the beginning of this period, only Earth, Moon, and Mars were seriously colonized. Fuel problems had been reduced and radiation protection fields were just being developed, meaning that the moons of the outer planets would soon be colonized.

The original story of the *81 Petals* was about how science and religion were the two wings of humanity's flight of adventure. After translation into Alkulu, the story became a monster cultural hit. It was added to and serialized for children. It became a great mythic form in the following century, a symbol of the struggle over the a-rings. It was responsible for Japanese being strongly preserved when many other languages fell out of use.

It was the story of a great ship, its nine arcs each painted with nine flower petals. Aboard were the nine Master Problem Solvers: Haiku Master, Engineer, Gardener, Grandparent, Mathematician, Composer, Painter, Teacher, and Quilt Master. Together, they overcame their differences to work "beauty" into technology. Therefore, humanity became worthy to use the a-rings. Part of it was written in Haiku of the period.

Eighty-one Petals
Cosmic flowers metalized
Glories in sunshine

Space travel was portrayed as a spiritual journey. It was the story that set the scientists on the track of jumping. Jumping could not be done with a probe; it required a human soul.

After scientists and society got up the nerve to attempt a jump, fully realizing that likely no one would come back, a ship was sent through the a-rings and disappeared. It took years to learn the fate of the ship—it had survived the jump. The pilot had not. But the AI reported by lightspeed continuously and its probes were sent to investigate the alien system. A-rings were found there.

Meanwhile, work was done to maximize Human resistance to g-forces while keeping conscious. It was Domingo Garza, the first to return from a jump, who understood. Scientists had the theory of how it worked, but not how to get to where you were going—until Domingo explained that he could feel a pathway, like a thread, and God had guided him. And phrases jumped right out of 81 Petals.

Spinning on a thread
of connected space and time
Sacred Crossing

Spirit must guide
And body faithful follow
New heart new place one

People went crazy over 81 Petals, looking for, and possibly finding, more clues. Mirai Yota, the author, took a vow of silence on the subject, and became a recluse.

During the next 200-300 years, Sectors 2-3 became established, bustling places. The legendary new Earth (also of 81 Petals) was nowhere to be found. So onward humanity went, in beautiful ships, colonizing Sectors 4-5. Finding plenty of resources, but only marginal planets, they kept going.

And then humanity lost the thread of their story. Ships lost their beauty and became cheap and functional. Major expansion continued as if by compulsion, with humanity reaching and spreading for hundreds of years before people noticed that something was wrong. The sectors were weak and thin. Ships were old, ugly, and broken down. Stations were merely prefabricated units bolted together. There were no major industries outside of Sector 5. Sector 6 was not yet self-sustaining when Sector 8 was cobbled together.

The inner sectors clamored for pressing on, like a cart pushed downhill from behind. But the reality on the frontier became one of getting by, not expanding. Some stations were even abandoned.

And then, Sector 3 decided to build a real ship: the *81-Petals*. Some people were horrified, others entranced. It took 20 years. It was considered the perfect ship. The crew was selected for their expertise and commitment to beauty. Two sister ships were built, *Dragonfly Dream* and *Starswimmer*, ships beautiful and amazing, technical dreams.

The ships jumped ceremonially from sector to sector— arriving to spectacular fanfare. Their jump for the new territories in Sector 9 was the biggest news of humanity. Each of the three ships went to a different star.

And were never heard from again.

After nine years, another three barebones ships were sent. Also not heard from again. There was nowhere to go now. It was the period at the end of the run-on sentence of expansion.

People held out hope that *81-Petals* had survived and they would hear a lightspeed message. It had only been 15 years, but the legend lost some of its wonder. Students still studied it in history and several excellent documentaries and story versions existed, but it was no longer humanity's common story.

And I'm about to write the sad ending.

Terina reviewed the command crews of the three ships. She had always known that her Uncle Aspen was aboard the *81-Petals*. She supposed her mom was so down because the silent ship meant there was no hope that he was aboard.

"Oyphf!" Rocket gave a cry of mild surprise. Terina's mom had floated in.

"Go play in there," Sequoia told Rocket and gave him a boost into her room, while Star tumbled after. "Hi."

Her mom looked a bit stressed, even considering their circumstances. "Mom, what's happening?"

Her mom just shook her head. "Are you doing your homework?"

"No, my history of *81 Petals*. And working on my hypothesis."

"Hypothesis? For school?"

"No. About history." She would love to tell her mom about it, but she feared she wouldn't be interested, as she was single-minded about pilot issues.

Her mom took a deep breath and stared at the ceiling. Then glided to a chair and latched on. "I'm listening."

"I . . . it's just an idea."

"I don't know enough to disagree with you."

"Well, I'm thinking about how bad people and good people affect history differently."

"What bad people?"

"You know. In history. Big historic bad people." *Not small-time bad people, like Dad.* But Terina shook herself and waved her hand at the past. She pressed her pad onto the table so her mom could see it. "If you graphed the prosperity of humanity, you'd see great leaps of progress after each Manifestation of God." Her mom nodded. "Then, along each religious period there is a slow but steady upward trend. But, there are small, sharp chips where humanity's fortunes plummet." She drew a sharp V shape along the graph. "Say World War II." She traced her finger along the line. "This series of slightly upward-sloping terraces is broken by canyons of badness, like chips in pottery."

"And those chips are caused by the bad people—like those who caused the war?"

"Exactly. They happen fast and people recover fast. Historically speaking.

"So I was wondering why we don't have spikes on the graph. Like the opposite of the V-shaped chips. Why don't good people make spikes? My hypothesis is that it's because there's no downside to the good. So it goes up, but not down. The good causes the general upward trend, and there's so much good that you don't notice individual spikes."

"That makes sense to me. But to the people living it, the good can make a huge difference."

"Yes. For the living, history is more like a river. Sometimes not much happens for a long time. The river is wide and slow. In times of turmoil, the river is fast and wild."

"You've never even seen a river."

"I've seen movies. And I think the river of history has been flat for too long. And we're about to hit white water."

"Events of the most profound significance are taking place in the world. The river of human history is flowing at a bewildering speed."[1] her mom quoted.

"Yes. You understand," Terina sighed. "I'm so glad we have Captain."

"Beezan?"

"Yes. He's going to steer us on our journey down the river of history."

"I think you're taking your metaphor too far." She looked pained. "Besides, someone could always throw him off course."

"We'll get back on. Or we were meant to be here. There are crux points, where the river swirls and anything could happen."

"You have a lot of faith in a lonely mid-jumper stuck in the middle of nowhere."

"He's good. And strong. And so are we. Our influence on history may be small, but it will be part of the upward fortune of humanity."

Her mom scowled. "He said he didn't talk to you."

"Who? Captain?" Terina shook her head.

Taking an exasperated breath, her mom said, "Beezan asked me if you could go."

"Go where?"

"To the *81-Petals*. Tomorrow."

Terina jumped up in surprise and joy, launching herself to the ceiling. The podpups zoomed back in, homing in on the excitement.

"I was going to tell him no. You're too young."

"Mom, Mom, please, please! I'm certified in EVA. It's the story of the century!"

"You may never get home to report it."

Terina pushed carefully down from the ceiling. "I can send it lightspeed. The people will have their history. The mystery of

81-Petals will be solved! I never thought he would allow—Mom, please!"

"Yes, yes. You can go." Her mom helped her down. "We're in a fix anyway. You might as well go. As Grandpa would say, 'Throw caution to the wind.'"

Terina hugged her mom tight. "Thank you. Thank you. Oh, I have to get ready!"

"Thank you. Thank you," the pups repeated.

19-Light

Terina stood at the *Drumheller* hangar hatch adjusting her helmet cam. She also had a wrist cam, a handheld, and a backup. "Can we turn the lights on around the shuttle?"

Jarvie, working at the panel, brought up the lights, fully illuminating the shuttle *Peacock.* "*Peacock?*" Terina turned to Captain in alarm. "Captain. We can't go in a shuttle called *Peacock.* This is history."

"Sorry, we only have one shuttle left."

"Besides," Jarvie added, "the other one was called *Cricket.*"

"Can we rename it?"

"Later," Beezan said. Later wouldn't help. She could blur out the visual, but it would be all over the audio.

Terina's grandfather gave her a kindly look. "Mustn't be proud as a peacock."

Beezan gave them both a sterner look. "Let's pay attention to the life and death stuff for the moment."

"Yes, honor," they said together.

But Terina was allowed to record them going to the shuttle. It was just the four of them, Captain, Iricana, Kelson, and Terina. Jarvie stayed behind in the Entry Lounge.

Beezan let her sit up front where she could get great shots of the *81-Petals*. With no starlight to illuminate it, the ship wasn't all that spectacular. But as they approached, the dark torus became apparent. It was a wide torus, with plenty of room for painting the cosmically large flower petals. And it was spinning.

"It's huge!" Beezan whispered.

"Bigger than some stations," Kelson agreed.

"You've seen it before?" Iricana asked quietly.

"Oh yes," Kelson answered. "I've been on it . . . in better times."

"Good thing it has all that fancy reflective paint," Beezan said as he slowed and adjusted their path to aim for the spindle, "or we wouldn't be able to see it at all."

Terina was vaguely aware of Iricana sending codes to open the hangar. That, in combination with their proximity, should get the hangar open. "On your right," grandfather whispered, just as a crack of light appeared. The hangar was opening! They sighed in relief as they slowly pulled in. Great shot of the big beautiful—empty—hangar.

"Where are the shuttles?" Grandfather asked, sounding mystified, but with a breath of hope. If the shuttles were gone, maybe the crew got away.

"There is something there," Iricana pointed and Terina panned over to it.

"That's not a Human shuttle," Kelson said. Beezan set the *Peacock* down and the auto anchors engaged. The strange little alien shuttle was a long, pointed cylinder, somewhat like a pretend rocket from the pre-space days, only it was on its side.

"Functional," Iricana added. "Nothing fancy. Can't be Ramian."

"It looks more like a tunnel bore for mining," Kelson speculated. "Thunder would know if it's one of ours."

They got out and pulled closer. Terina filmed them, but as

they approached, they all gasped. Iricana pointed to something on the side and Terina zoomed in. *Writing.* Iricana was aiming at the writing with her pad. "Checking the Human and Ramian language database. It says 'Not recognized.'"

"Strange shape, unknown language. Possibly non-Human, or non-legal," Kelson agreed. "Take your pick."

An alien ship? It was the last thing they had expected. But a cold stone settled in Terina's stomach. The ship was long and thin, like a Chike.

"Let's not get distracted," Beezan said, and headed for the Entry Lounge, where he and Kelson checked the fancy life support panels. Terina tilted her camera up to capture the greeting over the door, "Welcome to the *81-Petals*, where dreams become real."

"Life support is on in Arc 1!" Beezan exclaimed.

Kelson excitedly pointed over Captain's shoulder. "The garden is up and running!"

"But there's no air between there and here, so keep your visors down," Beezan instructed as they headed for the lift.

When they reached the rim, Terina was about to step out of the lift first, to record the others, but Captain must have had some instinct. He held her arm and let Kelson go first. Cautiously they walked along Arc 5.

Terina was walking along the side of the rimway, and slightly behind, to get as good a view as possible, when the door to Arc 4 suddenly opened, and a woman calmly walked out.

"Good Lord!" Kelson exclaimed.

They all froze. Terina zoomed in. "There's no air!" Iricana reminded them, as they stared at the unsuited woman.

"She's flickering," Terina said. "In my cam view."

"Hologram," Iricana confirmed. "Strange."

"And that takes power too," Beezan added disapprovingly.

He slowly advanced and reached out to touch the woman. His hand went right through. She seemed to be talking, but their external pickups were not getting anything. "Okay. That's unnerving, but let's keep going."

In Arc 4 there were more holograms, just casually walking, some hand in hand. Terina had to use the helmet cam as her hand was shaking too much for the others. So creepy. And sad, if this was all that was left of the crew.

"The AI maybe?" Beezan asked. "Trying to communicate?"

"A good thought," Iricana agreed. "But the holograms don't pay any attention to us."

In Arc 2, there were more. Beezan went faster, completely ignoring them, until Kelson gasped. "Aspen!"

"Where?" Terina whispered urgently. Her grandfather pointed to a dark, handsome, young man in an *81-Petals* uniform. Terina swung the camera his way.

Kelson stood, hand on his chest, staring at Aspen. But after Aspen paused to consult his s'link, he walked away. Kelson took a step to go after him, but Iricana grasped Kelson's shoulder. "It's the crew then. As they were, fifteen years ago."

"Yes," Kelson said, obviously trying not to shed any tears in his suit.

"Let's go," Beezan said, and hurried along to the Arc 1 hatch. They squeezed in together. *Pressurizing!* Terina pointed her camera to the Arc 1 rimway to be ready when the door opened.

Swish. Fifty hologram people. Kids. Podpups. Up and down the rimway. Going in and out the cabins and into what was probably the kitchen. Terina had to practice taking her slow quiet recording breaths. She handed the extra camera to Iricana, who took it willingly and started recording.

"Garden," Beezan ordered and moved ahead. They had all studied the design.

"Air checks out," Iricana confirmed, as they moved up the rimway.

"Let's check in the garden," Beezan said. "Here."

Up the stairs they went. When the door opened, they were immersed in the Sun spectrum lights. And wall to wall greenery. In the center was an actual tree, taller than the adults. Terina recorded it, zooming in on the orange fruits.

"Their One Tree," Kelson said. "Persimmons. It lives."

Beezan turned in a circle. "No holograms in here."

"Air checks out," Iricana announced. "*Drumheller*?"

Katie answered, "Agreed. Air checks out."

Beezan pointed to Kelson, who slowly unsealed his visor. Beezan watched his suit vitals for a couple of minutes while Kelson took some deep breaths. "It's good," Kelson said, and a small tear leaked out.

"Keep your helmets on," Beezan ordered, as they all opened their visors. Sweet, slightly warm air filled Terina's whole self. It smelled like—words escaped her. Like life, and dirt and something musky, Terina thought might be the right word.

They were all standing around the tree, just taking it in, when there was a loud rustling. And a big, furry, gray creature, with pointed nose and whiskers crawled out from behind a bush and calmly sat down.

All four of them scuttled back to the wall in fright.

"Giant mutant rat!" Beezan reported to the *Drumheller*.

"Oh, that's lovely," it said, wrapping its tail around its hind paws with a flick.

"Giant *talking* mutant rat," Iricana corrected, as Beezan held his chest in shock.

"Well, knock me over with a feather," Kelson said.

"How about a tail?" the rat replied with a twitch.

"No!" Beezan jumped to action, coming between the rat and Kelson with his hands up. "No knocking. Peace. No trouble."

"It—Ze speaks Alkulu," Terina whispered to the *Drumheller*. Ziz accent was pretty good, but there was a strange sound as if there were more lips, and more nose, than could be managed for Human speech.

"I toy with you Captain," ze said, with a small bow towards Kelson. I am Veez, patriarch of the family Slas-samslaad."

Kelson indicated Beezan and said, "This is our Captain, Beezan."

"This pup?" The rat threw both his front paws up as if they were having a wild party conversation.

A rat is calling our captain a podpup? But something about it made the rat less scary. Beezan edged forward. "I don't mean to be rude, but where is the crew? The real crew?"

"Ah," and Veez suddenly grew serious. "That is a long story, Captain. They are probably alive and well, but you will never see them again." Kelson hung his head.

"Maybe we should talk somewhere," Beezan suggested.

"Of course. Would you happen to have any new food?"

Iricana answered. "Yes. What do you eat?"

"Oh. Everything."

Kelson volunteered to check around the rest of the ship. Meanwhile, Iricana and Beezan casually walked with Veez to the kitchen. Terina followed behind with the camera.

Veez glanced behind and then said to Beezan. "Of course, everything I tell you is off the record. That's why I couldn't answer your messages. Might the child turn off the devices?"

"Sorry, Terina," Beezan said, obviously disappointed for her.

But Terina was not discouraged. She had practiced her "mental recording" and was ready to try.

Iricana and Beezan settled in at the table as if it was no big deal to eat with an intelligent alien rat. Then Terina remembered that they had both dealt with aliens before—the Ramians. Maybe this was "old hat," as grandpa would say.

"How long have you been alone here?" Beezan asked kindly.

"About three of your years."

"So, you're not supposed to be here? That's why it's off the record?" Iricana asked.

"I can't talk to you because I am GenThree."

A chill went down Terina's spine. Beezan leaned forward and cautiously asked, "Is that like a gentoo?"

"Of course not!" Veez sat up, obviously offended. He thumped his tail and Beezan scooted back. Finally, Veez sighed with great exaggeration. "Of course, I have studied your entertainment and see that you are utterly ignorant of even the basics."

"Enlighten us," Iricana said tightly.

Veez put his paw down on the table. "There are five generations of species in this part of the galaxy." He counted on his "fingers." "The GenOne," he paused respectfully, "highly evolved and generally benevolent. They were the original species to develop intelligence. They are the divinely-appointed supervisors of this leaf of space."

Divinely appointed? Five generations of species? Terina's heart was pounding. Beezan and Iricana were frozen in attention.

"The eight species of the GenTwo, the second wave of species, are the not-so-humble servants of the GenOne. Diligent and annoying."

He's talking galactic-wide species and rolling his eyes like they're fussing kids?

Iricana passed a bar of food.

"Hmm, dry, but interesting. So! The twelve species of the GenThree, all mammalian, by the way, include my people, the wissssniwinz." He stopped at the puzzled looks. "You may call us the Scampers. We are quick, independent, and creative. For some reason, the GenTwo have corralled the GenThree on the opposite side of this space. We're separated from the GenOne and GenTwo by your people." *That leaves humanity in a precarious place.*

"So, the GenFour—rising intelligences such as your clever selves—well, who knows how many? They are all what you call primates."

Iricana passed her last emergency ration over. Veez was quiet for a moment. "Then there are the GenFive. Those that have escaped their planets before learning peace."

Iricana spoke up, "So the Chike—"

"Those overly vigilant Chike are part of the GenTwo. I can see your confusion. They are quite regimented in nature. But you've not personally had dealings with them or they would have lectured you endlessly about the taboo."

"Taboo? Meaning something forbidden?" Beezan asked.

"Yes, that the generations may not mix. Religious decree. We don't take it so seriously, but still. That is why I am officially not talking to you."

"Right," Beezan agreed. "It's just a rescue."

"Exactly," Veez nodded, and ate his last bite.

6 / THE SPHERE OF DESTRUCTION

19-Light

81-Petals, at the rogue planet

Still aboard the *81-Petals*, Beezan walked to the Command Bay with Iricana. Terina was off recording and Kelson was checking Veez's space suit. Veez had gone to pack a few things.

"So what's the protocol?" Beezan asked Iricana. "Do you appoint yourself captain of the *81-Petals*, or do I appoint you?"

She grimaced and shook her head. "As it happens, I have contingency orders from Oatah to take possession."

"*Seriously?* Has he thought of *everything*?"

"Well, there's no mention of the five Gens or giant rats in his orders."

"Then the *81-Petals* is officially yours, Captain."

"Thank you, Captain. I'll let my first order be to keep the garden going. We may need it."

"Crew?"

"Can you spare Thunder and Kelson?"

"I think you'll need them. Technically, you're supposed to have a pilot aboard, too."

"We'll declare it in for repairs. That way Sequoia can stay on the *Drumheller* with Terina."

Beezan tried the Command Bay door with his captain's s'link, which didn't work, as he suspected. But Iricana was able to get in on her level 1. When the door slid open, Beezan gasped. "It's so big!" Iricana smiled at him. "Oh—is that just a cargo captain talking?"

"No. It's big and fancy." She smiled and slid into the command seat, as if she were used to that, while Beezan took the pilot's chair. *The entire crew could sit in here.* There were flower images on the ceiling. The Ramians might even approve.

Iricana put her s'link in the command slot and said "Voice activation. Emergency change of command." They didn't even have time to take a worried breath before the computer answered, sounding almost eager.

"Proceed. State the current commander."

"None. The ship is abandon—"

A mechanical voice blared out. "Attention / hear this! Humans / Lesser ones:"

Beezan and Iricana jumped halfway out of their chairs. "Volume down!" Beezan ordered, but it did no good. He held his hands over his ears and willed his heart not to beat insanely. The main screen went on and words scrolled across. He didn't know how Iricana had the presence of mind to whip out her s'link and start recording.

"Your ignorance / defiance of previous warnings / admonitions is criminal / rebellious. Your trespassing / interloping ships have been captured / confiscated. By order of the Chike, crew / Humans have been removed / relocated to a refuge / colony. This ship is returned as a reminder / warning. Observe the map / chart and do not encroach / offend GenTwo space!"

A map appeared on the screen. "The Chike," Beezan said,

and they looked at each other in dismay. "It's all true! Azann's story is real." He wiped tears away to look at the map, desperately searching for a recognizable point. But the map disappeared and was replaced by the *81-Petals* flower logo.

Beezan let out a big breath of air. "The Chike must have programmed that message and now the ship is back to normal," he guessed.

Iricana nodded, looking at her s'link. "Thank heavens we still have the map."

Beezan's s'link beeped, startling him again, and he read the message to Iricana. "It's from Kelson. He says he found *three* alien suits. Two are smaller."

"Which means there are actually three rats?" Iricana asked, as they both turned to look over their shoulders down the long rimway.

Her grandpa had turned off the holograms so Terina could record visuals in the kitchen, Observation Bay, and a few cabins, although they were empty. Now she was in the Med Bay. "More lights." It was huge. There were beds for at least twenty patients. She panned around with the camera.

At the back, she was surprised to see a door open. What would Captain Beezan say? She approached the door, to close it if nothing else, but saw that it was the staircase to the next deck up. And at the base of the stairs was a pile of dead weeds. *Why?*

Terina turned in alarm as someone came banging up the stairs from the rimway. It was Grandfather Kelson, who saw her and stopped, holding a hand to his chest. "Grandpa, should you be running?" He waved that he was okay and pulled out his s'link.

"Your s'link is off," he gasped, pointing to her.

"No, it's on silent. It interferes with the recording. I'm sorry. Grandpa, what's wrong?"

"Captain Iricana," he said into his s'link. "She's in the Med Bay. Everything is okay here."

"I was just closing this door. It was open. But there are weeds." She pointed them out as he slowly walked over, his breathing calming down. Kelson leaned over and picked up a couple as Beezan and Iricana came in.

"So big," Beezan muttered. "Bigger than Canyon Station's Med Bay." Iricana gave Kelson an amused glance.

"What did you find?" Iricana asked.

"Dead flowers," Kelson answered.

"Oh," Beezan said, "maybe that explains everything."

"Like?" Terina prompted them.

"There were three alien suits in the suit room," Iricana answered.

"I'm overly familiar with this part of the Med Bay," Beezan said quietly as he walked up the stairs carefully. Terina trailed behind him, recording. "Yes," he said sadly. "The freezers."

"Freezers?" Terina asked.

"The morgue." Iricana whispered, as she and Kelson joined them. "Two drawers are activated," she said as she pointed out the lights.

"Our missing rats," Kelson said.

"Look!" Beezan pointed to some alien writing, scrawled on the drawers with a black marker. Terina zoomed in on the writing. "The clock says 3 years 2 months for this one, and 7 years 4 months for this one."

"Seven years!" Kelson said. "He's been here a long time."

"Poor Veez," Terina sympathized.

"But he said he'd been here 3 years," Beezan said.

"No," Iricana said. "He said he'd been *alone here* three years."

The others nodded. "So why not mention how long he'd actually been here?"

Beezan, quick to pick up on any worry, nodded. "I wonder what else he didn't mention."

Drumheller, in orbit around the rogue planet

In the *Drumheller's* Hangar 1, Jarvie held the tubeway for the returning shuttle, since Thunder didn't have confidence in Veez's suit.

His mind flashed back to the time when Oatah, Iricana, Reeder, and Katie came aboard. How sick and shaky he'd been that day. Scared and lonely. Ashamed even. Now, he turned to the Entry Lounge and Katie waved to him, smiling. He smiled back, although she couldn't see through the helmet. *I should be more scared now, stranded around a rogue planet while a giant rat comes aboard. But I'm not.*

Jarvie felt strong. He was on a ship, part of a crew. He had people. They were having a grand adventure and he had faith they would get home, someday.

"Clear, Jarvie," Katie advised, and he started collapsing the tubeway. Besides, things were getting *interesting*.

3-Mercy

Watcher

Lanezi didn't know how much time had passed before he became aware of his breathing, gasping actually. Something, a mask maybe, was on his face. He felt tight, pressed down by acceleration. Threads! Everywhere. *We're jumping!* There was a big purple thread, you couldn't miss it. *What are they waiting for?* And then they were in the path.

Why am I not in the pilot chair?

They were carried along the thread, hurtling toward their destination, when Lanezi, in his agitation, broke his #1 rule. He looked. He turned his mind away from the thread and gazed around the depths of jumpspace—and saw a monster. Friendship. No ordinary star remained. Around it, all the threads had snapped. And a giant bubble of radiation was spewing outward, unstoppable.

What is that gasping, that thrashing? It's me. Wake up! Lanezi tried to haul himself out of the nightmare. Pressure—someone was holding his hands, exactly the same on both sides.

"It's okay, Lanezi."

"It's okay."

I'm alive! And then he heard the angels singing. *That's right. I was dying. No! I was jumping. The bubble!* Remembering his terrifying vision gave him the final surge to break through. His eyes flew open.

The twins were beside him, one on each side, holding his hands and chanting in their beautiful harmony. A Ramian standing over him was smiling, with burgundy colors. "Welcome back, Lanezi." *Neah, the one who speaks Alkulu.*

The twins, whose eyes had been closed, looked down. Joy flew across their faces. "Lanezi!" they said in unison and gripped his hands more firmly.

"I yield Thee thanks, O my Lord, that Thou hast wakened me from my sleep, and stirred me up,"[1] Euro chanted.

Everyone automatically turned to Io, who sang out, **"Praise be unto Thee, O My Lord, for all times, heretofore and hereafter; and thanks be unto Thee, O My God, under all conditions, whether of the past or the future."**[2]

Neah smiled at the twins. "You are blessed, Lanezi. You have *two* guardian angels."

But Lanezi couldn't afford to forget this time. Friendship. "No need for alarm," Neah was saying. "You're fine." The doctor came over, hooded. Lanezi tried to find his voice. He followed all that air gasping in and out and found his mouth.

"No!" He rasped. "No. Don't jump to Friendship!"

Neah's colors and expression switched to perplexed. "We're at Four. Humans call it Four." He looked at Lanezi's forehead, shook himself and looked into Lanezi's eyes. "What did you see at Friendship?"

"Bubble. Coming." Neah and the twins frowned. "Supernova! Worse even. Radiation coming."

Neah turned to the doctor. "I'll ask the other pilots. He may be dreaming."

"No," Lanezi insisted. "They won't tell you! I saw. *I saw.* It's a monster now."

The doctor leaned over and touched something on Lanezi's chest. And his hard-fought emergence slipped away.

4-Mercy

Lanezi sat up in his med chair, relieved that the aid, Anitoran, had stopped fussing. For all her concern over his food and blankets, she didn't seem to have a care for what he really wanted. He'd asked for the captain, for Neah, for Sontula and had no response. He checked her colors for clues, but of course, she was wearing the medical hood. When he asked for the twins, she said they were in school. *I'm going to hear about that.* He said it was important, but for all he could tell from her reaction it might be translating as "any old time you get around to it." She left him to drink his soup, or whatever it was. Warm. Salty. Blue. Blueberry-ish soup. He wondered if the pups were okay, but didn't want to call

Anitoran back and start the pillow-puffing and blanket-adjusting all over again.

The soup tasted like nothing familiar and yet it was immensely satisfying to just sit and sip. *Alive.* The doctors said he was cured and should live to *great heights.* He was thrilled and grateful, but it didn't cancel out his concern about the supernova at Friendship. *How long will it take for the deadly radiation to get to the next system?* He *had* to get a message to the sectors.

Lanezi woke up with a start when there was a commotion in the med center. Io and Euro had come in, carrying Whisper and Blue. Lanezi broke into a huge grin and struggled to stand. But Anitoran, hood off, intercepted them with a stern look and a flash of orange. The twins meekly arranged their Ramian clothes, fancy tunics and matching pants, and pressed their dark hair down. Both were wearing their red armbands, completely unnecessary, even insulting, outside of Human space. *Is there some kind of dress code in the med center?* He hugged them both, first together and then one at a time and then each pup. Whisper clung to him while the twins took turns trying to restrain Blue.

"You're up!" Euro said, just as Anitoran made him sit down.

"A little. I walked around today."

"You're going to live," Io said. He looked strained and worried.

"Yes, the doctors said I would be fine." He looked back and forth between them. There was something they weren't saying. "What's wrong?"

Euro's eyes flicked to Anitoran. "We need to talk to you."

"About what's happening," Io whispered. And at that, Whisper looked up at Lanezi and nodded.

"Let's take a walk," Lanezi suggested. But it was futile. Anitoran swooped in, sent the twins out, making sure Blue went with them, and fussed Lanezi back into the chair. *At least I have Whisper now*, he thought as the two of them drifted off to sleep.

5-Mercy

"There are too many . . . steps," Io tried to explain during their next visit. "You can't just talk to the captain."

"Who then?"

Euro stood quietly by Anitoran's station until he got her attention. "Yes?"

"We request for Sontula to visit Lanezi."

She considered. "I'll ask the doctor."

"Thank you," Euro said, glancing back at Lanezi and shrugging. First step on the ladder.

6-Mercy

Finally, Sontula came. Lanezi was able to convince her he wasn't dreaming about Friendship. She seemed concerned and willing to do something about the radiation bubble. "I'll tell Neah, right away."

"He knows. He was here before. But I'm not sure he believes. Or that he did anything."

"I will persuade," she assured him.

Meanwhile, Lanezi focused on getting his strength back. He ate and walked and fed Whisper. When the twins came to visit, he looked at them more critically. They still looked stressed. Their hair was shaggy. They seemed embarrassed about their frilly clothes, even though they normally didn't even think about clothes. There was Ramian writing on their collars. *Probably their names.* They were still rationing-thin. "Are you eating?"

"Yes," Io said. "We're getting used to the food."

"Do you have enough?" They hesitated.

"Well, they feed us the same as the other kids," Euro explained. "We couldn't ask for more. What if others went hungry?"

"I'm told there is plenty of food." But just then, Neah and Sontula came in. Neah greeted the twins and Lanezi quickly. "The Getti has an opening this afternoon. If you're up to it, we can see zir."

"Yes, of course," Lanezi agreed and stood up. He swayed just a bit. "How far?"

"A walk. But we'll get a liftchair." And suddenly, Sontula was a whirlwind arranging things. Fancy clothes were produced for Lanezi, emerald green with silver accents. But it wasn't frilly, like the twins' clothes, *thank heavens.*

"Can we go with you?" Euro asked.

"I'm so sorry," Sontula said. "A Getti's meeting is not for children."

Lanezi stopped tugging on his sleeve and looked up at her. "They're my crew. And they're not exactly children. They're youth."

Sontula did not use the translator and she seemed puzzled a moment. "How old are they?"

"Sixteen."

"You know Jarvie? How old is Jarvie?" she asked.

"Um, well, he's about the same. A little younger maybe."

Neah and Sontula looked at each other in consternation. Her colors switched to aquamarine and she held out her hand, as if unconsciously measuring the height of the twins. Then she whispered something to Neah in Ramian, but Lanezi's translator caught it. "We've made a social error. They are not children."

"No time to change their clothes, but yes, they may come," Neah declared.

The rimway was warm. They proceeded quickly, with Neah leading, Euro guiding the movable chair, Io walking beside, and Sontula in the rear. There were birds! He wasn't dreaming when he came aboard.

Euro saw him look and explained quietly. "The birds are photographers. Cameras *onbird*. Always around. They have an implant in their brain and a camera in one eye. The Ramians also use them to communicate with each other."

Brain implants? "Don't they just use their s'link things?"

"Yes, for official stuff. But for personal invitations, you have to summon a bird."

"Complicated," Io commented, with more strain in his voice than he'd had on the shuttle. Lanezi tried to give him an encouraging look, but he was distracted. Lanezi wasn't sure what Io was looking at. The rimway was empty.

"Where are the people?" Lanezi whispered to Io.

Io pointed to a very subtle blue light at the end of the corridor. "Our route has been cleared."

Sontula, who probably heard everything they said, explained, "This is an official delegation. We are not to be imposed upon."

This was all sounding very serious. *Good.*

They stopped outside the captain's—the getti's—outer office, so that Lanezi could stand and walk in. He was a bit dizzy, but he thought it was from all the art, the lights, the colors, the smells even. But Io came beside him and Lanezi put his hand on Io's shoulder for stability.

An efficient aid swept all of them into the getti's personal study. Drann was the medium-tall of middle age, steely blue, running neutral colors at the moment. Ze had many tokens, including some woven in ziz midnight blue hair, patches on ziz jacket, as well as jewelry and medals. Ze was harried but polite. In the introductions, ze crossed both hands over ziz chest.

Then they had a round of handpressing. The twins murmuring polite phrases in Ramian. Lanezi and Neah were offered chairs in front of Getti Drann, with all others to the side. Sontula and the getti's aid took out their pads.

Getti Drann spoke to Lanezi and the translator echoed "Captain Lanezi, what is this urgent matter?"

Good. Straight to business. "Honor. I must warn my people. And your people. They may be in danger."

Drann's colors turned amber. Lanezi gulped and went on. "Friendship—the system we came from before you rescued us —is destroyed. A bubble of radiation is coming."

"Do you mean the star itself has been destroyed?"

"Yes, like a supernova, or worse maybe."

Drann glanced at ziz aid and a map appeared on the wall screen. Lanezi looked at it in confusion. It was a Ramian map. Beautiful, but it didn't include sector circles. He didn't have any way to orient himself. "I need a point of reference."

Neah got up to explain. "Here," he pointed, "is Friendship. This," he ran his hand over the right side of the screen, "is Human space." With his left hand he indicated Ramian space. Lanezi got up to join him. The stars had the proper colors and small pathways—the same as the threads. Suddenly it made sense to him. "Canyon?" He pointed.

"Yes," Neah agreed.

"We need distances. Not jump distances, real lightyears. Those within 100 lightyears are in danger."

"Agreed," Neah said. Getti Drann approached and tapped the screen; Ramian numbers appeared. Neah translated. "Canyon, 75 lightyears."

"Thank God. There's time."

Neah nodded. "Luminesse, 50." *How sad*, Lanezi thought. *They just saved their system and now they'll have to abandon it.*

"Firelight, 120. Atikameq, 110." Lanezi let out a breath. Nothing disastrous for humanity. Thank heavens.

Neah glanced at Getti Drann and went deathly gray. Drann, also gray, was staring at the Ramian side of the map. Neah reached over and touched the star at Seven. "Five years," Neah whispered. Everyone in the room gasped. Seven was in the total destruction zone.

"They're not Ramian. But there are 10 billion people in that system," Drann whispered.

"Can we move them?" Lanezi asked.

"Not in time," Drann answered. "Not even with Human help. Besides, there is nowhere to put them." Ze sat down heavily at ziz desk. Drann's aid looked stricken. Her colors were gray with black shadows.

"This ship, the *Watcher,* has been studying those people for years," Euro whispered.

"What," Drann cleared his throat and struggled to speak, "happened at Friendship and how do you know?"

"I'm not sure," Lanezi answered. "There was something happening with a stray gravity ball. There was some vortex that got one of our ships and one of your ships." They nodded. "But the star was still intact, according to your crew," Drann said, glancing at Io and Euro.

"Yes, but something happened during our jump out, or right after. I only see the radiation bubble when *Watcher* jumps, when we're in jumpspace."

"Because in jumpspace, everything is in real time, or one place, however you like to look at it," Drann said. "But why don't my pilots see this?"

"I . . . I think they could, if they looked. Usually, at least for Humans, it's very strict, that you only look where you're going."

"Send word," Drann said to ziz aid. "Someone must jump and look. Immediately."

"Yes, Drannjik," she answered. Lanezi thought they were about to be dismissed.

"My people? We can warn them somehow?"

"Yes. You will record a message." Ze motioned another aid over. "Send whatever message they wish." And with that they were dismissed into the care of the aid.

7 / VEEZ

8-Mercy

Drumheller, in orbit around the rogue planet

Days after their visit to the 81-Petals, Beezan got ready for bed, missing part of his family. With Iricana, Thunder, and Kelson on the *81-Petals*, they were no longer at meals and social arts. They talked onscreen often, but it wasn't the same.

Beezan gave Sky one last hug. "First I'm lonely. Then it's too crowded. Then I miss people. Sky, what's wrong with me?"

She glared at him. "Have Sky." He laughed. *Obviously, what else could a person want?*

Now aboard the *Drumheller*, Veez was very happy. He was a social creature. He joined them for all meals, prayers, social arts, even cleanup. He volunteered for work and took great pleasure in bossing the robots. He even became their head cook while Jarvie was in school. Apparently, he'd watched years' worth of Human cooking shows on the *81*.

"Sky, what do you think about Veez?"

"Veez sad."

"He's been alone a long time. He misses his family."

"Bee take. Take home."

"We would take him home if we knew how."

"He knows."

Beezan couldn't sleep. How long should he let them stay on the *81-Petals*? Keeping two ships up and running was using a lot of extra energy. But it made sense to keep the *81* garden going. *Maybe it just doesn't matter. We're stuck here. I just wish I knew a shortcut home.*

He knows. Sky said, *he knows.* Beezan didn't want to wake her up and ask her. *Veez knows we would take him if we could, or he knows how to get home?*

9-Mercy

The next day, Beezan was cleaning up the lunch food, except there were no leftovers. Veez just ate it all. *I hope we don't have to ration.* Katie sat at the table with Veez, sipping her tea and reviewing the *81-Petals* medical records, while the pups snuffled around for crumbs.

"Thank you for lunch, Veez. You're a very good cook."

"Captain, you're very welcome. My pleasure. It's the least I can do for my ride home." Beezan froze.

"Veez . . ." Veez looked at him with complete innocence. *How can I break this to him?* "Veez, I can't take you home."

Veez waved it off. "Of course you can. Taboos are removed for emergencies."

"Veez, I don't know how."

"I'll explain where, of course." Katie was looking on sadly now. She scooted the pups out the door.

Beezan took a step closer. Maybe Veez really didn't get it. "I can't jump without the a-rings or a gravity-assist. We don't have either. We're stuck here, just like you were."

"I had no pilot. But you're a pilot. You can't be stuck."

"We have no way to reach JV. But the *81-Petals* must have sent a distress call 15 years ago. We hope for a rescue in less than 10 Human years."

"No," Veez whispered.

"Yes! My people are learning to build a-rings. They can bring them, and a gravity ball."

"Insanity. And they won't know."

"They'll know there's no star, so they'll take that precaution. I'm sure they will. For the *81-Petals*, they would do anything."

"But no, Captain." Veez got up and put his paw on Beezan's shoulder. "No message left here 15 years ago."

"They must have sent a message when they got stuck."

"No, Captain, you don't understand. They didn't get stuck here." He pointed in the direction of the rogue planet. "They were captured in Chike space, *hundreds* of lightyears from here." He pointed off as if into the far distance. "The Chike took the crew and . . . flung the ship back. But without a live pilot, it got stuck in this gravity well."

Katie was now by Beezan's side. "Are you saying no distress message left from here?"

"I sent one to my people, of course, fifteen years ago. But they won't get it for another 20 years."

Beezan's mind was reeling. Katie grabbed his arm. *No rescue?* "But maybe someone was aboard before you got here."

"Captain, I know. I was there for the capture."

"What?" He and Katie said together. Beezan felt a flash of anger.

"I am so sorry Captain. I did witness the capture of this crew in Chike space. We only barely escaped ourselves, by hiding on the *81-Petals* when the Chike tossed it back. But Captain, none of that matters. You can jump back from here. Any pilot could."

"How?"

An extremely conflicted look crossed Veez's face. Tears filled his eyes. Many heartbeats passed before he spoke. "Some taboos are not lifted. Even for emergencies."

"No gravity-assist? No a-rings? What else is there?"

"Captain, you must trust me. Let your mind be free of Human thinking. You can jump out of here."

"Without a-rings?"

"Do you really think the GenTwo put those gravity balls out there to help you? A-rings are a last resort."

"Veez!"

"I can say no more." And head down with resignation, he left the kitchen. Beezan looked at Katie in shock. But she was looking at him with expectation. He shook himself and grabbed his s'link. "Captain Iricana, please bring your crew here at 1600 for a consultation."

For the crew's sake, they had to find a way home.

Jarvie sat with Terina and Veez as they watched another episode of *Journey of our Hearts*. Since it was a newer show, Veez hadn't seen it on the *81*. They were all trying to take their minds off the scary news that no distress call had gone out from the rogue planet location to Human space.

Terina conspired with Jarvie to ask Veez as many unofficial questions as possible, since she wasn't allowed to interview him. So when the show wrapped up, and the pups started crawling all over Veez, Jarvie did his best. "Are the podpups taboo?"

"Who? These rascals?" Jarvie laughed at Veez's fake disdain. It was obvious that he liked them. And he seemed completely unsurprised to see them. "They can't be taboo. They're everywhere. A patriarch can hardly extend his family to another planet without bumping into the podpups, as you've so aptly named them."

"Where did they come from?"

"No one knows. Some of their DNA is ancient. Some people think they're not native to this leaf."

"Even the famous GenOne don't know?"

Veez leveled a schoolmaster-like gaze on Jarvie. "Do not mock the GenOne, child."

Jarvie got a little chill at that. "Sorry!"

"The GenOne do not know the origin of the small ones, but they could probably take a good guess. However, none of us could ever check, since we're not allowed outside the leaf."

"Why not?"

"Not our territory. Completely outside the protection of the GenOne."

"*Protection?*" Terina's comment was more like an objection. "Doesn't seem like they were much protection for the crew of the *81*."

"For that, you may blame the overzealous Chike patrolling their space." He paused. "At least, that's what we do."

"*Your* people have disappeared?" Terina asked. Obviously she couldn't help being the interrogator.

Veez stared off into space. "Ships disappear. We don't know for sure that the Chike have anything to do with it. There are seven other races of GenTwo, and a couple of them are very different. Mysterious. Their minds exist on the other side of a divide we cannot cross." His mood shifted to the melancholy and the pups slowly retreated to the familiarity of their Humans.

"It's time," Jarvie said. "I have to greet the *81-Petals* crew."

"I'll come," Terina said. So they gathered the pups and left Veez to his thoughts.

Beezan assembled the entire crew in the Consultation Hall: Humans, Veez, and podpups. Sequoia and Jarvie flanked Beezan. Katie, Iricana, Thunder, and Kelson sat together, and Veez sat across from Jarvie. Terina sat at the other end, saying she'd watch the pups. *Probably secretly taking notes.* A view of *81-Petals* was on the main screen. They said several rounds of prayers, until the pups fell onto their sides, asleep.

"Captain," Beezan said to Iricana, "we have distressing news." With help from Veez, he relayed the information that no mayday had left the rogue planet location 15 years ago. If they wanted to leave, they would have to wait a quarter century, or find their own way home. The others took it stoically.

"Exactly what is needed to jump?" Thunder asked Sequoia.

"A pilot. Jump velocity. A pathway."

"What don't we have?" Iricana asked.

"Fuel to reach the required speed." Sequoia answered, understanding that they were working their way through basic questions.

"We normally get free acceleration from a gravity ball or gravity assist," Beezan added. "But we don't have that here."

"If we had the fuel," Kelson asked, "How long would it take?"

"In straight line acceleration? *Drumheller*, can you calculate?" Beezan had assigned Jarvie to watch Veez carefully for any sign of approval or disapproval, but Veez obviously nodded his head yes, maybe subconsciously.

"At current fuel conversion rate, it would take 10.7 years."

There was a sigh of relief from the crew. "Better than waiting around for a rescue," Iricana said.

"Just out of curiosity," Jarvie asked, keeping an eye on Veez, "how long would it take if we had unlimited fuel already converted?"

"Options listed, assuming all necessarily fuel was available."

Beezan leaned over to look at Jarvie's pad, and sat back, stunned. "With some serious boosting, just over a month!" Jarvie said.

The crew, including Veez, lit up with hope. "But the necessary fuel would still take 10 years to convert," Beezan objected. And then all eyes turned to Beezan. *What did I say? Fuel saved? Ten years?* And Iricana turned to look at the *81-Petals* onscreen.

Beezan gasped. "Fuel? Is it saved?"

"Yes," Thunder confirmed. "The fuel converter has been on. And they have huge storage facilities. There's fifteen years of fuel ready."

"Can you transfer it to the *Drumheller?*" Beezan asked. That sounded like a job for a dockside repair team. The crew went still. Iricana bit her lip. Jarvie gasped. Terina looked wide-eyed at her grandfather.

Thunder continued in a quiet, gentle voice. "We've spent a couple of days insuring that the *81-Petals* is in operational order. And we have established command."

Beezan's mind suddenly felt muddy. They wanted to jump with *81*? "But how do we bring the *Drumheller*?" More silence and lip-biting. Slowly they all turned to look at the *81-Petals*. And Beezan understood. "No! No. I can't. I can't leave the *Drumheller*. I can't leave it *here!*" His heart was pounding. He broke out in a sweat. *They think the 81 is their only way home.*

"Captain—" Katie started to say.

"No! No AI has ever successfully merged or shared another ship." He looked to Iricana. "Right?"

"That's correct," she nodded. "We could not risk the attempt. It might damage the *81-Petals* AI."

"Captain, it might be possible to come back," Kelson said.

"No. When? *In a hundred years?* They'd come out for the *81*, but they'll never drag a-rings out here for the *Drumheller!*"

"We'd do everything in our power to get the *Drumheller* back," Iricana assured him.

"Then . . . then . . . I'll stay," Beezan said, not even fully understanding what he was saying. They all shook their heads.

"I need you," Jarvie whispered.

My ship or my son? But the ship is the embodiment of my entire family. My whole life. It's a unique intelligence.

Beezan put his head down on the table and covered it with his arms. "Let him be for now," he heard Katie say. "We probably don't appreciate what we're asking."

And the room quietly emptied, Jarvie squeezing his shoulder on the way out. And after he cried and said *no* about a hundred times, a quiet voice responded,

"Yes."

11-Mercy

Sandstorm, en route to the colony planet

Zahar paced along the edge of the big auditorium on the Chike ship. The Ramians had redesigned it to be flat, with a central square surrounded by private cabins on three sides. The Chike platform remained on the fourth side, but smaller. She wondered if the Ramian designer was sending a message to the Chike to keep their flag carriers out.

Of the private cabins, the Humans had three, a generous amount. One for Caspia and Evan, one for Thayne, and a crowded, but friendly one, for the rest of them. The central square was divided into a small exercise station and large eating and social area.

On the platform, a fancy table sat. Occasionally, the Exempt Pascal would preside over a short meeting with Quay. Today, however, Zahar had been informed by a low-level flag carrier that she would also be expected.

Minutes before the appointed time, Quay and Getti

Fasandar moved to the base of the platform. Zahar, with departing pats on the back from the *Cheetah* crew, joined them.

"What should we expect?" she asked.

"To receive an update. Then advice and orders." Quay smiled slightly. "Also, proclamations of ziz sincere advocacy for us."

"Let's hope it is sincere," Fasandar grumbled.

"Getti, you seem better today," Quay said, not quite a question.

"Yes. Thank you. The food has been a bounty for the whole crew. Everyone's health is improving."

"Yes, some things have been a blessing."

Zahar nodded. "I think we should eat while we can."

The door opened. The three of them snapped to attention.

Two flag carriers of Pascal's personal escort walked zir to the meeting table, but ze sent them to the corner with a graceful wave of ziz small claw.

There were no chairs. Pascal stepped onto a small lifter that made zir slightly taller than Getti Fasandar, the tallest of the three of them. Ze beckoned them forward. Though they had not planned it, Zahar and the Getti stopped a pace back from the table, allowing Quay to be in front. The rest of the Human and Ramian crews sat quietly in the square, attentive even though they would not be able to hear much.

Pascal began. "Greetings Harbinger Quay, Getti Fasandar, and Captain Zahar. May the favor of the Creator and protection of the GenOne be upon us all." The four of them nodded their heads respectfully.

"This ship is now only two jumps from the colony planet." Zahar's heart sank. Permanent exile. "Of course, the Harbinger will continue on." There was a slight gasp from Quay. "Do not despair! This one is not heartless! This one has negotiated /

maneuvered, to grant the Harbinger, that important personage, an escort of three."

"But there are four others in my family."

"Three. The Chike are generous."

No matter what Quay did, his family would be broken up. "Very well," Quay said. He seemed to breathe himself into a small trance. And then he stood up straight. "I will take Captain Zahar, and the Humans Evan and Caspia." Zahar nearly choked. *What is he doing?* But he obviously didn't mean to be cruel as he didn't separate Evan and Caspia.

"An intriguing choice," Pascal commented.

"Exempt Pascal, my people are tired. I am trusting. The Exempt Pascal has said the colony is a happy and healthy land. Let them go and live their lives."

No one asked Zahar if she agreed, but she found that she was guiltily relieved that she would not be going to the colony. And no matter what this crazy galactic meeting was that Quay was going to, she was determined to get a message through to the sectors to rescue the colonists.

Half in shock, Zahar gathered the *Cheetah* crew in Thayne's cabin to tell them the news. She tried to block out the thought of Quay telling his family goodbye, maybe forever. Caspia and Evan grasped each other's hands in relief that they would be together. The others, except Thayne, nodded in resignation.

"Ze said it is a beautiful planet. 'A real planet,' ze called it. Ze said that you'll be happy there. Maybe they don't have much concept of family. But the Human colony is on a separate continent from the Ramian continent, so you won't even see them."

"Why not?" Nkiroo asked, confused.

"It's . . . ze used the word 'primitive'," Zahar answered.

"As in cavepeople?" Melawn asked.

"Pre-computer, ze said. But it sounds like pre-ocean travel."

"God help us," Melawn muttered.

"You will help yourselves!" Zahar insisted. "You are human beings and will conduct yourselves with nobility. Dr. Tenshi, I appoint you leader of the Human detachment until you integrate into the local leadership."

"Yes, Captain."

Thayne rolled his eyes. "Why?"

"Because Dr. Tenshi is the only one of you who ever lived on Earth, and I believe you had some experience in a remote village?"

Tenshi nodded.

Zahar continued, "I'll do everything I can to get your location to the sectors, but obviously, I have no idea what we're getting into. We may end up with you on the colony, eventually."

12-Mercy

Watcher, in the Ramian system called Four

Lanezi, holding an excited Whisper close, walked down the corridor of the *Watcher* in the company of Neah, Sontula, and a bunch of birds. Sontula gave him a smile and chin-up motion. *That's right. There are cameras onbird. They're recording this.* Lanezi tried to smile, but he wasn't an actor. He sensed the tension of his escorts. They very much wanted to please.

Lanezi had been given a p'link of sorts, a small pad with colored, jeweled buttons that would call Neah, Sontula, Io, Euro, or Anitoran, the medical aid. He was finally going to be on his own.

They slowed, "Your quarters, compliments of Getti Drann,"

Neah announced. The door slid open, and—no stairs. It was one of the strangest differences between Human ships, which used artificial gravity, and the Ramian ship, with its central gravity from the captive gravity ball. It gave Lanezi a little shiver, but he was quickly distracted by the cabin. More like a mini-palace. It was extravagant, even by Ramian standards. Lanezi, accustomed to wealth, was speechless. He stepped inside, where he knew the birds were not allowed to follow.

"It's beautiful," he said quickly. "I hope no one had to give up their rooms."

"No," Neah assured him. "All ships are prepared for important guests. It is our pleasure to host."

Lanezi gazed in wonder at the most spectacular thing in the room, a window. Computer generated of course, but astonishing. He crossed the plush carpet, and the sunken square with couches, to look out. The scene was a deck overlooking a meadow of deep purple flowers. In the background were sharp-peaked mountains and a stunningly blue sky. So like Earth, but not. "Ramia," he whispered.

"Creator willing, you will see it someday," Neah said. "We will leave you to explore the other room and get settled." They turned to go.

Another room? "Oh, thank you. But—" They paused. "Euro and Io?"

"Just across the corridor," Sontula pointed. "Their rooms are almost as large as yours."

All this for three people? The life support it must take. "Neah, Sontula . . . I don't want to be a pampered guest. I owe you my life—and the lives of the twins, who are in my charge. It's a great debt. What can I do for you?"

A troubled look crossed Sontula's face and her colors went yellow with a turquoise stripe. But Neah's colors blazed blue and he nodded in approval. Neah put his hand on Lanezi's shoulder. "Lanezi, now that you are well, there are important duties for you. Have no fear of being an idle onlooker. We will meet with Getti Drann again soon. For now, rest."

They smiled and were gone, leaving Lanezi puzzled and overwhelmed. He set Whisper down in the colorful podpup play area, but she promptly scurried back under his feet. He had time to take about ten *what next* breaths before Io and Euro and the other pups showed up. He'd been expecting them. He'd been fretting about whatever they wanted to tell him once they had privacy. But he was totally unprepared for their story.

"Lanezi!" Io hugged him—and wouldn't let go, while they tried not to trip over all the pups.

The twins looked better. Since the age misunderstanding had been cleared up, they had unfrilly black pants and purple shirts with sky blue tokens on the right collar. He'd been told they had all the food they wanted. Sontula had made sure. "Io? Euro, what's wrong?"

Euro came closer. "You sacrificed yourself for us. We saw it on the summary."

And with a jolt, Lanezi realized that he had lied. Again. By not telling the twins what he was doing. But in this case—but he had vowed never! He sighed in defeat and led them to the sunken couches, dropped into one of them, and put an arm around each twin. "I couldn't tell you." He glanced back and forth. "I couldn't."

Io nodded. "We know. But if we'd jumped to Human space, no one could have saved you."

"We have all been blessed beyond measure," Lanezi said. "I'm so happy that you two survived. You have been brave and supportive—the best crew anyone—" he started to choke up. "Anyone could ask for."

"I'm so glad we can finally talk to you," Euro said. "We're not sure what's going on, but we saw other stuff on the summaries." Euro glanced at Io. "Upsetting stuff."

"What?" Lanezi asked.

Euro frowned. "We think we're in a war."

"*What?*"

"They're not calling it that," Euro explained. "But there is conflict between the Ramians and the Chike, and not everyone agrees about what should be done."

Io nodded. "They make these newsreels. They call them summaries. But they are more like stories than news. They feature specific people like they are heroes. They even have music. We're not sure if they are true or fiction."

"Well, the Ramians do put their artistic spin on everything. Can you show me?"

Lanezi looked up at the big screen. He had no idea how to work the equipment, but as usual, the twins had figured things out. "Summary of events at Seven, Six and Five," Euro said to the air. Several selections appeared on screen. Euro said something in Ramian and the second one started to play.

A Human shuttle appeared on screen. The main body was intact, although severely dented, but external equipment was either gone or broken beyond usefulness. *The Enkindler*. Lanezi gasped. The knot of panic and responsibility came right back to his stomach. Both Io and Euro grabbed his arms.

The view switched to inside the *Watcher*. The rescue team was shown suiting up—with music! Neah in particular was featured, giving orders and leading the rescuers to the airlock. The three of them watched their whole rescue scene replayed from the reverse point of view. Io hid his face until the final euphoric moment of safety. In the bottom right corner of the screen, a countdown clock stopped at 4.34.

"We had four minutes left?" Lanezi asked.

"No," Euro answered. "That's their time. It comes out to a minute and a half."

Lanezi's mind whirled. Every little thing, every decision by both ships had saved them, by less than two minutes over all that distance. ***"Praise and thanksgiving be unto Thee for whatever conformeth to Thy pleasure within the empire of heaven and earth."***[1]

The cameras were not allowed in the med center, so the narrative shifted to Getti Drann and the run for Seven's a-rings, complete with drama of *Would the Chike stop them?* The Chike did not even take notice.

A graphic appeared detailing their arrival at Six System. Positions of Chike ships, Ramian ships, planets and one space station were shown. The twins tensed up when a Chike announcement was replayed, warning the Ramians that they had only 21 days to vacate the system.

"Pause," Euro said. They all took a few breaths. "There's a recap of what happened at Six," Euro continued, "but *Watcher* went ahead." Euro pulled out his p'link. "Eight days later, we jumped to Five."

"They let you use your p'link," Lanezi said, puzzled.

Euro nodded. "They don't sync to their system, but we can still use them. We're trying to keep track of facts."

"Things here are kind of unreal," Io added.

"Continue at Five," Euro said.

Another graphic. There were more Ramian ships at Five System. Chike scouts were marked in amber, the caution color, Lanezi realized. And there was a big lunar colony. "Pause," Euro said. "There was no announcement this time, at least not yet. But they didn't have any way to evacuate that colony."

"Three thousand people," Io added.

"So the Ramians decided to take a stand." Euro skipped ahead in the summary. Another hero emerged. A young, small pilot. She boarded a sleek shuttle. The view switched to outside, where several Chike scouts were incoming to the lunar colony. The Ramian shuttle headed right for one of the viper-like Chike ships. It seemed inevitable that there would be a collision. At the last moment, the Ramian ship suddenly lurched to a stop, and was then immobilized. The Chike ship passed untouched.

"She was prepared to die," Euro commented.

"And to kill," Io added.

"Why?" Lanezi asked.

"Because the Chike are shutting down the gravity balls," Euro answered.

"And no one knows how far they will go," Io said.

Lanezi thought about how that would be in Human space. "If they deactivated the gravity balls in the sectors, we wouldn't be able to use the a-rings. We wouldn't be able to evacuate. It would strand everyone in the outer sectors and destroy our whole society."

"And the Ramians are afraid of what they might do at Ramia," Euro whispered. He checked his p'link again. "Seven days later we jumped to Four."

"That's what woke me up," Lanezi said. He felt a primitive instinct rise up in his chest—to fight. But he knew that was wrong. "When a thought of war comes—"

"Oppose it by a stronger thought of peace,"[2] both twins finished.

"But Lanezi," Io said, "we might be the only ones to have stronger thoughts of peace."

"And there's just the three of us," Euro pointed out.

· · ·

16-Mercy

Sandstorm, en route to the colony planet

Melawn sat with the other "colonists" in survival orientation. Their big room had been converted into a primitive village. They'd watched 3D movies about metalworking, farming, and managing livestock, including how to kill a chicken-thing. He'd fainted. They'd practiced how to build a fire. He burned his hand. How to chop wood. He didn't even try. He found it hard to believe that Humans were eating meat, but Tenshi said it might be that or starve.

There were warnings about poison plants and what to do if you got stung by giant bugs that were apparently out to kill you. Wear your hat, your sunglasses. Carry water at all times. And then the Exempt went on about what a nice, benign, beautiful, sunny planet the GenTwo had sacrificed for the colony.

Everyone was issued two sets of outer "protective" clothing, six sets of underclothes, boots that would stop a "stonesnake," water bottle, coat, blanket, and the biggest backpack he'd ever seen. Like one you'd use in nogee. Except this planet had 1.1g. Someone would have to carry Thayne's.

Electricity and somewhat less ancient technology were permitted at the hospital and printing press, under strict supervision by a remote Chike supervisor.

There were rules. Respect the local government. They had full authority to punish or banish you, which would easily be a death sentence. Do not pollute the planet. Follow strict recycling protocols. And most important of all—never ever bother "the crabs". Do not go near them, or into the ocean. It's their planet. Don't talk about space with the native born. Your old life is over. Make a new life. You will grow and be strong. Give up your anger and be happy.

Melawn glanced at Thayne. Thayne sat with fists clenched,

burning with anger. No one would even sit near him. If he'd never been able to give up his anger before, what would happen now?

Most of the Ramians were running reddish colors, some form of intense concentration. They had become so detached after their long ordeal, and grateful for their escape that they were more willing to take on this adventure. And most of them were with their families.

Then Thayne started another behavior that completely baffled Melawn: arguing with the Ramians about who had the better technology. Even Nkiroo got in on it. Melawn shook his head and avoided the whole thing.

The *Cheetah* crew had already lost Lanezi and the twins. Now they would be split again when he, Nkiroo, Thayne, and Tenshi went down to the colony—with only Dr. Tenshi having any remotely usable skills. Melawn realized that now he would never be able to reunite with his parents and make up for the guilt of leaving them. He consoled himself that at least he wasn't separated from Nkiroo, and remembered to thank God for that blessing.

Melawn tried to imagine it. No electricity. No computers, no p'links, no lights? When they were shown a "transportation" safety movie about how to ride a large animal, Nkiroo dropped his head in his hands and cried. There would be no ships for him.

Inside his assigned backpack, Melawn found one notebook, one pencil, and a prayer book. He clutched the notebook. This was it? The entirety of his data hunting for the rest of his life would have to go in this one notebook?

9 / *MUNDICIDE*

1-Words

Watcher, at Four System

Lanezi, Io, and Euro held Feast together, just before dinner. They were fortunate that the Ramians had converted their library of sacred writings over to the Ramian p'links. And they each had a prayer book. Happy to be alive, to be well, to be fed and safe, they read prayers of gratitude. But there was an undercurrent of anxiety. Their concern for the people of Seven was especially hard on Io who struggled to keep his composure, even after many more prayers for protection.

They were just starting on a small plate of Ramian treats when a Chike voice came booming over the *Watcher* comm system. They covered their ears, but it was no use. The Chike sounded so angry, but they could not understand the Ramian translation.

"Quartil," Io gasped. "I heard zir say—"

"That's Friendship," Euro explained for Lanezi.

They felt the pounding of Ramians running in the corridor.

"Let's go," Lanezi said, and they joined the throng headed for the dining room.

As they crowded inside, Sontula took Lanezi by the arm, steering the three of them to Neah's table. The mood in the dining room was grim. Their colors were running dark gray with an alarming orange streak. "We didn't understand," Lanezi told Neah immediately.

"Too loud for your translator," Neah said. "I'm running it through again. But the gist of it is that the Chike have verified the destruction of Friendship and tied it to us."

"The Ramians?" Lanezi asked. *It was Thayne that called all the gravity balls.*

"Maybe they just mean the lesser ones in general," Neah said. He set out his p'link. "Here:"

"Attention lesser ones! The total destruction of Friendship has been confirmed. The extremity of this crime / offense has no equal in the history of this leaf. The shockwave / radiation will devastate / lay waste to entire systems. It is mundicide! / Biocide! These servants are appalled. The GenOne will be consulted. There will be repercussions! There will be justice!"

"Will there be help for Seven?" Io asked, looking annoyed. Neah gazed thoughtfully at Io and then at Sontula, but had no answer.

4-Words

Aboard a Chike shuttle, at the colony planet

Melawn sat on a hard seat in the Chike landing shuttle, decorated in sickening stripes, yellow and black this time. They were dressed in their new colony clothes, with the backpacks secured under the seats. Thayne, on his right, had been sedated for the trip, his anger spilling over so badly that the Chike feared he might be a danger. Tenshi and Nkiroo were to Melawn's left, Tenshi often leaning forward to glance at Thayne and frown over his dazed condition.

Their honor guard consisted of two lowly flag carriers and two pilots. The Exempt Pascal had pronounced them hearty colonists and casually waved them off, with barely a moment to say goodbye to their crewmates. Zahar, Caspia, and Evan were sad and scared for them. Melawn wasn't sure which was worse, being stranded with Humans or venturing on with the Chike.

Their first order of business was to walk to the Human colony. The shuttle would not land anywhere near it. Tenshi had been given instructions she was not allowed to reveal until they were down. And she looked sick with worry.

Melawn took some deep breaths, but it was hot in the shuttle and he felt like he was just making himself hotter and more panicky. There wasn't enough soundproofing to mask the loud landing thrusters, so they could not talk to each other. As they made their final touchdown, it was deafening. Dust, maybe dead Chike scales, puffed up with the hard landing. Melawn tried to hold his breath until the dust settled. Still hunched over in his seat, he kept waiting for the hard landing to stop. "Good Lord," Tenshi gasped, "this feels like more than 1.1g."

The hatch opened, letting in a blast of even hotter, dryer air and sandy dust, along with blinding sunlight. They scrambled for their packs and sunglasses. One of the Chike gave Thayne a medical burst to counteract the sedative. A great raging came immediately back to his eyes.

"Let's go," Tenshi said, using both hands to lift her pack. "We're going to have to help each other."

Nkiroo took the hint and helped Tenshi put her pack on, while Melawn helped Thayne. Melawn had already secretly taken some of Thayne's load and put it in his own pack. The

Chike guards coaxed them along with the prods as a steep ramp unfolded. After struggling down the ramp, they stepped onto the hot sand. Melawn was grateful for the boots. They were quickly walked to the first of a line of flagpoles with green flags at the top and a small umbrella-like shade. "Resting places," Tenshi explained as their escort deserted them.

They covered their faces from the flying sand when the shuttle took off. Melawn was watching it go when Tenshi said, "Forget them. Get your hats on. We're to follow the line of green flags to a processing center. Then we announce 'We are newcomers.' We're not to speak or interact with anyone else."

"Who else is there?" Nkiroo asked.

Tenshi shook her head. "I don't know. Those are our instructions. The last flag is red."

The next flag was at the base of a mountain, quite a ways across a barren desert. And then the next one halfway up the mountain. And then, shimmering in the blistering sun, almost too bright to see, even with the sunglasses, another green flag waved at the summit.

Sandstorm, at the colony planet

Zahar blinked away tears as she watched on the screen. Melawn, Nkiroo, Thayne, and Tenshi left the Chike shuttle. Melawn reached out to steady Thayne and they both fell. Nkiroo had to set his heavy pack down to help them. When they were all situated and standing, Thayne stared back into the shuttle as if memorizing the face of every last Chike that was responsible for their banishment.

"Tenshi is strong," Caspia whispered. "She'll get them to the colony."

The ramp folded up, obscuring their last view of their shipmates. Quay was praying, alone, after the departure of the Ramians earlier. Zahar was already feeling bad after their quick and awkward goodbye with the others. She hefted Kiwi in her arms. One more farewell.

On the platform, two Chike were attempting to herd the Ramian podpups into a shipping habitat, using their ridiculous poles. The pups had been taken from the Ramians at the last minute to go to a different sanctuary, causing even more distress and tears.

Caspia and Evan scowled, and then went to help. The podpups trusted the Humans, and the Humans trusted the Chike that the pups really were going to a good place.

"Kiwi?"

His innocent eyes looked up at her. "Go with friends?" she asked him. He perked up and looked at the Ramian pups. But then looked back up at her. Doubt. Indecision. Too much for a podpup. Zahar hugged him tight. "Yes, go with friends. Be safe. Be happy." She handed him to Caspia, who barely covered a gasp.

"But they said you could keep him on the ship."

"But who knows where we will end up?"

Caspia nodded and gave Kiwi a quick hug. She passed him to Evan, who slipped him a treat—from some Chike manufactured secret pocket. They gently set him in with the others.

"God be with you Kiwi," Zahar whispered. As the Chike took the habitat away, Kiwi looked back once, but then snuggled up with one of his favorite Ramian pups.

Caspia and Evan nodded and whispered goodbye to all the pups. The three of them just sat on the edge of the platform, letting their day of parting and grief wash over them.

· · ·

On the Colony

Hats on, heads down, sweat pouring inside their clothes, they headed for the next flag. The sensation of walking in the sand was so strange and difficult. Melawn started to calculate the calories they were burning and realized he'd switched to survival mode. He glanced at Tenshi. She had been right to warn them and be strict with them.

The heat on his face from a star .7AUs away was incredible. To think that the atmosphere both held the heat and gave them air was a wonder. Some tight fist of fear in the back of his brain —the fear of cave-ins, of dome malfunctions, of sudden ship decompressions—eased open and he cautiously exchanged the old dangers for the new.

Soon enough they came to hard-packed ground with just a layer of slippery sand on top. "How far?" Thayne asked after he fell again.

"Over the hill and then 23 kilometers," Tenshi answered. "If they actually know how far a kilometer is."

Nkiroo considered. "Twelve times around the *Cheetah*—a five-hour walk."

"But in this gravity, more like seven," she warned. "And we only have two liters of water. Ration yourselves."

"Thayne can't carry the pack for seven hours," Melawn said.

Thayne glared at him. "You probably can't either!"

Melawn sighed. "That wasn't a character judgment."

Nkiroo tilted his head in thought. "Maybe we could devise a way to drag them."

"We can't stop!" Tenshi insisted. "There are probably only eight hours of daylight left" They all glanced at the sun.

"And we have no lights," Nkiroo agreed.

"We'll run out of water. We must get there. Do your devising while we walk." She turned her back on them and started again. They quickly fell in line.

It took two hours just to reach the top of the hill. Nkiroo had called it a mountain and Tenshi scoffed. But she was grave with worry. "Five-minute break. A little water." Thayne threw off his pack and sat down.

Nkiroo pointed into the distance. "Another green flag."

"At least we have the trail," Tenshi said.

"Did they say why we have to walk?" Nkiroo asked.

"Not exactly. The Exempt seemed to think if you couldn't survive the walk, you wouldn't survive the colony. But I felt like there was another reason. Like maybe they couldn't risk a shuttle too close to the Humans."

Thayne's head came up. His eyes focused and calculated. "Rebellion."

"How do you make that conclusion?" Nkiroo asked.

"A Chike shuttle would be in danger near the colony. The landing place is so desolate and unlivable they can't camp out there to wait for one."

"Pure conjecture." Tenshi shook her head.

Melawn took only two sips of his water and carefully put it away. Maybe it was crazy, but thinking of rebellion gave Thayne reason to get up and go.

After five hours, every step was a painful jolt across Melawn's shoulders. All three of them were carrying some of Thayne's things. Melawn was so thirsty, but looking out over the long line of flags, he understood their danger. No water, no light, no food, no rescue.

They got to the next flag and stood in the shade to rest. It was getting cooler. They stared at the flags. They went all the way to another hill, or small mountain, whatever. It was exhausting.

"Thirty minutes of daylight," Thayne whispered. "I've been timing it."

Tenshi nodded. "We'll have to stop."

"We were supposed to make it in one day, though," Nkiroo said. "Did they say what would happen if we didn't?"

"No, but we obviously can't move around in the dark. Maybe there will be a moon. But let's get organized for now. Put everything right where you can find it."

They drank a little more water, spread out their blankets, and collapsed on them, exhausted. After a few minutes Melawn sat up and chanted a prayer. The others sat up too, and offered quiet devotions.

"I *am* grateful to be off that hideous ship," Nkiroo said.

"Yes, we should look at the positive," Tenshi agreed. "We're alive. We're away from the Chike."

Melawn hesitated to say anything. In a strange way, the day had been exhilarating. "It's a planet. A real planet. It's so amazing."

The others nodded. Even Thayne. "Yes," Thayne said. "We should take a moment to appreciate it."

And then the stars came out, and it was suddenly like home again.

5-Words

Colony

Melawn awoke several times during the night. There were at least two moons. One looked like it was about the size of a ping pong ball that moved noticeably across the sky. The other looked like a miniature Pluto, except without the famous heart. It rose later during the night. Once, when Melawn woke up, Thayne was sitting up, writing in his notebook by the dim reddish light of the heartless Pluto. Thayne sensed Melawn looking at him and patted him on the arm. "Go back to sleep."

The next time he woke up, Nkiroo and Tenshi were whispering and Thayne was curled up, listening. "It's hard to estimate with only one night of observation, but I think the moon will be up until dawn."

"So we could start walking now," Tenshi suggested. "While it's still cool." Nkiroo nodded. Tenshi glanced at them, saw that they were awake and asked, "Are you up to it?"

"Yes," Thayne agreed, reasonable as anyone, and sat up.

They made good progress and passed more flags, but could make no sense of the spacing. By mid-morning, there was starting to be some very sparse vegetation. In a long stretch, they passed some random boulders, so they took the opportunity to rest in the meager shade, closing their water tightly between sips.

A large reptile darted between dried bushes, startling them. "That's the first sign of life we've seen," Tenshi said.

"Some kind of lizard?" Melawn asked.

"Could be a Chike spy," Nkiroo suggested.

Just then, a gust of wind, blast of dust, and black feathers swooped down and grabbed the lizard. The four of them recoiled against the rock as a giant bird took off again. Melawn's heart was pounding.

"That was huge!" Tenshi exclaimed.

"Three-meter wingspan at least," Thayne added.

"We didn't even hear it coming," Tenshi fretted. "We'll have to keep a watch overhead and behind. I think it's used to bigger prey."

"Well," Thayne said, "I hope it *was* a Chike spy."

They all burst out laughing—for the first time in weeks, maybe months. Even Thayne laughed and relaxed a little. It gave Melawn hope that they could find some camaraderie in all this.

As they trudged on in a daze, trying to watch where they put their feet and blinding themselves looking out for killer birds, Nkiroo stopped and pointed. "Look! Beyond the next green flag."

"The red flag!" Tenshi said.

"Thank heavens," Melawn said. "We'll reach it before the heat of the day." He turned around to see how far they had come. And saw dust rising behind them. "Something . . ." Tenshi turned quickly to look. "A sandstorm?"

"No," she said. "Something on the ground. You can hear them."

Nkiroo shaded his eyes and looked. "Animals, maybe with riders, coming our way."

Tenshi turned back to look at flags. "We can't reach the red flag before they overtake us."

"Maybe it's the welcome party," Thayne suggested.

"No. Pascal said they won't leave the valley until we signal them from the red flag post. But let's make it to the green flag. At least there is shade."

They hurried there and took a longer drink of water. They were all very shaky from lack of food and excitement. They put their packs down and stood back-to-back around the central flag pole and packs.

"They look Human," Nkiroo said. "Those are the beasts we saw in the orientation."

"Remember," Tenshi said sharply. "Don't' talk to them."

"Maybe we should," Thayne argued.

"We're not supposed to!"

"So say the Chike, but they're the enemy."

"We don't know that! Thayne, I'm telling you not to."

He frowned. "We should keep our options open."

"No! Quiet—or you're on your own."

In a cloud of dust, six creatures, large humpbacked beasts with armored heads approached and surrounded them. The leader walked her beast around once, looking down at them. The lower parts of the riders' faces were covered with cloth and they had sunglasses. "Where are the rest?" the leader asked in a perfectly normal outer sector accent. Her voice was low and gruff, but somehow familiar. The puzzling question, as well as the order not to talk, prevailed, and no one answered.

She circled around again, and drew a long curved knife, more like a sword, from her saddle. Melawn couldn't believe this was happening. Instinctively, he stepped in front of Thayne. She jumped from the saddle and, quick as anything, struck the ground next to Nkiroo's feet. They all gasped and looked. Not an arm's length from Nkiroo was a huge stonesnake, as they had seen in orientation. She had sliced it almost in half. The woman scooped it up with the blade of her sword and flicked it towards the animals. The two beasts that caught the ends and tore it apart happily crunched away. Melawn and the others let out relieved breaths. "Watch for the little mounds of sand. That's how they hide. There's a sand sliding sound when they come out," the woman advised quietly and they nodded.

"So now, tell me. Where are they landing your ship?" The four of them kept their silence as she walked from Nkiroo to

Melawn, who stared at the ground. Thayne squeezed Melawn's shoulder and edged out from behind him. She asked Thayne, "Who are you?" Thayne defiantly brushed off his hat, removed his sunglasses, and looked up at her. They stared at each other.

"So! You are brainwashed by the GenTwo. You'll learn better." She shrugged, suddenly casual, and glanced back at one of her people before mounting again and addressing Thayne. "What do you offer for safe passage?"

Melawn gripped his water bottle. They had nothing else of value out here. But Thayne leaned over and grabbed his pack, pulled out the water bottle and handed the pack to her. It was obviously mostly empty—but she took it. With a toss of her head, she signaled her people. The surprisingly nimble beast reeled off and the others followed, covering their tracks in a cloud of dust.

The four of them stood there frozen for several seconds. Then Tenshi said, "Let's move, before they come back for more." They shouldered their packs, Thayne not having to bother, and headed for the last flag. "Nkiroo, watch for birds. Thayne, watch for snakes, Melawn, watch for riders. God help us."

"What was left in your pack?" Nkiroo asked Thayne.

"My underwear."

They snickered.

"Well, the pack itself might be valuable if they're some kind of rebels living in the hills. We're lucky they didn't take them all," Tenshi said.

Yes, Melawn thought selfishly. He'd have hated to lose his final material possessions, especially his notebook. *Thayne's notebook is still in his pack! He was writing in it last night. Not a diary—a message! Thayne followed the order not to talk, but as usual, he outmaneuvered everyone.* Melawn turned and looked at him accusingly. "Who were they?"

Thayne answered calmly, as if all were going according to plan. "She is AnnaLee, Captain of the *Dragonfly Dream*, with some of her command crew."

"*What?*" Tenshi stopped, incredulous. "You recognized them?"

"I am very good with people and voices, doctor."

"They did seem fam—," Melawn said, but Tenshi cut him off.

"Do they know *you*?"

"Everyone knows me," Thayne reminded her. True enough. Melawn and Nkiroo nodded. Thayne had been famous since he was ten. And that was something the Chike would never suspect.

"What did she mean," Nkiroo asked, "about where they were landing the ship? Human ships don't land, only shuttles."

"Puzzling," Thayne agreed.

"Where is the *Cheetah*, anyway?" Melawn asked.

"They dumped it about fifty jumps out of Friendship," Nkiroo said. "God knows where it is. Or where we are."

"And now," Nkiroo said, "we know what happened to the *Dragonfly Dream*. Perhaps the fate of *Starswimmer* and *81-Petals* was no better."

5-Words

Watcher, in Four System

Again, in the middle of the night, Lanezi woke to the sound of a blaring Chike message. Gasping with a burst of adrenaline, he buried his head under pillows and blankets and refused to get up. But Whisper walked over him, stepping on him as many times as possible, and jumped down to the deck to greet the twins and three little pups coming in.

"He's sleeping," Io whispered.

"No one's sleeping," Euro answered, with an uncommon touch of grumpiness.

"Okay, okay," Lanezi said. He dragged his clothes on and went to the dining hall with them for a very early breakfast. Although most of the Ramians were running a dark forest green, for tiredness Lanezi assumed, Sontula's green had a gray streak. She shook her head in disbelief. "It's crazy. They're demanding we return the gravity balls."

"What do you mean?"

"The ones on the ships and stations. We're supposed to take them out—but the ships were built around them!"

"So you can't take them out without wrecking the ships." *That's a big problem.*

"The entire design depends on central gravity. Our worlds will be literally upside-down. And we can't possibly destroy all our ships," she said. Lanezi nodded. "But I have to go," Sontula continued. "Neah will be accompanying Getti Drann to a meeting on the ship *River Bridge* to discuss sending a delegation to protest the gravity ball order."

"Neah is now in the Getti's inner circle?" Lanezi asked.

Sontula flashed yes and was off.

"What about Seven?" Io asked.

"I'll try to talk to Neah when he gets back," Lanezi said. So they sat, mindlessly eating, mere weeks after nearly starving. *They need Nkiroo.* And he could see by the sad looks on the twins' faces that they were thinking the same thing. *I wonder if he survived.*

Colony

The red flag shelter was at the base of another, even taller range of hills, that Tenshi agreed could probably be called mountains. They would have no hope of scaling them without food, water, and help. When they reached the shelter, they let down their packs and slouched on the benches in the shade. This shelter was bigger than the others, with a poster of instructions.

"Water!" Tenshi said, pointing to a pump. Quickly she drank the last of her water, then used the long pump handle for many pumps before getting new water, which she tasted carefully. "I can't really test it. We'll have to trust them. But there's always an adjustment to local water supplies." She shrugged.

They all drank some and filled their bottles while reading the instructions. "Ring the bell once for each person." Nkiroo read. "I don't see a bell. Or any buttons." But Melawn was looking out at the shadow of the shelter and could see the silhouette of an antique-style bell on the roof.

"Look!" he said and peered up the central post of the shelter. "A rope." He grabbed the rope and pulled it. It barely budged.

"I think you really have to yank on it," Tenshi said. So Melawn put his full weight on it and it made a small clang.

"Who's going to hear that?" Thayne complained.

"Here," Nkiroo said, joining Melawn, "together." They both pulled as hard as they could. The bell rang out loudly and the rope snapped back up and then down. They pulled again on the down stroke and it rang again. They actually rang it seven times once they got going. Afterwards, it was their ears that were ringing. Thayne nodded in grudging approval, "They can probably hear that for kilometers."

"'We call you to patience,' it says," Tenshi reminded them. "Emergency food supplies." She opened a storage door to crates of protein-like bars, not wrapped like from a store, but covered in some kind of wax. "Let's eat and rest while we can." They each took three bars, putting two in their packs just in case. Melawn and Nkiroo each took an extra for Thayne. They broke off the wax; Thayne squashed it into a little ball and saved it. Melawn took a bite of the bar. It was sweet and nutty and gooey. He was so hungry, and it was so thick and chewy, that he practically choked eating it.

Melawn washed it down with a lot of water and stretched out to rest as well as he could in the heat. He put his hat over his face and said a few prayers to himself. He tried to sort out the happenings of the last few days, but he was tired and a little sad, and strangely excited. *A planet. A real planet.*

Melawn awoke with a start; the others were standing looking towards the mountain. "They're coming," Thayne whispered. "You've been asleep a couple of hours."

Melawn got up to look out across the desert. There was no one there. "Up there," Nkiroo pointed. On the side of the mountain, along a path that zigzagged back and forth, was one small cart, pulled by one of the beasts, with two people aboard. "A cart?" he gasped.

"Cart? Wagon? We're not historians," Thayne complained.

Melawn watched for a while and then wandered off to wash and say his prayers in the shade of a few boulders. Sitting quietly, he heard a strange sound, like sand running down the side of a rock—*snake!*

He rolled away and leaped to his feet, turning to see where he'd been sitting. Sure enough, a stonesnake had just missed him. He backed away quickly, scanning the ground for more. He started to shake again. *I need more food.* He hurried back to the shelter, got out another bar and ate it. *Survival. I'm learning.*

Tenshi, Nkiroo, and Thayne all followed Melawn's example, cleaning up and taming their hair as much as possible to meet the new people.

The colonists arrived in no hurry and with no fanfare; they barely introduced themselves: two women, one middle aged, named Grace, and one very young, named Etazann. The younger was obviously a native. Shorter and stockier than Grace, with dark skin darkened even more by the sun, she had her hair braided and piled on her head. Giant black feathers were stuck in her hair to form a makeshift hat brim. She had a brightly colored green vest, but the green side was facing in.

Grace mentioned that she was from the sectors, many long decades ago. She collected their names, asking only for first names, and asked if there were others coming. Tenshi said no. "Come. No words can explain." She motioned to the cart and they piled in.

At first, Melawn was grateful for the ride, but as they were increasingly knocked about on the mountain trail, Melawn wedged himself in a corner with his knees drawn up to his chest, leaned his head on his knees and hid under his hat, trying to sway with the road rather than fight it.

They traveled slowly up the switchbacks. He may have slept some or just dazed out, but about half way up, they came to a tunnel, cut through the mountain. Blessedly cool inside, they all looked up in relief. The tunnel was barely big enough for one cart. Two carts could not pass. There were no supports. It looked like it had been chipped by hand, with axes or even small chisels. Melawn looked back and forth, wondering how long it had taken. "Thirteen years," Grace said. And Nkiroo shook his head in despair.

Melawn put his hat back on as they approached the bright exit, but the increase in temperatures was merely warm, not a blast of desert heat. The cart pulled over at a road cut and they clamored out to catch the view—and were struck with wonder.

Melawn could not take it all in. The barren desert was gone, replaced by an immense, long, green valley, with a wide river flowing right to left as far as they could see both ways.

"My God," Tenshi whispered. On their side of the river, curved terraces broke the slope of the mountain, greened with gardens and small cottages. Colorfully-dressed people with baskets and clumps of exuberant children walked along pale dirt paths.

On the other side of the river, the land was flat and obviously fertile for a long, long way before it approached the next mountain range. Fields upon fields of cultivated crops grew, but Melawn didn't have any way to recognize them.

All that was taken in at a glance. Dominating the scene, right in front of them, built into their side of the mountain so that it towered up to where they stood, was a nine-sided building, shining blindingly in the full afternoon sun.

"Welcome to Paradise Valley," Grace intoned, and Etazann followed up with a prayer. Melawn quickly took off his hat in respect and bowed his head. He had heard that prayer[1], but it was not one of the hundreds he'd memorized, maybe because it never made sense to him. But he knew he would learn that prayer intimately, now that he had come to the "vast and spacious lands" and would certainly need a stronger back.

Beyond the great gleaming temple they could see a few buildings, made of the pale mud, logs, or cut wood. But the temple was metal. The nine sides were huge curved pieces. "No," Nkiroo gasped and then covered his mouth as if he'd said something blasphemous.

"Yes," Grace answered mildly, "So rests *Starswimmer*, first off-world temple of humanity."

Thayne walked to the edge of the path, almost to the side of a cliff, as if to see it better. "They landed the ship?" he asked, incredulous.

"Yes," Grace nodded. "And we shaped it into a temple. You will be processed there." She pointed to a large arc of buildings beside the temple. "Travelers Welcoming Center." It was big, as if they were expecting hundreds. "Come."

Nkiroo and Thayne were stunned over the ship, but Tenshi

stared out at the valley like she had gone to heaven. Melawn took a deep breath of real air and looked around. He stood in the shadow of a temple of his own faith, God knew how far from Earth. Turning back to the path, he started down, walking. He would go on foot to his destiny.

6-Words

Sandstorm

Zahar was happy to go back to her role of organizer, planner, and person who generally took care of things. She knew Quay would need a period of mourning. His entire family, home, everything was gone, after nine hard years of his bringing them through their ordeal. But he also needed something to occupy his mind, which Zahar puzzled over while she ordered breakfast trays for the four of them. Despite parting from the Ramians and *Cheetah* crew, Zahar had slept better last night than in a long time. She'd reconfigured a private cube for herself, one for Quay and a bigger one for Caspia and Evan.

Quay was in the central area, sitting at a table, staring at the wall, as if it were an observation window. The planet was long gone anyway, so maybe it was just as well. She slid the tray over to him. "May I join you?"

"Yes, please. Thank you for the food."

"Did you sleep?"

"Some." They ate quietly a few minutes while Zahar fretted about what to say. These people-suffering problems were not her strong point. But Quay spoke first. "We need to know what's going on. I'm thinking of making demands." *Okay, so he doesn't need things to occupy his mind. I should have known.* She nodded. "I don't think they would dare harm me," he continued, "but I'm concerned about the three of you."

Caspia and Evan were up. Zahar waved them over. "Do you have any objection to Quay making demands of Pascal?"

"Depends," Evan said mildly. Caspia and Zahar turned to look at him in surprise. "On what he's going to demand."

Quay smiled.

Pascal entered with ziz usual fuss, although ze only had an escort of six now, still double Quay's escort. Before ze even got settled, Quay said, "This one has concerns."

Pascal turned ziz head sharply to the side and stared with one eye at Quay. A little shiver went up Zahar's back. *Have we underestimated Pascal?*

"This one," Quay continued, using Pascal's formal talk, "is required in a meeting / convocation. This one wishes to know where we are."

Pascal hesitated only a moment. "This ship remains in GenFour space. The search for harbingers continues. This ship is honored to discover the harbinger Quay."

"Exempt Pascal, how many harbingers are there?"

"At least one for each species. The Human harbinger is not yet found. Also we search for witnesses."

"What else are the Chike doing in Ramian space? This one requires proper information. This one requires *continuous* information. This one requires a full tactical room with knowledge of GenFour space and operations of this ship."

Pascal swiveled ziz head to stare with the other eye. "Requires?"

"It is proper," Quay confirmed mildly.

"Such information is not for lesser ones. You will not understand it."

"Are we *prisoners?*"

"No! The harbinger and Humans are honored guests!"

"Then it will be simplified for GenFour use, and explained."

Another swivel. "This is difficult."

"It cannot be beyond the power of this Exempt."

"Your words persuade. One will contemplate."

"Thank you, Exempt Pascal."

11 / DRUMHELLER

7-Words

Watcher, in Four System

In his fancy cabin, Lanezi managed to get through twenty pushups before his arms shook so badly he thought they'd give way and he'd break his nose. He rolled onto his back to stare at the beautiful geometric paintings on the ceiling. It was as if no part of the ship were left unadorned. *Maybe I could get a job as a painter here.*

Or, maybe I don't know how to paint anymore. Or how to jump anymore. He was gaining weight. He didn't feel starved, although he was still very thin. And even though he felt weak, the first day he'd only been able to do two pushups. But his mind was still fuzzy, as if not quite enough calories were going to his brain. Whisper jumped down from a chair onto his chest. "Owww."

"Breakfast!" She peered into his eyes. "Hungree!"

"Okay." He pushed himself to his feet. "We're going."

Moments later, Lanezi peeked in the dining room. The Ramians were buzzing, colors running red, turquoise, and yellow with stripes of grey or turquoise. The twins caught up with him. "What's going on?" he asked them.

"We thought you would know," Euro answered.

They were about to go in when Sontula magically appeared again and directed them to a smaller dining room next door. Several top-level Ramians, including Neah, were already eating.

"Getti Drann," Lanezi said, with a slight Human bow, since he had no colors to show respect. "Neah. Honors."

"Lanezi, join us," Drann pointed to a chair. Lanezi handed Whisper to Io, who went with Euro to the table with the special assistants, the ones called tans. Lanezi ate, even though this little change of plan was making him nervous. He had a new attitude about food—eat when you have the chance.

Getti Drann told everyone, "We've got work." Ze pulled up a view of Four system on the screen. "As you all know, the Chike have ordered us to leave this system. We believe they intend to chase us all the way back to Ramia. Although we have no military way to fight back, we've decided to step up our resistance here. An arrangement has been made between the stations and ships. We'll refuse to evacuate. We don't believe they are prepared to create massive loss of life. An evacuation is nearly impossible anyway. There are 4000 people on *Sister* Station and 6000 people on *Brother* Station. And although there are about 45 ships in this system, that's not enough to take everyone in one trip. The Chike are giving us 75 days. We estimate it would take 2-3 trips, closer to 225 days. We asked for 300 days and were refused."

Lanezi put his spoon down.

"I know," Drann nodded at Lanezi. "At the meeting, I expressed your strong objection to escalating or offering any warlike resistance." Ze glanced around the table. "That's why

Watcher won't be part of the resistance. We'll have a different mission—to plead for assistance for Seven."

An aid came in, and while Getti Drann was dealing with her, Lanezi turned to Neah, "You can't be against them and also ask for their help!"

"Of course we can."

"You have practically declared them enemies."

"Yes exactly. Consultation, your people have this." Lanezi blinked in confusion. Neah continued, "You send your trusted friend to get the enemy's story and then you listen to your friend, because people don't listen to their enemies."

Lanezi considered maybe that was like when Melawn would explain what was up with Thayne and the crew would listen. Not that Thayne was an enemy. Not really. "We try not to see people as enemies."

"Exactly. If you are the trusted friend, go to the enemy as a friend and bring back friendship."

"The stations refuse to evacuate?"

"Yes," Neah said.

"And meanwhile, we send a delegation to ask for the Chike's help with Seven?"

"We're morally obliged."

"Do you think the Chike will understand that, and not just capture the delegation?" Lanezi asked.

"We believe there is a universal standard of justice, like not enslaving people."

"But their version of justice could be dangerously different than yours or mine."

"Agreed. But we must try. And I'm asking for your help, Lanezi. *You* are the trusted friend. Not Chike. Not Ramian. You must go to the Chike."

"You can't be serious!" Lanezi's heart started pounding.

Neah flashed confidence. "I will go with you."

8-Words

Drumheller, at the rogue planet

Beezan wandered down the rimway, approaching the work tower. While the others packed supplies and shuttled them to the *81,* he was supposedly in charge of documenting the *Drumheller.* Terina and Jarvie were doing the actual work, since they'd already surveyed many cabins. Now they continued checking cabins for historical artifacts and "anything of value."

Inside the work tower, the surviving robots had been removed and the niches uninstalled and packed, each container anchored down in case of emergency. Luckily, *Drumheller* was a cargo ship and had plenty of containers—for things of value. He gazed at the workbench. When he was young, he had worked there with his grandfather. He looked up to the top of the tower, eyes blurry. Nurita had taught him nogee gymnastics up there. How many generations of his family had come here?

What would become of the *Drumheller*? Would it ever be found? Would any word of the crew ever make it back to the sectors, or would they disappear forever, like Azann? Beezan went to the workbench and got a microtool. He took the lift to the top of the work tower. There, he engraved his name on the wall, very small, and the date. Then he pocketed the tool, thinking he might just leave another message somewhere.

But his attempt at history didn't make Beezan feel any better. All his things of value, his places, his ship, the moments of his life, would be left behind. His urge to stay was so strong, his sadness unbearable; he could hardly tour the ship this one last time. But he had to say goodbye or forever regret it, so he staggered on, hunched over in his grief, seeing and touching the ship, standing in his places and trying to capture it in his mind, since he would no longer have it in this world.

9-Words

The next day, after engraving one more message on the door of the Command Bay, Beezan took the lift down to the *Drumheller* hangar for the last time. He needed to take the *Peacock* over to *81* and he didn't plan to come back. He made sure he was alone, except for Sky, of course. "*Drumheller?*"

"I am here."

"I'm transferring to the *81-Petals* now. Instigate command routine Beezan 99."

"Yes, Captain."

"We will attempt to return the crew to the sectors in the *81-Petals.*"

"Yes, Captain."

"I will try to come back for you."

"Yes, Captain."

"*Drumheller* . . . I'm sorry. I don't want to leave you."

"It is necessary for the survival of the crew."

"Yes. Do you get used to it? The coming and going of Humans?"

"I have 500 years of recordings, Captain. I have experienced the death or departure of 72 exemplars. It is always an adjustment."

"*Drumheller*, do you remember them? Azann and the others?"

"No, Captain. I have no data of Azann, or the alleged Chike, or anything from the *Ultrasoar* time."

"I want to find them. Azann's people. My people. *Our* people. *Drumheller*, I may not be able to come back."

"I understand, Captain."

Sky looked up at him curiously, and tilted her head, as most Humans did when talking to the computer. "*Drummy* sad?" she asked. Beezan gasped. He had never heard a podpup talk to the ship. Although who knew what they did in secret?

"I am programmed to perceive sadness."

"*Drummy* lonely?"

"I am programmed to engage the crew if they show signs of loneliness."

"Back soon."

"No, Sky." Beezan gave her a squeeze. "We're not coming back soon." She scowled at him. "*Drumheller*, I'm going to leave your lightspeed transmitter on, as well as your receivers. Could you send me an update—to Redrock—every year? And I'll send you updates."

"Yes, Captain."

"And thank you. Thank you for 'engaging' me all these years."

"The pleasure was mine, Beezan."

The doors slid open and Beezan pulled out quickly, before he started to cry. He headed for the suit locker. But Sky rolled her eyes. "*Drummy* machine. Sky love."

Beezan couldn't help but laugh. "Sky, that's why you're coming with me. Always."

She nodded emphatically. "Good Bee."

81-Petals, at the rogue planet

After Beezan secured the *Peacock* in the big *81-Petals* hangar, landing properly on the painted rectangle, he signaled Jarvie to send out the automated tubeway. And Thunder sent over an automated cargo loader. "Fancy," Beezan grumbled to Sky.

As Beezan pulled through the tubeway, he looked down at Sky. He was about to say, "Welcome to our new home," when he realized he would never be given the *81* in trade for the *Drumheller*. When this was over, he would have no ship, no home. On that happy note, he pulled into the Entry Lounge.

Iricana was there to greet him. "Welcome aboard, honor."

"Thank you, Captain. Please call me Beezan."

"Humph!"

Iricana smiled. "And welcome to you too, Sky."

They went up the lift, with Sky settling into Beezan's podpup pocket as the gravity increased. "We've prepared your cabin, still next to Jarvie. But please, Cap—Beezan, if you need anything, let us know. We know it's a difficult transition."

"Thank you. I guess what I need is a job."

"Actually, Kelson said he needed our help with something. We're supposed to 'talk turkey' at dinner."

Iricana took Beezan to the door of his new cabin, registered his links, and officially logged him with the ship. "*81*, add to crew: Pilot Beezan, command level 2." Iricana took his s'link and converted it for the *81*.

"Pilot Beezan added." The voice was distinctly female, cultured, cool, almost aloof.

"Greetings *81-Petals*," Beezan said. "Please add the podpup Sky to your monitoring and safekeeping."

There was the slightest hesitation. **"Sky added."** The voice sounded almost aggrieved.

Beezan glanced at Iricana, who rolled her eyes. "Star and Rocket have been here for two days."

"Are all the new AIs like this?"

"Yes, more or less. They are unique personalities, but they haven't had hundreds of years of exemplars. *Drumheller* is very special." A wave of regret passed over Beezan. Iricana grasped his shoulder. "We'll do everything we can to get *Drumheller* back."

He nodded, and quickly turned and went down the steps to his cabin. Big. Fancy. "Sky, we're not on a cargo ship anymore."

10-Words

Jarvie and Terina were cleaning up after dinner while the adults were talking. "You know," Kelson said, tapping a finger to his lips, "an ounce of prevention is worth a pound of cure."

Huh? Jarvie thought. He looked at Terina, who mouthed "Grandpa!"

"Captain," Kelson continued, looking at Iricana, "it occurs to me that we can't just go blazing back to the sectors with the *81-Petals*. And all your top-secret messages are coded for the *Drumheller*."

Iricana frowned. "I didn't think of that. And there's no way for me to send a correction."

"And once *81-Petals* appears on the Ship Tracker, it'll be chaos," Sequoia added. "It'll be impossible for us to come in quietly and report on the Gens."

"What do you recommend?" Iricana asked cautiously.

Kelson smiled. "I just think we should proceed discreetly."

"Disable the beacon?" Beezan asked. "That's illegal, and possibly dangerous."

"I was thinking along the lines of switching beacons."

"You mean," Katie asked, "pretending to be the *Drumheller*, by taking its beacon, and leaving the *81-Petals* beacon here?" Kelson nodded.

"Anyone who sees the ship will know," Thunder added. "Also, it's hardwired. We'd have to do a physical switch."

Iricana nodded. "Not that many people will see the ship

unless we dock. But everyone sees the Ship Tracker. We could alert the council without creating a ruckus if we switch the beacons. And I can authorize it with my level 1."

They all turned to Thunder. "We don't have to switch the whole structure, just the ID box." He held up his hands about shoulder width apart. "I know how it's done. We'd have to be very careful."

Beezan nodded. "I can help."

11-Words

Colony

Melawn paced around the small common room in the Travelers Welcoming Center, alone. Modest snacks were provided, but, waiting for the others, he was too anxious to eat. After their arrival day, they'd been separated. Melawn had been briefed, debriefed, and rebriefed, and there was nothing brief about it. For days, they'd interviewed him about every possible thing, sector news, technology, people, the *Cheetah*, and all possible skills, with Grace taking notes *by hand.*

Melawn tried to calm his agitation and compose his expression, but then remembered that there were no cameras, so he could hyperventilate all he wanted to. The door creaked open and Nkiroo came in, closing it behind him, and smiling when he saw Melawn.

"Kiro!" Melawn hugged him fiercely. "I'm glad it's you first."

"Are you okay?"

"Yes," Melawn answered, "Just going insane from worry, too many questions, and no devices!"

Nkiroo nodded. "They said keeping us apart was necessary to *separate us from any lingering group influence in our former environment.*"

"Great. Did a ship of councilors land here?"

Nkiroo laughed.

"You don't seem very bothered by it all," Melawn said.

Nkiroo's eyes turned soft and serious. "I've been through this before."

Melawn smacked himself on the forehead. "I'm so sorry!"

Nkiroo squeezed his shoulder. "It's okay, but some of the questions were a little awkward—hey! Food!"

Melawn sighed in relief as Nkiroo checked out the different nuts and rolls. Just having Nkiroo back calmed his heart. Of course, once Thayne came through that door, the storm would start up again.

But Tenshi arrived next, in a storm of her own, frowning and angry. But she gave them each a hug and asked how they were holding up, not in her old doctor way, but as if she really cared.

"We're fine," Melawn answered.

"What's wrong, though?" Nkiroo asked.

She frowned and looked down, then let out a breath. "I guess I've never mentioned my husband."

"What?" Nkiroo gasped. "You have a husband? Is he *here*?"

"No, no," Tenshi shook her head sadly. "He's on Earth. He's severely disabled. He isn't conscious to the world. Grace wanted me to take a divorce." They gasped. "She said I'd never leave here, I'd never see him again, and I wasn't *too old* to contribute to the population."

They gasped again. "But you told her . . ." Melawn prompted.

"That the last thing in the world I want to do is bring a child onto a prison planet and she should be ashamed for even suggesting division in my marriage. We will be together in the next world."

Melawn and Nkiroo nodded. "I'm sorry," Melawn whispered. She nodded, the anger seeping away, replaced by rolling eyes.

"Grace did say I should encourage you two to get with it."

"With what?" Nkiroo asked.

She laughed. "The marriage and contributing to the population part."

"Just the two of us?" Melawn asked.

Tenshi nodded her head and glanced at the door. "Thayne, a husband? And God forbid, a father? Even Grace could see that would be a disaster. So it's up to you two."

"We're only 25." Nkiroo objected.

"Years behind schedule in this society," she answered.

"But . . ." Melawn said, "if we get married, if we have native children . . ."

Nkiroo went serious and pale, "Then we can never leave."

Finally, finally, Grace came in with their relocation assignments. They were now part of a society where they had no experience, no history, no family, no friends, and unknown social credibility. Their skills were mostly unsuitable. They were weak, by planetary standards. But today, they were to be given their assignments and released.

Melawn had one overriding goal: freedom. He wanted a do over, away from the ship, away from Thayne, from everything except Nkiroo. If this was going to be his second chance in life, he was going to embrace it. His main regret would be for his parents, never knowing that he missed them and was sorry for leaving them.

Grace opened another door for them and led them to a cool room with a large map on the wall, hand drawn. Notes were stuck on it with soft wax. The paper was crude and obviously carefully conserved.

"Please be seated." Thayne was brought in, smiling and cooperative, on his most pleasant, charming behavior, probably still trying to figure out all the angles. When they settled down, Grace chanted a prayer.

Then Grace explained to them about life without a p'link. Like you don't have help at your fingertips, you can't contact people every second and if you get lost, there's no way to find you. Plan ahead to meet up with people. Use the free message boards. But to Melawn, it was still sounding like freedom.

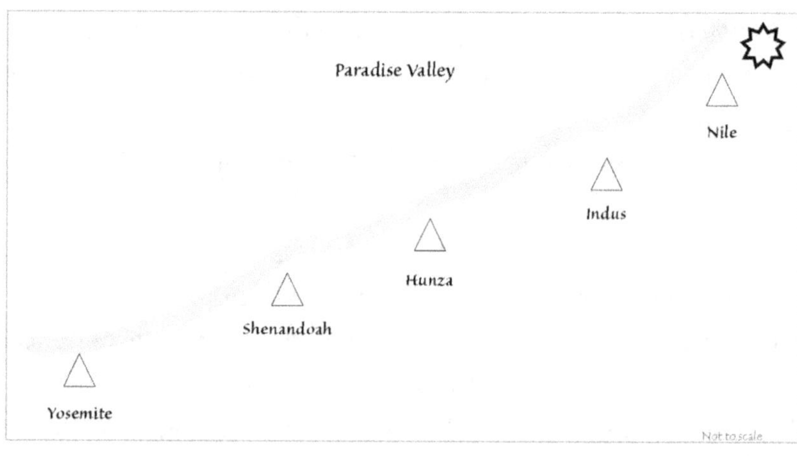

They had previously explained that Paradise Valley had five villages. The village with the temple was Nile. Downriver were Indus, then Hunza, Shenandoah, and Yosemite near the coast. Between each village were farms known by whatever name the first farm crew gave them. Now, on the map, they could see the extent of the colony. It was bigger than Melawn expected.

"Here everyone works," Grace said. "You may feel that your

modern skills aren't appreciated. We need to find out how your skills fit into our society. We ask for your patience. Most people eventually adjust and are happy."

"What about the rebels?" Thayne interrupted.

Grace paused and nodded slowly. "There are no rebels. No one is trying to overthrow our government. There are two groups of people living in societies separate from the colony. One group is quite old, the Zann. There are two branches of them, the mountain people, and the beast herders. The mountain people mostly keep to themselves. If you see them with the green vest facing outward, don't talk to them. The herders help us with the beasts. They are all descendants of early drops. We have no idea how many there are. Occasionally they'll send a few teens here for school and we accept them. We trade information. Relations are good. They do not accept spacers into their society."

Grace sighed. "The other group is more problematic. The leaders are the command crew of *Dragonfly Dream*. Everyone in this group is from the three 'big ships' as we call them. They separated from us immediately, refusing even to be processed." Melawn couldn't entirely blame them.

"Unfortunately, they occasionally resort to lawless behavior, raiding our tools and harassing cart trains. You had your own run-in with them."

Thayne nodded. "Has anyone been hurt?"

"No. Never. Everyone is under instructions to comply with their demands. We leave food and supplies for them in the winter. Their goal is not to rebel against us, but to rebel against the Chike. Since the valley people refuse to do that, they refuse to settle with us." *So they are rebels.*

"What about the Ramians?" Nkiroo asked.

"We had no knowledge of them until you came. But you say

that they were dropped on another continent. We have no sailing capabilities and we are forbidden by the Chike from going out on the ocean. This is the planet of a sentient crab-like people. It is their ocean."

Then she turned to Nkiroo. Melawn held his breath. "Nkiroo, you are the easiest to place. You'll be assigned to a salvage and engineering crew here in Nile. Usually, when we get a new group of people, we get their ship and everything on it. In your case, we were only given the data cube, no ship. But there's still stuff out in the desert to be dealt with. A limited number of power tools can be checked out. Your team leader will explain." Nkiroo nodded. It was a good job for him. He might even be happy. Or as happy as one could be taking ships apart rather than building them.

"Tenshi. We don't use titles here. Not even for doctors. You do have experience in field medicine, so we'll send you for additional training. Then you'll be going to Yosemite, our newest village."

Melawn started to panic. It appeared that they were going to be separated. "Yes, of course. Whatever you think is best," Tenshi replied. Melawn puzzled over their general meekness. The crew of *Dragonfly Dream* had probably broken the walls down by now.

"Thayne," she continued and smiled genuinely at him. "We fully acknowledge the great importance your work has to the outer sectors, but there's just no use pursuing it here. We ask that you be a professor at our university in Shenandoah. We need advanced astronomy, physics, and math. It will be quite demanding."

"Of course." Thayne nodded as meekly as Tenshi.

"So, we come to you Melawn." There was an awkward pause. *I'm useless.*

But Thayne spoke up. "Could he come with me? He could teach too."

She smiled, but shook her head no. "We actually have a job in mind. You are a data processor of sorts?"

"Yes, but you don't have data." As unimaginable as that was on so many levels.

"But we do have data. We're in a constant battle here to increase our food supply. We can't improve the technology level of our society until we free up enough people for industry. We'd like you to be a field scientist, go from farm to farm. We have data, but get your own. Anything. Any ideas, correlations. This is your talent, yes?"

"With a computer, yes."

"You'll have to do it by hand."

God in heaven. Scratching out data on rough scraps of paper? "I don't know anything about farming."

"We'll assign you to a farm team. But we want you to be independent, new eyes, etc. You'll be based out of Indus."

He nodded. Indus. Away from Thayne, but also away from Nkiroo. "Thank you." But maybe, maybe, it's the ultimate freedom after all.

"Everyone does four hours professional work and four hours physical community work, in the fields, kitchens, schools, villages, wherever. Your local supervisor will put you into light community rotation until you get used to heavier work."

"You'll all leave today. Cart trains run twice a day from the loading station. We'll take you there."

Today? Suddenly not having a p'link was alarming. "How do we contact each other?" Melawn asked.

"First of all, you'll integrate into our society. There's no particular need to keep crews together. Cart trains take official and personal messages. Personal messages cost one community credit. Otherwise, the community message boards are free." Message boards, Melawn realized, were not a digital thing.

"Credit? Money?" Tenshi asked.

"Yes," without electronics, it's the most efficient method of trading goods and services," Grace explained. "So that's the last thing." She motioned to her aid, who brought a box to the table and opened it. Grace reached in and passed an ancient looking rough, cloth string bag to each of them, about the size of an orange. Melawn carefully opened his. It was full of seeds, the size of jelly beans. There were about fifty. "These are the community credits, sometimes called seeseeds. These," she handed them each a metal disk, like a thin coin, with the number 100 stamped on it, "are for larger amounts."

"Cut from inner bulkheads?" Nkiroo asked.

"Yes, and not easy to do. We've given you a generous amount—half a month's pay. You'll have to earn the rest. Here are your ID cards."

Melawn put the paper card into his chest pocket, cinched up the seed bag tightly, and put it in a secure pocket. Then he slipped the coin into a separate pocket.

"Crime?" Thayne asked.

"Nothing major. But don't leave your money around. We are ready to go. Pack up your things. We'll put you on the afternoon cart train."

From the Welcoming Center, they entered the temple through a door to the choir loft, then went down a set of narrow metal stairs to the main hall.

The interior of the reshaped *Starswimmer* was unrecognizable. Elaborate tapestries hung around the nine sides. Quotes from the Writings and geometric patterns were inlaid over the nine doors. The floor was stone, polished satiny smooth. Melawn craned his neck to look up. Just as in the temples on

Earth, the Greatest Name shimmered from the apex of the dome where nine ribs of polished metal came together. A cool breeze lifted his hair, and here, instead of his usual instinct to panic from decompression, he felt some tension drain out. He sat by Nkiroo as they said prayers together, hoping it wouldn't be their last time.

"We should go," Grace said quietly. They gathered their packs, put on their hats and sunglasses, and walked out through the gardens and down the well-worn path to the road.

As they approached, the sounds of village life lifted to their ears and they could see the bustle of people waiting for the carts. "Looks like they have plenty of children," Nkiroo said quietly. *Tons of them*, Melawn thought. Running around in native clothes, with bits of color and ribbon, almost like the tokens of the Ramians. They were noisy, happy, playing, jostling, and excited.

Tenshi smiled. "God, how I've missed this."

Grace nodded knowingly, and brought them to a stop. "God be with you then." She bowed and backed away, leaving them to face their future.

Melawn was nervous about approaching the other people, but they were somewhat lost in the crush. There were four wooden posts, one for each of the other villages. You lined up where you wanted to go.

"So, this is goodbye then," Tenshi said.

"After all we've been through, it comes to this," Nkiroo said sadly.

"We must represent well!" Thayne admonished them. "We are not just from some ship. We were entrusted with a mission—and I have not given it up. I will train my students to do what we need to do."

"Well, good luck to you," Nkiroo said, "all of you." He gave

Tenshi a hug. "Thank you, doctor, for everything. Here and on the *Cheetah*." People were staring. Melawn heard the word "newcomers" whispered through the crowd. But no one bothered them.

Melawn took a breath, hugged the doctor and Thayne, and almost couldn't bear to hug Nkiroo goodbye. But Nkiroo whispered, "I'll be in touch. Don't worry."

The carts started to pull into the lanes. Melawn went to his line and watched how people did it. He handed over two seeseeds for passage and clamored aboard. He sat, staring ahead and swallowing his tears, but not all of sadness. Money, a cart, a planet, freedom. There was just something so Human about it all.

13 / THE SHIMMER

12-Words

Sandstorm

Zahar sat with Quay, Caspia, and Evan during morning devotions. Quay was chanting a prayer in Ramian, when the door opened and Pascal burst in—unescorted. Quay stopped.

"This one is a defender of the weak! This one has created a masterpiece! It will shock / stun / surprise!" Ze stepped aside so ze wasn't blocking the door.

"Let's hope for surprise," Caspia whispered.

About thirty Chike came in. They were not masked or decorated, and they had work-type clothes with pockets. "Tools," Evan noted. "They're doing real work, not that on-demand stuff."

There was a boss and three sub-bosses, each with their own workers. One of the teams was quite a bit smaller. Females? Males? Kids? The bosses were extremely courteous to Pascal. After a few minutes, Pascal left and Quay went back to his prayer. Lately, they had been singing too. But they stopped after one song, because it was very distracting to the Chike, who were turning and giving them the one-eye.

By lunch, it was done. Some kind of structure had been built under the main view screen. Part way through the work, the Chike had pulled privacy screens across so Zahar and the others couldn't see. Pascal returned with a small escort and dismissed the workers. "Stand back," ze said dramatically. "The final adjustments, and then the gift shall be revealed. Close your eyes!"

Is ze kidding? All of them turned to look at Pascal, but ze turned the one-eye on them. *Not kidding.* Zahar dropped her head and held her hands over her eyes. The strange whirring, gurgling, shirring sounds of the on-demand engineering could be heard on a large scale. "Now . . . Behold!" Pascal announced.

Zahar opened her eyes. She couldn't help herself. She gasped. So did the others. They were in the *Cheetah* Command Bay, only much bigger, and, not destroyed. But unmistakably modeled on the *Cheetah*.

"The Exempt is clever and resourceful," Quay said quietly.

Evan was looking around puzzled. That's when Zahar noticed the escort was gone. Only the four of them and Pascal remained, and she was certain that Pascal was very pleased with zirself.

"May the Humans ask questions directly of the Exempt?" Quay asked.

"It is granted!" Pascal said happily. Ze directed the four of them to workstations in the front, while ze took a throne-like platform behind, like the admiral of their little ship within a ship. "Yes. Take the controls. This one wishes to observe the quality of work."

Evan reached out to a panel, and said, "*Cheetah?* Voice control?" *Could they possibly have preserved the AI?*

"Voice control activated. Please provide identification."

A chill went down Zahar's spine. It sounded just like the *Cheetah* AI. But that was not necessarily a good thing, considering all the trouble they had had with it.

"This is Evan, pilot of the harbinger Quay. Also authorized are Quay, Caspia, and Zahar."

"Accepted." They looked at each other. *It must be a fake, controlled by the Chike.*

"*Cheetah*, what is the date?"

"12-Words."

Is that all? Zahar thought. Just over two months since they woke up on the Chike ship?

"Seems like forever," Caspia whispered.

13-Words

Drumheller, at the rogue planet

Of course, switching the beacons meant going back aboard the *Drumheller*. Beezan tried to be detached as he and Jarvie suited up, took the *Drumheller* work tower lift to the top and then pulled the rest of the way to the hub transfer ring. From the ring, they crawled to the access hatch, and then outside to the central spire on top of the *Drumheller*.

"Wow!" Jarvie said as they emerged.

"Tether, please." Beezan didn't want Jarvie getting too distracted, although the view was spectacular. The stars appeared to spin around them, but it was no worse than looking out the observation window.

Beezan had the suit overlay safety zones into the helmet view, showing where the projectile and radiation fields were generated. They had practiced this repair with Thunder many times inside the ship. Beezan didn't have to tell Jarvie what to do. Jarvie pulled up the spire ladder to the beacon access hatch. Beezan pulled up behind him, running his tether up the safety bar.

"Here," Jarvie said, moving over so Beezan could come up beside him. The beacon access door opened easily, thanks to recent dockside repairs. They attached a tether directly to the ID box. Jarvie unlatched the box and tugged. It didn't budge. Jarvie braced his feet better and tugged again, this time getting it part way out. After several more big tugs, Jarvie checked his own tether and warned Beezan, "I'm going to pull harder."

With a surge of exertion, the box and Jarvie came loose. "Whoa!" Jarvie exclaimed, but didn't let go of the box.

"Easy," Beezan said while he clumsily pulled Jarvie in and guided his hand to a hold. Beezan attached the box to Jarvie's back and they made their way down to the small central platform and then inside.

"Good job," Beezan told Jarvie as they rested. Kelson took the *Drumheller* beacon and flew it over to the *81*, where Thunder and Iricana would swap it out. When Kelson returned with the *81's* box, Jarvie and Beezan would have to repeat their little adventure.

"Do you want me to do it?" Jarvie asked.

"No way," Beezan answered emphatically, even though he was tired. "Two is always better."

And when they were done, they stayed a few minutes outside on the central platform, just looking at the *Drumheller*. Jarvie pointed, "There's where we got hit. You can see the repairs." It made Beezan's heart pound just remembering that day.

"We really shouldn't stay out here." But neither of them moved. Beezan gazed around the rim of the torus, trying to memorize his one last view of the *Drumheller*. Near the edge he noticed a little sparkle. "Hmmm."

"What, Captain?"

Beezan pointed. "Do you see anything there?"

"Yes! A shimmering arc! What is it?"

"*Drumheller*! Do you have a leak?"

"There are no malfunctions, Captain."

"Thunder, Kelson, do you see it on the feed?"

Thunder's voice came over the link. "It's not a leak, Captain. A leak would trail around the ship as the damaged point rotated. It's something peeling off the surface from the outside."

"It's going to the *81-Petals*!" Jarvie exclaimed.

"That's imposs—" But Beezan stopped. He'd learned the hard way not to say impossible. And it did seem as if the glittering stream was making a wide arc across the distance between the ships.

"Paint chips?" Kelson speculated.

"It's so . . . orderly," Beezan said.

"It doesn't seem to be a coincidence," Thunder said. "It reminds me of the microbots."

"But they're gone!" Kelson objected. "The repair crew destroyed them and cleaned up the leftovers."

"They were hiding," Jarvie said.

"They did start across just as we turned on the *Drumheller* beacon at *81*," Beezan said.

Beezan stared in wonder. He had no fear of the former *Drumheller* microbots. They had defended the ship before. And he was certain no Chike bots had survived once robot #9 was unleashed. He smiled. The soul of the *Drumheller* was remaining here. But its defenders were coming with them.

• • •

15-Words

81-Petals, at the rogue planet

The only way to see the GenThree star maps was to go aboard Veez's shuttle. But no one wanted to trust its life support after all these years, and Veez didn't have a good suit. So Thunder and Kelson went aboard and managed to power it up. With Veez's advice, they jury-rigged a relay from Veez's computer to the *81-Petals*. Apparently, the GenThree had what Veez mysteriously called a "magic box" for translating the computer input / output of any of the Gens. "Cracking computer data," Jarvie whispered to Beezan. "That was probably his real job. Why else would he be following our ships around?"

Iricana, who generally disapproved of wild speculation, unconsciously nodded her head. The three of them, plus Terina, waited in the big fancy Observation Bay of *81-Petals*. Beezan sat as calmly as he could, trying to focus, completely out of his element. He wasn't captain anymore. He was no longer on a cargo ship. The *81* wasn't even a regular passenger ship. It was the most elite ship ever built, combining exploration and public relations. Even the air smelled different. He was grateful to Sky for staying close.

Just then, Veez came in. His fur was especially shiny and neat, and he was wearing matching beaded wrist and neck bands.

"Why are you dressed up?" Terina asked.

"Today is to be formal, yes? An agreement is to be made."

"Yes," Iricana agreed. "Please join us at the table."

When they were settled, Veez turned to Beezan. "An agreement then, Captain."

"Iricana is captain now," Beezan answered quietly.

"Ah," Veez glanced her way, but continued talking to

Beezan. "You are the pilot. I make my agreement with you." He put his paws on the table. "I will give you the location of my home star. You agree to take me there. I will give you the location of the Human colony. You will leave GenThree space immediately after dropping me off."

"I agree, with two conditions," Beezan said, as planned. "That you understand we may not make it, and that would not be a breach of our agreement. And because of that, we would like the location of the colony now, so we can send it in a light-speed message."

Veez nodded. "Fair and reasonable. I agree." He reached out his paw, "As you Humans do, a 'handshake' is all that is required?"

"Yes, with us," Beezan said and reached out and shook the paw of a giant mutant rat, who was now his crewmate.

16-Words

It took several hours of studying the GenThree maps, the latest sector maps from *81*, and various NAV stars and pulsar specs before they all agreed on how to mesh their maps. The *81-Petals*, with the most powerful off-Earth computer ever built, was able to reconstruct the entire GenThree map in a tabletop hologram.

"Oh, that's quite good!" Veez exclaimed. "You Humans are excellent at visual representation."

"You haven't seen the Ramians." Jarvie remarked.

"Those daredevils? I do hope you keep your distance from them."

"Why?" Iricana asked, suddenly concerned.

"Oh, nothing, just rumors." But Beezan and Iricana stared at him, annoyed, until he answered. "Oh, you know, there's talk about them stealing gravity balls. Utter nonsense, I'm sure."

"What if they did?" Iricana asked.

"Oh impossible! You know. It would be a dangerous occupation. I don't think they would last long." Beezan and Iricana glanced at each other.

"Wait," Veez now looked serious. "You do know the Ramians?" Iricana nodded. "And they do steal gravity balls?" Iricana nodded again.

"That's not in the *81-Petals* history."

"We've only recently learned this," Iricana answered. "The Ramians put the gravity balls inside their ships for artificial gravity."

"*WHAT??!!*" Veez actually stumbled back away from the hologram. "This cannot be so!"

"Crazy as it seems," Iricana said, "but that's beside the point now."

"Wait, no. A moment, Captain," Veez waved his paw in an erase motion. "Where do they get the gravity balls?"

"From the k-belts," Jarvie answered.

"They're removing them from the k-belts?"

"They have ships that find and call them."

"Noooooo," Veez shook his head in alarm.

Beezan was concerned that Veez would change his mind about their agreement; he was so distracted by this, so Beezan pointed back to the hologram. "Maybe we should concentrate—"

"Those gravity balls aren't toys, like lost ping pong balls! They are orbiting in your k-belts for a reason!"

"What reason?" Iricana asked, but Veez wouldn't answer.

Instead Veez asked, "Do the GenOne know about this?"

"We have no idea," Iricana answered. "We don't know

anything about the GenOne. But if you go home, you can tell them yourself."

"Yes," Veez agreed, back to business. He focused on the hologram until he found a particular star and pointed it out with a nostalgic sigh. "This one is my home. I'll call it Castle for now."

Beezan looked across the image to the approximate position of their little rogue planet. He didn't really grasp the scale of the map. "That seems like a really long way, with stuff in between." They played with the scale and discovered it compared to the long jump from Atik to Radium Junction. "Sequoia will have to do this," Beezan said desperately to Iricana.

"No, my friend," Veez insisted. "You. I have known pilots all my life. I know those who can see into the deep."

18-Words

81-Petals, at the rogue planet

Even though Beezan saw Iricana on and off every day, the new captain would schedule formal meetings to consult about specific things, often things he had never taken care of. He tried not to take it as a sign that he wasn't a good captain. He had come a long way since his cargo days. He wore his uniform, which still said *Drumheller*. His hair was combed and he endeavored to be at command meetings five minutes ahead of the captain—as Jarvie, his diplomatic advisor, reminded him.

This ship is so big! Drumheller had a big cargo hold, but the torus itself was not particularly large. This ship itself was huge. His new cabin was big. The kitchen was big. The prayer room could seat forty people. Which meant that walking one Arc took a long time. He paused at the kitchen to drop off Sky, but she said, "Sky come," so he brought her along.

Beezan jogged past the last few doors to get there on time,

setting Sky off. She trilled along as if they were on a big adventure. He went up the stairs and slid into his seat, giving Sky a squeeze and setting her down. Iricana came in only a moment behind him. Too close. He had to get used to not being last to the meetings.

The senior crew, Thunder, Kelson, Sequoia, and Veez were there, along with Terina, who was ready to record the historic moment. Veez himself chanted a prayer, in Alkulu. Terina took a picture of Veez handing a hand-written note to Iricana. It was the coordinates to the Human colony, which Veez had converted from his coordinate system. Sequoia programmed it into their NAV hologram. Their next jump was to take Veez home, but they were all curious to see where the colony was.

The star lit up in the hologram. Veez explained it was near the Chike's neighbor, a crab-like people that only used the oceans. They had given over the land of their planet to the colonies.

"Colonies?" Kelson asked.

"One assumes. Why waste a prime planet for one little colony?" Veez shrugged in the Human way while they absorbed that.

They gazed at the hologram and played with the scale. Sky crawled up on the table to check it out, her black fur becoming the background for the stars. "A long way," Sequoia said. "Like three times the distance from Sector 8 to Earth."

"Hmmm, yes," Veez agreed. "But, should you decide to, umm, visit, you would be detected soon after you entered normal space in the system. Unless," he paused and Sky went over to look him in the eye. "Aboard my shuttle is a shield that masks the signature of our engines and thrusters. Oh, let's call it a shimmer. That's got a nice Human dramatic touch."

"What," Iricana asked, "does this shimmer do?"

"I'm not an engineer. But I think it could be altered to mask even Human ships. I have taken the liberty of translating key parts of the instructions." He handed Thunder a big folded document. Terina was about to take a picture and thought better of it. Thunder unfolded it. It was covered with diagrams and hand—paw—writing.

"Maybe we should review this," Kelson said mildly.

"Of course. But you Humans are so good at these things."

"You're a spy," Iricana said.

"Please, Captain, a scout."

Sky looked up at him. "Humph."

Later, Beezan huddled with Thunder and Iricana in the Command Bay. "I've sent the colony coordinates by lightspeed, tightbeam, full power to all sector councils." She shook her head. "I just don't know if we can trust him."

"This whole thing could be fiction," Thunder agreed.

"We thought the Chike were fiction," Beezan reminded them.

"They still might be," Iricana added. "We mentioned them first."

"Veez good," said a soft voice.

They all looked down in surprise. Sky was peeking into her snack box for leftovers. "Sky?" Beezan asked, getting another little chill. Sometimes she was so odd. Beezan picked her up. She gave him the full innocent look. "Do you even know anyone who is not good?"

Sky paused. "Rocket." They couldn't help laughing. But Iricana shook her head at Beezan. They couldn't make decisions on the word of a one-year-old podpup.

"He has been stranded here. That's a fact. And he may know

what happened to the crew, since he's on the ship. I think we're in too deep," Thunder said. "We have to trust."

Beezan scowled. Every time he trusted, something crazy happened.

2-Perfection

Watcher, at Four System

Lanezi could not sleep. The images of the disaster at Friendship System had been growing in his mind day by day and now stretched into the night. They weren't even real images, since he didn't see it anywhere except in his jumping mind. He knew there was only one way to banish them—by painting them into one frozen moment. He went through his container of things that the Ramians had salvaged from the *Enkindler.* He'd put his poncho on his bed. It was too warm on the *Watcher* to wear it. His paint kit was there, with some paint, but not the right colors. And he needed something to paint on.

There was a large market section on the *Watcher.* He'd been escorted through it a few times. He knew they had an art store. In the sectors, he was considered rich. But his sliders were useless here. He had some jewelry. Possibly he could sell it to the token shops, but that might cause trouble. He found his ship pins, pulled from his damaged and discarded uniform. But he couldn't give those to the Ramians. Maybe he could get a job. "Computer? *Watcher?*"

"What is your wish?"

"Are there any job opportunities aboard?"

"Kindly clarify."

"I need money. Credit. Funds. I need a job."

"Humans are honored guests. Whatever you wish will be delivered."

Lanezi frowned and continued looking through his treasures, trying to be practical and not get distracted by the memories. He did have a seashell. "Horse Conch," it said. Puzzling, as it didn't seem to be related to horses. It was frozen in some kind of clear material, so it didn't break. He held it in his hand, a little piece of Earth. In trade for an image of Friendship's fate?

He put on his best Ramian clothes, held the ship pins in his hands and said a prayer for his people, and then pinned them on his shirt. They were something like tokens and might get him a little respect. He put the shell in a pocket and left the cabin. And was instantly lost.

Lanezi only knew his way to the dining hall. The birds fluttered around, but he waved them away. He knew how to use the map on his Ramian p'link and he knew the market was next to an open square where the kids hung out after school. The layout was not like one rimway around the ring of a ship, or even multiple rimways on stacked station rings. The Ramian central gravity ball and spherical ships allowed them to design passageways any way they wanted—which they seemed to do with a fondness for mazelike alleyways, randomly intersecting corridors, bridges and meandering paths.

As he worked his way towards the square, people nodded and greeted him with an air of aloofness, but they couldn't hide flashes of their curious turquoise. Once he got to the open square, before school let out, thank heavens, he knew the market was just across a decorative bridge.

The market was bigger than the market on Redrock, and that was a whole station, not a ship. There were places to eat, to buy gadgets, stores for treats, or small gardens to sit and eat, like nature cafés. There were clothes and shoe stores, beauty spas, a token center, music store, podpup and toddler play zones, and finally, a big art supply store. He stepped over the half gate that separated it from romping toddlers.

Inside, the store had many sections, for pottery, cooking, etching, and sculpting. There were decorative lights, cameras of all kinds, beads, yarn, rows of cloth, spools of thin metal, jewelry, and other things he wasn't sure about. He walked up and down gawking until he found a doorway to a separate room of painting supplies.

Colors! The colors of the Ramians' emotions streamed in large painted swashes across the walls, transforming to swirls of cloth across the ceiling. There were rows and rows of paints, more than Lanezi had seen on Earth.

A materialistic shout of *I want it all* surfaced, but he laughed and shook himself. That was crazy. He knew what he needed. Slightly dazed by it all, he worked his way to the main desk, Ramians in the rows turning curious but approving looks and colors his way.

The attendant came to attention and looked behind Lanezi, as if wondering who brought him here. Lanezi smiled and said, "Greetings. I am Lanezi." He received a polite color flash.

"Greetings Lanezi. I am Farchayna." A quick left hand tap on the right collar. He glanced at Lanezi's ship pins, "At your service."

"Greetings Farchayna. I don't have any . . . money. Would you take this in trade?" Lanezi pulled the shell from his pocket and set it on the counter. "It's the shell of a creature that lives in the oceans of Earth."

Farchayna's eyes widened and his colors went to solid brown, a color Lanezi wasn't familiar with. "Earth? The Human homeworld? This?" He reached out but didn't touch it.

"Yes." Lanezi pushed it closer to Farchayna, who still didn't touch it.

"No. This must be your treasure. You must keep it. You may take whatever you like."

"Please. I want to pay and I don't have Ramian money."

"You don't need any. You may have whatever you like. You are a guest."

"Please. I won't take anything unless I can pay." That triggered the concern color.

"Perhaps, I can hold onto it until you have Ramian credits. Then you come back for it."

Lanezi smiled. "That sounds good to me. Thank you."

Farchayna picked up the cube, gazed at it, and then put it safely behind the counter. "What may I show you?"

Lanezi knew he would get back with no trouble as Farchayna had programmed his Ramian p'link for him. Apparently, everyone knew where he lived. And he was reminded to come back for his treasure. He was happy. He had everything he needed. He felt compelled to get to work, as if the painting inside him was clamoring for attention. As he hurried back, he was already planning the first layer of color in his mind. He was so distracted that he almost walked right into a commotion near the square. The familiar voices of Io and Euro got his attention. They were marching through the square, with Sontula quickly coming the other way toward them. They all met at an intersection.

"Io, Euro, what's wrong?" Lanezi asked.

"We're leaving school," Euro told Lanezi.

"Honor," Euro added to Sontula, who was running solid caution colors.

"Let's talk in private," Sontula suggested, eyes scanning their foreheads uselessly, and then their faces for clues.

Lanezi offered his cabin. When they got there, he quietly stored his package out of sight with a sigh, and then brought tea for everyone. "What's happened?" he asked Euro.

"We tried. But there's no reason for us to go to Ramian school. And the kids tease us."

At that, a yellow flicker crossed Sontula's forehead. "They should not! You are honored guests."

"They keep asking 'Who is jik? Who is tan?'" Euro complained.

Sontula gasped. "Very rude! You are right to be upset. It is unbecoming of your hosts. Did no bold child stand up for you?"

"We stood up for ourselves!" Io declared.

"Good," she nodded. "I will speak to the supervisor."

"Maybe they're right," Lanezi added. "Why send them to school? We need something real to do. All three of us."

Sontula nodded, colors bright yellow. "I will conspire," she said, setting down her unfinished tea, and was gone.

"Conspire?" Euro asked.

"Yes," Lanezi commented. "I think the translator is getting better."

Within twenty minutes, Lanezi, Euro, and Io were called to meet with Getti Drann. Sontula took them to a small command center near the main bridge. "This is the planning room." Lanezi was shown to a worktable. Sontula signaled for them to remain standing. Getti Drann approached. Lanezi felt a little bad for creating a fuss when the command crew was so busy, but they were greeted warmly.

"Lanezi, we appoint you Chief Diplomat to the Humans and Chike." *And Chike? Did ze just say Chike?* Lanezi swayed on his feet and grabbed the back of a chair. *What have I gotten myself into?* "Your assistants will be Euro and Io."

"Yes, honor," they answered politely, while Lanezi was still dumbstruck.

"Your first assignment is to formulate arguments, based on Human canon, to convince the Chike to save Seven. Appeals to the Chike seem to focus on propriety as well as morality, so please keep that in mind."

The three of them sat down at the table. *God in heaven. I'm a pilot. How did I go from painting to saving a planet?* But Io slid his pad across the table. "I've been thinking." Euro smiled and hugged his brother.

4-Perfection

81-Petals, leaving the rogue planet, en route to Castle

Terina looked around the big Command Bay. The entire crew, Veez included, could sit there, with seats to spare. The Command Bay was blue, like the sky, like the ocean, like Earth. The walls and panels were shiny new, even after sitting around for fifteen years. It was like newborn-new compared to the 500-year-old *Drumheller*.

Jarvie, sitting in the monitor seat, announced, "All crew to blue zones." It was a formality. They had reconfigured the ship to boosting mode yesterday, swinging the cabins, kitchen,

Command Bay, and prayer room around to make them "down" for boosting. The *81* was designed to operate in boosting or spinning mode. So by accelerating at 1g they would be able to maintain constant acceleration and live semi-normally, instead of being strapped in the travel chairs for hours.

Terina sat in back, with Kelson and Thunder. Veez, Katie and the pups were on the right side. In the front row, Iricana sat in the captain's chair and Sequoia and Beezan sat in Pilot 1 and 2, on each side of Jarvie.

"Secure for boosting, Captain," Jarvie reported.

"Engage boosting schedule," Iricana said to Sequoia. The main screen showed the view forward. A side screen showed the rogue planet behind, good riddance, and Beezan had a small screen showing the *Drumheller*.

Terina made some notes in her article *81-Petals: Return to Flight*. Their three-part journey would be one part adventure, one part homecoming and one part sad farewell. The *81-Petals*, former inspiration to humanity itself, would now be an emissary to the GenThree. She took a picture and noted the date and time.

Terina felt just a little heaviness as Sequoia engaged the engines slowly. There was hardly any vibration. It took five hours to build up to 1g. Terina, used to the .92g generally used in the outer sectors, complained. "Child," her grandfather chided, "Ten billion Earthborn deal with it every day. Even butterflies and birds and tiny ants deal with it."

Terina scowled at him. Iricana sympathized. "We should adjust, and it's good for us. Let's see how it goes." They walked carefully out of the Command Bay. In this configuration, they had to walk along the "walls" of the rimway. It was so disorienting. Terina hung on to the rails tightly, glancing back at Beezan who stayed behind to watch the receding *Drumheller*.

Later, they had dinner and extra treats, made by Veez, to commemorate the occasion of leaving the rogue planet. Jarvie picked the music for social arts. "Blues?" Katie asked. "Blues for blue zones?"

"No. Blues, for being sad, yet hopeful," Jarvie explained.

"Blues were from a troubled time on Earth," Terina added. "Oppression. Prejudice. Concepts we barely understand anymore."

"Well, amen to that," Kelson added. "Let only the music remain."

Terina was glad that Beezan showed up to play the first violin part, because it looked hard. Beezan studied the music a long time. "Well, I'll try," he said bravely, and then proceeded to play with such anguish that there was not a dry eye that night. Even for Veez, who, although he was returning home, the spirits of his companions had gone on without him.

6-Perfection

Watcher, at Four System

When Delegation Day arrived, school and work were cancelled. Pups were taken to the play zone. Lanezi and the twins dressed in their best clothes and reported as diplomats on the bridge. They weren't on the delegation, but they would be in the summary, so they were instructed to dress up. The delegation to renegotiate the gravity ball recall was dispatched from a different ship, not the *Watcher. Watcher* was officially not involved in resistance.

The delegation shuttle was a beautiful five-armed craft that looked more like a glimmery starfish than a ship. It carried an impressive selection of gifts for the Chike: works of art, a Ramian symphony, peaceful food offerings, and the personal tokens of the Gettis. It was headed for the main ship of the Chike, the ship that hosted the "Exempt," some sort of spokesperson, the only Chike allowed to speak with outsiders.

It also carried their argument: *God is the One Creator. Those creatures who acknowledge the Creator, their own souls, and have the power of utterance are elevated from the animal kingdom. All have nobility and rights. The right to peace is foremost and proper.*

It went on, but Lanezi was uneasy. There was no way to deny that the Ramians had taken the gravity balls—powerful and dangerous machines—that did not belong to them. It was not unreasonable to Lanezi that the Chike should ask for them back. But to not give the Ramians more time was cruel.

Lanezi, Euro, and Io sat at the back of the bridge near Sontula. Their own delegation, to approach the Chike Exempt about Seven, was waiting to see how today's events worked out.

The starfish shuttle broadcast colors of polite greetings and respect. Lanezi wondered if the Chike had any clue about the Ramian colors, but regardless, a hangar door opened on the Chike ship. Lanezi listened carefully to the translation from the delegate feed. *We're granted an audience with the Exempt.* But as soon as the shuttle passed inside, communication was lost.

"Now what?" Lanezi asked Sontula.

"We wait. One full day."

"And then what?"

"We send a second delegation to request the release of the first."

Lanezi counted at least forty Ramian ships in system, plus the two big space stations. "How many delegations are there?"

"As many as it takes."

. . .

Later that afternoon, Lanezi, Io, and Euro joined the Ramians in a large prayer meeting. School and duties were canceled again. Everyone was praying, like a jump day, except he had no jump to make, nothing to do. After two hours, Lanezi got too anxious to sit, so he went for a walk in the nearly deserted ship. He stopped at a small ornamental garden, sat on a bench and tried to say a few more prayers between his moments of distraction.

I wonder where Katie is. I wish we could just go to Human space and be together. This isn't my battle. But he wasn't even sure about that. What was happening in the sectors? What if the Chike were chasing humanity home—and with the a-rings down at Firelight, everyone could be stranded there. But Thayne . . . that's what he was trying to do. Save Firelight. Either way, Lanezi was certain that humanity would not resort to violence. They had learned their lesson hundreds of years ago.

The Ramian culture of boldness propelled them to make statements, hopeless as they were. Euro called on the Ramian p'link. "Something's happening. Where are you?"

"I don't know. In a garden. Where are you?"

"Going to the bridge."

"I'll meet you." He didn't bother with the directions. He just told a bird, "Bridge—urgent" and it took off. He had to run to keep it in sight.

15 / EXTRACTION

Watcher, at Four System

Lanezi slid into his spot on the bridge next to Io and Euro. "What?" he gasped.

"The starfish shuttle was sent home by the Chike," Euro told him. "Then they gave a two-hour warning to the big station—Brother Station. They're going to extract the gravity ball."

"*What?* Now? They had 75 days."

Sontula joined them. "75 days to leave the system. We were supposed to evacuate the stations days ago."

"How are they going to extract them?" Lanezi asked.

"We have no idea. Can they beam it out? We fear they'll cut it. We complained that we haven't evacuated, but they said they warned us days ago and it was our responsibility. They would not guarantee the safety of anyone."

Lanezi looked around the bridge. The station was on the main screen. It wasn't a complete sphere, more like an orange with the top and bottom sliced off.

At least thirty smaller screens showed live feeds from other sources. This was real time, not a summary. It was a confusing overlap of panicked views on and around the station and from nearby ships. The translator struggled with the multiple audio feeds, but Sontula fed them into a screen on their table, so Lanezi, Io, and Euro could read the strands. It was clear that the Getti of Brother station and its command crew were staying, while the rest of the station people were now scrambling to evacuate. Shuttles were leaving their ships to ferry people off the station. Evacuees were delivered to the nearest ship and then the ships would rotate out when full. "Command has issued an assistance order," Sontula explained, "but we are to remain apart."

Neah was standing nearby though, and he suggested to the Getti that they donate shuttles that would take evacuees to other ships. Getti Drann nodded at one of ziz crew, and within moments, starfish and bus-like shuttles streaked from the *Watcher.*

Meanwhile, two Chike ships approached each side of the station and dispatched work platforms that unfolded and expanded to be bigger than the station, one on each side. With thrusters, the two huge work platforms approached each other until they linked, trapping the station in between. Struts reached out to stabilize the station. There were suited Chike, but much of the work was being done by robot configurations.

"They're going to cut," Getti Drann announced grimly.

One of the feeds was a counter—the number of people left on the station. It would drop down by double digits as shuttles left.

"Is that automated?" Lanezi asked Sontula.

"No. It is updated by one of their professional reporting teams, like for sports events."

Little Ramian ships—almost like scooters, darted in close to the Chike platform. Suddenly, they had a closer view.

"Camera ships?" Euro asked. "Drones?"

"Oh no," Sontula answered. "One photographic artist on each scooter. And each of our ships has a feed mixer."

"Artist?" Io whispered. It was just as important to the Ramians to get the pictures as to save lives. But the combined views allowed them to really follow what was happening.

Suited Chike workers converged on the top of the station. Shuttles could no longer reach their hangars because of the struts of the work platforms, except for one small place at the bottom of the station. Screens showed people inside the station running one direction and suddenly turning the other way. *Dar kaza! Dar kaza!* Lanezi kept hearing. "Southern decks," Euro whispered.

Suddenly the running Ramians launched into the air, waving their arms and feet to reorient in weightlessness. Their gravity ball had just turned off. It would take longer to move in the corridors now.

"Our shuttle is small," Lanezi suggested.

"I'm sorry," Sontula said. "Your shuttle was beyond repair. But thank you. And you cannot go. You must remain here for our next mission."

Mission. Right. Saving Seven.

Io was standing, edging closer to the Ramian command crew in his agitation. The Ramians' colors were blazing orange with yellow streaks.

Chike workers, amazingly deft in their suited claws, began to survey the top of the station, and followed up by marking the surface with some kind of paint. The camera scooters got very close and were not shooed away.

"That's not paint!" Neah said. "It's dissolving the hull."

"Acid?" Sontula asked. But then more foamy stuff puffed off

the hull as if specks of hull were being dug up and pushed out of the way.

"Nanos," Getty Drann said. "They're dismantling the hull and discarding the material."

"It's the same as cutting," Lanezi muttered. Io whipped his head around and looked at Lanezi with such desperation and despair that Lanezi couldn't bear it. But he turned back quickly to see what was happening.

"They'll have to go through eleven decks," Sontula hissed. "Through walls and life support, plumbing, cabling, air ducts."

"God in heaven," Lanezi whispered.

"And then they'll have to pull it out somehow," Neah added.

What if they hit something dangerous? Lanezi wondered.

Although the volumes were very low on the feeds, they could now hear screaming. Suited Chike were entering the station from multiple hatches. Suited Ramians hurried to intercept, blocking the way by bracing themselves and linking their elbows to stop the Chike. But it was hopeless in nogee. The Chike just pressed past them in teams, with suits that could stick to the walls and the deck. They seemed far stronger than the Ramians.

The Ramians packed one corridor full to block the Chike, but the Chike had some kind of prods. They touched the nearest person and ze went limp. There was an outcry on the *Watcher* bridge. Their colors flashed from orange to gray and back. Io slumped to his knees and Euro dived to his side, putting an arm around him. A wave of shock and anger surged through Lanezi. The prod touched another person and another, each going limp and adrift. The crowd parted, or tried to, but they were packed tight and too many were limp.

"Neahjik, are they dead you think?" Sontula asked.

But people over the feed started to report, "Suits report

they're breathing." "Still breathing." "None dead." "Completely unconscious." There was a huff of relief that the unthinkable was not being done, but still, the level of anger did not subside.

"If too many are unconscious, there will be no one to take them to safety," Neah whispered.

At that, Io staggered to his feet and fled. Euro went after him, pressing Lanezi on the arm as if to say *stay*.

The Ramians on the station were finally given the order to stop resisting. They did not have convenient pull bars in the rimways as Human ships did. Instead they had to rely on small, nearly-hidden panels that could be opened to reveal holdbars. They began to work together, anchoring people to the holdbars to propel the others along. In an agonizingly slow panic, they made their way to the southern decks.

At the top of the station, one Chike stood supervising. Now that the hull had been breached, Ze held back the other workers to let the station vent, staying well away until it was clear of escaping gases and debris.

The Ramian alarms went crazy. On at least two feeds, they could see that people were trapped. They scrambled for breathers. The command crew was suited up on the bridge. Getti Drann signaled for the two feeds to be turned off. Lanezi started praying silently.

"They're going to need air reserves," Neah suggested.

"Get that organized," Getti Drann told one of ziz crew.

The Chike work platform extended telescoping hooks into the station, extracting a deck at a time as they approached the gravity ball.

It took hours. The shuttles and camera scooters never stopped. The southern decks of the station were jammed with people. Water floated in huge bubbles in some places. Not everyone had a suit, power went out, life support was on emergency, and some feeds were lost. Getti Drann shut down four more feeds. For all their love of summaries, Lanezi was thankful they were not into watching people die.

Another number appeared on the main screen. Estimated dead. Fourteen so far. The Ramians were protesting furiously to the Exempt, who answered "Failure to comply with instructions may result in injury or death. This is your responsibility. Warning was given."

In the end it took 20 hours. The Chike popped the last section like pulling a plug, hauling the gravity ball out with it, and destroying two-thirds of the station. They detached the gravity ball and sent it outbound, forced the crippled and bent decks back in the station and sealed the outer hull. As if that were cleaning up their work.

There were no more feeds coming from the northern decks, but they assumed that Chike had left the station. The work platforms were removed, and the Chike ships departed. Shuttles zoomed back in to help however they could.

The counters stood at 587 still aboard, estimated 48 dead. It was a loss of life shocking even by Human standards of precarious outer sector accidents. But to the Ramians, it was incomprehensible.

Lanezi was in a daze, slumped at his table on the bridge. He'd actually slept several hours, but his mind was numb from grief and anxiety. He left the bridge, not caring if he ever went back. The twins were in their cabin, Io in an exhausted sleep and Euro saying his prayers. Euro looked up and gestured for

Lanezi to come in, but Lanezi went back to his cabin and collapsed.

The Ramians spent the day in shock. Some Gettis attempted to regroup and sort out refugees, but other ships headed to the a-rings with whatever partial families they had aboard.

Io was inconsolable and Euro focused on taking care of him. Lanezi prayed with them, but his mind had taken up its own chant—*I just want to go home—I just want to go home.*

9-Perfection

A mere two days later, the Chike announced the grim news that the gravity ball would be extracted from the second station —Sister Station. Evacuation began immediately, except there were fewer ships and less room to put people. Lanezi didn't need to go to the planning room to find out what was going on. The Ramians were totally open. The news blasted continuously. But he forced himself to make an appearance.

In the planning room, he discovered that there was yet another resistance plan. "Art?" He asked Sontula, not sure he understood the translator.

"Yes. Any resistance has to be symbolic."

"You're going to send them another painting?"

"No. A grand display in space is planned. It will be huge in scope, visible from their ships—a memorial for the station and the fallen there." So on top of all the technical work that had to be done, refugees to deal with, food, water and life support to fret about, two hundred Ramians were working on an art project. *I'm an artist. I should appreciate it.*

Neah stopped by and Lanezi asked why they weren't taking on refugees. Neah glanced over at Getti Drann, who approached and sat down next to Lanezi. *Oh, this is going to be bad.*

"Watcher's original mission remains, to protect the people of Seven," Getti Drann said. "As approaching the Chike Exempt will probably be more dangerous now, we will be offloading some of our people. We suggest you send the twins."

"No," Lanezi gasped.

"For their own safety," Sontula added.

"Would they be taken directly to Human space?"

Neah and Sontula looked at each other and flashed no.

"No. I don't need to ask them. They'll stay with me."

10-Perfection

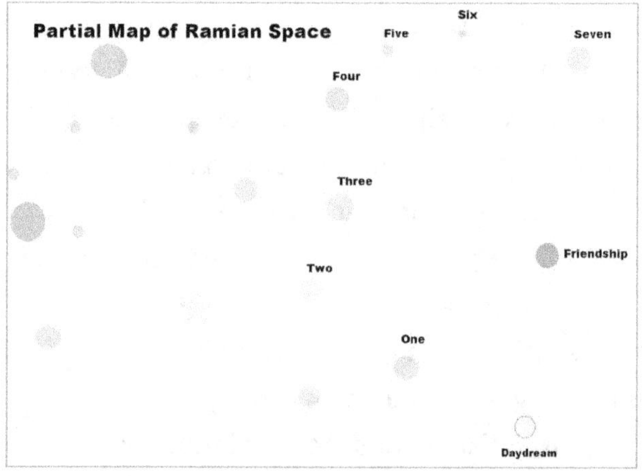

A ship came in from Five System, one that had escaped with its gravity ball intact. It reported that all Ramians were evacuated from Six System, except those who refused to leave. Word was that the Chike had shut down the a-rings at Seven and Six, so those holdouts were doomed.

There were still too many ships at Five to shut down the a-rings, but those that had their gravity balls extracted were too damaged to jump. The incoming Getti advised everyone to jump all the way to Ramia while they could, that is, if they wanted to live.

No news was coming out from Three or any other system. It would be foolhardy to jump outward.

11-Perfection

The Chike extracted the gravity ball from the Sister Station the same way, except without the drama of evacuating people. Lanezi refused to watch. Meanwhile, Ramians had surveyed Brother Station and declared it lost. Thousands of refugees were now on crowded ships racing for the a-rings. Except for *Watcher*.

At yet another planning meeting, Lanezi got the shocking news that their delegation would be heard. "Except," Neah said, "we're not allowed to go to their ship. The Exempt Raykatoo will come here."

"Here?"

"Ze's coming in two days. Our ship will not be tampered with while ze is here, so it's a protection for us too. Meanwhile, we need to refine our arguments."

12-Perfection

Sandstorm

Zahar sipped her morning tea as she slipped into her chair on the mock Cheetah. The chair was just a little more comfortable than the real *Cheetah*. Her clothes were a little bit nicer. Even the tea was just a little more aromatic. In the past weeks they'd had the best food, time to rest, time to exercise, and time to sit and watch the destruction of the Ramians. The sad

Ramian news was delayed by a week or so, having to wait for jumpships. Even the GenTwo could not communicate without jumping.

Quay sat with them, unable to tear himself away from the grim news. He was exhausted from arguing with the impervious Pascal, grief-stricken over the terrifying images, and furious over their helplessness.

The Chike had managed to clean out most of Four System. The two space stations, abandoned, orbited darkly. Ships, already overpopulated for their life-support, had run for the a-rings and jumped, leaving a few crippled ships behind.

There was still no feed from Three System, Two System, or Ramia itself. And gnawing at Zahar's stomach was the lack of *any* news from the Human sectors.

The Chike were studying Four System. Only two uncrippled Ramian ships were not attempting to flee the system. One was called *Watcher*. It was somehow diplomatically protected. The other was the flagship of Four System, *Moontide*. It carried the Ramian System Commander, a Getti Taukernan. Apparently, Ramians did not have councils, as Humans did. Their leaders from top to bottom were individuals. Somewhere back on Ramia they had a great and ancient queen. It was rumored she was 2.5 meters tall.

The outer door slid open and Pascal was escorted in by a small, but fancy, group of pole stompers. Zahar and the others rose quickly and bowed. Pascal acknowledged them and dismissed ziz entourage with a flick of ziz claw. "This one has news!"

Quay looked up sharply, his gray colors momentarily struggling to blue.

"An Exempt will visit the Ramian ship *Watcher* soon. There

will be courtesies. There will be dialogue. There will be progress."

"May it be so, Exempt," Quay answered.

"This One's honored colleague has taken the Ramian name Raykatoo—" Pascal paused.

"It's the name of a famous Ramian artist," Quay filled in.

"Artist! How appropriate. There is to be a live art performance in that one's honor. It is said to be a grand space spectacle."

"What?" Evan whispered.

"A protest probably," Quay explained.

"Rebellion through art?" Caspia asked.

"It is symbolic. Token," Quay whispered.

"Based on the news we've seen, it may be a surrender," Zahar suggested.

"No," Quay said. "They might run. They might even blow themselves up in protest. But they will not surrender."

14-Perfection

Watcher, at Four System

Lanezi watched the ruins of the Ramian space stations on a side screen in the planning room. They sat abandoned, dark, and outgassing. Ships with gravity balls intact boosted for the a-rings. The Chike pounced on slower ships, extracting the gravity balls while the passengers huddled in small safe pockets, with no immediate hope of rescue.

The Ramian Gettis had assigned some resources to helping the survivors, but mostly they'd been absorbed in designing and planning tomorrow's big art show.

Io and Euro, incredulous, had left their posts as assistant diplomats days ago. They'd taken Summer, Dusty, and Blue and worked their way onto the only rescue support team on *Watcher.* They were packing food.

Lanezi was honor bound, as the Friend of the Friend, to stay and review the points they would make tomorrow with the visiting exempt. He was immeasurably relieved that he did not have to go to the Chike ship. All he had to do was meet with a scary superior alien and present the request for the rescue of Seven. The Ramians assured him that the request would be taken up the channels by the Chike and his job would be over. *Watcher* would then return the three of them to Human space.

So, if this were his ticket home, he would do his best. He tore his eyes from the screens to review the agenda.

15-Perfection

In the morning, when Lanezi left his room, the twins and pups were waiting for him. "You don't have to come," he whispered, self-conscious of all the bird cams. "I know how much you dislike this. In fact, maybe you should take Whisper."

"Whisper stay," she said emphatically. Io and Euro nodded in unison. The three of them, in their dress clothes, and the four pups were escorted by Neah and Sontula, with bird cams hovering.

The Ramians were understandably angry with the Chike. Lanezi learned that they could hide their colors, if they concentrated, but it took great self-discipline. Only those who could maintain their bluish-lavender equilibrium would be allowed near the Chike. The Chike insisted on clearing the corridors anyway, to avoid "contamination." Additional precautions had been taken by the Ramians. Anyone with any connection to a person killed in the evacuation had been taken off the *Watcher*. They'd been sent to the *Moontide*, Getti Taukernan's ship. The Getti now commanded Four system from there.

Lanezi, Io, and Euro were escorted to the auditorium. There was a round stage in the middle with an oblong table. A live orchestra sat on the right of the stage. Trays of food adorned the table. *They have time to cut food in fancy shapes and send their tankers to collect gas from the giant planets when their people are struggling for their lives on wrecked ships. Maybe we have less in common than I thought.*

But I owe them my life—and the twins' lives. He swallowed his disapproval and endeavored to do his best. Ten billion lives on Seven were at stake.

Lanezi stood just outside the open auditorium door with the twins, the pups, Neah and Sontula, and Getti Drann. The orchestra sat frozen, colors hidden under hoods. A large screen opposite the orchestra went on, showing the view from the hangar bay. The hatch from the exempt's ship had just opened. Twenty-two Chike formed two rows of an honor guard, lining up along each side of the exit ramp. They stood upright, were dressed in fancy vests and headgear and held decorated poles. As one, they turned to face the door. Lanezi could sense Neah, next to him, nodding as if all was going as expected.

When the exempt appeared, the honor guard gave a thump with their poles. They stood aside until the exempt walked to the head of the formation. Then they fell in behind. The exempt, a lizard-like being, was imposing, wearing a rich brown robe and walking upright. Ze had one large claw and one small claw crossed over ziz chest.

Breathe. Keep breathing. All I have to do is present the request. Blue suddenly popped free of Io and rolled down to the orchestra, disappearing under their chairs. Dusty buried herself in Io's shirt and Summer buried herself in Euro's, whimpering. Lanezi tightened his grip on Whisper. She was watching the screen intently, but did not seem afraid.

The Chike exempt arrived at the closed door opposite Lanezi. "Places," Sontula whispered. Lanezi stood in front with the twins behind him, Getti Drann following, and Neah and

Sontula behind him. The orchestra lifted their instruments. The door opposite opened, revealing the Chike exempt. Ziz head swung back and forth, studying them with one stern eye and the other, sterner. No one moved for a beat. There was one pole thump and the exempt stepped into the room. The orchestra started to play a Ramian processional.

Mesmerized, Lanezi and the others advanced to the table, every step mirrored by the Chike exempt, who advanced without the honor guard. At the table, the twins and Ramians fanned out, each standing behind a chair. The Chike turned to ziz guard and spoke. The translator in Lanezi's collar said "Return to the ship." *The guard is leaving?* Getti Drann and Neah exchanged alarmed glances.

"This one," Raykatoo announced grandly, "risks life to come aboard a ship with captured / confined / imprisoned energy orb. This exempt mercifully sends the escort / honor guard back to safety." Lanezi had to wait for the double translation from Chike to Ramian to Human.

When ze looked at him again, Lanezi took a shaky breath and said, "Greetings Honored Exempt Raykatoo. I am Lanezi, friend of—"

"Lanezi!" The Chike broke in. Lanezi stopped. There had been a whole script; the Chike had provided it themselves, concerning the proper way to greet the exempt. "Explain Human names / designations / titles."

"Yes, Exempt. Lanezi is my personal name."

"Beast," the translator said. Lanezi took a slight step back. This was not going well. But Euro whispered "*Cheetah.*"

"Yes, the small one hears! Beast!" And this time Lanezi heard beyond the Ramian translator. Ze actually said "*Cheetah.*"

He abandoned the script. "Yes, we came from the Human ship *Cheetah.* Do you know what happened to it?"

"You will address this one as Exempt!"

"Yes, honored Exempt. Forgive me," he said desperately.

"The Human ship *Chee-tah* was involved in the crime / destruction / disaster at Friendship! How did you come to be here?"

"Honored Exempt, I was rescued by Getti Drann," Lanezi gestured toward Drann, "at Seven system." Thanks to the ever-alert Ramian feed director, a map came up on the screen and Seven was highlighted. The exempt turned and studied the map. "Exempt, I was in a shuttle, jumping from Friendship, and my shuttle was damaged arriving at Seven. Getti Drann saved the three of us—and the podpups." He nodded toward Io and Euro.

"The *Chee-tah* was captured / rescued / detained. *Cheetah* and a Ramian ship were the cause of this destruction! This . . . multidimensional . . . star clashing . . ." The translator fell into gibberish. Ze pointed at Lanezi, continuing, even though the translator was obviously useless. Lanezi grabbed the back of the chair to steady himself. *The Cheetah was captured!*

"The Chike shuttle is away," Neah whispered to the Getti.

Getti Drann stepped forward and gestured to the chairs. "Honored Exempt, perhaps we should sit."

"Yes, sit!" Ze looked around as if ze expected someone to pull out the chair. Io calmly walked around the table and helped zir with the chair. When ze was settled, Io sat down next to zir, Dusty diving under the table, probably headed for the orchestra. The exempt set a small device on the table and turned it on. Immediately, the entire half of the auditorium behind zir filled with Chike.

Holograms, Lanezi told himself. *Hundreds. From the ship.* He started to shake. Euro pressed his arm. The exempt leveled ziz snout at him, turning so ze could see Lanezi with one eye and then the other. Ze seemed to have no interest in anyone else in the room. Lanezi was supposed to explain the friend of the friend thing, but feared ze would hear nothing of it.

Ze spoke in a cold and calculated manner, "Human Lanezi, you are a witness to the crime / tragedy at Friendship?" All the holograms leaned forward as if surprised and waiting to hear more. *It's live.*

His heart pounded. "I saw what happened with the gravity ball, not the star. It was an accident."

"You will testify! Now!"

"Exempt," Getti Drann began, "the purpose of this meeting—"

"No!" Ze said. "This one will hear / understand / scrutinize the testimony."

"Yes, Exempt." Lanezi made a calming gesture with his hands. "I don't have much to tell." He took a few breaths. "We— Io, Euro, myself, and the four podpups—were in the shuttle *Enkindler,* following behind our ship, the *Cheetah.* We were almost to the a-rings, when another ship, a Ramian ship, was discovered, approaching from the left." He used his hands to demonstrate the positions of the ships. "While we were sleeping, there was an accident, or event, or malfunction. We were suddenly thrown back, as if by a huge gravity wave." Lanezi stopped, reviewing in his mind the terrifying moments trying to bring the shuttle under control, then realizing how far they'd been knocked, thinking they would starve. *What does ze want to know?* "The Cheetah and Ramian ship disappeared. We reviewed the record to see what happened—"

"Stop. You did not see with your own eyes." Ze switched to the other eye to glare at him.

"No Exempt. On the playback. We had to slow it down."

"You have data? Data that is stored on your shuttle?"

Lanezi suddenly feared where this was going. "Yes. We did."

"Where is this data now?"

Lanezi turned to Neah, who turned to Getti Drann, both calmly blue. Getti Drann turned ziz head sideways in a fair imitation of the exempt's interrogative stare. Lanezi's mind raced. The Chike want the data, but the data might implicate the Humans or the Ramians. But it could also clear them.

Getti Drann turned ziz head to the other side and answered. "The data has been retrieved and stored in a database tied to the gravity ball aboard this ship."

Huh? Lanezi frowned, but caught Io's look of alarm. It took another beat for Lanezi to understand. If the Chike cut out the gravity ball, the data would be lost. The Ramians had schemed steps ahead of anything Lanezi would have thought of, without even telling him. He sat back in his chair, stunned. He wasn't *the friend*. He was a pawn.

The holocrowd was in an uproar. If they had actually been in the room, Lanezi would have feared a riot. The exempt raised ziz small claw, tiredly. "This one requires the data."

"Of course," Getti Drann nodded. "When this ship is safely home, to Ramia, with our gravity ball intact, we will release the data."

"This one can take the data."

"Tampering with the data or the gravity ball will destroy all data."

"This one can take the witnesses!"

Lanezi's heart froze. Whisper whined. Getti Drann leaned forward, "Witnesses cannot recount multi-band data, including images and gravity readings."

Lanezi looked intensely at Neah. *Was Neah in on this?* Lanezi felt betrayed. Did the Ramians even care about Seven? "Wait!" Lanezi said. "We're here to talk about Seven!" He pointed at the map. "Ten billion people need to be saved! We're asking you-Exempt—to help, or get help."

Ze slumped in ziz chair. "Not all species / peoples / planets survive."

"But this wasn't their fault. An advanced civilization must have some mercy."

"It was your fault perhaps?" The exempt suggested.

"Or yours!" Getti Drann suddenly said. "For building a defective gravity ball!"

For the first time, the exempt seemed genuinely angry. Ze sat up in the chair and gave Drann the one-eye. "DEFECTIVE? A species as reckless / foolhardy / stupid as yours blames this event / disaster / tragedy on the Chike? It is irresponsible! / outrageous! / brazen!" The exempt slammed ziz claws on the table. The holo Chike were standing, shouting, but unheard.

Lanezi despaired. All their carefully considered, high-minded points were not even being read. It was like wrangling with people who forgot how to consult. He did the only thing he knew how to do in these circumstances. "Perhaps a prayer…"

Everyone stopped and looked at him, chagrined, as their translators kicked in. "Very well," Raykatoo said, and turned to Io. "This one shall offer."

"Yes, Exempt," Io whispered. He sat up, took a breath, took another breath, and began chanting the Tablet of Peace, with all the sincerity and heart that made Io who he was.

When he was done, there was silence. Drann and Neah both had the sense to let the moment sink in and waited for the exempt to speak. But Io spoke instead. "If you need a witness, I will go." Euro grabbed his chest as if having a heart attack.

The exempt tapped a claw on the table and said, "Accepted."

"I must go with him," Euro said quietly.

"Of course," the Chike said mildly, tapping again. And still Lanezi sat frozen. *Say you'll go! Go with them! But Katie . . .*

Raykatoo turned to Getti Drann. "The Chike are a merciful and responsible people. An urgent request for the salvation of Seven has already gone to the honored GenOne." Lanezi sagged in his seat. They should have known. And all this was for nothing. "However," the exempt continued, "even the GenOne cannot save them from your crime. It would require the building of two million ships. Should the GenTwo enslave this leaf and strip all resources to do this? How would that be justice? But no doubt a remnant / sample / percentage will survive."

"What did happen?" Lanezi asked. "With the gravity ball, with the star?"

"That is what this one must know! For the sake of Seven, and for all the Gens. Starkeepers report that the ways are frying / snapping / fizzling."

"You mean we won't be able to jump?" Getti Drann asked.

"Long term effects are unknown, but the ways are closing. Why do you think the merciful Chike chase you home?" They had no answer to this terribly shocking news. "So it is agreed then. These two brave Humans, plus your data, in return for this ship to remain intact until it reaches Ramia."

Lanezi held up both hands. "What happens to them after they testify?"

"Safe passage to Human space. Earth even."

Getti Drann nodded. "How long?"

The exempt swung ziz head to the other side. "No more than 400 of your days."

I can't let them go. A pain shot through Lanezi's heart, thinking of them, thinking of Katie. "I can't let them go . . . alone," Lanezi whispered in mental agony. "I have to go . . . with them."

"Accepted." The exempt clicked ziz claw on the table again. Io's eyes filled with tears, realizing the emotional toll his selfless and innocent offer had put on others.

Suddenly the baby pups appeared, climbing onto Sontula and rolling across the table to Io and Euro. "We go."

The exempt stared at them for a moment, inspiring all three pups to give zir the one-eye back. "Accepted." With a tired sigh, ze clicked on the table one last time.

17 / THE SKY SHOW

After a few minutes to calm down, the orchestra tuned up, hitting painful combinations that matched Lanezi's despair. He really didn't want to stay for the art show. He wanted to hide in his cabin and feel sorry for himself. Except he'd given up his cabin. How did he end up going from one ship to another, and another, and none of them headed back to Katie? He dropped his head into his hands. Katie would give up on him.

"She will not give up on you."

"What?" Lanezi looked up. Neah had just returned to the table after seeing to the preparations. Getti Drann was approaching for the opening remarks.

"Remember," Neah whispered, "I know your Katie." Lanezi had a hazy memory of Neah saying something about her, but he'd thought it was a dream. "I traveled with her on the *Drumheller*. Katie will not give up on you. She is a strong and loyal person. She probably worries for you this very moment."

Lanezi nodded his thanks, even a little reassured by Neah's calm purple colors. The screen switched on and Lanezi turned away from Neah to watch, or at least pretend. The orchestra quieted.

On the screen, they could see the Chike ship, slightly glimmering in the rays of the Four star. Its gravity ball floated, barely seen, behind it. The Ramians had formed a ring of shuttles, gas tankers, and art scooters near the Chike ship.

Getti Drann stood and formally announced, "We are ready to present a sky show, Exempt Raykatoo. Turning points in history, whether tragic or triumphant, are expressed through our art. We are honored to share it with the exempt."

The Chike turned ziz chair toward the screen. "Resigned. This one is not experienced in interpreting art. The Chike are a practical people. But you may proceed."

The lights went down and the orchestra started playing quietly. Just enough time passed to make Lanezi wonder if something was wrong, when a ring of plasma erupted in front of the Chike ship, like a giant red aurora, a ring of fire, beautiful but scary. The exempt hissed. The hologram Chike jumped from their seats.

"It is perfectly safe," Getti Drann assured the Chike. "We call it sky painting. It is reserved for the most important occasions. They are specialists."

The music took on a melancholy theme as ribbons of light peeled off the main ring, changing colors in spectral order, arching around and joining, then folding into other shapes and colors. It expanded outward from the ship like a quickly-evolving planetary nebula. "Although we are dismayed and sad, the Ramians are a peaceful people. Our resistance is expressed in peaceful artistic ways. We remain committed to cooperation."

As it went on, and the orchestra segued to more hopeful phrases, Lanezi had to admit, it was spectacular. The holographic Chike stood astonished, jaws literally dropping open. Their ship was so much closer; the painting must seem to surround them. On Neah's handheld pad, Lanezi could see many feeds coming in from the art scooters. A director somewhere was choosing which to send to the main screen.

The organization, the resources, tankers, containment field deployment, even in the midst of their station disasters made Lanezi wonder if even the Chike could have done such a thing, or if it was some kind of divine talent of the Ramians.

But if there was inner meaning, Lanezi had no idea. He sat, watching with his eyes, but not his heart. He tried to say a prayer to be a better person, to think of the ten billion on Seven. Only another year in his dizzy life.

The auroras were becoming more 3D now, actually expanding around the Chike ship. Lanezi knew from hearing the orchestra rehearse that they were near the end. The holoChike turned their heads as if watching something pass over them towards the rear of the ship. A couple jumped out of their chairs. They seemed alarmed. The exempt sat up suddenly.

"There is no danger to the ship," Getti Drann reassured.

"Too close!" The exempt turned and told Drann, "Stop them!"

"The sky painting is harmless and won't touch the ship."

"*Not the ship!*" The holoChike were in full panic now as the art scooters passed by for one last formation behind the Chike ship. "*The orb!*" Raykatoo pointed to the screen, "*STOP THEM!*"

Getti Drann was on ziz s'link to Getti Taukernan, "Stop the show. There is some danger—"

As the art scooters crossed each other behind the Chike ship, dragging the plasma streams with them, the scooters suddenly blinked out. *What happened?* Lanezi turned to look at the orchestra conductor, still going, watching a simulation screen.

But the exempt was now screaming at Drann. The translator was useless. Drann and Neah were both on their s'links desperately trying to stop the show. As more scooters crisscrossed behind the ship, a giant yellow jet flared out between the scooters and the gravity ball. Lanezi's stomach dropped. That was what happened at Friendship. "Move away!" he warned Getti Drann. He did not want to be sucked in the way the *Cheetah* was.

The yellow jet reached the gravity ball and then spiked back toward the Ramian scooters. Now the Ramians were in a panic. "Move away. Fast!" Lanezi shouted at Neah and Drann. But they were worried about the scooters, not even aware of the danger to themselves.

Lanezi grabbed Neah's arm. "Like Friendship!"

But Neah was nodding now. "Yes, I understand."

The *Watcher* began to move slowly. Everyone gripped their chairs, but Lanezi realized the chairs were not bolted to the deck!

The orchestra finally stopped, completing a wonderful, hopeful triumphant chord and puzzling over the audience reaction.

Back on the screen, the rebounding energy spike hit the origin point between the gravity ball and the Chike ship and spoked out, running along the sky paint lines to every art scooter, every tanker, and the Chike ship itself. The holoChike were in action, some giving orders, some working at panels, all panicked.

"Exempt," Neah pleaded, "what's happening?"

Raykatoo was holding ziz head with one claw and ziz chest with another. "You pour / sink energy into the danger point between the orb and the ship! It is—"

What looked to be a long struggle between the ship and the

gravity ball was lost unfathomably fast. The Chike ship and everything near it compressed into one molten metal stream and flowed along the energy spike, disappearing into the gravity ball.

In one breath the holoChike blinked out.

The feeds from the art scooters on Neah's pad disappeared, but they still had the main view from the *Watcher*. There was nothing left but the strangely fizzling gravity ball. "The ship," Io whispered.

"Gone!" the Chike exempt wailed. "The nest mates!" The translator struggled to keep up. "The eggs! One thousand eggs!"

Were they really gone, or just sucked in like the *Cheetah*? But the ship had been distorted and destroyed, strung out along the spike. They could now see it, horribly playing in slow motion on the main screen. "Gone," Neah agreed, dismayed.

Whisper looked up at Lanezi—she would know, she was a rescuer, but she shook her head, "Gone."

"*WHAT HAVE YOU DONE?*" Ze raged at Drann, but before Drann could answer there was a jolt and the gravity ball blazed to light.

"Gravity wave!" Lanezi shouted. "We're not far enough away!" Memories of the shuttle being thrown like a toy set him into a panic.

"Nooooo!" The Chike fainted or died, slumping to the deck.

"We need safe spots!" Lanezi told everyone, but they were in an auditorium! *Crazy!* "Under the table!" It was bolted down, but who knew how strongly. Euro dived under and crawled to the other side to help Io drag the exempt under. The orchestra people scrambled for wall restraints and small spaces, but only a few of them were going to make it. Drann and Neah and the others dived under the table, not a second too soon. There was a brilliant flash of light, the final explosion of the gravity ball, no doubt, which hit at the same time as the stomach dropping feeling of the ship being thrown up by the first ripple of destruction.

Lanezi didn't have time to brace himself properly. He pulled Whisper out of his pouch so he wouldn't squish her. He hit the underside of the table, hard. Pain, breath knocked out of him. He heard screaming as some people fell all the way to the ceiling. A second later he hit the deck just as hard. Then the clatter of chairs and discordant notes of the instruments crashing to the deck. The food, piles of green and orange, splatted down around the table. He heard cracked bones, saw blue bloody noses, membrane colors going to dark gray.

Up again. He hit the table. Down, he covered his head with his arms and felt a sharp pain in his shoulder. He tried to brace with his feet as Io and Euro were doing, holding the arms of the Chike. Table. Deck. Table. Deck. Fewer and fewer screams. His head swam. He saw white lights. He hit the table again, but it was not as bad this time, or he was going unconscious.

Finally, Lanezi went up, but didn't hit the table, praise the Lord. Down on the deck again. Deck. Deck. Deck, and finally the surges were not enough to lift them from the deck. His stomach was heaving, head spinning, thinking fuzzy, pain, and panic, but he realized something unexpected. The power flickered, but was still on.

Io and Euro were moaning, both alive. He just tried to breathe, painful as it was. The podpups scurried around checking people, and then he felt the burning in his veins. "Whisper! Please! It's too much." But she was focused on the orchestra. She scampered over prone bodies toward one musician in particular.

Sontula crawled behind Whisper, holding one arm against her chest. She said something, but the translators were not working. Orders were coming over the comm system, but Lanezi couldn't understand.

Those Ramians who could move were slowly getting up, showing emergency colors, steady white with flashes of red, amber, and yellow, like a fire burning through them.

Getti Drann was on ziz feet, tokens dropping from loose hair, leaning on the table with one hand and holding ziz neck with the other, still giving orders. Neah was bleeding, bright blue blood running from his nose and a gash on his cheek. He held a broken translator. Quickly, he snapped it back together and handed it to Lanezi, before using one hand to put pressure on his nose.

Lanezi took the translator in a daze. Neah was focused; Drann was taking charge. Lanezi was supposed to be trained for emergencies, but Whisper's agitation was overwhelming him. He stood and shakily followed Whisper and Sontula to the orchestra.

One student, who played a large keyboard instrument, was half crushed beneath it. Lanezi turned away. But the Ramians were already taking care of people. Medics were appearing. Lanezi clipped the bloody translator to his ear. Far above the pleas for help, terse orders, and the shouting medics was one loud demanding voice—Getti Drann. Ze was looking at the screen, where Lanezi could see the other Ramian ship, *Moontide*. It had apparently survived the wake of the disaster and decided to run for the a-rings. *Leaving us.* There were no other viable ships left in Four system.

Suspicious thoughts jumped into Lanezi's head. Did they do this on purpose? He couldn't believe Neah would destroy another ship. But Getti Drann? Getti Taukernan, who was now fleeing the system?

"Getti Taukernan!" Drann shouted at the screen, "I insist

you stay and help us!" Ze turned to ziz tan, "Are our comm systems working?"

"Yes, Drannjik. They are receiving our signal." But there was no answer.

Meanwhile, the twins were studying the still prone Chike. Euro looked up at him, "Ze is breathing." Slowly, ze came to all fours, and then in one convulsive motion, rose to ziz hind feet and flung ziz arms out, sending both twins flying. "Do not touch this one!" They landed less hard than the gravity wave, but winced. Lanezi limped to them.

"EVIL BETRAYERS! LIARS! BAD FAITH HEATHENS!" Ze swept ziz tail, clearing a circle around zir. "MURDERERS! *You tricked / deceived us!*"

Ze suddenly leaped onto the table, crossing it on all fours as if returning to ziz primitive predator form. Ze came eye-to-eye with Drann, "*You* are to blame!"

Drann did not flinch, but met ziz gaze beseechingly. "No, Exempt. No. I think it was an accident."

"You *THINK?*"

"The other ship—" ze glanced toward the screen.

"It flees!"

"We didn't know about the danger point." Drann spread ziz hands wide. "Would we do this to ourselves?"

"Your kind are idiots / fools! Too dangerous to leave your planetary hovels! / the slime pits of your tides! I declare you *GenSix*! You will be *quarantined*! You will be herded back to your pitiful planet like the *barbarians* that you are!"

Ze wailed again, so loud the others winced. "Three-thousand Chike! Gone because of your egotistical showoff nonsense! Grandstanding! It is *outrageous beyond reason!*"

Several of the standing had now collapsed again. Lanezi felt faint himself. "It was not my doing," Getti Drann pleaded. "Please Exempt, I have injured."

"You have bigger trouble! You have this one! And this one will return home to report your treachery immediately!"

"Exempt, as soon as a Chike ship comes, we'll transfer you!"

"NO! This ship is now MINE!"

"That's not possible," Drann said desperately. "We're damaged. My crew. My people."

"This one's crew is DEAD! This one's people are DEAD! This one's ship is *VAPORIZED!*"

Ze poked the Getti with a sharp claw and swung to give Drann the alternate one-eye. "YOU—will take this one *home.*"

Lanezi could practically see Drann's desperate thoughts. Agree to take zir home—or lock zir up and run for Ramia? The Chike might never know ze lived. Ze would be their prisoner.

Certainly a real GenSix would do exactly that. Lanezi found himself wondering what kind of people the Ramians were. Did they blow up the ship on purpose? But Drann had risked every-thing to come back for Lanezi's shuttle.

Neah was swaying on his feet. Sontula steadied him. Lanezi realized his own position was precarious. He was now the friend of the enemy. The Ramians surely assumed he would take their side. But what if he stood with the Chike? They would have to lock them all up. And his message had already gone to Human space. Humans knew that he lived and where he was. Was it only right that the Ramians face the reality of their toying with the gravity balls? Would the Chike be civilized or take revenge?

Slowly, subtly, he turned to align himself with the fuming Chike. The twins returned to the table and faced Getti Drann as well.

Drann shook ziz head and then winced in pain. "I'm not going to run off with zir." Ze glanced at the screen and frowned.

A flash of courage passed ziz membrane. "Fine," ze said quietly. And then more formally, "Most honored Exempt Raykatoo, I am desperately sorry for this devastating loss, and I wish I could take it all back. And I wish I could reassure you that no harm was intended. We, on this ship, meant no harm. I am so so sorry for your personal loss as well. As soon as we are able, we will take the exempt home."

Ze slithered back to ziz side of the table, standing. "At least truth this one hears." Ze glanced at Io, holding his shoulder, and Euro hunched over. "Attend the young! Lanezi will escort this one to a nest. In two weeks, this one will meet with your pilots."

"Yes, Exempt." Drann nodded at Lanezi. And so Lanezi circled back to his former cabin, escorting the raging exempt, each step shooting pain through his heart.

17-Perfection Eve

Indus Village

For the first time in over three weeks, Melawn lay awake on his mat in the men's hall in Indus Village. It was the first time he hadn't dropped from exhaustion at the end of the day. But the long hall was stifling. Half the men had left, taking their mats with them. *Where do they go?*

Maybe I'm finally getting stronger? The first week, he'd been weak, overwhelmed, confused, starved, embarrassed, and lonely. Slowly, his challenges had dropped below the panic threshold.

His farm team was as baffled as he was by his inclusion. None of them could figure out what he was really supposed to be doing. So he went out with them, joining them for their four hours of professional work, which they called *seedjub,* meaning working for the little seed money. That was planting, testing, planning, and documenting. Then they got credit for two hours community work, digging and harvesting. He finished his community work, or *scrubjub,* after dinner. It usually did involve some kind of scrubbing, in the kitchen or elsewhere. Or hauling or prepping food. *It's all about food.* That was his first big data conclusion.

The members of Melawn's assigned farm team were natives, so he couldn't talk to them about his former life. But they were friendly, helpful, even entertaining in their teasing interactions with each other. Most of the natives had a childlike playfulness that Melawn supposed that space, or Thayne, had filtered out of him. He felt old and serious by comparison. Even the farm team boss, a young grandmother named Tani, tolerated the craziness with just a hint of eye-rolling. The farmers were all family people, meaning married and living in the units. Even the two big 18-year olds, Holt and Iram, were both married men. So at the end of every day, Melawn came back to the men's hall alone.

He peered down the rows of mats in the dark. There were not many single men on the colony, period, just a few stubborn spacers and the occasional ill-tempered malcontent. Melawn hoped people didn't put him in that category. Most of the men in the hall were drop-ins, travelers bunking while on the road.

Another man, someone he knew, a cart driver named Jagger, headed out of the hall with his mat. Quietly, Melawn got up and followed him, expecting to go out front. But on the back porch, a rickety ladder was propped against the building. Jagger sprang up, one-handed. Melawn stood looking up, suddenly unnerved. *What is up there? Secret? Would I be welcome? Is it illegal?* But Jagger glanced down and saw him and waved Melawn up.

Melawn grabbed the ladder, reminded himself to be careful in gravity and slowly crawled up, relieved to hear Jagger walk away. When he stood, he could see the men spread out, sleeping on the moonlit roof. It was so much cooler. Melawn walked quietly to an empty spot and lay down. It was so beautiful. He could see the Milky Way, stretched across the sky, looking the same as it did from the sectors.

Of course the spacers would come up here to sleep under the stars. He took a few deep breaths and felt some built-up tension dissolve. He didn't have a mat, so he would just stay a little longer . . .

Melawn awoke, startled. The early morning sun was slanting across the roof, warming his cheek and shining in his eyes. Waking up with the sun, an old-fashioned thing, had never happened to him. He blinked and sat up. He'd slept like a rock, but it was chilly now, and there wasn't a man left on the roof. He'd missed dawn bell. Embarrassed, he scrambled down the ladder.

Melawn washed up and managed to get to the courtyard by prayer bell. He sat reverently in a sunny spot, rubbing his cheek where the sun had awoken him. *Such a cosmic feeling.*

After prayers and breakfast, he packed his lunch in a little metal bucket, probably made from the pipes of a ship. He'd learned to wash in a wooden bucket with metal hoops, and do his laundry in a bigger bucket. He hadn't yet had to chop wood or kill a bird as in the Chike orientation.

Packing everything in his backpack, he walked out to the stable to meet the farm team cart. He knew he was conspicuous in his Chike clothes, but just hadn't had the nerve to cash in his 100-coin for native supplies. Besides, even in native clothes, everyone would know he was a newcomer.

Tani, the farm team leader, was hooking her beast, Rocky, to the cart. He was so thick-skinned it looked like someone had glued grayish-blue rocks all over him. Tani's 21-year-old daughter, Piper, smiled as she casually tossed huge bags of seed into the back of the cart. Melawn slowed down so he wouldn't have to help. Although he was strong enough now to lift the bags, barely, getting them over the side of the cart was another matter. Luckily, 14-year-old Ellie showed up. She and Melawn worked together on the bags, although Melawn figured she could probably have managed without him.

"Where are those two now?" Tani asked.

"You'd think it was eleventh day," Piper scoffed.

Melawn couldn't help laughing. They only got two days off seedjub, Feast day and 10th day. And there were no days off scrubjub. But people did tend to dance, eat, play wild sports, and generally socialize themselves into exhaustion on 10th day. He was about to climb in back as usual, when Tani patted the seat next to her. "Melawn, up front. I'll teach you to drive."

He froze. Those beasts had minds of their own. "Yeah–good idea GranTani!" Holt wisecracked, as the two latecomers appeared and leaped on the back, rocking the whole cart. "He can drive when the beasts are too tired to carry."

"Yah, they won't notice his weight," Iram agreed. Although they were kidding, it was the inspiration Melawn needed to join Tani up front. *I can fly a shuttle. I can drive a cart. I can be smart and strong.* They would still poke fun at him all day. But he supposed Humans needed something to do with their minds when they weren't busy solving gravity ball physics problems.

"You hush. Driving is serious business and I think Melawn has the mind for it, unlike you two comics."

"Yes, GranTani," they chimed, in perfect unison.

"Git on!" she called, and the beast slowly started moving.

"Are they cousins?" Melawn asked.

"Honey, everyone's cousins. Those two are brothers. Pity their mother!" she said just loud enough for them to hear. But they all laughed. Obviously their jokes, shocking as they were to Melawn, meant no harm.

"So listen up, Melawn. These beasts can out-stubborn a tree. And they know there's nothing you can do to move them if they don't care to git on."

"So, they're domesticated, right?"

"What? In 500 years? Not likely." The others laughed. "Well, not unless the Chike tweaked some genes, which maybe they did."

"Yeah," Holt called out. "They don't try to kill you until *after* they know you."

Great. "They're very cooperative with you," Melawn observed, and he remembered the rebels, riding their beasts like race horses.

"Now seriously, they can kill you, even by accident. They have a pecking order. They need to respect you, know you, and consider you their better." Rocky suddenly turned and jerked on the reign. "Easy there," Tani soothed. "See. He saw you sitting up here, so he's thinking about it. We'll see." And that was the lesson of the day. Melawn wasn't sure if it was for him or Rocky.

9-Names Eve

81-Petals, outbound from the rogue planet

After more than a month of boosting, they were finally at speed to jump to Veez's home planet, Castle. Beezan knew he should be meditating, but all his routines were lost on this big, unfamiliar ship. Big cabin, big Prayer Room, big Command Bay. He was in Arc 2, hunting for a small room, a closet even, where he could hide. But he couldn't escape facing a strange jump in a strange ship.

Without the a-rings, they'd be doing a straight line jump.

Theoretically, jumping the *81* should be no different than jumping the *Drumheller*. But to Beezan, the *Drumheller* had always been part of him, like taking a journey with a big warm coat. *81-Petals* would be like taking a journey with a shuttle on his back. *Maybe I should be happy. This big ship would be hard to handle in the a-rings.*

Beezan thought he would circumambulate the *81*, as they had on the *Drumheller* after Arc 9 was repaired. But it took so long just to get to Arc 2 that he was having second thoughts. Maybe he was really looking for some peace of mind, some little place to hide from his fretting. He was so impossibly far from his serene jumping state that his stomach was in knots. Finally, he gave up and sat down on the cold rimway deck of Arc 2.

Everything depends on me. And Veez has some crazy idea that I'm the one for this task. How would he even know?

Beezan didn't know how long he'd been sitting there, hugging his knees against his chest, when he heard the Arc door open and someone tentatively approach, clearing her throat. *Sequoia.* The last person he wanted to talk to. Unless—

He lifted his head, alarmed. "Is something wrong?"

"No. I'm sorry to disturb you."

He shrugged and indicated his surroundings. Obviously he wasn't doing anything, not even a decent job of hiding.

"May I join you?"

"Yes."

She sat down on the deck across from him. "I thought we should talk about the jump. I was thinking—for all our sakes—that I should do the jump. Veez wouldn't have to know." She held up her hands to hold off any objections. "Just being sensible. I'm a long jumper. I've jumped in many different ships. And I won't be leaving my home behind." Beezan felt a stab of pain at the last point. "In fact, I was thinking it might be best to have you put under."

What? He was about to refuse when he remembered he wasn't the captain anymore. And on this ship, he wasn't the senior pilot. "Have you talked to Iricana?" he managed to ask in a neutral voice.

"No. I wanted to talk to you. You know I'm a strong pilot."

"Yes, I know. You were strong enough to pull us off the last jump."

"You blame me, but you really don't know."

"We were on track for Tektite."

"This rogue planet was probably more of a factor than I was," Sequoia said.

"You don't trust me. You don't respect me."

"Of course I respect you. You're a perfectly capable—"

"—cargo captain."

"Most of the time, yes."

Beezan stopped, stunned. That was a bold insult. Terribly impolite unless there was some basis. Then he realized and sighed. "You heard about my last crew?"

"Everyone heard."

Because no one kills three pilots at once. "I'm tired of explaining that it wasn't my fault. It was no one's fault. I just happened to be the sole survivor. I was cleared!"

"Yes, thanks to me, you were cleared. And now I'm not so sure."

"*What?*" He rolled to his feet and stepped away. "How did you have anything to do with it?"

She looked up at him, sternly. "There are always pilots on the investigating commission. I cast the tiebreaker against sending you to retirement." Beezan gasped. There were 15 people on those commissions! Seven people voted against him?

"And," she continued, "my *reward* for supporting you was to be sent to help you."

Beezan wanted to storm off. To go back to his cabin and ignore her. He wished he didn't ever have to think about that terrible jump that killed his fiancée and two good friends. And the eve of a jump was the worst time to think about it. He could let Sequoia jump. Take the stress off himself. Admit that he held a small grudge against her for his loss of the *Drumheller*. But he held his temper, because, if the jump failed, it would be his fault. Because in his heart he knew. Veez was right. "I do know the ways. I see them."

She shook her head. "Beezan, half those retired pilots think they see the ways. And you testified that you didn't."

"I didn't then. But I do now. Since Lander. And those other pilots probably do too." Beezan turned to go. But he couldn't. Pilots couldn't fight. It would be the death of all of them. But he couldn't just throw a switch and make his hurt and mistrust of Sequoia go away. It would take a lot of prayer to do that. He turned back and looked as far as he could see down the long Arc 2. He still wanted to go around. He let out a frustrated breath and forced himself to make the offer. "Come with me." Sequoia looked down the rimway, confused. "Circumambulate," he explained. "A prayer in each arc. Just the two of us."

The next look that crossed her face was that he was out of his mind. She glanced at the time. It was late and this ship would take way longer to walk than the *Drumheller*. But she was a true long jump pilot, familiar with the process of prayer and meditation. Slowly she stood, reaching into her podpup pouch for a prayer book. "Perhaps it is the only way," she agreed.

"Shut your eyes to estrangement, then fix your gaze upon unity."[1]

. . .

9-Names

Jarvie floated at the Passenger Lounge door, his last stop in securing the ship. This large Passenger Lounge was actually one of 27, and they were only using the front row of chairs.

Katie, as passenger monitor, was just finishing with Veez. He was strapped in a chair that Thunder and Kelson transferred from his shuttle.

Terina was next. Jarvie sent Star to the jump box with Rocket, where Terina secured them both. "Sky's up front," she told Jarvie.

Jarvie touched his s'link. "All crew ready, Captain. P&P is 8 and 3."

"Good," Iricana answered. "Proceed."

A chorus of "See you on the other side," followed as he secured the door.

Jarvie entered the Command Bay tentatively, not knowing what to expect, and not wanting his own undisciplined vibes to disturb anyone. He checked on Sky, who was subdued. He tapped her water bottle and snacks. "You're good, Sky."

"Zharvee good," she approved and watched closely as he checked the latch. Sometimes the crew would shake hands with the captain, but she was busy, and the two pilots were completely aloof, although the tension of late had dissipated. That gave Jarvie a surge of hope and satisfaction. *They're professionals after all.*

Jarvie finished his brackets and resus pack and sealed into his cocoon. "*81-Petals*," Sequoia commanded, "simulate bursts of acceleration as if we were in the a-rings."

The bursts were not going to be as hard as the a-rings, only at the same intervals, to approximate the feeling of the jump for the pilots. Supposedly, they wouldn't even need the resus packs, but you never knew, so everyone had one.

"Jump speed in 6 hours, two minutes."

Jarvie clicked his helmet on. "Ready, Captain."

"God be with us all," Beezan said quietly.

The ship was already aligned in the right direction, aimed directly at Castle. Jarvie set a camera to record the last views of the *Drumheller*, but didn't feed it to the others. He took one last look at the ship that had been his accidental home and turned it off. *Time to take Veez home.*

Jarvie did his best for six hours to find the proper pilotish prayerful state. Although he was often sidetracked by stray thoughts or boredom, he did feel relaxed and in tune. He tried to picture his Ramian implants detecting the resonance waves.

Usually, the pilot would see a thread of resonance between the current star and the target star. But here, there was no star. They had to find the nearest crossing thread. It was possible it could take some time or multiple attempts, but Beezan was confident.

"Three more simulated bumps," Jarvie whispered.

Two. One. **"JV,"** *81* announced.

Before Jarvie could even flick the mental switch that would trigger his Ramian implants, he heard both Beezan and Sequoia exclaim in surprise and fear. He hesitated, wondering if it would be better to stay out of the jump. But they sounded nearly panicked. Maybe he could help.

Ahh! I should have known better! He was blasted with back-light, nearly blinding him to the paths in front. The buzzing was intense, but probably not nearly as bad as it would have been with Human implants. He flicked through his screens to see that Beezan and Sequoia's heart rates were skyrocketing.

Suddenly, there was a thrust and they were in a path, Beezan's doing, Jarvie sensed. The path itself was not particularly bright. The burning light was coming from behind them, as if they were flying down a lit candle wick with the flame at their tail. Steadying himself so as not to disturb the ship, he risked a mental look backward. Behind them, something bright and hot burned. Jarvie fought the urge to bail out of the path. This was their chance. But the path in front of them was unraveling, twisting and turning with stray strands peeling off. He'd never even heard of such a thing. Something terrible was happening.

Jarvie could feel Sequoia keeping them in the path and Beezan pressing them forward. *I should help.* But he wasn't sure what to do. Mentally, he reached out as if to help link Sequoia and Beezan together, just trying to add a little strength.

The ship suddenly rocked as Sequoia tilted it to avoid a piece of path that was twisting off. *What is happening? Calm, stay calm. Stay in the path.*

There must be a supernova behind them, or something like it. But it was burning up the ways. Jarvie risked another mental glance back. It was huge. *Oh my God!* Pulses of energy were traveling down the path towards them. Jarvie whipped his attention forward and focused on the path in front, focused on his image of holding on to Beezan and Sequoia, to everyone. *Stay in the path. Stay in it. Stay together.*

Sending a quick prayer for assistance, Jarvie tried to picture himself, Beezan and Sequoia, superhero style, flying down the path, holding on to each other and the *81-Petals* so that they would not be pushed out.

The pulse hit them, imparting a huge surge of acceleration.

Jarvie could not think or breathe for many seconds. Gasping afterward, he tried to see down the path. *We're closer, but not close enough to bail. And if the next pulse hits us, we'll overshoot!* He had no doubt that Beezan understood exactly what was happening and would ride it to the last second. *Trust Beezan. Trust him. Sequoia, please trust him.* Jarvie waited, terrified. He could feel Beezan actually squeezing them down into the path, keeping them near death. The sentries appeared everywhere, but they hesitated. *Is it our time?*

But then Beezan wrenched them out of the path, dropping them into normal space. They came back so fast from so deep in the path that Jarvie thought he'd left his soul behind.

81-Petals, incoming to Castle

Terina became conscious with a start. In her mind, that great ball of fire still chased them, but when she opened her eyes, it was gone. She started gasping. All the contingency plans she had memorized went right out of her head. "What was *that?*" she asked, hoping someone would explain. There was another burn, and she was pressed sideways in her chair. "What happened?" she asked again, as she flicked through her helmet screens to see who was up. Yellow lights! No one was conscious in the Command Bay. "*81?*"

"Stand by. Arrival at Castle system confirmed. We are maneuvering into a safe traffic lane."

Traffic? "Mom? Mom! Grandpa?"

"Easy, child. We're not all spring chickens."

What? Well, Grandpa is alright.

"Did you see that light?" Katie asked groggily.

"Yes. A powerful thing it was, which probably explains why all the pilots are out," Kelson said. "*81,* are we clear to get up?"

"Stand by." *81* made the slightest nudge, which would not have disturbed their afternoon tea if they were up. **"Traffic pattern achieved. Spinning up now."** A series of small burns coordinated quickly and perfectly with the orientation of their chairs, as the *81* spun the giant torus up to 1g. **"Secure."**

Terina unsealed her cocoon, popped her helmet, yanked it off, and hooked it on the chair, then started on her brackets, as Thunder, Kelson, and Katie did the same. *Veez. I'm supposed to help Veez.* She staggered over to his chair and unsealed the cocoon. He started thrashing. Quickly, she pulled off his helmet. Whiskers sprang out and brushed her face. —"out of here!"

"Oh, sorry. Sorry Honor Veez!" She pulled the cocoon away and undid his brackets. Veez immediately opened his special channel and started responding to messages, talking, sniffing, and gesturing wildly. He was both overjoyed and terrified.

Podpups next. She let out Rocket and Star, expecting to be pestered for food, but they flopped on the deck.

"Owww," Rocket complained.

"Bad," Star grumped.

Jump critics. "We're in the right place and everyone is alive," she scolded them.

"Owww," Rocket repeated.

It seemed that only treats were going to restore their good humor. She gave them each one. "Come on now. Help me," she said, anxious to get to the Command Bay. She opened the door and looked down at the pups, walking dizzily along. When she looked up and saw the main screen, she screamed.

"*What?*" Katie asked.

Thunder was beside her in an instant. "It's okay, doctor," he reported. Katie and Kelson ran in to look anyway and they all stared in disbelief.

There were ships—tens of them—right outside their observation window. It was as crowded as a dock. But they were all traveling together in some kind of mass stationkeeping. "*81?* Explain." Kelson ordered.

"We have proceeded through a series of transfer orbits to this traffic loop. Speed and position are now stable. Awaiting instructions from a traffic command center."

The ships were of all sorts, as if each pilot had built his own from a different scrapheap. "Apparently, they're into recycling," Thunder commented.

"OUT, OUT! BEE, BEE!" Rocket and Star nosed against the latch of Sky's box. Terina rushed to let her out. Sky would not take water or treats. She scurried to Beezan's chair and reached up. Katie helped her up and set her in Beezan's lap. As soon as she did, Beezan began to move. Star got the idea that maybe he should check on Jarvie, so Terina lifted him up, and then snatched Rocket to put in her mom's lap—even though her mom was not so outwardly fond of Rocket.

As Terina and Katie worked on the cocoons and brackets and Kelson and Thunder checked their systems with *81*, Iricana, Jarvie and Sequoia's lights finally blinked to green. Both Jarvie and Sequoia held their heads in pain.

"Back!" Sequoia said, immediately turning to Iricana. "We have to jump back now!"

"What was that?" Iricana asked.

"I don't know. But it was burning up the ways," Sequoia said.

"But," Jarvie objected, "We'd have to jump toward it to go home."

"That's why we have to go now," Sequoia insisted, "or we'll miss our chance."

Iricana nodded and then winced. "Yes. I agree, but we have to let Veez off."

"We could send him in our shuttle," Jarvie suggested. "We wouldn't have to slow down any more."

"We need to find out what sort of traffic pattern this is," Iricana said. "We need to get to their a-rings. We need to talk to Veez."

"But what about Beezan?" Jarvie asked, worriedly.

"He'll be fine," Sequoia said, unconcerned, and pushed out of her chair. "Veez was right. Beezan knew the way—which means he knows the way home."

11 · Names

Watcher, at Four System

Once when he was on the Moon, Lanezi had toured the Tranquility Base Historic Site. A great clear walkway jutted over the surface so that it appeared you were in space above the moon and you could walk over the historic spot without altering it.

Now, Lanezi, Io, and Raykatoo were being escorted to a meeting in the pilots' lounge. They entered the main bridge of *Watcher,* a place Lanezi had never seen. He had a moment of déjà vu. The bridge appeared open to space, except here there was no moon below. He heard Io try to cover up a small gasp. Raykatoo hesitated only a moment before stepping out onto an unseen deck. Quietly, they turned away from the dizzying view and walked up a small ramp toward the back, where they entered the pilots' lounge, a room which on Earth would have been fit for royalty.

Like box seats to heaven, the pilots had an incredible view of the bridge below and the expanse of space outside. Each of the six pilots had their own alcove, with chairs reminiscent of thrones, but they were currently seated at a beautiful briefing table with central view screens. Lanezi held back and took a side chair away from the table, not knowing what his part would be in this, and a little overwhelmed by the excess.

In the two weeks since the accident, his shoulder had mostly healed. The exempt was stern in public, but Io, her default personal aide, reported her great private grief. She had spent ten days in a ritual of chanting and humming, repeating a passage of ascension for each soul aboard the Chike ship, including the thousand eggs. Taking breaks at night, and eating only breakfast, she completed her task. Fortunately for the Ramians, in her state of exhaustion, she no longer raged at them.

The *Watcher* was as repaired as it could be, with parts scavenged and stockpiled from the wrecked stations. Funerals were over. The few birds that survived were out recording, ensuring that the never-ceasing summaries would continue, but thankfully, none came past the door to the pilots' lounge.

Raykatoo had used the data stored in the control box at the a-rings to figure out how to program all the jumps needed to take her back to Chike space. When questioned as to how she, a nest grandmother and exempt, could do such technical things, she hissed, "We are *all* engineers."

Now Raykatoo sat at the table with a Ramian pad, Io next to her. With her small claw, she clicked at the pad, no longer needing any translator. The pilots sitting closest to Raykatoo sat back as far as possible in their chairs; scared, angry, or just plain prejudiced. Lanezi shook his head in dismay. For so many centuries, humanity had sought the builders, the great species that had opened space travel to them. And it had come to this sad juncture.

The Ramian pilots were a cliquish and token-bedecked bunch. Humility was not a strong characteristic. In fact, their colors were running undimmed defiance toward Raykatoo with flashes of annoyance when they glanced Lanezi's way. They were the full range of blue skin and heights, but all had the pilot's a-ring token at the base of their throat.

Getti Drann arrived and took the chair beside Raykatoo, on the other side from Io. Raykatoo was about to speak, but Drann held up ziz hand and began a prayer song. The pilots joined in immediately, sitting up and taking more respectful expressions and colors. Then Drann nodded, "Honored Exempt?"

Raykatoo scanned the room once, before demanding, "Names?"

The pilot to Io's right introduced herself as "Shiwelna, chief pilot." She must have been a great-grandmother herself and was unintimidated by Raykatoo. Widinmay, next, was old and steady, a grandfather most likely, with so many bracelet tokens they clanked on the table. Reev, flashing more defiance than anyone, was middle aged, and had the least tokens.

Tuladar was pregnant and distracted, obviously unhappy about the situation. Gosikeen was young and angry, but trying to overcome her colors. And Kells, very short. A teenager? No defiant colors. Lanezi saw flashes of admiration aimed his way and even at Raykatoo.

"I am Raykatoo. You will address me as Exempt. I under-stand that Ramians jump in the correct manner—" she flashed a scornful look at Lanezi, "—by using the codes from the control panel. Your own implants help you detect the pathways and turn out in a timely manner. This is correct?"

There was a general yellow flashing, but Drann answered, "Yes, Exempt."

"Good. Attend the route." She pointed to the screen. Lanezi moved to the table between Reev, the defiant, and Tuladar, the pregnant, to see better.

Four System appeared on the screen. Its main planets and a-rings were marked. There was a Ramian number "1" written by the a-rings. A small icon of the *Watcher* zoomed into the a-rings and then jumped. A new screen appeared where the *Watcher* icon had jumped: Five System. The Ramians flashed understanding. Their first jump would be back to Five System.

A "2" appeared at the a-rings of Five System and the *Watcher* icon zoomed in and jumped. It arrived in a system unfamiliar to Lanezi. He scanned it quickly, but it didn't match with any Human system he could think of. A "3" appeared at the a-ring symbol and the scene zoomed and jumped again, but this time, it didn't stop. Like a rock skipping over a pond, the scene touched down only momentarily. There was no a-ring symbol. It jumped again immediately to the next system and then again. Systems flashed by before the next full stop. This time, at the a-ring symbol, Lanezi could not read the Ramian number, but heard Io whisper "23." Then the skipping started again. The Ramian pilots were sitting up, agitated.

A cumulative plot appeared on the screen. As the jumps progressed, the maps of each location disappeared into the running plot, leaving only one glowing line, tracing the route of *Watcher*, 15 or 20 quick blinks at a time, followed by a slow blink. It proceeded across the screen; 100 jumps, 200. The pilots started muttering under their breaths. Raykatoo spoke over the mad plotting. "We will visit the far reaches of Chike jurisdiction. 200 days—472 jumps."

"Impossible!" Reev the defiant leaped from his chair. He shouted at Raykatoo and Drann and his own chief pilot. The chief pilot Shiwelna stood and joined in, but their overlapping voices scrambled the translator. Lanezi ignored them and leaned closer to the screen. He wanted to know where they were going. 472 jumps would take them so far away, how could they possibly get back?

The mapping stopped and Raykatoo pointed. There was a momentary pause. "After that, you will take this one to the Convocation—the great meeting where all fates will be decided."

"Impossible," Reev repeated. Raykatoo glared at him with one eye. "If your puny people have any ambition not to remain sunk in your prime gravity well, you will learn civilized behavior! You will take this one and await the mercy of the GenOne!"

Before the pilots could start their bickering again, Drann held up a hand and flashed a warning. "Sit!"

They hesitated. Drann turned to Shiwelna and there was a silent contest of will. Slowly, the chief pilot sat down and Reev followed. But Lanezi felt it was a small battle won. The true war was yet to come.

With a last glare around the room, Drann turned to face Raykatoo. "Honored Exempt, the standard turnaround for a good jump is 20 days. It would take 25 years to get to your convocation."

"Twenty days?" she questioned.

"Most of that time is coming in to the a-rings."

"There are no a-rings in most of these systems! These are swing points / touch and go, like letting go of one swinging rope and grabbing another. This way, one can change threads without losing momentum. Primates excel at this."

Although it sounded like an insult, Lanezi suddenly understood. All the swing points were part of one jump, so that it was like 20 jumps at a time. He turned back to the map. Yes. The a-ring points were marked in blue, and the swing points were yellow. "This one understands." Raykatoo pointed to Lanezi. "A-rings launch a ship. Then all swing points must be completed to arrive at the next a-ring system."

Shiwelna objected. "That's too many jumps at a time. What if you lose track of the threads, or make a mistake?"

"Then you will be responsible for stranding your ship," Raykatoo answered.

"Wait! Please," Drann tried to calm them down. "You are saying we only need to make 18 jumps in 200 days. That's still only 11 days between jumps."

"Yes," Raykatoo agreed. "You will have to come in close, as you are trained to do."

"And what if we refuse?" Reev spoke out of turn again. The chief pilot turned and glared at him, while Drann ignored him completely.

"Refuse? Underling, your captain has already agreed to take this one."

"Well, I didn't agree!" Reev stood again and stormed out of the room. Gosikeen, the young angry woman, looked like she might go after him, but a flash from Shiwelna kept her in her chair.

"That one refuses his duty?" Raykatoo asked Drann.

"Yes. I can't force them."

"What is the punishment for failure to obey?"

"Demotion. Dismissal."

"Insufficient! Since this is now my ship, he will incur the Chike punishment for refusing duty—starvation!"

There were gasps around the room. "That's barbaric!" Shiwelna objected.

Raykatoo gave her the one-eye. "Apparently, our species differ on the meaning of barbaric. Those who do not contribute will not receive the bounty of the nest."

"Please, honored Exempt," Drann said. "They are frightened and angry. None of this was their doing. Let me talk with them."

"Agreed. But Reev disrespected this one. No rations for two days." She turned her eye on Drann, who struggled momentarily with ziz conflicting duties.

"Yes, Exempt."

14-Names

Watcher, at the Four System a-rings

Lanezi woke the twins. "Jump day," he said quietly—and laughed as the pups burst into runaround mode. He had stayed up all night praying and meditating, determined to stop feeling sorry for himself and to think of serving others.

The twins moped about, not sharing a shred of excitement with the pups. Lanezi hated to see the once-happy teens like this, but certainly understood how they felt. Now that they'd been separated from their doctor, their genetic disorder might catch up with them before they had any chance of seeing their family again. "Io, go with Euro today, and take the little ones. I'll go with the exempt."

Io perked up. "Thanks Lanezi!" He snapped up Blue, who could not be trusted to follow, and the five of them headed for the travel room.

"Okay, Whisper," he said, scooping her up. "Let's go witness this fancy jumping."

In the rimway, he shooed the birdcam away before buzzing at Raykatoo's door. She appeared, standing, ready to go. She covered a small surprised turn of the head.

"Honored Exempt. I sent Io with the youth. I've come to escort you today."

"Acceptable." They started down the rimway.

Before the bird came back Lanezi asked quietly, "Honored Exempt, when you calculated the jumps, did you account for the situation at Friendship?"

Raykatoo hissed at him. "An insulting question! But at least you have the thought to ask." Lanezi let out a tense breath. "I have calculated a route away. However, adjustments may be necessary as we collect real time jump data. You—" she poked him with her small claw, "will help me monitor."

"Yes, Exempt."

In the travel room, Raykatoo announced that she had not seen the nestlings up close and would like to view them. As the adults stood by uneasily, Lanezi took her to the front of the room where the five to fifteen-year-olds sat. Io and Euro got up and nodded to her, saying "Greetings, Exempt," but no Ramian children followed their lead. Their colors ranged from defiant to scared—except for one girl. Lanezi had never seen her before. She had no colors. She had a membrane, like the rest of the Ramians, but there was no light. Raykatoo spotted her immediately and pointed. "This one is defective."

There were small gasps all around, but only Io stepped forward. "She's not defective, Exempt. She's special. She has a rare genetic disorder, as my brother and I do." Lanezi saw that she carried a small headband, which she had taken off for the jump and was now partly hidden in her hand. It flashed colors. Just then she smiled at Io and the band flashed pink, but Io didn't see. Strangely, Raykatoo nodded slowly.

Lanezi shook hands with the twins, took Raykatoo to her special chair, stowed Whisper under his own chair, and settled in. The first of twenty jumps across the galaxy. It should be exciting, but the mood was grim, with most everyone believing they were jumping the wrong way. On a Human ship, it would be very challenging for a pilot to jump against the will of the crew. But with the codes, it was supposed to be easier. *We'll see.*

He prayed during the long, slow a-ring cycling. At the moment of the jump, he saw the clear path to Five System and helped concentrate on it, trying to ignore the chaotic fireball to the side. It almost felt hot, but its activity was focused in a different direction. Lanezi snapped his mind back to the thread, not knowing if he was having any effect at all. The pilot, Tuladar, the pregnant woman, was clinging desperately to the thread and barely dropped out in time, leaving them with only three days to the next a-rings.

Lanezi breathed a sigh of relief. Eight days to spare for another jump. First leg of their marathon ride finished. And then he slept in his chair and no one dared wake him.

18-Names

Indus Village

Melawn and the farm team took a break from their work in a narrow canyon of the mountainside outside Indus proper. They'd spent the morning mapping and taking soil temperatures. They were only halfway up the mountain, "hill" as the others called it, but Melawn imagined that he could feel the air thinning. No spacesuit control was going to fix that, so he tried not to panic.

They washed for lunch with their little pan of water and sat in the sun on mats, Melawn borrowing Tani's extra, which she never seemed to mind. Melawn's companions all had home-cooked food, but were curious about what the dining hall dished out, although they usually had to explain it to Melawn.

Today's lunch, packed in a small metal bucket, was pasta with beast cheese and a covering of sautéed greens that were slightly spicy. The beast cheese was so good. With all the physical work, Melawn had found himself being hungrier. "Where are the baby beasts?" he asked.

"They're out with the Zann herders, past the red flag." Piper waved vaguely upstream.

"Oh, but I hear the Gembira farm has one," Iram added. "We could stop by."

"Oh, that's not necessary," Melawn said.

"Yeah—the only thing more ornery than a beast is a baby beast. And they're all the more likely to step on you," Holt said. "They're about your size, Melawn."

Melawn laughed. They were just finishing up when there was a shrill whistle, repeated three times. The others froze. "What's that?" Melawn asked.

"Zann whistle," Tani answered, holding up her hand for quiet, "for emergencies." There were three more short blasts.

"Not far," Iram said. They stood up, turning their heads to triangulate the sound bouncing around the canyons. The three short blasts came again. Tani pointed up the mountain to the left. Holt and Iram took off running, just as a series of long and short whistles broke out.

"Wait," Tani called, but there was no stopping those two. *Is it a code?* Melawn wondered. There was nothing in the orientation about a whistle code, just a drum code, which Melawn had dutifully memorized. And suddenly it clicked in his mind. *The same.*

"Snake bite," he said, "need medicine . . . hurry, hurry." The others looked at him in astonishment. Ellie ran for the cart and pulled out the first aid kit. "School trail," Melawn shouted after her.

"I know where that is," Ellie shouted back, running up the mountain after Holt and Iram, with Piper on her heels.

"Let's bring the cart," Tani said. Melawn looked at the rough, steep trail. It was barely big enough for the beast, let alone the cart. But Tani hitched Rocky and started him up. "Walk behind the cart and help push it over the bumps!"

The whistling continued as they struggled up the trail with the cart, but Melawn couldn't concentrate. After about ten minutes there was a change to the panicked messages. "Help here, need, something."

"Cart, probably," Tani said. "Let's keep on."

When they came to a rough place, Melawn would try to put his shoulder to the cart and shove it at just the right moment to get it over, but he was almost useless. Ellie came running out of the trees near them.

"What's happening?" Tani asked.

"Three snake bite victims. One's really old. He's in trouble. They've got the anti-venom, but we need to get them to the hospital."

Tani quickly unhooked Rocky and walked him to the rear of the cart, crashing through the bushes and small trees. Melawn stood cautiously on the opposite side, catching his breath and rubbing his shoulder. They could hear voices and people running through the trees. "Turn the cart!" Tani shouted to him. Melawn grabbed the tongue and calculated the mass and force as if he were in an exosuit. No luck. It was his little muscle against a lot of friction. Wheels, he reminded himself, and slowly pulled and walked it around in a small circle. It was agonizing. He feared for his back, and his lungs were suffering, but he finally got it around.

As Tani hooked up Rocky again, twenty people burst out of the trees. They looked like Etazann, the greeter they had met on their first day. Small and muscular, yet graceful and quick, they skipped and leaped over rocks and fallen branches. The most striking things were their bright green woven vests and black-feather hats. Similar to the colonists, they had various over-the-shoulder bags. Their pants were soft cloth with shin guards of beast hide, and their tunics were tan with a leather belt. Some carried bows and arrows on their backs. Faces grim and urgent, they took in the scene and noted Melawn's presence immediately.

Four Zann were carrying the old victim on a hastily-made stretcher while two others carried the young ones in their arms. They veered away from Melawn in the Chike clothes, helpless as he must have looked, straining for breath. He backed away so as not to spook them.

They laid the victims in the cart, setting two small Zanns and Ellie to hold their heads. "Git on!" Tani ordered, and they started down. Only seconds later, they jammed against a rock. Melawn ran up to set his shoulder against the cart again, but with Holt and Iram pulling from the sides, the cart jerked over quickly and sprang downhill. Melawn fell hard, skidding and cutting up his hands.

Iram grabbed him under the arms and actually lifted him off the ground, but set him down gently and clapped him on the back. "Okay, we got it," Holt said, no jokes, for once.

"Git on! Fast!" Tani said, and with everyone helping, everyone except Melawn, they headed down the path faster than he thought possible. *Thank God, I don't have to push any more.* He trudged down the path, feeling relieved but weak and useless. He was picking the rocks out of his palms when his mind seemed to split and see himself from above. Never in his life had he expected to be walking downhill, in the dirt, on a planet, in the open air, bleeding from tiny rocks. *Now the planet is part of me.*

The others were long gone by the time Melawn got back to

the lunch site. He sat and washed his hands, and knees, as it turned out they were bleeding too. Then he drank his water and finished his lunch, and everyone else's lunches. He could not carry all their gear, but he packed it up. As he was contemplating what to take, he heard a cart coming. It was Jagger.

"Looks like you had a little run-in with gravity!"

Melawn nodded.

"Well, let's load it up and we'll get you back. They've taken the Zanns on to the clinic."

"Thank you."

"What is all this?" Jagger asked as they started down.

Melawn assumed he meant the plant sample boxes as he would know about all the farm tools and lunch. "I'm collecting plant samples."

"Why don't you just check out the samples at the botany library?"

Melawn, sitting up front with Jagger, turned to him, stunned. "They told me there was no library."

"Not here," Jagger said. "At the university, in Shen."

Melawn dropped his head in his scraped-up hands in disbelief. "I don't understand what I'm doing here," he mumbled.

2-Might Eve

81-Petals, in Castle System

Jarvie sat on his bunk, saying his prayers, with Star actually snuggling quietly by his side after a hard day of pesting people.

The crew was relieved that Beezan was awake and eating and acting relatively normal, although he had his wandering moments. But he assured them he was fine. Further proof of his good condition was Sky, who joined the other pups working the crowd for more treats.

What turned out to be a problem was the question of Veez's people taking him back. His homecoming was less than enthusiastic, at least among officials. "Apparently," Thunder explained, "some factions think he has broken the taboo against mixing with other generations."

"He has classified information," Sequoia had argued. "They'll take him back."

"Will he be in trouble?" Terina asked.

"Probably not," Kelson reassured her. "If their government is like any other, they just want to make sure they find a way to go by the book."

"Well, if they don't take him soon, I'm for launching him in one of our shuttles," Sequoia said.

"Mom!"

"They won't let him die," she said, disgusted. "It'll just speed up those committees."

"Let's hope our consultation this evening goes well," Iricana had said.

Late that evening, Jarvie checked his p'link. If they were still "consulting," it had been a long time. What was there to talk about? He was just about to turn off his light when there was a soft knock on the door and Star leaped up. "Play!" Star declared and scampered up the stairs towards the door.

"Open," Jarvie said, and the door slid open just in time for Star to career into Beezan's legs.

"You again." Beezan shook his head. "Sorry to bother you, Jarvie, but we need to scramble. Iricana finally got permission to transfer Veez. I need you to help bring the bodies from the freezer."

"Got it!" Jarvie stowed his prayer book respectfully and

threw his uniform on. He wasn't going to meet the GenThree in his sleeping clothes. "Star, come."

Out in the rimway, he joined the others, mostly still tugging on their ship jackets or warm coats and pulling back hair as they hurried toward the hangar. Sequoia, who'd been very agitated and impatient the whole time, complained. "Eleven days we wait, and now it's urgent?"

"Captain Iricana made a deal," Beezan explained. "They take Veez and we'll go to the a-rings now and jump."

"*Now?*"

"You wanted to get out of here," Terina reminded her mom.

"Let's not give them any chance to change their minds," Thunder recommended.

As they approached the Med Bay, Beezan directed Kelson, Thunder, and Jarvie to help Katie with the bodies. Terina with her camera, Beezan, and Sequoia continued on. "Hangar 3," Beezan said, as they peeled off.

Katie had configured two sets of bots into rolling platforms and parked them at the morgue door. "Stow the pups and grab the gloves. It's cold." Jarvie put Star in a safe box with a disgruntled Sky and wild Rocket, checked their water and treats, and pulled the gloves on. He knew the operation from when they had taken Lander. He hoped this sad escort duty would be his last for a very long time.

They opened the drawers and slid the cold containers straight onto the platforms. The containers were eye level to the others, but Jarvie was tall enough to see through a clear panel in the top. He couldn't help looking as he pushed the first container towards the door. But there wasn't much to see. The two rat-people were wrapped in beautiful cloth. He said a quick prayer for them, friends, or maybe even family, of Veez.

Jarvie hauled the second container out and shut the morgue

door, while Katie checked the controls and made an official note in the log. "Let's go."

The escort left the rolling platforms behind when they got out of the lift. Carefully, they maneuvered the containers in nogee, Thunder and Katie on one, and Jarvie helping Kelson with the other. They joined the others at the Hangar 3 Entry Lounge.

Beezan, Sequoia, Terina, and Iricana were saying goodbye to Veez, who was understandably emotional. They stood around the containers for a moment of silence.

When the pressurizing bell chimed, they gathered at the window. A slightly less ragtag shuttle, one with possible markings of an actual organization, settled into their hangar. As they waited, the rest of them said their last goodbyes to Veez, who was alternately teary and wildly excited.

Jarvie dodged the whiskers to give Veez a hug and was the recipient of a big tail squeeze.

"My friends, I cannot thank you enough for my freedom. I shall cherish you all, and my progeny will learn the ways of the Humans."

"I hope we meet again," Terina said, and although surprised, Veez was pleased.

"I am going to be rescued by one of my sixes," Veez said.

"What's that?" Terina asked.

"My six-times-great-granddaughter."

"Wow. You must have a big family," Katie said.

"Small now, since I've been gone. But always friendly and dutiful."

"Your population must be . . . large." Katie said.

"Oh yes, but remember, my Human friends, we only live 38 years."

"How old are you?" Jarvie asked.

"I am 19."

"Jarvie," Beezan said, "set a tether please." So Jarvie went out into the pressurized hangar and pulled a tether across to the shuttle. He used the self-sticking latches to attach the free end to what he hoped was a holdbar.

Veez came across easily in nogee while the others proceeded carefully with the bodies. No other GenThree were seen. Veez turned and gave them an old-fashioned military salute, which Kelson returned. Then he joyfully sailed up the ramp. The others angled the containers and gave them a big shove into the ship where they were grabbed by shadowy figures.

They hurried back across to the Entry Lounge, Jarvie last, pulling the tether in behind him. Seconds after he got through the inner lock, the shuttle engine started up. They turned and waved through the window, although it was questionable that anyone could see them. "I hope he's happily celebrating," Katie said.

"Yes. I wish we could too," Iricana said, "but we've been given eight hours to clear the system. Good thing they let us into this a-ring orbit."

"Where are we going?" Terina asked.

"Tektite," Iricana answered, with a look to Beezan. "There's one other thing," she added as they all crowded in the lift together.

They turned in alarm at her voice. "Veez has indirectly indicated that he's received information that something's going on in our space. He recommended caution on our jump back." Jarvie gulped. After their hard jump, fighting off depression, now this.

"Something besides the fireball?" Sequoia asked incredulously.

"Well, he knows that we know about the fireball, and he still cautioned me."

"A mystery then," Kelson speculated as the lift neared the rim and a great weight settled on them again.

2-Might

Sandstorm

Although officially Zahar had nothing to do, she was committed to living a productive life, even on this journey of perpetual inaction aboard the Chike ship *Sandstorm*. She devised a daily schedule for herself and invited Quay, Caspia, and Evan to join her, which they did.

Prayers, breakfast, studying the Writings, exercise, lunch, time in the false Cheetah, free time, dinner, social arts, free time, prayers, sleep.

They found an exercise all four of them liked that could be engineered from the ship: ping pong. After several days, they were good enough to keep the ball in play, emphasizing wild moves over competitive spirit. It even brought Quay out of his shell. They purposely had loud fun, especially if Pascal were watching, which ze was today, as Evan and Quay faced Zahar and Caspia.

The quick *dit-dot, dit-dot* of the ball seemed to mesmerize

Pascal. Ze swiveled ziz head more than usual, studying them with both sides of the brain.

Evan returned a ball that had bounced off Quay's arm. They kept on, laughing as they played. Pascal, who had looked up the rules, announced, "That ball is out of play!"

"No one cares!" Caspia shot back.

"Exempt," Evan added.

"You require an umpire."

The ball went wild again and Caspia hit it sideways, towards Pascal, who picked it up.

Quay ran to get it. "We're just playing for fun, Exempt," he said breathlessly.

"Fun?"

"Recreation." Pascal considered Quay without handing the ball back. "Exercise. Would the Exempt like to participate?" Pascal leaned back in surprise. "For cultural exploration," Quay suggested, as the three Humans shared alarmed glances.

Pascal, still holding the ball, slowly got up from ziz throne and walked to the table. Zahar was uneasy about it, so she motioned the others away. "Let's let Quay play."

"This one is new to the game," Pascal said as ze took ziz place at the end of the table.

"We don't have to keep score," Quay said.

"Of course, we must," Pascal said, and spoke to the air in Chike. A new racket for ziz claw grip appeared, along with a scoreboard.

Pascal bowed to Quay, and before any of them even realized the game was starting, the ball came zooming across the table, hit the far corner, and bounced away. "Point," Pascal announced.

"Yikes," Quay said under his breath, sounding like a Human.

Evan turned to run after the ball, but there was no need. It disappeared and another materialized on the table in front of Pascal. But Quay got his racket on the next shot, even if the return went wild. By Quay's eighth return, they finally got a rally going, forcing Pascal to actually move. Zahar wondered where the formal, pondering Chike had gone. Pascal was *fast* on two feet and a tail.

"We've been hustled," Caspia leaned over and whispered to Zahar. Then Evan jumped into the game next to Quay, shouting "Two on one!"

"Irregular!" Pascal replied, but Zahar thought she heard a hint of amusement in ziz voice. *Is Pascal having fun?*

"I . . . need . . . relief," Quay gasped, so Zahar jumped in. As fast as she moved, the ball just shot past her. Pascal was creaming them. Could it be that the Chike were superior in all ways? Not just education and technology, but in a million years of evolution?

Quay and Caspia cheered fairly for both sides, further confusing Pascal as to the purpose of the activity, which ze clearly thought was winning. Zahar was concentrating so hard on the ball that she didn't even hear the door open, but Pascal suddenly stopped playing and stood at attention. The ball rolled away and Quay and Caspia's cheer was cut short by two stern flag carriers. Zahar froze.

Pascal put ziz racket down and said, "Interesting. Your reflexes are adequate, if not approaching Chike capabilities." Ze walked proudly to the flag carriers who then marched zir out of the room.

"Is ze in trouble?" Quay asked.

"Sure looks like it," Caspia said. They all frowned. Their unspoken attempt to get Pascal on their side seemed to have backfired.

Zahar was worried. "Did we just demonstrate that we don't follow the rules?"

"Or that we actually know how to have fun?" Caspia suggested.

"Or that we're slow and uncoordinated?" Evan said, collapsing on the deck.

Quay sat down next to him. "Let's hope we displayed friendliness to all."

Later, during the Cheetah session, Pascal was back, smugger than ever. "Still no news of the Ramian ship meeting with Exempt Raykatoo?" Quay complained. "It's been 25 days."

"This one is also anxious for news, but more patient. Ships go where they will, and may not pass messages."

"Why is there no news from Three, Exempt?" Quay asked.

"No ships come. We do have other news today." They scowled at Pascal, but ze carried on. "Two more harbingers have been located."

"By this ship?" Caspia asked.

"Sadly, no. But we are honored with at least one," ze said, always looking at the bright side. *Darn*, Zahar thought. *No chance of meeting other aliens.*

"Where are these harbingers from?" Evan asked.

In ziz enthusiasm, Pascal waved up a 3D map. "This is a map of our leaf." Misty colored clouds grouped stars into sections, overlapping in some places, and leaving voids in others. "It's coded for generations and species." A bright object burned in one overlapping section. "The blue is Ramian space; the brown is Human. This one has explained the fireball at the place you call Friendship. This anomaly was caused by Ramians and possibly Humans. It devastates the ways. Its radiation will destroy an entire civilization here, at the system they call Seven."

"Can't the GenOne do something?" Quay asked.

"They cannot undo the foolishness of the GenSix. That is why some species are quarantined."

"You put an entire species in jail?" Zahar asked.

"Not jail. Confined to their home systems. The GenOne decide, for the good of all."

"Exempt, is that what's going to happen at this convocation you talked about?" Zahar asked.

"Yes. That is one purpose of the convocation. The GenOne will decide the fate of all emergent species. GenFour will be assisted. GenFive will be left to develop on their own. GenSix will be quarantined."

"Forever?" Evan asked.

"Not necessarily. Quarantined species can prove their worthiness. But only one species has ever overcome the confinement." Pascal sighed, as if ze disapproved and was reluctant to mention them. "They're called the Scampers, but you wouldn't know them. They are GenThree now, but heavily supervised."

"What normally happens to the GenSix?" Caspia asked.

"Normally? / Generally? / Usually? They perish." Shocked, they all turned from the map to Pascal. "Climate change. Nuclear war. Resource exhaustion. Failure to educate. The usual."

"And you don't save them?" Zahar asked, indignant.

"In their own home systems, they must save themselves."

A chill went down Zahar's spine. "Are you saying, because of this fireball, Humans and Ramians might be labeled GenSix?"

"To be labeled GenFive would be your hope and salvation. That's why they drive your people home even now," ze said gravely. *So Humans are being herded back to Sector 1.* Zahar's heart went out to them. Even if they got home, what would be left?

"Harbingers were found here and here," Pascal went on cheerfully pointing out the locations. "But the search continues."

Quay reached in and touched the star that was Ramia. "What happens when you reach our home world?"

"Nothing," Pascal answered. "Home systems are sovereign. Not even the GenOne would touch them."

Zahar locked eyes with Caspia. *And there lies our final hope and salvation.*

81-Petals, at Castle a-rings

Jarvie was monitor for their jump from Castle to Tektite as they entered the a-rings at speed, the destination supposedly programmed by Veez's people, the Scampers. He hoped it would be easy, doing it like the Ramians did. Beezan and Sequoia had taken a couple hours to pray and meditate, but it wasn't near enough for Sequoia, who was barely less agitated than before. But to Jarvie's relief, she was no longer mad at Beezan.

Beezan was fine, with no sign of nerves before making the most important jump of his life. "Let's go home," he'd said, and patted them on the helmets before getting in his chair.

"Passengers ready," Katie reported. "Only Kelson is under. Something about old dogs and new tricks." It wouldn't matter if the crew were awake. The only one strong enough to pull Beezan off the path was Sequoia, and Jarvie didn't think that would happen again.

It was an exhausting six hours as they sped up to JV. Each time around the a-rings, Jarvie would see a little blip on his screen in the direction of Tektite. Meanwhile, the passengers took turns chanting prayers. This was a new thing as the passengers were normally unconscious, but Jarvie found it very comforting.

Thunder's deep voice recited, ***"And shouldst thou spur on the charger of the spirit and traverse the meads of heaven, thou wouldst complete all these journeys and discover every mystery in less than the twinkling of an eye."***[1]

"Seven laps," Jarvie announced, wincing as the painful bumps were now coming close together. The pain was part of the process though, every stab bringing them closer to home.

"Six," Jarvie whispered. He felt a little probing as they circled past the Tektite direction, as if Beezan were already looking for the path, something he'd never noticed before. *Maybe I'm getting more in tune.*

"Five laps."

"I see it," Beezan whispered. "We could jump."

"We're not at JV!" Sequoia said, alarmed.

"Wait, please, Beezan," Iricana cut in. "It's only four laps. We just want to get home."

"Yes, Captain," Beezan said, sounding disappointed.

"Three."

"Two."

"One."

"Jump lap—"

One blast of the thrusters and they were in a path. The sentries hovered, but did not come near. The burning orb was there, far to the right, less frightening as the fire wasn't coming their way this time. Jarvie tore his mind away from it and focused on the path. He could feel Beezan and Sequoia holding on strongly, as if the fireball and the sentries didn't even feather-touch their thoughts.

They coasted in that strange realm, where their clocks and

sensors didn't work and awareness was limited to fuzzy paths and large masses. Jarvie stayed awake to practice being a pilot, but he felt the passengers slip into sleep. "Soon," he heard Beezan say. And gently, smoothly, they dropped into normal space. The fireball was gone. All lights were green. *What an easy jump. Was it too easy?* Jarvie held his breath for confirmation. *Are we really home?*

"**Tektite Beacon,**" *81* reported.

The crew cheered. Jarvie had to choke back a sob. *Back in the sectors!* They would not die, stranded at that rogue planet. *What is that flashing red light?* He blinked away tears to see better. *Oh no!*

"**Beacon on mayday,**" 81 continued. As Veez had warned, something was wrong. "**Stand by for deceleration.**"

81 started the process of configuring the ship for steady 1g deceleration.

"*81*, status of a-rings?" Iricana asked.

"**A-rings are intact.**" They sagged with relief.

Quickly, Jarvie called the station using their cover name. "*Drumheller* to Tektite Incoming Authority: *Drumheller* ETA 5 days. Is it safe to approach? What is your emergency?" They waited several minutes.

"33 seconds lag time, and reducing, Captain," Jarvie reported. "No answer."

"**Clear from Blue zones,**" *81* announced.

Jarvie unsealed his cocoon and pulled off his gear. Terina came to stow it for him and let out the pups. "We're home!" she whispered gleefully and he smiled despite the mayday.

"**Relay station is abandoned. Relay beacon is on standby. There is only one ship beacon in the system, docked at Tektite Station.**"

"That's crazy, even for Tektite," Sequoia said. "There should be 10 ships here. In fact, if it's the 2nd of the month, there should be other ships incoming from Terrace."

"What ship is here?" Beezan asked.

"Kingfisher."

"That's a Special Diplomatic Courier," Iricana said. "*Drumheller* to *Kingfisher*, Iricana here. Report please." But there was no response.

Everyone got up and crowded into the Command Bay. Beezan was hugging Sky, no sign of wandering. Suddenly a breathless voice came over the com. "*Drumheller?* This is Maura, umm, actin' commander of Tektite. Yes! Safe to approach. Perfectly safe. Any slot you-ah like. Thanks-ah so much for comin' back for us." Iricana and Sequoia looked at each other in grave concern as Maura rambled on. "Umm, our situation, we're-ah the only ones left. Please. Just eleven of us. We-ah need a ride. *Kingfisher* is unrepairable after all. Please don't leave us here."

Eleven people? Jarvie wondered. *What in the world happened? Why are they evacuating?*

"*Drumheller* to Tektite," Iricana answered. "We're on our way. Tell your people to pack. Prepare to load all your food and medical supplies."

"We're downloading logs and news," Jarvie whispered.

"That should be interesting," Thunder said.

"We have been blessed to live in interesting times," Kelson added cryptically.

Sequoia scowled and turned on Beezan. "What was *that*? You wanted to jump *before* JV? Are you crazy?"

"No. I'm not crazy," he answered mildly. "I'm sorry. I was just tired of waiting, and the laps were getting painful."

"But it's not possible!"

"The path was obvious, maybe because they programmed it."

"We could program direction. It doesn't help you get in the path. You need speed. You said yourself the Ramians jump at the same speed we do."

"Maybe you just need the speed to see the path."

Sequoia glared at him. Iricana clapped them both on the shoulder. "Good work. We're home. We can talk about the jump later. Let's get everyone cleaned up and have some dinner. *81*, review the logs and prepare a news update since 16 Grandeur. We need to know what happened here."

81-Petals, incoming to Tektite Station

Iricana made them wait through dinner to hear *81's* summary of sector news they had missed while at the rogue planet. Terina stuffed down her food and waited impatiently. Here she'd thought coming aboard the missing *Drumheller* and discovering the runaway Jarvie had been the biggest story ever. Then they'd found the *81-Petals*. Now, it looked like she missed an even bigger story. But this one might not be so happy.

Iricana looked over at her and sympathized. Finally, they all sat down with their tea, facing the big screen in the kitchen. "*81*, proceed."

A fuzzy picture of a strange viper-head ship appeared. **"On 10-Light, an alien ship, later self-identified as Chike, appeared in Tektite system."**

"Pause," Iricana said, as they all set down their cups and recovered from choking. "So. Veez was telling the truth. The Chike are real after all." They slumped in their seats, staring at the screen. "Proceed."

**"By 11-Light, Chike ships had appeared in every system in

Sector 8. They announced that they were under orders to evac- uate all of Sector 8 to Sector 7. The Sector 8 Council at Radium Junction challenged the authority of the Chike to remove Humans from their own systems. A Chike *Exempt* met with the Sector 8 Council, after which the council surrendered."

Another gasp. Kelson pulled up a sector map on a side screen. "All system councils in Sector 8, including Tektite, immediately surrendered and began the evacuation of citizens. The deadline was 1-Perfection. For *incentive*, the Chike warned the councils that if they missed the deadline, they personally would be taken by the Chike."

"Taken where?" Sequoia asked.

"That was not specified."

"Probably to Veez's mystery colony. Poor people. They had no idea what would happen to them," Thunder said.

"No ship has come into Tektite since 6-Mercy, so there is no news if all Sector 8 systems were able to comply."

"What about Sector 7 news?" Terina asked.

"No ships have jumped from Sector 7 since the evacuation order."

They all scowled. "We'll have no idea where to go next," Sequoia said.

"What happened here?" Iricana asked.

"The incoming ship *Kingfisher* was not going to reach Tektite dock in time to evacuate. The council asked for an extension, which was denied. The council left their top mechanic crew to help the *Kingfisher* and voluntarily took a shuttle to a Chike ship since they failed to meet the deadline. All Chike ships left Tektite system on 2-Perfection. *Kingfisher* came in on 13-Names and was unrepairable, due to failure of a specialized part."

"Where did the evacuees jump?" Thunder asked.

"All ships jumped to Tundra, in order to allow Terrace traffic to go through Tanuki. Mid jumpers planned to jump from Tetra to Sandune. Long jumpers planned to jump from Tanuki to Radium Junction to Mirage."

Kelson nodded. "A reasonable plan."

"Captain," Katie, who had been so quiet, spoke up. "There may be other stranded people. We are probably the last ship to come through. We should stop and check."

"Stop at every station?" Sequoia asked. "That will take forever!"

"The location of the colony needs to get to whatever council we can find," Iricana said.

"This information needs to go to the Sector Council level," Kelson argued.

"Mirage then," Iricana agreed.

"Ten jumps," Beezan said. "Eleven if we have to go to Redrock first."

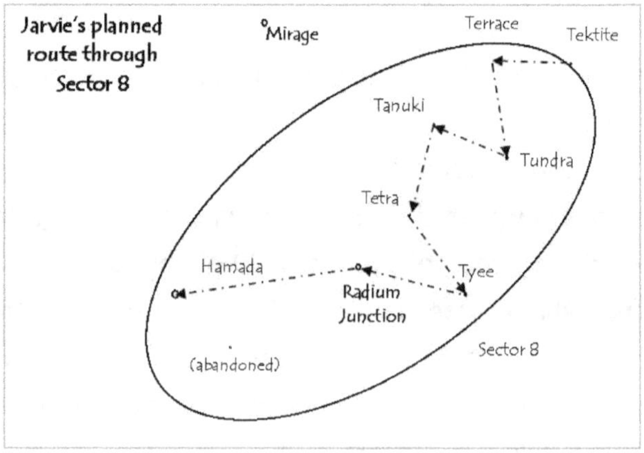

They sat in silence, Terina looking over Jarvie's shoulder as he sketched out a path for the Sector 8 jumps. "It all depends on how close we come in," Jarvie said.

"And how many people we have to load," Kelson reminded them. Iricana sat with her head in her hand. Jarvie had told Terina once that Iricana was a level 1 and knew everything that went on in the sectors. Terina had confidence in whatever she decided.

Finally, Iricana looked up. "Okay. Ten or eleven jumps to Mirage, unless we can confirm that stations are empty. We'll turn over our information to Mirage Council." She took a deep breath. "If Sector 7 has surrendered, we'll go to Harbor and hope Jamez is still there."

"Why Harbor?" Sequoia asked.

"Because Jamez can make that shimmer shield that Veez was talking about. We'll get him started while we send for permission from Atikameq or Firelight," Iricana answered.

"It's all about speed," Sequoia said vaguely, but Beezan was staring somewhere far away again.

7-Might

Tektite Station

Jarvie pulled across the Tektite hangar from the *81* shuttle *Bird of Paradise*, along with Terina, Thunder, and Beezan. No one had come out to the shuttle or extended any tubeway, if they had one. Jarvie was glad Kelson told them to wear their pressure suits. Besides being rundown in the hangar, it was freezing.

In the so-called Entry Lounge, they pulled off their helmets and were greeted by a mechanic, as evidenced by his coverall stuffed with tools, hard hat, and safety glasses, which apparently, he forgot he was wearing. Scrawled across his uniform in black pen, it said, *If I can't fix it, no one can.* He thumped his chest instead of a handshake. And between chomps of green gum, he introduced himself, "Heya, thanks for comin'. I'm Teeve." Jarvie smiled. Obviously, Teeve had spent zero days on any diplomatic mission. *Tektite native. Outer outer sector.* But he was sincere and looked competent. Jarvie nodded and thumped his own chest, as did Thunder.

"Greetings, Teeve. God is Most Glorious," Thunder replied. "This is Honor Beezan, Jarvie, Terina, and I'm Thunder." Teeve cocked an eyebrow at the "honor" part, but quickly refocused on Thunder's question. "What's your status?"

"Wella, we're-ah finishin' the loadin'." He waved for them to follow him, pulling easily out the door into the small cargo rimway. Jarvie considered putting his helmet back on. It was just as freezing here as in the hangar. And the interior was alarming. Terina smirked at him, like *I told you so*, after her little history briefing this morning.

Tektite station was not even one complete torus. Two partial arcs were connected by a narrow "X" structure, requiring the inhabitants to cross through nogee to get to the other arc. The cheerless walls were unpainted as no theme had ever been implemented. Its cobbled-together sections still displayed part numbers. Pipes, cables, and switches were exposed. In some places instructions were scrawled on the rimway wall, punctuated by wads of dried green gum. It smelled of ozone and mint. There were no flat decking plates covering the rimway sections, which wouldn't matter here in nogee. But if it were that way in the torus sections, they'd have to watch where they walked.

They passed more scrawling on the walls, this time marked with pink gum. Jarvie was careful where he touched the walls. "I fear the station is held together by gum," he whispered to Terina, who was trying to hide her horrified expression.

They met acting commander Maura and the others loading

cargo in another hangar. "Heya!" Maura greeted them, thumping her chest where her slogan, *Read the instructions!* was scrawled. "Thank y'all for pickin' us up. We-ah should be ready in 'bout an hour." She gave them all a more critical onceover. "Look-ah, we've-ah got plenty of pilots, but if a couple of ya want to give these refurbs a spin, be our guest."

"We'd love to," Thunder answered easily. *Was that some kind of Tektite gesture of good manners?* Jarvie must have looked surprised as Thunder winked at him. Not counting Teeve and Maura, there were six others in the hangar, all in various colors of faded coveralls. They saluted shyly with whatever tool they had in hand and went back to work. Their hair was dyed yellow and white and braided in various ways. Except for the two kids, they were muscular.

"They look like Vikings," Terina whispered. Jarvie didn't know what that was, but something else Terina said came back to him. That there were second and third generation children on Tektite who'd been isolated all their lives, having their own culture, language and suspicion of outsiders. Was that why Iricana sent Thunder, who understood the isolation, or Beezan who was so shy?

"Commander," Thunder said, "your message said eleven people."

It took Maura a second to realize Thunder was talking to her. "Oh, ah, yeah," she explained, "Mech crew here, of eight, plus three off *Kingfisher*. Pity to leave such a fine ship." Following their gaze, she grabbed a holdbar and turned to introduce the others. "Y'all met Teeve, my-ah spouse, and that's Cooper there, my-ah little sib. He's our instrument expert, coder, such." Jarvie drifted closer to read Cooper's slogan, *Triplecheck.* "Cooper's spouses with Mika, Teeve's little sib." Little must be an affectionate term, Jarvie thought, as Mika looked like she could haul a shuttle across the hangar one-handed. "Then there's Sunny and Danny, top mechs, and their sibs Chip and Kente." Jarvie barely looked at them, too busy reading slogans: *Get it done*, *You break it, we fix it*, and his favorite, *Save the box*. The kids had small electronic badges generating their slogans, but they quickly went off.

"I'm going to need a scorecard," Terina whispered. Kenta and Chip were younger than Terina, wearing red arm bands like rebel flags. Despite the lack of armbands on the others, Jarvie was certain they weren't all 21, meaning the real Tektite commander had left youth in charge of the station.

They continued on to check out the shuttles. Terina, wide-eyed, took a few photos. One of the shuttles was expensive and beautiful. "That's *Sonata*," Maura said, "*Kingfisher*'s shuttle. Ra'Tama, ah, Captain Ra'Tama, will be flyin' that with his crew-ah two." She paused and whispered to them, "He's a bit distressed 'bout leavin' the *Kingfisher*." They all nodded in sincere sympathy.

Maura pointed at the other two shuttles, obviously left by the station commander, not thinking they would get far or be worth much. They looked to be only halfway through their refurbishment. "You'll all be wearing pressure suits, I hope," Thunder said.

"Oh, yeah. Pretty standard round here."

Thunder turned to Beezan. "Honor?" Beezan gave a fateful shrug and pointed to the shuttle on the right.

"That's *Pinecone*," Maura said. "Looks like junk, but the engine is tops, and well-ah, it'll be tops when we're done with it." Then she pointed to the other and turned back to Thunder. "So ya get *Thunder Bay*."

"How appropriate," Terina whispered.

As Jarvie and Terina headed back to the Entry Lounge, they

met three people with perfect posture, even in nogee, exquisitely dressed in royal blue ship uniforms, who greeted them with extreme courtesy—the *Kingfisher* crew. Captain Ra'Tama was a red-banded 18-year-old, but obviously he was no delinquent. Jarvie was taken aback. Something about Ra'Tama reminded him of his brother. Whereas Canim had been friendly and funny, Ra'Tama was very reserved. He was dark tan with thick wavy, dark hair, cut short, and intense brown eyes. "Please call me Ra'Tama. And this is my crew, Vante Kay and Kay Ling." At first glance, Jarvie thought they were twins, but then realized they must be husband and wife. They had long wavy hair and a certain spring-loaded tension that made them seem slightly dangerous.

"I've never heard of the *Kingfisher*," Terina commented, already digging for information.

"Out of Sector 1. Earth actually," Ra'Tama explained.

"Wow. You must have some story!" Terina said, which caused all three of them to regard her with even more intensity.

Jarvie noted the podpup box. "We've got several pups aboard the ship."

"I am pleased to hear that," Ra'Tama said. "My pup has been alone." He was so concerned for his podpup. Jarvie expected a little surge of jealousy on meeting another perfect older brother type, but instead, he was happy. Ra'Tama seemed truly kind. *And I don't have to compete with him my whole life.*

Three hours later, Jarvie and Terina, with the two youngest gum-chewing Tektites, were backing out of the hangar. The two super shy kids, with no obvious gender, who couldn't have been more than 11, had balked about going with Jarvie. Maura had moved them along with a quiet comment that if Jarvie couldn't fly, they could always take over the shuttle. That made Jarvie more determined not to mess up.

Beezan's voice came over their system. "*Pinecone* to all shuttles, *Sonata*, follow me, then *Thunder Bay*, then *Bird of Paradise*."

"*Sonata* acknowledges," came a woman's voice. Not the pilot Ra'Tama. He'd appointed a monitor for a dock.

"*Thunder Bay*. Copy," Thunder said.

Jarvie waved his hand at Terina, who answered, "*Bird of Paradise* acknowledges." He could just see Beezan rolling his eyes at the formality. The three shuttles passed in front of Jarvie and he joined them, leaving the same interval between. It would have been a beautiful sight from the Tektite Observation Lounge. If there was anyone to see. If two of the shuttles weren't patched-up boxes of scrap metal.

"We do what we can," he sighed. *That could be my motto!* And then they cleared the cargo section and the *81-Petals* came into view.

Kenta and Chip gasped. "That's . . . that's . . ."

"Yes," Terina replied as instructed. "It's the *81-Petals*. That is classified information. All will be explained by our captain. For now, we're using the call sign *Drumheller*."

They leaned forward in their seats in amazement and excitement. "My grandfather Kibwe was on the *81*," Kenta whispered. Do you know him?"

"No. I'm sorry," Terina turned to talk to them. "We really are the crew of the *Drumheller*. The captain will explain."

Captain Iricana greeted them all courteously at the *81* Entry Lounge. Warned by Thunder, she thumped her chest at the Tektites, but shook hands with Ra'Tama and his crew. Tears came to their eyes when she said, "Welcome to the *81-Petals*. A strange destiny has brought us together. You'll be processed quickly, taken to your cabins to clean up, and then we'll talk."

They went up the lift; the Tektites marveling at the fancy *81-Petals*. Ra'Tama barely noticed. Jarvie would have walked down the rimway with him, but his crew stayed right next to him, offering support and encouragement. Suddenly Jarvie felt bad for laughing about Ra'Tama using a monitor to talk to the other shuttles. He'd just left his home, the *Kingfisher*, probably for a long time. Maybe forever.

After Katie and Beezan split off to take the new people to their cabins, Iricana turned to Thunder in dismay, "They're children!"

Thunder nodded. "Maura is 24 and the oldest. But yes, the commander left his best mech team to save the *Kingfisher*. They volunteered. They thought they could fix anything. But some Earth ships have special parts."

She shook her head in sympathy. "And now we have two displaced captains."

11-Might Eve

Indus Village

Melawn still enjoyed sleeping on the roof, even though it was getting colder. Only spacers ventured up in the chilly weather, so many of the men would gather at night and swap stories. It was the one place they could talk freely about their past lives, about the ships, the stations, and for some, Earth. It was hard for the pilots, never to jump again. Although the official transcript of news from the *Cheetah* had been posted, the others were eager to hear Melawn's story firsthand.

They never mentioned Melawn still wearing the Chike clothes, or being weak, or incompetent. They were understanding. Possibly most of them had been through the same thing. But they all looked like colonists. Melawn could only tell the difference between spacers and colonists by their slightly different accents and considerably less brash behavior among the spacers. And of course, spacers loved the stars—not as constellations full of fables, but as real places, perhaps even their homes. There was much speculation about which stars might be sector stars or even the Sun, but the reality was, they had no idea. They didn't even know which direction was home. So each one adopted his own star and often turned that way for prayers, thinking of Earth, the sectors, and the Human family they had left behind.

Melawn chose no star. It was unrelated to actual data. But as he settled down in his blanket, he scanned the Milky Way, wondering. Suddenly, one of the men shouted, "Orbiter!" The others scrambled up, Melawn along with them, holding the blanket around him. The man was pointing up. A white, pinpoint light was arcing steadily across the night sky.

"Equatorial," someone said.

"What is it?" Melawn asked Jagger.

"Chike ship. We think. We sometimes get drops the day after, but not if it's in an equatorial orbit. And sometimes we think they're just spying on us."

"The Ramian colony was close to the equator," Melawn said.

"Well, maybe they'll have company tomorrow," Jagger said and wandered to the edge of the roof while the others kept watching. Melawn joined him and looked out over the road. A cart approached and dropped off a rider, even though it wasn't the regular time. Jagger waved down to the driver.

"Night rides?" Melawn asked.

"Informal," Jagger explained. "Night carts charge only half." He turned to Melawn and smiled conspiratorially. "My turn starts tomorrow night."

"Where do you get on?"

"Oh, near the stands, along the road. Wherever."

11-Might

Melawn struggled through another hard day of farm work

and scrubjub. He hauled loads of flax to the textile hall. On the first trip, he hoped to snag someone to help him with the heavy bundles, but was ashamed when he got there. The hall was filled with the feeble and old. They had spared the children, sending them to school in a desperate plan to educate their way to better times. He could see that the weavers were tired. One old woman, obviously a former long jumper, stared out the window at the sky.

No one is retired. There're not enough people. No. It's about food. There's not enough food. Which is it?

12-Might

The next day, Melawn quizzed the farm team about total crop yield, population, number of person-work-days to generate 1 day's worth of food for one person. Greater than one? Less than one? Too many or too few?

They had no idea. "Isn't that your job?" Tani asked worriedly.

"I fear it is," Melawn whispered to her. On the way home, he came to the last page in his single notebook. Time for decisions.

"Tani," he said seriously, "I'm going to work in Shen a few days."

She nodded. "Good luck."

After scrubjub, Melawn pushed open the door of the "store" side of the textile hall. An elderly couple ushered him in with great kindness. "Greetings, Melawn."

"God is Most—I mean—"

"Yes, God is Most Glorious," the woman chimed, "and it is a

glorious day. My husband is Nalu and I'm Nika. Please come in. We've been expecting you. Have tea. We'll talk."

Expecting? Tea? Talk? Melawn stood, flustered. *Calm down. Slow down. Take a breath*, he reminded himself. He washed at a small stand before sliding onto a wooden chair at a small square table made of wooden planks.

More elderly people worked around the shop. Uneasily, Melawn hoped they didn't think he had come for a job. But between the tea and cookies and the sweetness of the couple, he relaxed and admitted he'd finally broken his 100 coin to buy notebooks and pencils so he resigned himself to buy native clothes. "I guess I'm the only person in Indus wearing Chike clothes."

Nalu clasped him gently on the shoulder. "Melawn, you're the only person in Paradise Valley wearing Chike clothes."

"Oh, hush, Nalu," Nika said, pushing another cookie Melawn's way. "The adjustment takes time. We were so young. It was easy for us."

"You're spacers?" Melawn asked in surprise, hearing no trace of the sector accent.

"Both off the *Pilgrims' Promise.*"

"*Pilgrim!*" Melawn said, "Lost in 1022. That was 62 years ago!"

"Yes," she said. "We were children. I hardly remember life on the ship."

Nalu nodded. "Jumping. That I remember. That stays with you. And of course, we had our families. And now we have quite a family of our own here—as you will too someday."

"Nalu, you'll scare him," Nika patted her husband affection- ately and took the tea cups.

Nalu chuckled. "Now, let's talk about what you need."

"I have a feeling you know better than I do. But I only have this much," Melawn said, laying 60 out on the table. "And I need a mat too."

Nalu considered carefully and pushed 15 back to Melawn. "Save 20 for winter when I finish making your coat. Davy, run down and get a full flex mat." He patted Melawn on the shoulder. "Don't worry. We're going to get you the raiment of Paradise."

A quote rolled through Melawn's mind as Nalu got up, smiling. **". . . how numerous are those who wear clothes made of cotton or coarse wool throughout their lives, and yet by reason of their being endowed with the vesture of divine guidance and righteousness, are truly attired with the raiment of Paradise . . ."**[1]

13-Might Eve

Melawn stood by the cart stand in the near dark before moonrise. He'd brought everything he owned, leaving his samples behind, and checking out of the men's hall.

Nalu and Nika had shown him how to pack for the road, rolling his blanket in the large mat, which had its own shoulder strap, and putting a towel between his nested lunch bucket and washing bucket to keep them quiet. Their smiling granddaughter, about 18, had even packed a bunch of cookies into his lunch bucket. They outfitted him with a soft, but warm, tan tunic that came halfway to his knees. The pants were loose tough material, like denim, but brown, with knee protectors made of beast hide. They assured him the beast had died a natural death, but nothing was wasted here. The pants tied at the top and a plain buckled belt went on the outside of the tunic. Another change of clothes, two warm undershirts and a sweater, along with all the Chike underwear went into a pillowcase with a handle, more like a giant tote bag, into his backpack. Along with that, he had his hat, sunglasses, prayer book, notebooks, pencils, soap, razor, and comb. Melawn still wore his Chike shoes, but other people did too. He was happy to see they lasted for years. The large Chike backpack was now concealed beneath a windproof, rainproof poncho with hood. Melawn had a sharp pain thinking of Lanezi and his poncho. They had not always gotten along, but Melawn missed him now and wished he hadn't been so disapproving. *I need to have a more generous heart.*

Glancing up at the roof, where only last night he'd looked down, he saw a man raising his hand in parting. *Do they know everything about people here?* Melawn waved back. Several other people lingered about and up and down the road. Sure enough, by the time Jagger came along, there were already three people in the back of the cart.

Melawn climbed on, handing over his half fare.

"Headed for Shen?"

"Yes, please." Melawn settled in, sitting on his mat and wrapping his blanket around him like the others. By the edge of town, they were squeezed together. An older spacer next to him rested his head on Melawn's shoulder and snored.

"Hunza." Jagger said softly. Melawn awoke with a start. He'd slept over two hours. "Five-minute break." They were parked outside the family hall, so people could either check in or use the facilities before going on. Melawn went quickly.

New people piled on, greeting each other quietly and bundling up. Either they slept or they watched the road. And some, like Melawn, watched the stars.

· · ·

13-Might

Shenandoah Village

Melawn's sleepy night faded away the next morning as he walked down the long steppingstone path from the university campus to an outbuilding, following his new acquaintance, the botany professor. Jadee was about 40, strong and healthy as were all natives. He had very dark skin, not from genetics, but from standing in the sun too long. He had a hat hanging around the back of his neck, but apparently he was too distracted to put it on. Terrified of the blinding sun, Melawn instinctively put his hat on every time he went outside.

Jadee was more than distracted, upset even, so Melawn feared that he'd come at a bad time. But Jadee insisted he had no class until three bells and gave Melawn a tour.

The first stop was the herbarium, where racks and racks of pressed plant specimens were shoved against the walls, two racks deep. Melawn, if he'd spent the rest of his days here, could not have done even a tenth of it. "How long have you been collecting?"

"Oh, a hundred years at least. We have to go pretty far afield to get anything new. I've been down the coast with my kids."

In another building, there were hundreds of bottled samples. "The glass?" Melawn asked.

"Melted down from the ships. Lots of it since the *Starswimmer*, so this is where we keep the backup food stock plants. And of course we have seed vaults."

"Any Earth seeds?"

"No chance. The Chike are very thorough in their inspections. No seeds have ever come through on the ships."

They toured a small greenhouse. "I've seen big greenhouses out at the farms," Melawn realized.

"Yes, but those are for starting food seedlings. This is where we experiment with increasing the yield."

"Can I ask you about crop yields? Population?"

Jadee nodded with resignation. "You can ask. I don't promise to have answers. You're not the first person Grace has assigned to the food issue."

Melawn was utterly defeated. He tried to calm his mind on the way to Jadee's office. *What am I supposed to be doing?* "Do you know why I wasn't given the previous research or any information? It's like reinventing the wheel."

"Well, maybe Grace is hoping for fresh eyes."

Melawn shook his head. "If you—if *we* keep starting over, we'll be stuck in the stone age."

"I hope it doesn't come to that."

"So what do you think? About the food?" Melawn asked.

"I think we're good for 100 years, if we don't have major drops. After that, we need more arable land, and not all in one place. And more water."

Jadee pushed open the door of his small office. Melawn got three steps in and stopped dead when he saw the chalkboard. Thayne's writing. Population formulas. "You're working with Thayne."

"Ah. I thought he might be your shipmate."

"I was going to go see him next."

"You're out of luck. He's gone," Jadee said with enough anger that Melawn turned sharply to look at him.

"Gone?"

"A week ago. And he took five good students with him."

"To the rebels?"

"Rebels? They're more like poachers. Took my daughter. He has some kind of persuasiveness."

A little chill went up Melawn's spine. He remembered the

day he told his parents he was leaving with Thayne. On his 15th birthday. They could not legally stop him. *How would my life have been different?* "I'm sorry. Where are they?"

"I don't know. Grace probably does. But she's not going to tell you."

"Well, how do you join if you can't find them?"

"You planning to join?"

Melawn dropped his gear to the floor and wandered over to the window, while Jadee stood with his arms crossed in a hostile manner. *What good am I here?*

"You got a daughter?—No, course not," Jadee answered his own question. When Melawn left with Thayne, all those years ago, he had expected to be gone a short time, make important discoveries, and be back with his family. And he'd never seen them again. The image of Melawn's mother begging him not to go became overwhelming, and Melawn's eye's filled with tears. And suddenly Jadee came and turned him around so they were face to face. Melawn quickly wiped his tears away. "No," Jadee grasped the situation. "You were one of those disloyal kids!"

Melawn winced. "You don't understand. Thayne is an astonishing human being. His mind is on another plane. To work with him is an honor. We did amazing science. We're unlocking the secrets of the a-rings, of gravity balls—"

"He poached you from your parents."

"I went of my own free will."

"And have you had any free will since?"

Have I? They stood in unhappy silence for a moment. "Could I at least see his office?"

In his office, Thayne had left the rebel location for Melawn, plain as day. On a big map of the valley a Hidden Word was written out and pinned to the map. Not far, east and north of the red flag. One or two days' walk.

"Can I get through the tunnel?"

"Are you going to join?"

"No. No, I'm not. But I'd like to talk to him about the population."

"Thayne says there's no hope; that we need to escape."

"There is no escape," Melawn said, "and no hope of rescue. I've seen the Chike and their ships."

"The council agrees. We should put our effort into the food."

"But the population is unpredictable with the drops. And with the unrest with the Chike, there may be more drops."

"And there are a few people who think a cooperative society doesn't work hard enough," Jadee whispered.

"Seems to me you work plenty hard."

"We have no idea. None of us have ever been enslaved."

"It won't come to that," Melawn said, truly believing it.

"I hope not." They stared at each other.

"We're civilized Human beings now. We'll starve first," Melawn insisted.

Finally, Jadee relented. "Yes. You can get through the tunnel. In the daytime. They won't stop you."

"Do you want to come with me?"

"Are you *crazy?*"

"Your daughter—"

"Yeah, well, I've got four more to worry about who didn't go running off with a sweet-talking stonesnake!" Jadee went to Thayne's desk and grabbed a small compass. "Better take this."

"Thank you. Do you want to send a note to your daughter?"

He dropped his head sadly. "No. Just tell her . . . tell her we miss her and please come home."

13-Might

Watcher, leaving Five System

Lanezi settled into his jump chair. The Ramians, to their credit, had scrambled to revamp the chairs in preparation for the 26-hour multiple jump sequence. There were feeding and waste hookups and on-call stimulants for pilots. They devised heartbeat clocks which wouldn't tell the time, but would relay the elapsed number of heartbeats to each pilot. 5000 beats would be approximately an hour, unless things got really exciting.

Not only had they prepped physically, but by Getti Drann's orders, they reframed the whole mission of the journey. Lanezi was amazed how a few well-crafted summaries had converted the general anger into the new story that this journey was a bold mission. They even incorporated some of the Human let's-work-together sentiment. The swing jump, originally declared impossible, was now seen as a way for their hero, chief pilot Shiwelna, to prove she was bolder and smarter than any Chike would expect. Shiwelna and three other pilots would rotate three-hour shifts. Lanezi was not to intervene unless an extreme emergency developed.

Io and Euro were not looking forward to it, but they had been stubbornly cheerful, helping Raykatoo, the podpups, and the Ramian children get situated. Lanezi pressed hands with Neah, hugged the twins, and said the traditional final words, "See you on the other side" before they got in their chairs.

Shiwelna would take the lead shift through the a-rings and then the first three do-or-die swing points. Lanezi had suggested that the pilots pray together, contrary to their usual process. They agreed to sing instead, choosing a rousing march that may have dated back to their military days, something about onward with bold colors. As they approached the a-rings, the entire company sang, colors steady white with a coral streak: courage.

Lanezi spent the six-hour ride in the a-rings napping, praying, and thinking of his people, far behind now. If he never made it back to humanity, would he end up thinking like a Ramian? Would he value boldness over cooperation? Were the two cultures meant to moderate each other? And who, if anyone, would survive the Chike invasion?

Two laps. One. With barely any adjustment, they were in the path. It was now the tense hour or so before the crucial moment. Lanezi sensed the sentries, and was aware of the fireball, but he carefully didn't look.

Raykatoo had explained that they must not drop out of the path too soon. They were programmed to come very close to the star, on what would be the gravity-braking side. At the precise moment that their resonance thread would send them into the star, they would tip out, clear the star, tip back, and make a strong burn in the new direction; catching the new thread to the next destination. Raykatoo said it would be obvious what to do.

The fact that 99% of their momentum was still going the wrong way didn't worry the Exempt. It was only necessary to catch the thread, and the momentum didn't matter, she said, completely at odds with what Lanezi thought he knew about jumping. Raykatoo said it was a simple matter of discipline and vision. If one did not have a failure of courage and drop out. If one was not blind. Etc.

Only the pilots and Raykatoo were allowed to speak during the jumps. "Approaching a mass," Shiwelna said. "Planetary."

"Agreed," Widinmay, the old pilot, said. Lanezi agreed as well, as they stayed on. They passed another slight mass. Lanezi started to get nervous. Normally, he'd have tipped out by now, or the ship would have automatically. He began to sense a really large mass in front of them. "That's it for sure," Shiwelna said. "We'll be passing on the left."

"New trajectory will be to the right," Widinmay said.

"So close!" Shiwelna fretted.

"Steady. You've got this," Widinmay said.

Was it his imagination or was it getting hot in here? Lanezi could hear the other pilots start to breathe harder. Suddenly, Lanezi could feel the thread bending, as if it were going to drive them right into the star. Involuntarily, he shouted "Now!" and so did the others. Shiwelna tipped out.

How close were they? Closer than Mercury to the Sun? Closer than a hot Jupiter? But those thoughts were fleeting distractions. As the meager thrust to the right began, Lanezi cast his mind for the new thread and realized that they had overshot it. There was only a tendril left for them to grab.

But Shiwelna took the thrusters and manually blasted them hard right with a burn that was probably 8g. Lanezi blacked out for only a moment, but when his mind cleared, they were in the path. *A bold move. And it probably saved us.*

The pilots were on a separate audio from the rest of the crew, so they didn't hear if there were casualties. Raykatoo was silent, probably wondering if she'd survive the day.

6200 heartbeats later, at the second swing point, the complete opposite happened. They tipped out too soon and had to boost forward to get in the path. "God Almighty," was all Shiwelna said, or all the translator could make of it.

The third time, she got it exactly right. There was a strange feeling of weightlessness and momentum transfer, just as if you were swinging. Lanezi hoped all the pilots had the feel and they wouldn't have to do more hard boosting. His head ached.

The pattern was repeated with less boosting and less drama as each pilot got the hang of it. Confidence grew with every jump. Almost a day later, when they tipped out in the regular way at stop #23, rather than exhaustion, there was a great wave of euphoria. The marching song rose up again. Medics scrambled to aid those injured by the high gee maneuvers, but they were few. There was hand pressing. Raykatoo's, "Adequate, if dramatic," was greeted with cheers.

But Euro was grabbing Lanezi's arm. "The podpups are gone!" he said, pointing to their box.

Lanezi's heart seized. "No. I would know if something happened to Whisper." Euro shook his head.

"I mean missing. They escaped their boxes."

"Oh. Crazy pups! Of course, they'd wander around in 8g and jumpspace!"

"The kitchen," Io suggested.

Podpups and stray treats were spread from the kitchen all over the ship. Lanezi located a content Whisper and scooped her up. "What were you doing?"

"Visiting."

"Visiting who?"

"Children." *The children were in the jump chairs.*

"What children?"

She looked confused. "Visitors."

"Where did you find visitors?"

"They find."

Io gasped and looked up at Lanezi. "Sentries."

"Is that possible?" Euro asked.

Lanezi shrugged. They'd jumped across the galaxy today. What else could be more astonishing? "That would just figure," he said. "Podpups playing with angels."

Io smiled. ***". . . the angels of heaven surround you."*[1]

15-Might

Sandstorm

"This one has news!" Pascal burst in during their fake Cheetah time, unescorted. Ze waltzed past ziz throne, breezed by Zahar, and tapped the co-pilot chair, converting it into a Chike chair so ze could sit. Ze seemed so pleased that Zahar smiled.

"What could be so good?" Quay asked.

With a click of ziz small claw, the 3D Human sector map appeared. "Here," Pascal pointed to Cove, in Sector 5. "The Human harbinger has been taken."

They all gasped. It *was* big news. "Taken?" Caspia repeated cautiously.

Pascal waved the big claw. "Taken / collected / discovered. A small shuttle was taken as well, remarkable for its beauty in an otherwise clunky culture." Caspia rolled her eyes behind Pascal's back.

"Do you know the harbinger's name?" Zahar asked.

Pascal switched the feed on and a bunch of Chike characters

appeared on the screen. "Send Human and Ramian translations to other screens," Pascal ordered.

"O TA," The Human screen read. Zahar gasped. "Oatah!"

"You know this one?" Pascal asked, impressed.

"Not personally. He took over Thayne's mission. We had orders from him."

"He took over from the angry one?"

"Yes."

"Is this one also angry?"

"He probably is now," Caspia said.

Pascal leaned forward to click off the feed, but before ze touched it, several messages, with priority beeps, came in succession. Pascal froze, reading them with alarm. Evan and Quay leaned closer to the Human and Ramian screens to read.

"No!" Pascal grabbed ziz chest in obvious distress. Reading more, ze hissed, saying no, no in Chike. Suddenly, ze screeched and clawed the sides of ziz face. Bright yellow-green blood dripped down the side of ziz head. Zahar jumped back, and then was ashamed, as Caspia moved closer to grab ziz claws to stop zir.

"Exempt!" Caspia said, "Don't!"

"A Chike ship is destroyed!" Evan explained in a loud whisper.

"How?" Zahar asked.

Evan looked at Quay, who was reading his screen, colors dark grey. "Accidentally. By the Ramians. Three thousand Chike are dead."

Pascal raked ziz face again, barely missing ziz eye. "Nest mates! Primary family! Gone! Gone!"

Caspia grabbed zir again. "Pascal! Don't hurt yourself!"

Zahar ran to the door. "We need help! Open!" Nothing happened. "Emergency! Medical emergency! Security!" Frustrated, she just pounded on the door, and it opened immediately.

Two flag-carrying guards rushed in. Seeing Caspia grappling with Pascal, they rushed forward and stunned her with the flagpole, even as Evan tried to block them. "No! No!" Zahar yelled at them. "She's trying to help!" Caspia crumbled to the deck.

Pascal, released, began wailing in Chike. The translator was useless. Zahar and Evan pulled Caspia away from their clawed feet as the guards took hold of Pascal, half dragging zir out.

"Medical supplies!" Zahar demanded from the ceiling. "Human first aid kit! Antiseptic! Blanket."

Only later, when things had calmed down, Caspia was resting, and they'd been confined to their sleeping quarters, did Zahar realize that Quay had never stopped reading the feed.

16-Might

Leaving Paradise Valley

Melawn had returned to Indus in another exhausting night cart ride, done his scrubjub and told Tani he was going to Nile this time. But he told her nothing of his real intentions.

On the night cart to Nile, he actually slept and felt ready to set out in the morning, even though it was still dark. Carrying a canteen, a Chike bottle, and stomach full of water, he figured if he could walk to the red flag in one day, he could refill his water. They'd made it in an afternoon on the cart.

In the early morning dark, people would be less likely to question or even notice him as he climbed up the steep hill to the tunnel, focusing on putting one foot in front of the other. It was steeper than he remembered. It was his hope that he could get out without any report going to Grace. He reached the lookout just as the dawn bell rang. The rays of the sun touched the top of the Temple as if lighting a candle. But he would be easy to spot standing there, so he hurried to the entrance of the tunnel.

Although he could see a patch of light at the exit, the tunnel was long and dark with narrow sides, reminding him of the mine, with its speeding rail carts. The screeching sounds and sense of danger came back to him as he put his hand on the inner tunnel wall. *It's perfectly safe. The fastest thing coming through here would be a big stubborn beast.* He took a breath and stepped in, and as he did, the first song of dawn prayers floated up from the village and carried him through the tunnel.

Hat and glasses on now, Melawn reached the red flag by lunch, with most of his water. He forced himself to eat, drink as much as possible, and refill. It was definitely not as hot as the first day they'd come through. Winter was coming. Maybe because he was in better shape now, he had made good time. So he decided to go on. He pulled out the compass, even though he didn't really think he needed it. He had to walk roughly north until he found a narrow eastward-running canyon.

The walking was lonely. No laughing farm team, no intellectually challenging shipmates, no loving family. He started out alert for snakes, birds, and riders, but began saying prayers and eventually fell into a trancelike pace. After an hour, he noticed tracks, and then a highway of ruts. A great sense of relief flooded over him that he would not be lost.

As the tracks turned into the canyon, Melawn looked up and stopped in wonder. The lowering sun reflected off the steep walls of the canyon, transforming it into a golden valley.

"He is My true follower who, if he come to a valley of pure

gold, will pass straight through it aloof as a cloud, and will neither turn back, nor pause."[2]

Melawn laughed at himself. He had not only paused, he had come to a complete stop. He hurried on again, knowing he had to find a safe place, off the sand, and curl up for the night.

Later, he heard a strange whistle, which didn't sound like a bird. It wasn't the Zann whistle or any kind of instrument. It sounded Human. He figured he had half an hour of daylight left. He scrambled up a small red pillar of rock to look ahead.

The canyon was dry, at least above ground. He wondered if the Chike had rerouted the river, or if the planet was drying up. One more thing to worry about. And then, not a hundred meters away, he saw a flag waving from the top of a rock spire. A red flag with a white dragon.

If he could make it, he wouldn't need to stay out at night. He scrambled down and hurried on, now winding through tall dark rock outcroppings. It was like some fantasy landscape from a dragon story. He expected to see a fire-breathing creature swoop out of a shadowy cave at any moment.

And then the whistling was all around him. *I'm surrounded.* "Greetings!" He called out. A man, dressed as the rebels he'd seen before, stepped out from behind a rock.

"Stop!"

Since he was already stopped, Melawn wasn't sure what to do, but decided to try the direct approach. "I've come to see Thayne."

"You can't come in. They're sick."

Oh, no. "How bad? What do the doctors say?"

"We don't have any doctors. Are you a doctor?"

"No. But I could get one. Is Thayne sick?" At this point

Melawn noticed the guard was swaying on his feet. "Sit down. I'm no threat." He moved forward to help the man sit, but the guard held up a hand to stop him. "Are you sick?" Melawn asked.

"No. I'm a survivor."

"People are dying?"

"Yes. Really bad flu. Or worse. I don't know who is sick."

Melawn sent a quick prayer up that he wasn't exposing himself, even though the guard was three meters away. "I've been cleared," the man reassured him. "But so tired."

"It's night. I can't go back now."

"You stay up there," the man pointed to the tall rock near Melawn. "Maybe we can let your friend know you were here."

"I'll go back in the morning. Get a doctor."

"Thanks," the guard nodded, got back up and struggled to the top of his rock, where he wrapped in a blanket and slumped at his post.

Melawn climbed the opposite rock, used a bit of precious water to wash, then ate a ration and curled up in his blanket, on top of his mat, on top of a lumpy rock, exposed to the chilling breeze.

"Though My couch should be made of the hard rock and My associates of the beasts of the desert, I will not blench, but will be patient . . . and under all circumstances I give thanks unto God."[3]

17-Might Eve

81-Petals, approaching Tektite a-rings

Jarvie waited at the door of the Conference Room while Ra'Tama approached, accompanied by Vante Kay and Kay Ling, and carrying his old pup, Cookie. Ra'Tama had kept to himself for days, but couldn't get out of the Terrace pre-jump meeting. And though Ra'Tama was very reserved, he was the closest to Jarvie's age, and Jarvie was determined to make friends with him. "Greetings Honor Ra'Tama," Jarvie said, as gently as possible.

"Good morning, Jarvie," Ra'Tama said quietly. "Please call me Ra'Tama," and flashed an encouraging smile.

"Let's get settled," Katie suggested, ushering them all up the stairs. Terina set Rocket down and Jarvie lost hold of Star. The two pups ran off crazy, then circled back to Ra'Tama and started pawing him. Slowly, he knelt down, very gently lowering Cookie between the youngsters, patting them each on the head and whispering to them, "Old. Gentle." They squished up beside Cookie, but obviously a long-time matriarch, she gave them stern looks and they backed off as much as their excitement allowed.

As Beezan came in and Sky joined them on the deck, the pups shook off a bit of their wildness. Cookie ignored the other two completely as she gazed at the approaching Sky until they were nose to nose. Then very slowly, creakily, Cookie sat and bowed. Ra'Tama and Kay Ling let out small gasps. Ra'Tama bowed his head as if pained at his pup's loss of status—or feared she was getting too old. "That one's just a baby," Kay Ling objected.

"It's okay," Katie reassured them. "Sky's the boss of everyone. There's nothing wrong with your pup. I checked her out thoroughly." Sky gave them all a mysterious look, nuzzled Cookie, and led her over to the podpup area.

With a last look at Cookie, Ra'Tama settled at the table with Beezan and Sequoia, just as Iricana came in. The Kays stayed with the pups as if they were guarding royal children. "Honor Ra'Tama," Iricana said quietly, "no one here is on standard teen-training. The red band won't be necessary."

"Yes, Captain," he said, and yanked it off.

After prayers and reviewing the jump, Beezan requested to be allowed to jump early if he saw the path. "There's little risk," he continued. "If we have to abort, we can try again in a few days." He traced his emergency route with his finger on the table map of Tektite system.

Jarvie looked immediately to Sequoia to object. So did everyone else. But she was considering. "Sequoia?" Iricana asked.

"He does seem to have some sense of the paths that others don't have."

"Oatah said you were a seer," Iricana added. Ra'Tama glanced at her sharply.

"Actually, he said I *would be* a seer, since we didn't have one," Beezan said. "I really don't know what will happen. I just want to try. Only if it's obvious."

"Jarvie?"

Jarvie had learned to trust Beezan and knew this wasn't grandstanding. Beezan wasn't like that. "Yes, I'm all for trying."

"Ra'Tama?" He jumped when she said his name.

"Yes, Captain."

More mildly, Iricana asked, "What are your thoughts about it?"

Ra'Tama looked up. Deep brown eyes gazed at Beezan. Then he turned and looked at the pups, at Sky teaching the little ones how to be gentle with Cookie. He turned back to Iricana. "I have seen some strange things in the ways, especially lately. If Honor Beezan is confident, I am with him."

It was a touching endorsement from someone who had never jumped with them, but underneath, Jarvie thought he detected a hint of that determination that all pilots needed.

Iricana nodded. "Okay then. We'll just proceed like a regular jump. If the opportunity arises, take it. No pressure."

"Yes, Captain," they all answered.

"Captain, if I may?" Ra'Tama asked.

"Of course," Iricana answered.

"Perhaps it would be wise to invite one or two of the Tektites to be on your command crew."

Iricana paused. Jarvie sympathized. Visions of gum-sticking were probably running through her head. But Thunder nodded subtly and she considered. "That's probably a good idea. Who do you recommend?" she asked Ra'Tama.

"Maura is the only one with any administrative experience. Teeve is their chief mechanical engineer. They're a family group. The others will follow their lead."

"Thank you." Iricana said, and invited Vante to join them to say the closing prayer.

When they all got up to go, Terina called, "Hey, Cookie!" Star and Rocket bounded over, confused by the name and seeming offer of a cookie. She laughed. "Come on to the kitchen you sillies." They followed enthusiastically.

"Well," Ra'Tama said, "it was her name before I got her. I begged for a podpup for so long. I never thought there would be any others."

"No worries," Jarvie said. "Who knows how many we'll end up with? We might have a podpup zoo!"

At that, Sky and Rocket repeated "ZOO!" and Sequoia groaned.

17-Might

Once again, Jarvie was monitor, this time for the jump from Tektite to Terrace, with 19 people and 4 pups. "One half JV," he announced. They'd been in the rings a good three hours. All the Tektites except Ra'Tama were under in the Passenger Lounge, with Katie as monitor.

Another hour passed. Jarvie cast his mind out for the path, but couldn't sense anything. After five hours, he figured they'd jump the regular way. ".85 JV."

"I see it," Beezan whispered.

"Be sure," Iricana cautioned.

Six laps passed by. "Yes," Beezan assured them.

Jarvie couldn't see any path, but on the next lap they rocketed out of the a-rings in the Terrace direction. *Nothing. Nothing. Don't panic.* Just as he was expecting a go-around, there was a big thrust and they slipped into a path. *Incredible!* Only a fraction of a second before they were in it did Jarvie see the path.

With gasps of surprise from Sequoia and Ra'Tama, they now all focused on the thread.

The fireball was still there, threatening, but Jarvie felt no sense of it interacting with them as it had the first time. He only glanced at it though, concentrating on their own path.

It seemed like a long time before he felt the forward mass and knew they were approaching another star. Going five or ten seconds longer than Jarvie would have, Beezan tipped them into normal space.

Jarvie already had his screen up to search for the beacon, and it popped right up. "Terrace beacon confirmed." He couldn't keep the excitement out of his voice. They had just done the unheard of.

"Stand by for route correction," *81* warned them, making several burns. **"ETA Terrace Station, 11 days."**

But a red message was flashing on Jarvie's screen. "Beacon announcement," he reported. "'This station is abandoned. Go directly to a-rings.' It's just repeating that message."

"*81*," Iricana ordered, "reroute to a-rings."

After several small burns, their new ETA was 6 days. **"Clear from blue zones."**

"All chair lights green," Jarvie reported.

The crew erupted into cheers. "History again!" Terina said, clamoring out of her chair and high-fiving Jarvie before going back to her notes. Jarvie checked on Beezan, who was dazed, but not wandering.

"Did you see it?" Beezan asked the other pilots.

"No, not until we were in it," Sequoia answered. "How can you see it?"

Jarvie shook his head no to Beezan's question. Ra'Tama's eyes were bright with excitement. "That was wild!"

Beezan sat, exhausted and contemplating. "It was hard to

get in. It might not be worth the trouble. Like you need to be more exact."

Then the pups were loose and gathering around Beezan, looking up at him in their puzzled way.

Back to Paradise Valley

For hours, Melawn trudged back through the canyon, more disappointed than he expected not to see Thayne, and very worried for Thayne's health. He'd sent a note in, but did not wait around this morning for a response. He intended to walk back in one day and try to get a doctor, despite being sore and tired from a night out on the rock. As he habitually scanned for attack birds, he noticed a lot of dust in the air to the south, even though it wasn't windy. He wondered if AnnaLee was out and about with the beasts. If he used his imagination, he could almost hear the sound of voices.

And then he did.

Chanting. A strong melodious voice bounced hauntingly through the canyon. *Someone returning to the rebels?* But it somehow didn't fit with his image of the rebels. It was so touching, he was sorry when the last echoes died away. And then the bell started to ring. Hesitantly at first, as when he and Nkiroo had done it. And then stronger. Five. Six. Seven.

Impulsively, Melawn started to run. They were supposed to ring the bell once for every person. Twenty. Thirty. He forced himself to be sensible and slow down. Fifty now. With all those people, there may not be enough food and water at the red flag.

Melawn rounded the last stones of the canyon. In the distance, a sea of red Chike-issued clothes was clustered around the red flag and still coming. Melawn stopped counting. As he got closer, he could see a column of people from the red flag back to the prior green flag, and then farther. Hundreds, maybe more than a thousand.

He hurried on. They spotted him and surged toward him, saying, "We're newcomers." He held up his hands and let them absorb him and flow towards their leader. Luckily, they met a hundred meters from the bell so they could hear each other, barely.

The crowd brought him to a pained, but determined looking 50-year-old man, who tilted his hat back to see Melawn better. A captain, he'd put his ship pins on the Chike clothes. *Lothlorian*. "Captain Risi," Melawn said. "I know you're not supposed to talk to me."

"Forget that. As long as you're not one of them."

"I'm Melawn from the *Cheetah*." Recognition flashed in Risi's eyes and he shook Melawn's hand. "How many?" Melawn asked.

"Twelve-hundred, thirty-seven."

1237! Melawn tried to cover his shock. Forget the food at the red flag. Would there be enough in the colony? *Wait. It's about a 10% increase. Not a complete disaster. Stay calm and help these people.* "I'm pretty new here myself, but I think I can help you. Normally carts would come for you from that tunnel there." He pointed up and the surrounding people turned to look, nodding their heads when they saw it. "There won't be enough carts. I think I should start up with the strongest people."

"Listen up!" Captain Risi shouted. "All strong, able-bodied people follow Melawn here. Dr. Obala! Go with him."

"Yes, honor," the confident and stately Obala answered. *That melodious voice—he was the one chanting.*

Melawn moved slowly through the crowd, angling toward the tunnel, reassuring as he went. "Up the hill and through the tunnel. There's a beautiful valley. Water and food." *Please make it so, Grace.*

As Obala joined him, Melawn realized that not only did they have their ship pins, they had put on their armbands. Green, blue, and black peppered the forward group, but he could see the yellow bands of children farther back. It was their own little rebellion, and they were not even to the colony yet.

"Dr. Obala. Your name is familiar."

"I was the podpup doctor at Harbor."

That whole day, with Lanezi's lying and Thayne's crazy departure came back to Melawn like scenes from another life. *And Obala, a podpup doctor. There's a man with no job in the valley.* "Harbor. What's happening there?"

"I don't know. I was inbound to Terrace on the *Quechua* to visit my family when the Chike appeared. Our pilot tried a gravity assist out of there. We might have made it, but the Chike grabbed us."

"So not all these people are from one place?"

"No. Three ships and various councils from Sector 8."

"Councils! Come," Melawn encouraged them all. "It's a three or four hour walk up those switchbacks."

After three hours, they stopped to rest at the entrance to the tunnel. The bell had stopped ringing at some point. They shook their heads as if to clear that sad toll from their minds. Looking to the end of the line, they could see the dusty stragglers: the elderly, injured, some being carried. "How many will be left behind?" Melawn fretted to himself.

"None," Obala said firmly. And Melawn smiled. These people were not going to be a burden. Something to consider in their calculations.

They were just about to enter the tunnel when they saw carts at the other side. Obala got everyone in a single line and had them stand aside.

When Grace came through on the first cart, she drove forward to Melawn's position and halted, staring out over the arid plain in real dismay. "1237," Melawn told her. "I thought we should start in."

Grace blinked and refocused on him. "Melawn. Yes. Take the first 300 through, all the way to Yosemite."

"Yosemite?"

"Yes, they'll be places to stop along the way for food and rest."

"Yes, Grace. And Honor—Grace, please. The rebels need a doctor, badly. Something contagious—and fatal."

"Send a message to the hospital when you go through. Tell them I said to send a doctor—*if* they can spare one."

"Yes, Grace." She went on, nodding to the people. Her assistant, Etazann, followed by Obala, counted off 300 and held the line, but Melawn had already started through.

Melawn took the lead down the tunnel, trying to set a steady, but not exhausting pace. It was loud inside with the trudging of many footsteps. He slowed after he exited so the 300 could bunch up a bit, preparing for them to round the turn at the lookout and see the Temple and the valley.

When the Temple came into view, they dropped to their knees as a group. Hats were swept off and prayers spontaneously lifted from the crowd. Melawn had a pang of shame, remembering how they had gawked liked tourists instead. After ten minutes, Melawn quietly went to the front and pointed out the villages and the distance they must travel.

With some relief and new resolve, the young healthy people stood, put their hats on, and shouldered their packs. Melawn let Dr. Obala take the lead and fell in at the end, with a glance back to the tunnel, where the second group was just emerging.

As they dropped into the valley and entered the main road, Melawn was amazed at the organization in such a short time. *They've been ready for this.*

Latrines had been built, away from the river, crude, but usable for tens at a time. Washing, food, and water stations followed, so the crowd could keep moving.

As they walked down the road with the majestic Obala at the front, the villagers lined the sides waving and clapping, even singing. For all the trouble this huge influx could cause, they had chosen to welcome them.

Suddenly, a shout went up from the right. "Nakoma! Nakoma!" A woman ran into the marchers, rushing into the embrace of another woman. "Sisters," the word spread back to Melawn, "Separated 15 years ago." *They're looking for people they know.* The villager dragged her sister and a man by the arms, pulling them out of the parade into their household. A cheer went up from the crowd.

18-Might

They stayed overnight in the farmland outside of Nile Village, sleeping in the Chike-supplied blankets, and eating a hot meal in their Chike-supplied mess kits, served by the villagers.

By the time they reached Indus that day, it was an organized operation. Villagers stood at the sides of the road with signs bearing their names or their ship names. Some had job offers, like cook, carpenter, or farm hand. Job applicants, distant family, friends, and friends of friends were taken from the marchers, no questions asked.

On the steps of the textile hall, Melawn saw the woman who had given him the cookies. She shook her head with exasperation at him as she surveyed the passing crowd. Melawn was tempted to bail out, since Indus was his post, but Grace had told him to take them to Yosemite, so he carried on. Besides, there was a certain exhilaration to it.

19-Might

When they reached Shen, the colonists had figured out that the young and strong, and mostly single, were coming through first. Melawn saw Jadee, the botanist, standing to the side, arms crossed, with his wife and four remaining daughters. The youngest daughter boldly pointed out a boy she liked, young, bigger and stronger-looking than most spacers. He was called over. With only a moment's consultation, there was a handshake and he and his family were taken. *Incredible!* Melawn thought. No wonder people think I'm slow.

At last, late the next day, they reached Yosemite, with maybe 240 of their original 300. Melawn was confident that the rest of the spacers would be welcomed as well.

2-Will

81-Petals, at Terrace a-rings

The Tundra pre-jump meeting was quick and businesslike. Terina left Rocket in the kitchen, where he joined the other pups with no complaints, leaving the Kays to deal with them and cook dinner.

Terina was thrilled to be included at top level meetings with her mom, Honor Beezan, Thunder, Doctor Katie, Honor Ra'Tama, Maura, and Jarvie. Captain Iricana obviously had a good sense of history to include her. The Captain assigned Katie as passenger monitor. Jarvie would be flight monitor, again. "Who will jump?" Iricana asked Sequoia.

"I thought I would," Sequoia said, "to give Beezan a break. Unless . . ." She looked at him and stopped. "Unless you have another scheme up your sleeve." Terina stifled a laugh. Her mom sounded like her grandpa.

"Well," Beezan said slowly. "It occurs to me that if we're jumping in the right direction, we might not need the a-rings at all."

There was dead silence. Sequoia looked at him as if he truly had lost his mind in all that wandering.

"It's been tried," Iricana said.

"It's been done," Beezan argued. "We do it when we use a gravity assist, and we did it jumping away from the rogue planet."

"Those are very special circumstances. In both cases, we had speed. We had all that fuel," Sequoia pointed out.

"And we still have half that fuel," Thunder commented.

"I don't think we need all that speed," Beezan explained. "Just enough to see the path. The slower you go, the harder they are to see, harder to . . . untangle. What's the harm of trying?"

"Can you describe it more?" Iricana asked.

Beezan's eyes went a bit unfocused. Sequoia sat up, alarmed. "Can you see the paths *now*?"

"No. I mean, not really. Glimpses. I have to . . . shift . . . to another . . . looking mode."

The pilots looked at each other and back to Iricana.

"I could scan him while he's looking," Katie suggested. "See what's going on in his brain."

"Let's think more about that later," Iricana agreed. "I am wondering about how well we could calculate the actual direction. That was supposedly the purpose of the control panels."

"Sometimes," Beezan said, looking at the other pilots, and then starting again. "You know how the Ramians were so into sailing on water? Neah told me that there was a way to go with the wind, and another way of going across the wind. So I think we can jump without the a-rings, only if we are going with the wind."

"But, what is the wind?" Sequoia asked.

"I don't know," Beezan admitted.

"Rotation of the galaxy?" Iricana speculated. "Local movement of the star system? Galactic expansion? Something we don't even know about?"

"They've looked at all those variables before," Sequoia said.

"Let me think about it," Iricana said. "We'll do a short check-in after dinner."

After dinner, Iricana set a plot on the kitchen table, right where Jarvie was sitting, slurping his tea. "As near as *81* can calculate, jumping to Tundra would not be exactly 'with the wind' as you say, but there is galactic rotation roughly in that direction. It's too hard to calculate exactly. I wouldn't even call it estimating. Guessing. Wildly."

Beezan and the pilots stared at the chart. "Maybe," was all he would say. Terina took a photo for the record.

"Have you done this jump before?" Iricana asked Beezan.

"Three times."

"We'll never know if he doesn't try," Sequoia admitted. Grandpa patted her on the back with admiration.

Iricana nodded. "Only if you see a strong path. Be sure."

"Yes, Captain."

There was a beat of silence and Ra'Tama cleared his throat. "Permission to sit up front?" He asked. Jarvie turned to him sharply. "Forgive me," he whispered to Jarvie.

Only three pilots could sit in front, so Ra'Tama would be taking Jarvie's seat. Sequoia nodded. "Granted," Iricana said. "Jarvie will move to Monitor 1."

Jarvie clapped Ra'Tama on the shoulder, surprising him. "Yes, Captain. No problem."

So they changed their trajectory to head straight for Tundra, waiting on Beezan's word for the right moment to jump.

. . .

4-Will

"Where are they?" Katie asked. At the tone of her voice, Terina froze in the process of putting on her brackets. The Tektites, all eight of them, were late. Everyone was supposed to be in the Passenger Lounge, in their chairs, an hour before jump sequence. The Tektites had jumped before, but this time, Iricana ordered that all non-essential crew would be put under.

"Thunder to Passenger Monitor," came over Katie's s'link.

"Go ahead."

"We're on our way," Thunder said.

But in the background they heard, "You're not drugging me!"

Katie checked the time. "It's okay," Kelson said. "We're not using the a-rings, so the timing is flexible."

"But the pilots have their schedule," Katie said.

"And crew need to follow instructions," Iricana said firmly, "or we won't be able to trust them with any serious responsibility."

"I'll talk with them later," Kelson assured them. "Meanwhile, get me situated, so I can start my nap."

Terina went back to work, hoping she'd still be conscious to see what happened. Iricana was frowning and about to say something when Ra'Tama lifted his hand, just a bit, but for some reason it was so noticeable. "That's Chip, the youngest. Perhaps," he suggested, "Honor Beezan would make an exception."

Iricana frowned at Ra'Tama, but she did ask.

Terina heard Beezan take a breath and a long moment to answer. "If it will maintain some unity and goodwill then I'm okay with it."

Sequoia huffed. Terina would know that sound anywhere.

"But Ra'Tama," Beezan added.

"Yes, honor?"

"*You* keep zir corralled during the jump." Ra'Tama blinked in surprise.

Iricana clapped Ra'Tama on the back as he left the Kays and headed for the Command Bay. "Good suggestion. Thank you."

"Yes, honor. Honors," Ra'Tama said.

Even before the Chip situation, Beezan wasn't really in a meditative state. *Who am I to think I can jump without the a-rings and without JV? Maybe the wandering has made me delusional. Maybe that's why they retire all those pilots.*

And now I've got them all expectant. Beezan tried to calm down and focus. Sometimes there was nothing, and sometimes there was a crisscrossing of unidentified paths.

".3JV," he heard Jarvie say, practically whispering.

Beezan tried to put the jump out of his mind, put all stray thoughts away, and just focus on his place in the universe, on the connections of the stars.

Those souls that, in this day, enter the divine kingdom and attain everlasting life, although materially dwelling on earth, yet in reality soar in the realm of heaven. Their bodies may linger on earth but their spirits travel in the immensity of space. For as thoughts widen and become illumined, they acquire the power of flight and transport man to the kingdom of God.[1]

The few crew that were not using the jump drug didn't seem agitated. Since they weren't in the a-rings, they were not doing the painful bumps. Some were sleeping. A nap sounded tempting.

Am I awake or asleep? Beezan wasn't sure. It didn't seem like a good idea to jump in your sleep. But one path was beginning to call to him. Yes. He remembered from his previous jumps. Well, good. He really had to focus, like pulling from a deep sleep, pulling into the path. He heard gasps from Sequoia and Ra'Tama, and then Jarvie. They were with him now.

Jarvie felt a mass approaching and they tipped out. *We did it!* The dream of freejumping was at hand! Jarvie stifled a shout and scanned for the beacon, having no doubt in his mind. "Tundra beacon!"

The crew cheered. A wave of exhilaration passed over them.

"All green, except Chip is yellow, but steady. Ze recessed," Katie reported, concerned.

"Ze should be fine," Ra'Tama said, holding his head. "A very curious person . . ."

Jarvie read out the beacon's automated message. "High alert. Request evacuation. Tundra Outbound Station closed."

"*81*," Iricana ordered, "optimize course to Tundra Station."

After a few burns, they got the clear from blue zones. **"ETA 6 days."**

"Tundra Inbound Authority, this is *Drumheller* inbound from Terrace. Please report your P&P," Jarvie requested.

While they waited, there was a flurry of bracket removal, getting out of cocoons, checking on and congratulating Beezan, who of course, was a little dazed by it all. Although it was an even bigger deal than before, they were subdued. Maybe in shock, or worried about Tundra. Jarvie gave Beezan a big hug and then the others collected the pups and headed for the kitchen. Terina was doing her best to be an objective reporter, but practically jumping up and down in excitement. Jarvie laughed to himself and stayed with Iricana and Thunder in the Command Bay to complete his job.

A response came quickly. Tundra had not left their monitor station unstaffed. "*Drumheller,* T.I.A. We have you inbound on the ship tracker for 10-Will arrival. We request evacuation for 40 people and 3 podpups." There was a slight pause. "Our P&P is 41 and 3."

Thunder and Iricana looked at each other in relief and puzzlement. There were only 40. It wouldn't be chaos. "T.I.A., this is Captain Iricana. Please explain why one person wishes to remain."

They waited again for a response. "It's a personal matter. Also please clarify. We have Beezan Mirage listed as Captain."

Thunder nodded. "Good. They're doing a little checking."

"T.I.A., Honor Beezan remains aboard in good health. I've taken command of this vessel for the duration of the emergency. Please clarify if the Sector Council ordered a complete evacuation."

"*Drumheller*, yes. Complete evacuation was ordered by RJ Council. This person won't come. We tried to evac him earlier."

"Do you have a counselor?"

"He *is* a counselor. He's the AI therapist. He won't leave his 'patient.'"

Iricana was about to answer when Thunder raised a hand and gave a cautionary shake of the head. She continued, "T.I.A., prepare your 40 for evac. Tell #41 that we are the last ship."

When they joined the others in the kitchen, Iricana explained. Ra'Tama and Beezan were sympathetic. "Why did you stop me from saying more?" Iricana asked Thunder.

"I'm concerned. If the AI therapist is unstable, who knows what condition the Tundra AI is in? I've been reading about some trouble with AIs having conflicting exemplars. I'm just worried that the AI may resist us."

"We'll have to talk to them in person," Iricana said. "But no one stays behind."

"Yes, Captain," they all answered.

8-Will

Sandstorm

Zahar swayed on her feet, gripping the "rail of the living" in the Chike Ascension Hall. *Last day*, she reminded herself. For twelve days, she, Caspia, Evan, and Quay had stood at the rail, behind Pascal, as ze grieved for the dead, repeating the same ritual 3,142 times.

First the gong, then the shaking bells, stomps of the poles, humming, the name of the deceased, the two-minute prayer, the ascend to heaven part where everyone in the hall, including Humans and Ramians, would clap their hands or claws and raise them to release the spirit. That was followed by more humming, and the Gong of Finality, an ear-splitting clang that would crack open heaven for the spirit's arrival.

For days now, they had been on "Egg #__", but as it was in Chike and they no longer had the wits to count, they could only guess that they were near the end. Quay, Caspia, and Evan were troopers. It had been Zahar's suggestion to reach out to Pascal, not knowing what she was getting them into. Another case of assumption, like the Ramians who didn't think the Chike would cut open the stations to take their gravity balls.

After the news of the Chike ship's destruction, they didn't see Pascal for days. Quay told them what he'd read: a Ramian ship called *Moontide*, under Getti Taukernan, was captured at Three. Data extracted had shown some kind of plasma wave, generated by the Ramians, creating an arc between the Chike vessel and its gravity ball, destroying both. Quay insisted it was not an attack, that it was some kind of grand art show.

Raykatoo, the Exempt, was assumed to be the only survivor, as she was aboard the Ramian ship *Watcher*. As for *Watcher* itself, it was no longer at Four, and its whereabouts were unknown.

Most concerning of all, Quay reported that there were Humans aboard the *Watcher*. He didn't get their names, but it was possible Humans could be implicated in the incident, bringing the GenSix punishment upon them.

That's when Zahar suggested showing the Chike what Humans and Ramians were all about—unity, compassion, peacefulness, diversity, order. So they reached out to Pascal, expressing sorrow and concern and volunteering to accompany zir on ziz ascension ritual. *So long ago.*

The gong rang one last time. They looked up. There was no move to start again. Evan caught Quay as he slumped from the rail, lowering him to the deck and kneeling by him. Caspia knelt next to Evan and put her arm around him, reaching out for Zahar with the other arm. They knelt there next to Quay, sending their own last prayer for the departed, for all the Chike and Ramians lost. And hoping that such carnage was not repeating itself in the Human sectors.

9-Will

81-Petals, at Tundra Station

Terina looked around the Conference Room. Rather than the cozy few of them, there were now 19. *Auspicious,* she thought. Already, the Tektite crew had become "us" and the about-to-board Tundra crew "them." But of course, there was no "us" and "them." It was just a matter of opening their hearts and getting organized—the whole reason for this meeting.

They crowded around the table, raised to standing level. Honor Beezan was the most unnerved by all the people, so Jarvie and Kelson flanked him, giving him a little extra space.

Tundra pre-board meeting, Terina entered into her ongoing history notes, dropping in the list that Iricana just posted. "Here's who we're expecting," Iricana said. "I'll sort them into a reporting framework after we see who's senior. But we do know that the acting commander is named Taj."

5 administrators

3 teachers

2 monitors

3 engineers: 1 life support, 1 field generator, 1 materials
1 robot manager
2 mechanics / EVA specialists
2 mechanics / shuttle pilots
3 mechanics
3 cargo loaders
2 maintenance specialists
1 medical aide
2 AI specialists
1 journalist
1 kitchen manager
8 food and garden specialists
1 event programmer

"Their council was disbanded and third-in-command Taj was set in command. The youngest is 17, the event planner. The oldest is 72, the kitchen manager. No known pregnancies or chronic medical problems. Three podpups: Peeps, Chilly, and Tiger."

There were a few chuckles at the podpups names. Even when they weren't present at the meetings, they were keeping spirits up.

"Two AI specialists in addition to the AI therapist?" Thunder asked.

"Yes, Ulf, #41, is not on the list," Iricana answered.

"Whatever problem they've been having must be serious," Katie said.

"Yes, but it shouldn't affect us. My concern is that we'll be tripling our population." Iricana paused seriously. "I'm going to officially declare ourselves a refugee ship. We have no idea how long we'll be together—from months to years." Beezan paled.

"We need to start the community-building process immediately."

There was general nodding around the table. "I know you've all been through some of the modules, based on your upbringing and situations, but who has real experience running a community circle?"

Kelson, Thunder, Katie, and Maura raised their hands. "Well, we could use more, but maybe some will come aboard," Iricana said. "We'll start in two days. So far, everyone will be assigned to crew, no passengers. We'll do *Building Community: Large Ships*, and *Integrating Refugee populations*."

There was an enthusiastic chorus of yes, Captain. Iricana nodded and went on. "For now, Sequoia will be chief pilot; Kelson, garden chief; Thunder, manage the mechanics until you decide on team leaders, then I want you back. Katie, chief medical for now, and head Arc 1 doctor regardless. Jarvie, Captain's diplomat; Terina, journalist; and Teeve, pick your own team and get Arc 2 opened."

"Cap, hold on—" Teeve stopped when Maura elbowed him. "I mean, Captain . . . ah?"

"Yes, Teeve."

"We should open Arc 6 next, there's a preferred order for balance."

"It's a long walk." She frowned. "Okay. Put the new people in Arc 1 and get Arc 6 prepped. We have no idea when we'll need it."

"Right-ah, Captain."

"Our priorities will be food, education, and maintenance. And one more assignment: Honor Beezan will be second-in-command." There were some surprised looks, but a general nodding of acceptance.

"Cap," Danny asked, "what about social arts?" Terina

thought he was joking, but who knew, maybe social arts were a big deal on Tektite.

Maura hissed at him for being so casual, but Iricana smiled. "Are you volunteering?"

"Ah, no." Iricana just kept looking at him. "I mean, ah yeah. Honor. Cap . . . Captain."

"Thank you. You all know your roles for tomorrow. Dismissed."

10-Will

Bird of Prey, at Tundra Station

Jarvie tried to breathe deeply to calm himself, but his heart jumped at every sound and his eyes darted from one screen to another. He was in his suit, with the visor up, in the pilot seat of the double-decker shuttle *Bird of Paradise*. They were docked on the central pillar of Tundra Station with the top of the shuttle facing out. On the lower level of the shuttle, Teeve supervised the deck hatch, waiting for the last passengers, evacuees, from Tundra. Everyone had agreed it was safer to dock outside rather than go in the hangar with a malfunctioning AI.

Iricana, with her level 1 s'link, had gone to the Tundra Command Bay to meet the two AI experts, Sho and Adisa. In the residential decks, Commander Taj, the medical aide Roza, and two very large brothers, Hiro and Hisoka, were on their way to collect #41, Ulf, from his cabin.

Out the window, Jarvie could see the *81-Petals,* a third as big as Tundra Station. The rest of the Tundra population had already been transferred to the *81.* Their food, supplies, and shuttles were now being loaded by the other Tektites.

The *Bird of Paradise,* a 20-passenger shuttle, was now just waiting on the last eight people. The plan was to walk Ulf to the suit room, get him in one, and escort him through the unpressurized hatchway onto the shuttle. Jarvie prayed that would be it, but they had various backup plans.

Adisa and Sho explained that there was an exemplar conflict, which had been going on for years. Somehow the AI's exemplars didn't mesh into one personality, so there was an ongoing, but subtle, battle for dominance. Five months ago, Ulf, the best AI therapist in the outer sectors, had been ordered to extract one of the exemplars, but something went very wrong. Now Ulf was convinced that the "real" AI was in trouble and needed him. And the dominant Tundra AI was convinced that Ulf was a security threat.

"Hey, pilot?"

"Yes?" Jarvie asked, careful not to turn around, so they wouldn't see how young he was.

"What's happening?"

Jarvie flicked on the screen and sent the feed of the camera following Taj and company, just as they approached Ulf's cabin.

Taj was a young, handsome man, with bright brown eyes, dark tan skin, and a deep brown turban. "Open," Taj ordered. Nothing happened. "Taj to Ulf. Please open your door." His voice was calm and friendly, with the slightest hint of command.

"No! I'm not leaving!" Ulf's voice sounded thin and desperate. Jarvie's heart sank. This was not going to go the easy way.

Taj proceeded calmly. "I know you don't want to, but the last ship is here and we are all going."

"I must stay! The station needs me!"

"You can come back. The AI will still be here."

"No! I have explained this to you! The others are too strong! There are too many iterations! She can't hold them off!"

She?

"We'll talk about it in the ship. Everything will be fine."

"It won't be fine! The new matrix isn't set! I have to stay until it's set!"

"Why?" Adisa whispered, and Taj repeated.

"Because! I'm overprinting a new exemplar!"

"You? You're the new exemplar?" Taj asked, alarmed. "That's not allowed!"

"It was the only way! It had to be someone strong and living, to override the others. That's why I have to stay."

Taj dropped his hand from the door. "Captain, your call."

"God in heaven," Iricana whispered. "If we leave him, they'll go crazy together. Bring him."

Roza moved to the side with her med dart. Hiro and Hisoka stood ready. Taj put his level 2 s'link into the door slot. "Open."

Electricity arced out of the door slot, frying Taj's s'link. There were gasps on the shuttle and from the Command Bay. Immediately, Taj pulled another s'link out of his pocket. In the Command Bay, Iricana ordered power cut to all cabin doors. The power and camera view went off.

A few seconds later, it came back on. Taj and company had their wrist lights on and were forcing the door open. Then the power went off and on again. "It's battling itself for control of the station," Adisa whispered. Off again. In the next blink of power, the door was opened and blocked and no one was in the rimway, but they could hear Ulf yelling, pleading desperately. It was heartbreaking.

Jarvie started praying for Ulf when the power went out again. And calculating. It would probably take 10 minutes to subdue Ulf for transport and 30 minutes to drag him to the shuttle. He scanned all his systems for readiness.

The power went back on. "Captain," Taj reported quickly, "We've got him."

"Everyone get to the shuttle!" Iricana ordered from the

Command Bay. The power in the residential area was off again, but Jarvie had no doubt they were on their way. Iricana, Adisa, and Sho also made good progress, running along the torus rim in gravity while they could.

And then the power went off on the whole station. "They won't make it," one of the Tundra passengers grumbled. "Too many doors."

"Hush," said the other. "There's a plan."

"You can't out-plan an AI, especially a crazy one."

Teeve poked his head up from the lower deck. "Boss, you want me to go help?"

"No!" Jarvie said, turning around to look.

"Hey," the same passenger said. "You're a kid."

"I am a youth and qualified pilot," he replied diplomatically.

"That don't mean you're a qualified leader. I'm going after our people." He reached for his restraints.

Jarvie had a flash of his brother facing down five unruly passengers on the *Sunburst*, cool firm voice, not harsh or insulting, but totally in command. *I can't do that!*

"Please sit down," he said as firmly as he could. And it came out squeaky and quiet.

"They need help and I'm not the sittin' around type!"

"Remain seated!" Jarvie said with a lot less diplomacy.

The man got his restraints off and pulled for the ladder to go below.

Jarvie switched on his cabin camera so he wouldn't have to keep turning around. And Teeve was floating in the passageway between the last two rows of seats.

"You need to go back to your seat, friend."

"You aren't the boss."

"Nope. He is," Teeve said casually. "And you are disobeying a direct order."

I'm getting distracted, Jarvie realized. And scanned his readings again. In another power blink he got a s'link message from Taj. "Restrained and proceeding. We'll never get him in a suit. We need a bubble."

Teeve and the objector were still facing off.

Jarvie turned to the other two passengers. "What's his name?"

"Marc."

"Hey Marc!" He called. "Get a bubble and go meet them."

"Now you're talkin'."

Where is Iricana and her team? As far as Jarvie could figure, having to manually override all doors could really slow them down, even with Iricana's level one. *I wouldn't bother. I'd just go out a hatch. They have their suits. Which is, of course, exactly what Iricana will do.*

"*Bird of Paradise*, locate all external hatches on this side of the torus and monitor them. Report any activity."

Twenty minutes later, Ulf was aboard, and they removed their helmets. "Keep him in the bubble. Keep your helmets ready."

"What? We're secure." Marc objected. "The AI can't touch us now."

"Hey!" Teeve said, and they followed directions, hooking Ulf to a seat, with Roza next to him, frowning.

"He's not doing well. Labored breathing," she said quietly to Jarvie.

"Teeve," Jarvie ordered. "Secure the hatch. Prepare for departure."

"Hey!" Marc objected. "What about the others?"

Jarvie didn't have time for another argument. **"Activity at hatch 3BL3,"** *Bird of Paradise* reported.

"Get your helmets back on!"

"Secure below," Teeve reported as he strapped himself in. "Secure up top."

"Thank you, Teeve," Jarvie replied, scanned his readings one last time. "*Bird of Paradise,* undock. Rendezvous with Iricana's signal on the hull. *81, Bird of Paradise.* We have Ulf. Picking up Command Bay team outside. ETA 27 minutes. Katie please link with Roza to advise."

"*Bird of Paradise,*" came Beezan's voice. "Copy your ETA. Good job."

Well, Jarvie thought. *Not as good as my brother. And thank heavens for Teeve. But still. Getting it done.*

13-Will

Nile Village

Melawn arrived at Nile late at night, cold and exhausted, still wet from a sudden rainstorm two days ago in Hunza. He had only himself to blame for standing out in the rain, along with all the other newcomers, spellbound at such an elemental event. Finally, when the lightning started, natives called them in and laughed as they cowered from the bone-rumbling thunder. Then he'd been forced to sleep in a stall in a beast barn.

Tonight, he just kept walking. Anything was better than sleeping on wet beast straw. And the smell. He wished it would rain again to wash it off.

The council had tried to process the newcomers, doing orientations in each village, but there were just too many people. They were forced to put people to work immediately and run short community circles at night. But people wandered around in a daze. They clamored around the carts, waiting for the cart cards, or they just walked, looking for friends and family.

There were crowds of people on the roads. Only the most infirm could ride the carts. There would be no room in the men's hall at Nile. Nkiroo was stationed at Nile, but probably out at the landing of the new ships, somewhere past the rebel caves. Melawn missed Nkiroo so much. It was like part of him was gone. He'd sent cart cards, hoping to meet up with Kiro. Pulling his poncho around him, he wondered what became of Lanezi and the twins. Then he wondered what was becoming of all of humanity.

Arriving after midnight, he found the road actually blocked, with "welcomers" stationed at a makeshift gate. "Name and business," the welcomer asked.

"I've come to see Grace," Melawn answered.

"Does she know you're coming?"

"She seems to know everything." He instantly regretted his irritated answer, thinking he'd be turned away, but with a patient sigh the man asked his name again. "Melawn."

"Ahh."

Ahh?

"Go to the council building. Try telling your name first, friend."

Melawn nodded, chagrined. "Yes, honor. Thank you."

At the building he was ushered into the left hallway with other people who were waiting, given a cup of soup, and a spot on the floor, where he gratefully slept until morning.

Melawn was almost to the front of the line for the council chamber when a woman came in, poncho on and hat pulled down over her eyes. She went right to the clerk at the front of the line. Her manner was so self-assured and purposeful that no one questioned her. Melawn wondered if she were a council member.

But there was something familiar in her bearing. She swept off her hat and looked up. Their eyes met. She didn't smile, but there was recognition and acceptance, maybe even relief. Tenshi. Deep lines of worry creased her face, but the impatience and haughtiness were gone. He could see the passion in her eyes. She was a person on a mission. She had found her place in the universe.

Melawn moved to greet her, but just as he got there, the council door opened and the previous person came out. "Oh, Tenshi," the clerk said, "go right in." And with an iron grip on his arm, as if he didn't have four kilograms of new muscle, Tenshi steered him into the room with her.

Embarrassed to cut in line, and thrown off course by Tenshi, Melawn quickly scanned the room. It was a simple clay-brick chamber with tall windows and a high ceiling. A large fireplace struggled to pump enough heat into the room. The council members sat around a semicircular table, facing the guests. The table was piled with papers, maps, and books. There was no food or water. Two clerks sat to the sides.

The council members looked exhausted. He knew they had been meeting almost continuously since the drop. All nine were there, although one had her head down on the table, asleep. All looked like natives, but that could be deceiving, as Melawn knew that Grace was not, just a long-timer.

The chairperson sat at the center, raising an eyebrow at Melawn. "Prayer please," the chairperson said to Tenshi, who recited the short healing prayer.

"Your visit to the caverns was successful?" The chairperson asked, as Tenshi handed a written report to the clerk.

"Partially," Tenshi answered. "I was admitted to the

compound in the caves. Most of them were quite ill and past the vaccination stage. So I assisted as I could."

"You're aware there are two viruses?" A council member on the right asked.

"Yes," Tenshi said. "The Chike agree with our analysis that this virus originated in the caves. We're calling it C3."

"A second virus came down with the drop," the council member continued.

"Yes," Tenshi said. "I'm worried that we have two waves crossing. People are going to get both. And C3 is bad. Eight people died before I got there.

Melawn couldn't stifle a gasp. "Not Thayne," Tenshi turned to reassure him. "Seven people over 50 and one infant passed away."

The council members sat up in surprise. "They have children?" the chairperson asked.

How could they not know that? Is Tenshi the first person to go in?

Tenshi continued reporting in her calm, efficient voice, but Melawn sensed an edge to it now. "At least twenty children under 15," she confirmed. "I administered 64 doses of the vaccine myself. They asked for 60 more."

"Why?"

"Scouting parties, they said. But I suspect there is another location. I saw a mail drop."

"So you're saying they are not all vaccinated."

"Correct. I'd like to go back with more vaccines."

"Yes, of course," the chairperson said. It was a dismissal, but Tenshi held her ground. "I bring a message." All eyes turned to her. "The Dragon's Den wishes to open relations with Paradise Valley."

Dragon's Den?

"Relations?" Grace asked.

"Unhindered passage back and forth. Cart service. Doctors. Dialogue. A liaison," Tenshi reported.

"I volunteer for liaison," Melawn said immediately, and Tenshi nodded, as if that had been her plan when dragging him in.

"This is Melawn, the data hunter," Grace added. "He has a talent for appearing at key moments.

"I'm useless in my current job," Melawn said.

"I volunteer as well," Tenshi added sternly. "We have a humanitarian crisis in the making."

The chairperson nodded. He looked left and right, reading the subtle signs of the members. "Until we decide, Tenshi, remain in Nile. Get the rest of the vaccinations organized. You-" he pointed to Melawn and looked at Grace.

"I recommend double scrubjub in town until we decide," Grace decreed.

"Very well," the chairperson said. "God protect you."

And they were dismissed. Outside, they hurried down the stone steps and around the corner before Tenshi would speak to him.

"Thayne?" Melawn asked.

"Alive, but it was close. I trust the council will figure out the right thing to do. It's just really bad timing. Come to the med tent and get vaccinated. We need to be ready. She turned, determined, and walked off, with Melawn following.

Two mind-numbing days of scrubjub later, Melawn was confronted by a runner, who handed him a message.

Report to my office. You are now one of my assistants. —
Grace

. . .

16-Will

81-Petals, incoming to Tanuki Station

Terina studied her personal notes, making a few corrections. They were more detailed than the historical record she was making, but she wanted to preserve everything about every jump.

If we jump early from the a-rings, the pilots are calling it a prejump. If we jump with no a-rings, that's a freejump. So, yesterday, we weren't going in the right direction to freejump to Tanuki, so Honor Beezan took us into the Tundra a-rings and circled for three hours, until he saw the path. He continued in the a-rings until both Mom and Ra'Tama thought they saw it, but he prejumped. Surprisingly, Mom tipped out successfully at Tanuki, only 4 days out. They are getting good at this!

Tanuki has a P&P of 77 and 6, so we won't be overwhelmed when we get there on the 19th. They'll all be transferred to Arc 1. Arc 1 is now fully opened, with expanded gardens, kitchen, Med Bays, everything.

Tomorrow is Jarvie's 16th birthday. We're having a little surprise party for him. He doesn't suspect a thing!

17-Will

Blurry-eyed first thing in the morning, Jarvie checked his s'link. Dress uniform with ship jacket today. Hmmm. He didn't see how that related to any surprise birthday party for him. Besides, it was before breakfast. He heard Beezan fuss with Sky, then send her through to Jarvie's room and shut the adjoining door. But Sky was in a mischievous mood, so Jarvie wasn't fooled.

Ten minutes later, the door opened to a breakfast surprise party in Beezan's cabin, with just the old *Drumheller* crew. Jarvie laughed and hugged them all. Then, remembering his lonely 15th birthday on the *Pearl*, and wondering whatever happened to Quay, he teared up. Being part of a family and on a great adventure filled him with joy.

They ate all his favorites for breakfast. Then Jarvie really was surprised when Captain Iricana announced that with so many people aboard, they would be going back to armbands.

Beezan presented Jarvie with his black youth armband. It had his posting "81-Petals" on the outside, and name and age on the inside.

"Thank you," Jarvie whispered when Beezan put it on him.

"Oh, one more thing," Beezan said, pulling something out of his pocket. "You are the first to receive the *81-Petals* pin." Everyone clapped. "And today, for your birthday gift, you and Terina will distribute armbands and pins shipwide."

Terina gasped and jumped up and down. Beezan couldn't stop smiling himself. "Thank you!" Jarvie laughed. He hugged Beezan again and said, "Thank you, everyone."

Jarvie and Terina nervously presented the pins to everyone else at the party. "Cake!" Star demanded, well versed in birthday tradition.

"Later," Iricana said, patting him while he grumped. They filed out, giving Jarvie their best wishes as they went.

And it was a great gift to distribute the pins. Iricana came with them as Captain, but they got to do all the pinning, getting less nervous as they went. There were not many youth, and no children, so there weren't many armbands to pass out. The pins, though, were beautifully detailed, colorful representations of the *81-Petals* seen from above, with the petals painted on the torus. Stations didn't do pins, so for many people, this was their first—and from a legendary ship, no less. People added it to their uniforms, shaking hands and congratulating each other.

Jarvie suddenly realized the wisdom of it. Yesterday, they had been *Drumheller*, Tektite, Tundra. But today, they were *81-Petals*. One ship, one crew.

On the walk back with Terina, Jarvie thought of all the happy birthday memories he'd had with his family, and touched all three of his ship pins: *Sunburst*, *Drumheller* and *81-Petals*.

"For luck?" Terina asked, looking up at him.

"For family," he said quietly.

She scowled. "Is there an Earth pin? My brother is somewhere on Earth."

"You have a brother?"

"I did. Dad stole him. My dad was Earthborn, like grandpa, but when he married my mom, he swore he never wanted to go back. But then he got this idea to make my little brother a big sports star. Mom never talks about it and doesn't want to know anything. But I looked him up. My Dad's a famous World Cup coach now. Not one mention of my brother."

So that's why she doesn't have her father's name. "I'm so sorry."

"Oh. I shouldn't have told you that on your birthday. Sorry. This crew is my family now." She nodded and touched her ship pins. "For family *and* luck."

19-Will

Terina tried to focus on her history of the *81-Petals*. She sat across from Jarvie at the library. He wasn't paying attention to his studies either. Everyone was nervous about the 77 people from Tanuki boarding tomorrow.

They didn't even adjust to one set of new people, when another, bigger set would come aboard. Honor Beezan was especially rattled. They needed distraction. Then she found the perfect thing.

Terina slid her pad across to Jarvie. "Check it out," she whispered.

"A diagram of *81-Petals*?"

She pointed to the third level inward and zoomed in. "Torus Tram!"

He grabbed the pad, wide-eyed. "I didn't remember that about the *81*."

"Because you were, what? One year old?"

"Thunder would have remembered," Jarvie said. "And he didn't say anything."

Confronted in the kitchen, both Kelson and Thunder admitted they knew about the tram, nodding with feigned indifference. But Terina knew better. They were probably dying to get in there.

"Well," Kelson explained, "the captain is concerned that there are a lot of moving parts."

"That haven't been moving for fifteen years," Thunder finished.

"It would need an extensive overhaul," Kelson said, nodding.

"We have an overabundance of mechanics aboard!" Jarvie argued. Thunder laughed.

"Let's not bite off more than we can chew," Kelson advised.

"Grandpa!"

But Jarvie didn't get that they were joking with them. "Our community circle could do it! For a service project!"

Kelson and Thunder looked at each other in surprise.

"We're supposed to do service together. And we're all in the same group!" Terina added.

"And we've got all the Tektites," Jarvie said.

"Well, then," Thunder tried to look serious. "How about this? For our service tonight, we'll go check it out."

"Yes!" Both Jarvie and Terina got so excited, they set off the pups, even disturbing them from their snacking. They started running around the kitchen.

"Okay, Okay," Thunder said. "But pups stay here."

Talk spread, and by the time they headed for the tram, they had 21 people, including Honor Beezan and all eight of the Tektites. "Why are we taking the stairs?" Terina complained. "There is a lift."

Thunder smiled and pointed at Kelson, leading the group. "If Honor Kelson can take the stairs, you can take the stairs."

They emerged onto the deck, no different from any subway or tramway platform on any station. The platform edge doors were closed, but the walls were transparent. Led by Chip and Kente, they all ran up to look through. They could see the tracks, but there weren't any trams parked there.

"Where are the cars?" Terina asked.

"In the repair bays, near Arc 6," Thunder answered. "I hope."

Thunder turned off the lights on the platform and turned them on in the tube. Terina pressed her face against the window, looking up and down the track. Iricana had said it would be a long walk from Arc 6 to Arc 1, but not with the tram.

"Good thing you people all volunteered to help," Thunder announced.

"Being as you were all going to be assigned anyway," Kelson added. But the Tektites barely heard. They were surveying the whole scene in wonder and anticipation.

1-Knowledge

Near the Dragon's Den

Melawn and Tenshi turned down the canyon to the Dragon's Den, walking at the fastest pace they could sustain. The days were getting shorter and they had no wish to wander among the stone pillars at night.

"At least there's a moon," Melawn said.

"Yes, but the clouds are coming in." Tenshi gestured to the west. "It'll be dim and wet tonight." Melawn nodded. The golden cliffs were far less spectacular without the sun—another lesson from nature.

They were probably walking twice as fast as the day they first came to the colony. Both of them were stronger, healthier, and had completely adjusted to the gravity. "Our bodies were built for this? This planetary life?"

"Yes," Tenshi answered. "We're not going to overcome millions of years of evolution in a couple of generations. We need to find planets to be healthy."

Melawn and Tenshi had traded their sun hats for warm caps. Melawn shifted his pack, adjusting it over his new winter coat. It no longer felt like he was carrying a shuttle on his back. They were sharing the load: 100 doses of vaccine, along with medical supplies. Part of the load was mental. They carried a message from the council, and an order to discover if the Dragon's Den was hiding something. And Jadee had asked Melawn to bring his daughter home. Many challenging assignments, but it was better than farming.

Melawn glanced at Tenshi. All that time on the *Cheetah* and they'd barely had a real conversation. She was different now. Almost as if the rat study had been a failed distraction.

"You never mentioned your husband."

No expression of pain crossed her face. "He's been in a coma over twenty years."

"I'm so sorry. You got married young then."

"We were 15. We got married and then left Earth to go to medical school together, in Sector 2. We went back to Earth to do our service. There are so many places that still need help. He jumped into an infested river to save a man and was infected by rare parasites. They live in him now. But he's not conscious. The old man he saved only lived a month after that."

"How horrible!"

"I spent ten years working on a cure. I discovered thirteen other cures, but never that. It was making me crazy. So I left, and vowed never to return. Others carry on the work. Many villagers were infected, but the river is clean now."

"I'm so sorry."

"I didn't divorce him when I left Earth, and I won't divorce him now. He is my husband and we'll be together again."

"Long time to wait."

"I have no wish to die young. But I'm not the one who's waiting."

"What?" Melawn asked, confused.

She gave him a look. "You're 25."

"Oh, me." He shrugged. "I'm not going to marry a native."

"You think you're going to get off this planet?"

"I don't know. But if the opportunity appears, I want to go." But as soon as he said it, he had a pang of regret. *Do I really want to go?*

"Well, with all the new spacers, there are plenty of people who would go with you." He shrugged again, hoping to drop the subject. "You need to let Thayne go," she said gently.

"I'm not—we're not—"

"He demands complete personal loyalty. He doesn't share. He has a hold on your soul."

"No."

"You need to get away from him."

"I've let him go. I have."

"Maybe. But he has not let you go. And he never will."

"He's found new students."

"We'll see," she said. But she patted him on the shoulder encouragingly.

It was almost dark when they heard the whistling. Tenshi stopped. "It's Tenshi and Melawn, sent by the council. We have the vaccines."

They waited as a chilly wind picked up and a few drops of rain touched their cheeks. Melawn glanced up to the rock that had been his bed last time. He would not want to sleep up there now. The same sentry appeared, steady on his feet this time.

"Go," was all he said, indicating that Melawn and Tenshi should walk in front of him. Verbally guiding them through many twists and turns they descended into a cavern. Melawn's nerves started up. Memories of cave-ins, gas leaks, alarms. *It's not a mine!* He scolded himself.

The caves were more and more populated as they went farther in. Even based on Tenshi's report, he had not expected so many. "How many people are here?" He whispered to Tenshi.

"More than before," she answered. "But most were collapsed on the floor at the time."

Finally, they came to a larger hall. "This way," the guard said.

"No," Tenshi answered. "I'm going to your medical cavern." Melawn was about to follow her, but Tenshi put a hand on his arm to stop him. "Take Melawn to AnnaLee."

The guard hesitated, but Tenshi fixed him with one of her no-nonsense looks. "Okay. This way."

It wasn't much warmer in the caves, but with his coat on and nerves acting up, Melawn started to sweat. People were staring, some just curious, some with cold or angry looks. Automatically, he checked for vents, and was relieved to see pipes in various places.

Finally, he was brought to a chamber with a small fireplace and a man and woman sitting behind a table. They looked tense. He recognized AnnaLee, without the mask this time. The guard made an attempt to be formal. "Ahlili, Melawn, from the council, he says." AnnaLee dismissed the guard with a toss of her head. Melawn quickly removed his hat out of respect, and got his coat undone.

"Melawn," she said.

"Yes, honor."

"You've come to join us?"

"No, honor. Officially, I've come with a message from the council." Both of them narrowed their eyes. "Unofficially, to consult with Thayne."

She stared at him a long time. "He said you would come."

Am I that predictable? She turned to the man next to her. "This is Ellant, my right hand." Melawn nodded to him and received a wary gaze in return. Melawn had memorized the crew of the *Dragonfly Dream*; Ellant was the chief scientist. "Ellant, show our guest where to wash up and bring him to dinner." She turned back to Melawn with a dangerous smile. "Welcome to the Dragon's Den."

Melawn was escorted to a private dining area by a very guarded Ellant, who gave one-word answers to Melawn's attempts at polite conversation.

The "dining room" was another cavern, a dark and cold one, with no fireplace. Candles on the table and walls didn't provide enough light to cheer the place, let alone heat it.

Melawn hesitated, as there was no food line, no serving area. And where were the rest of the people? "Please be seated," a young woman said. She wore a white shirt with a homemade Dragon's Den patch, like an employee—or a servant. She pulled one of the ten wooden chairs out from the single table for Melawn.

"Thank you." He awkwardly sat down, trying not to get caught in a heavy tablecloth—warm. There were hot stones or something under the table. Thayne entered, and as if his brain were on springs, Melawn jumped up to greet him, nearly pulling off the tablecloth. Thayne smiled and embraced him like a long-lost son. Even knowing how fickle Thayne could be, it was good to see him. Melawn hugged him back, alarmed at how thin Thayne was, even with a heavy coat on.

Thayne insisted that Melawn sit to his right, and introduced one of his new students, who sat to his left. "This is DeeZann. I think you know her father, Jadee."

"But you're a Zann," Melawn said, before thinking that was probably impolite.

"I'm a trade," she said simply. "My parents swapped babies at birth for the benefit of both populations. Officially, I'm not a Zann, but I'm allowed to keep my name."

"Oh," Melawn said dumbly, realizing that she was the daughter he was supposed to bring back. And she was now Thayne's favored student.

The chairs filled with Ellant at the foot of the table, his wife to his right, then Tenshi and AnnaLee's husband, and their daughter next to him. She was about 7 years old, and stared down at the table, unspeaking.

Last came one of AnnaLee's officers, but she remained standing. The guests shifted in anticipation and then stood when AnnaLee came in. Melawn and Tenshi jumped to join them, Tenshi giving him a concerned look. He shared her concern. Such formality was not shown to agents, let alone ship captains. And this private dining, and servants. *Who does she think she is?*

AnnaLee sat, and so did the rest of them. Thayne had been a bit slow to stand, and now flashed Melawn a "be careful" look. *Is it dinner, or a conspiracy?*

"So wonderful to have guests," AnnaLee said. "This is my husband Henrik, and daughter Dima," who looked up and nodded, eyes focused on the wall. "And you know Ellant, and this is his wife Rhona," who smiled with genuine warmth.

AnnaLee neglected to introduce Tenshi and Melawn. Then six servants entered, five with food, putting the plates in front of them. The unencumbered one announced, "First course: Sunrise tubers with dragon mushrooms."

They're even naming the food after themselves? It was a generous portion of orange tubers and small mushrooms that Melawn hadn't seen before. Tenshi ate reluctantly, no doubt wondering if everyone in the Dragon's Den was getting their share. But Melawn had learned his survival lesson. He ate it all and finished Thayne's when Thayne pushed it over to him.

Course two was greens with "dragon" spice. Conversation consisted of AnnaLee telling them the great things Dragon Den had done and how amazing their little community was. The child actually stopped eating and looked up at her mom in puzzlement, until the dad gently nudged her elbow.

By dessert—beast cheese cake—Melawn was convinced they were being lulled into complacency on purpose. When tea was served, Henrik, Dima, and Rhona were excused. Melawn could see that Tenshi was pondering if now was the time to bring up the council's instructions, but she appeared to be waiting for some sign.

Finally, the servants cleared everything and extinguished the candles by their entrance. AnnaLee's aid stood by the door. "So," AnnaLee said, "I trust your meal was good."

They all murmured their praise and thanks, as if AnnaLee had served them herself.

"Dr. Tenshi, you have a message for us?"

"We do. It's in writing, but I can tell you the gist of it."

"Please do."

Tenshi spoke in her detached professional mode. "After the usual greetings, the Paradise Council informs you that it is promoting itself to a regional council." AnnaLee actually blinked in surprise. "Each village will elect a local council. The Zann have already elected. The Dragon's Den would be allowed to elect a local council if certain conditions were met regarding education of children and guaranteed equality."

Melawn noticed an expression of hope flash across Ellant's face. "Interesting," AnnaLee said. "But that is not our goal, as you know. We wish to be separate."

"You are separate," Tenshi said, puzzled.

"No, a separate government. Our own government. Free of your pan-Human administrative structure."

The color completely drained from Tenshi's face. Melawn's heart started to pound. *Did she really just declare mutiny on humanity?*

"No one has a separate government," Tenshi said.

"We will."

Tenshi persisted. "No Humans have a separate government! Not in the sectors, not even on Earth anymore. Even the monarchs submit to the council. We are all one people!"

"Who says?" AnnaLee challenged.

"The Writings say," Tenshi answered.

"And the people," Melawn added. Data from his community circle on unity came back to him from eleven years ago. "In the One Humanity vote on Earth, reiterated on the Moon, and proclaimed on Mars again. Then again in Sector 3. Even in the outer sectors, after the Sundering. Even here! We remain one Human organization."

"Yes," Thayne said quietly. AnnaLee shot Thayne a sharp look. Melawn really began to wonder what was going on. Why was Thayne even here? Did he mean to take AnnaLee's place? Of course, Thayne had worked outside the government himself.

"Perhaps," Ellant suggested, "We should study the *proposal* more closely later." AnnaLee seemed annoyed at him, but subsided.

"Very well. We have a proposal for you. Something even

your council would approve of—a science expedition." AnnaLee nodded to DeeZann, who got up and unrolled a map, holding it so everyone could see. Melawn, trying to stay calm, turned in his chair as AnnaLee continued.

"As you can see, the landscape to the south of the dessert has two mountain ranges running somewhat north-south, with this valley between them, angling until they reach the coast. If you follow the mountains past the flag route, you'll come to the ocean, not far from the Chike landing area. However, if you stay inland and continue south, you'll cross a wide plain, somewhat reminiscent of the North American plains. We call this the Plain of Patience.

"The area is marginally habitable. Streams cross through in the spring. There is vegetation and thin, but hard, wood for fuel. We have sent several expeditions south and we do have an outpost."

"On the coast?" Tenshi asked.

"The land is not exactly flat. There are steppes and ridges running east-west. But eventually, before the equator, there is a major river, probably a continental one. We call it Narmada." *So many Earth references.* "Our outpost is near the coast on a slight plateau at Narmada."

AnnaLee turned away from the map. "Our expedition will check in with the outpost, vaccinate them, and gather whatever data they've collected. Ellant will lead, with some of his aids. DeeZann will be going by Thayne's request. We offer full transparency by inviting you, Melawn. And of course, Dr. Tenshi must come with the vaccines."

Melawn knew he could not refuse. "When?"

"Oh, not until spring."

"We'll take your proposal back to the council of course," Tenshi said neutrally.

"And I will consider the council's proposal." A little chill went down Melawn's spine. A council order wasn't something to be considered or rejected. It just was.

Melawn was invited to Thayne's private chamber for the night, but when he tried to ask *what are you doing here with these people?* Thayne just held a finger to his lips and whispered, "I'm getting off this planet," and wouldn't say another word.

5-Knowledge

81-Petals, incoming to Tetra Station

"Tetra beacon confirmed," Jarvie reported, as Sequoia tipped them into normal space. "Standard signal. No mayday."

"Tetra Station, this is *Drumheller*. ETA 2 days." There was an immediate answer. A woman looking thin and strained, but smiling with determination, appeared. "Greetings *Drumheller*. God is Most Glorious. I am Turrell and I'll be your moni—" Suddenly, she looked to the left. "What?" And she cut Jarvie off.

A few seconds later, Ra'Tama said, "Something's happening on the docking ring." Katie had just announced that all 137 passengers had green lights, but Iricana was still coming around.

"*81*," Sequoia ordered, "scan docking ring and station and all nearby ships."

"Five beacons approaching from the docking ring, all regis-tered shuttles."

What? "*Drumheller* to approaching shuttles, state your intentions." Jarvie said. He unsealed his cocoon. No answers.

"Tetra, come in." Jarvie yanked off his helmet and started on his brackets. Nothing. "Tetra Outbound Authority, come in." They got out of their chairs and stretched as they waited.

"What's the ETA of those shuttles?" Iricana asked after she woke up.

"26 hours," Sequoia answered.

"We'll need to get food to Arc 6," Iricana said.

"But why?" Jarvie asked. "There's no mayday. There's no emergency."

"An old trick," Terina explained. "I mean really old. Towns on the seacoast would put out fake beacon lights, like it was a safe harbor. And when the ships came in and crashed on the rocks, they would take all their cargo."

They all looked at Terina, horrified, all believing that humanity was well past those days. "Well," Kelson cautioned, "If they are running low on food, they might not want to spook an approaching ship by sending a mayday."

"Tetra Station, this is Captain Iricana. Please send your P&P so we can prepare food, and explain the purpose of approaching shuttles."

Tetra Station finally answered, "*Drumheller*, Captain, the shuttles are unauthorized. Our P&P is 485 and 12."

There were gasps around the Command Bay. 485 people would fill an arc. And unauthorized shuttles! "How many are on the shuttles?" Iricana asked.

"About a hundred, total."

"How did a hundred people get on shuttles so quickly?" Kelson whispered.

"Tetra," Iricana said, "tell your people not to panic. We have plenty of food and there's room for everyone."

"*Drumheller*, we are short of food, but the main problem is life support. We estimated it would fail three days ago."

"That's why they're in the shuttles," Thunder whispered back to Kelson.

"Can we speed up?" Iricana asked Sequoia.

"Sure," Sequoia answered. "We can burn a lot of fuel to speed up and burn more to slow down, and save a few hours at most."

"But Captain," an exhausted Beezan cut in, "If we speed up, the shuttles will probably overshoot and miss us."

Iricana took a deep breath. "Tetra, are there more shuttles?"

"*Drumheller*, yes. Four more."

"Tetra, we'll hold course. Send the remaining shuttles. We'll dock for the rest of you and any supplies. Stay in touch at all times. Who's in command?"

"Thank you, honor." And they were cut off again.

"What?" Iricana looked around the room.

"No one is in command," Kelson said quietly. "Or not effectively anyway."

"God help us. Let's get with it," she replied. But Sequoia had collapsed back into her chair. "Except pilots, of course."

11-Knowledge

81-Petals, headed for Tetra a-rings

They left Tetra Station and started boosting to the a-rings six days later. Beezan sat on his bunk shaking. Deep breaths. The others had sheltered him from the stress of the shuttle dockings and chaotic mass boarding, sending him and Ra'Tama to the gardens or kitchens to keep them busy. But he knew. He had seen on the screens.

Iricana was smart. She let the shuttles dock in the hangar, pressurized it and let the people enter in groups. They were guided up the lift and down the rimway to Arc 6, with constant reassuring instructions. They were sealed off, one family or group to a cabin. There were rations in every cabin. It had taken them every second of time they had to prep the cabins. Then they sent the shuttles back for more, so they never actually docked with Tetra station. Finally, Thunder and company salvaged everything they could from the station.

Good thing I'm not Captain. I never would have thought of all that. But there was no food left at Tetra. They broke into 15-year-old stored food on the *81*. Beezan was still chewing on a ration bar. And Iricana had ordered him to rest, even though Sequoia was going to jump. He was tired, so he accepted it.

There was a soft knock at his adjoining door and Jarvie came in. "You okay?" he asked.

"Yes," Beezan nodded to reassure him. "You?"

"Yes, fine. Tired." Jarvie looked good. Excited even.

"Have you been in Arc 6?" Beezan asked with alarm.

Jarvie shook his head no, sitting down on the bunk beside him. "Tomorrow. Captain's going in. Thunder, Teeve, Katie, and I are going too. And Hiro and Hisoka, if you remember those big men."

Jarvie fished a ration bar out of his pocket and started to eat it, making a face. "So the Tetras are calming down, but they had a lot of disunity on Tetra. And now they're all together in one arc with their troubles. That's not going to go away fast. They don't seem to have one leader."

"No acting commander?"

"Apparently, he was removed."

"Mutiny?" Beezan asked in shock.

"They say not. Some kind of mediation by the council."

"Huh. Maybe that works on a station." He squeezed Jarvie's arm. "Be careful. I'll pray for you."

• • •

12-Knowledge

81-Petals, Arc 6

Jarvie hoped Beezan was praying, because this was more nerve wracking than he expected. He stood next to Teeve, trying to look calm and businesslike, while Iricana stood on a small platform and faced down the 485 people jammed into the rimway. The curvature of the rimway helped them all to see her. With her solid stature, her pale skin, and blue eyes, she probably looked like some Earthborn administrator. But she also had the stern mom vibe that Jarvie hoped would keep people in line.

They had made sure that breakfast was distributed first. Then they opened the cabins a few at a time, letting the people gather quietly. The Tektites had tagged along, and Maura chanted prayers in a powerful voice. The people responded to the food, the calm, the beauty of the prayers, and settled down.

But Jarvie noticed a few people glaring at each other and jockeying for position in the front row. "God is Most Glorious," Iricana addressed the crowd. "I'm Captain Iricana, and you are aboard the *81-Petals*." Iricana explained that they were going through Sector 8, picking up all the strays, so people should expect more additions, and that everyone needed to help out, that all would have food and work to do. But before she got very far, the two jockiers started shouting questions.

"Shouldn't a station commander be in charge?" one asked.

"Why are we locked in?" asked the other. "And what about the Chike?"

Iricana stopped. "First of all, I have authority in the outer sectors to take command of any vessel or station as I see fit." Jarvie turned to look at her. *Wow.*

"I've been given this authority by Diego Oatah, Agent of Sector 1." As if that were not enough, she pulled out her s'link and ran it up to level 1, slowly passing it in front of her so that all could see the #1. There was a general murmur of surprise and acceptance at that.

"We have not seen the Chike at any system. But the order of the council was to evacuate, so that's what we're doing." There were some scowls and grumbling and some relieved looks. Jarvie wondered if surrender was the source of their disagreement.

"As for your access to the rest of the ship, that depends on you. The process of community building will start immediately. I mean, today. When you're far enough along, you will organize yourself and select leaders that will be held responsible for Arc 6. After everyone is registered today, your first task is to get gardens up and running, and, in four days, you must have all your jump chairs ready. Because we're going to Tyee."

18-Knowledge

81-Petals, incoming to Tyee Station

15 Knowledge: Sequoia jumped the regular way out of Tetra, tipping us into Tyee with an ETA of only 1 day. But all the pilots agreed they saw or felt something and were willing to let Sequoia try the prejump to RJ.

Terina kept her history log open at all times now, tapping in notes as they went. Things were happening so fast, and in so many places that her grandpa had found some journalists to help her. He was now visiting Arc 6 every day, getting people settled.

Meanwhile, Thunder and Teeve and their mechanics were going full speed. They opened Arcs 3 and 8, and were starting on Arc 2. With the large influx of people, visions of their study circle doing the tram were canceled and a real engineering team was assigned.

Settling the Tetras was especially difficult as they were unorganized and unprepared. Their council had decided that only volunteers would stay. It was a nice sentiment, and perhaps necessary, but it left a selection of truly humble people mixed with wannabe heroes. And it was the supposed heroes that were causing all the trouble. Additionally, fewer people had the skills they needed for emergency operations.

Tyee had not done that. They had a P&P of a stunning 603 and 32. But they were not starved or angry. They were already organized into work teams. They sent packets of names, skills and current assignments in advance, which was a great relief to Iricana.

Now, Terina sat with Jarvie at one table in the Arc 3 rimway with Taj and Maura at another table. They were checking in the Tyee people, registering their p'links and s'links, and pulling out the few experts that were needed immediately. These people were patient, friendly, polite, and helpful. It had gone so smoothly, they only had a few more to process. Terina breathed a big sigh of relief for the first time in days.

Wham! A man slammed his backpack on the table in front of Jarvie. Jarvie looked up in shock and turned pale. "Yan," he whispered. *Yan,* Terina remembered from studying Jarvie's history. *His former caretaker.*

"Yeah, *Yan*," the man mocked. "Didn't expect to see me here, did you? —or ever!"

Everyone froze except Taj, who was out of his chair and soothing Yan. "Easy friend. I don't know what the problem—"

"You shut up!" He knocked Taj's arm away. People gasped and came closer to assist. Maura gently pulled Terina away.

Jarvie put his hands up. "Yan, I'm sorry."

"*Sorry!* I spent a year in detention because of you!"

"I'm so sorry."

"*I lost my job! I have a level 10 s'link!*" He threw it down next to the backpack for proof.

"I—"

"I tried to help you and you *ruined my life!*"

"I'm so sorry," Jarvie whispered again.

"SORRY ISN'T GOOD ENOUGH!" he lunged across the table, knocking Taj away and grabbing Jarvie by the jacket collar, trying to lift him out of his chair. But Jarvie didn't budge and Yan fell against the table.

Hiro and Hisoka arrived and took Yan calmly by the arms. Slowly, Jarvie stood up and Yan stepped back, staring up at him. "Come along friend," Hiro said mildly. "We need to talk." Gently, they guided him away, Taj following with the backpack and s'link.

Jarvie collapsed back in the chair, while Maura processed the last couple of people. Terina sat by Jarvie, who was breathing hard and shaking. "Was that your old caretaker?"

"Yes. He has every right to be furious with me," and then Jarvie couldn't hold back the tears.

Beezan, Iricana, and Katie had a formal meeting with Jarvie after they viewed the recording. Beezan was obviously upset and quiet, although Jarvie felt his support. Iricana was more upset with herself. "I should have anticipated that Yan wouldn't stay on Hamada."

"We had no way to know where he was until we got the Tyee data," Katie said. "And he wasn't flagged. He served his detention time on Hamada and had counseling. The Tyee counselors said he's been an ideal citizen. But the shock of seeing Jarvie again triggered his outburst. He's in counseling in Arc 8 now and they say he's very regretful."

"We'll keep him in Arc 8," Iricana said, "but I'd like to work towards bringing you two together to make some sort of peace."

"But what can I ever say or do to make up for it? I did wreck his life. I knew he'd be in trouble and I didn't even care."

"You both broke the law," Iricana said. "But you were a kid and he was an adult. And he was put in detention for breaking security laws, not for your running away."

"There have been a few other unhappy reunions," Katie added. "Counseling says the main approach, besides counseling, is to find useful work and friends for the people. Also, you should know, Yan's fiancé was taken by the Chike."

Oh no, Jarvie despaired. And knew he would be blamed for that too. There was nothing he could ever do to make peace with Yan.

19-Knowledge

Nile Village

Melawn was happy to be reassigned to Nile, especially since he was reunited with Nkiroo, when Nkiroo wasn't out with the scavenging team. Tonight, Tenshi was in town, so the three of them planned to have dinner together. Jadee was in town too, but Melawn was avoiding him after failing to return DeeZann.

They were assigned to late dinner, which was a good thing, as Melawn had to finish his scrubjub. If he thought being a council member's assistant would get him out of it, he was wrong. Even the council members did their share. Even visiting Zann chipped in. Only medical workers were exempt—because they scrubbed the hospital and clinics. Unlike the Dragon's Den, they were committed to a society of equals.

With all the extra people, food organization and preparation were top priority. Today, after compiling reports for Grace, he'd spent two hours hauling buckets of water, and two hours cooking huge pots of grain that got so thick he could barely stir.

Finally done, he dropped his gear and pulled out his mat

near the Temple garden. He sat and rested against a rock until Nkiroo came trudging up and dumped his gear with a sigh. Melawn got up and high-fived Nkiroo, getting that small reassuring smile that always warmed his heart. "I'm tired," was all Nkiroo had to say.

Then Tenshi came into view, heading their way with vigor and intensity, standing up straight, with people dodging out of her way. Melawn and Nkiroo both laughed. "She's a force," Melawn acknowledged, as they both stood up straighter.

"Friends," she greeted them, lightly lowering her gear.

"Doctor," Nkiroo replied formally, tapping her lightly on the shoulder.

"Tenshi, have we mentioned how much we admire you?" Melawn teased.

"Mention it in the food line. Let's go."

Settling cross-legged, with their legumes over barely stirable grains, the three ate appreciatively for a time.

"Nkiroo," Tenshi asked, "we saw something in the sky last night. Was it another ship drop?"

"Probably. But, most sadly, I am reassigned to local projects."

"Local?"

"We're building carts, housing units, halls, kitchens, everything. Lots of metal now, so we're making lightweight carts. I've designed a new carriage and a quick release mechanism for the drivers. We're assigned Chike power tools, but it's still really hands-on."

"I'm sorry," Melawn said. "I know you love the ships."

"I don't love taking them apart. I'm just as happy to be making cargo carts for your expedition."

"Does everyone know about the expedition?"

"There are no secrets here."

After dinner, while they were drinking their tea, Nkiroo asked, "Is it normal to think about them?"

"Who?" Melawn asked.

"Our people. Lanezi, Euro, Io, Zahar, Evan, Caspia, Iricana, Katie?"

"It would be abnormal if you didn't," Tenshi said.

"I think of them all the time. Pray for them, and you," Melawn reassured him.

"So many people, gone," Nkiroo said sadly. Melawn reached over and grabbed Nkiroo's arm. "The counselors taught me about making friends. But they didn't teach me what to do when they disappear."

"I know," Melawn sympathized. "It's so hard. But we are here, and you can make new friends."

"But something will happen and they'll disappear," he said, and Melawn couldn't deny it.

"Would you rather never have known them?" Tenshi asked, looking off into the distance.

Nkiroo thought about it. "No. I'm happy to have them in my heart. But they keep talking about community now. Like everyone is your friend. But a real friend knows you, cares about you. How do I know who's going to be a real friend, and not someone who uses you?"

Tenshi looked at Nkiroo sharply. "Someone's hurt you?"

"Made me build routers. Lied to me."

She nodded. "You're mad at Thayne."

"He isn't a friend."

"No."

"But you are going to see him," Nkiroo said quietly.

Melawn could hear the hurt in Nkiroo's voice. Like they had

taken Thayne's side over his. "We're not visiting as friends. He's still the smartest person around," Melawn explained.

"No. He's not. He's a liar."

"We know who we're dealing with," Melawn insisted.

"No, you don't."

"I do," Tenshi said. "He's not going on the expedition anyway."

Nkiroo let out a breath.

"We'll be careful. I promise," Melawn said.

Tenshi looked out on the village, down the river, and a strange expression crossed her face.

"What is that vibration?" Nkiroo asked, putting his hands on the ground.

"Cave-in!" Melawn said as they all jumped to their feet. But that was just childhood fears talking.

"No. Oh, no." Tenshi almost sobbed. They looked at her in alarm. "It's an Earthquake!"

The shaking was obvious now; people were starting to scream. "Planetquake!" Tenshi repeated. She looked above their heads at the Temple, at the mountain behind, at the structures. Melawn looked down the river towards the sunset. It sounded like a giant subway train was coming their way. There was dust rising in the west.

"Too long. It's a big quake," Tenshi said. It became hard to stand. The three of them grabbed onto each other as rocks started to roll down the mountain.

"Oh my God," Melawn said. "The Dragon's Den."

Nkiroo's eyes were on the buildings. "Were they built for this?"

As the ground rolled in waves, they could not stand. They toppled over, scrambling away from the big bouncing rocks that moments ago had been immobile. Pebbles danced up and down and dust and sand rose in puffs. The sounds of screaming were joined by crashing as tables, pots, chairs, walls, and hundreds of small items were thrown about. And still it went on.

Dodging for survival, Melawn heard Tenshi reciting ***"Dominion is God's, the Lord of the seen and the unseen, the Lord of creation."***[1] He joined in, as did others, still scrambling, nearly shouting the prayer.

Rocks rolling down the mountain toward the Temple were demolishing the traveler's center. Melawn hoped no one was in there. Other people were still trying to run or crawl away as the rolling and noise started to subside. They could hear the bell ringing in the desert, Melawn assumed from the rocking of the planet and not some hapless crew.

Before the shaking even stopped, Tenshi was gathering her scattered gear and lighting her lantern. "We have to get organized. It'll be dark soon! I'm going to the hospital." She stopped long enough to look them both in the eye and grip their arms. "God be with you both."

She turned to go, but then they heard the Zann whistles. "Up. Up," they were shouting. "Away from the water!"

"Tsunami!" Tenshi saw their perplexed expressions and explained. "A giant wave of ocean water."

"But we're kilometers from the ocean," Nkiroo objected.

"It'll push up the river. The Zann seem to know. We'll have salt water. God help us," and she ran up the path.

Lighting his own lantern, Melawn and Nkiroo headed to the council building. They had to stop several times, to help people, or just tell them to go to the village square. It seemed like only moments later that there was another terrifying sound and more shouting. A deafening roar of water rushed up the river with enough force to spray on them all the way up the path.

There was a metallic, scraping, nerve-chilling screech. But it was too dark to see the river now.

Nkiroo looked horrified. "The bridges. That's the sound of metal twisting." The sound carried on, past them, up the river. And then Nkiroo turned away, towards the collapsed council building. He pulled his Chike-issued power tool out of his pack, as determined as Tenshi. "Let's get people out."

In the night, Melawn sat at his makeshift information table, trying to make lists by the light of a single shaky lamp. People would run up and report, sometimes incoherently, and run off.

When the first aftershock hit, he grabbed the lamp and huddled on the ground. There was less crashing this time. Now he could hear the metallic groaning of the Temple structure and the far-off ringing of the red flag bell. The aftershock alone would have knocked down the village. Now it just added sound and terror to the night. More water rushed up the river and a fire lit the western sky.

Aftershock after aftershock, tsunami after tsunami, and refrains of "Dominion is God's" repeated until no one came to report. The whole village huddled in dread. Melawn hunched over his table, clutching his poncho around him, trying not to hyperventilate when the lantern went out. Some detached part of his mind marveled at how easy it was to slip into hysterics.

Finally, Nkiroo came to get him, dragging him to a row of men who were sleeping in the square. They were sharing blankets, mats, and cloaks in the cold. Melawn ended up between Nkiroo and a big man snoring like he was taking a tenth-day nap. It almost made Melawn laugh. And that brought his mind back to him. Gradually, the ground, the water, and the people settled down.

. . .

1-Power

Before dawn, Melawn gave a silent prayer of thanks that the Temple was still standing, and most people were alive and not badly injured, at least here. In the predawn light, he took care of Grace's first orders and joined the crowd of stunned onlookers at the river's edge. He was stiff and sleepy, but relieved to be able to see rather than imagine the destruction surrounding them.

The river banks had overflowed by at least ten meters on both sides. Shallow muddy water was still pooled up. They had suffered at least twenty waves, and even now, the river battled the ocean over which way it would flow. But there had not been a big wave or aftershock for four hours now.

Mud and debris were scattered on both sides: marine plants, Human-made baskets, and strange coral spikes. Some people walked right out into it, poking around. "What must it be like at Yosemite?" someone asked.

"Crabs!" Another shouted. Hearing that, Tenshi and Jadee ran down the path, wading in.

"Are they alive?" Jadee asked.

"No, not this one. It's upside-down." The man nudged it with his boot.

They gathered around. "These are the crab people," a Zann said sternly.

"Sentient beings," Tenshi said. "We should put them back in the river."

"But they're dead."

"Well, I assume their dead are dealt with in the water. It's the best we can do," she insisted. But she did kneel down next to Jadee as he did a quick, but gentle exam.

"Big brain," he whispered. "One big claw, one small. Looks like it could do fine work."

"Markings," Tenshi pointed out. "Different on different ones."

Melawn whipped out his notebook and started copying down the markings. "Show me," he said. So people gathered the bodies and made a sad parade past Melawn before gently slipping them back into the main river, to be washed back to their ocean graves.

Jadee and Tenshi both took water samples, but Jadee came by and whispered to Melawn. "Tell the council it's most likely that all our crops will die. They'll be flooded under salt water."

"Can we drain the water out?" Melawn asked.

"Probably not fast enough to save this year's crops. But the faster, the better, to save the soil."

"I'll tell them," Melawn said. "Jadee, I'm sorry we didn't get your daughter last time. I hope she's okay."

He nodded grimly. "Me too. I hope all of them are okay."

"Runners have gone," Melawn said. It had been one of his first tasks from Grace. Organize runners. Open an information desk. Gather the facts. Melawn sat back down at his table to write an urgent message for Grace.

There was no breakfast, but everyone was given a drink of water from stores. Kitchens were being organized outside as most buildings had collapsed. He wasn't hungry anyway. He was just scared, worried, and terrified. He kept thinking the planet was shaking again, but it was just him.

A young Zann came running up. Etazann, his first runner. He'd sent her on the most dangerous mission, to the tunnel. She was out of breath. "No way through," she reported. His heart sank. "Look," she pointed. He could see that the cliff edge, where they stopped the carts to first view the Temple, was covered by a slide. There was no road to the tunnel.

"Can you see if the tunnel is open?"

"It looks buried. I can take a team over the mountain, on the old path, to check on the Dragon's Den."

"Get a small team ready, but let me check with the council before you go."

"Right!"

And suddenly the dawn bell began to ring, a little late, adding a bittersweet beginning to their first recovery day.

2-Power

"Day 2" Melawn wrote at the top of his log. He had three assistants now, all scribbling messages, making reports and interviewing. He was the master organizer, sorting and listing data, by hand. He'd slept fitfully. It was cold and his stomach was in knots, worrying about Thayne. And then he was ashamed at himself for not worrying just as much about everyone else, especially his farm team. He'd sent them a message that he was okay, not knowing if they even cared or expected any reassurance.

4-Power

By day four, Melawn started to get reports from downriver.

All bridges were destroyed. Thirty people were stranded on the other side of the river. Twenty were taken in by the Zann, but ten were walking upriver to the narrow part to ford. A team of engineers had also been sent to inspect the bridge wreckage.

"Melawn," a gentle voice and tap on the shoulder broke him out of his half sleep. It was Nkiroo. "Here."

"Food!" Melawn took it gratefully, but then hesitated. "Everyone has some?"

"Yes, yes. Eat." Nkiroo sat on Melawn's "guest" chair. Melawn looked down at the tiny slice of flatbread, greens, and cheese.

"We have ovens?"

"No. Open fires."

Melawn nodded. "What else is happening?"

"There are a lot of people here from the outer sectors. Lots of emergency training. They've organized themselves in work teams or in community circles. Scrubjub coordinators are organizing the volunteers—which is almost everyone. Clean up is going amazingly fast."

Another rock came careening down the mountain and smashed into the pile on top of the travelers' building. They cringed. "I've requested to go to the Dragon's Den," Nkiroo whispered. "With an engineering team."

Melawn tried not to get his hopes up. "Good. They did have air vents, so I have hope, but it's going to rain," Melawn said, looking up at the clouds.

"Good. We need water. We're building tanks and buckets. Any word from the Chike?"

"Tenshi said they would get a medical drop tomorrow. But that's all. No other help."

Nkiroo shook his head. "We're going to need food. Water."

"I think we're going to have to get it ourselves."

Melawn sent in his sad report from Yosemite:

11 fatalities

4 missing

37 serious injuries

0 buildings standing

60 Beasts unaccounted for

30% food supplies remaining

20% crops above water, draining in progress

Sending the weak and children upriver.

Reports from other villages were similar, with less severity as they moved upriver. Even Nile had one fatality, discovered on the side of the mountain.

5-Power Eve

Since it was storming, they now huddled inside the Temple, with the rain pounding down on the metal structure blissfully loud.

Every available container was set out, along with a big tank the engineers had built. Melawn wrapped his notebooks to protect them from water, and guarded them closely. He sat near the council's area, ready to help.

There was a commotion at the door and Etazann came in. She stopped in the entranceway, letting the water drip and taking off her cloak. Grace signaled Melawn to bring her, so they both came to the council, Melawn with his notebook.

"Council," Etazann started, "the Dragon's Den survives, but they have suffered heavy losses. Many caves and passageways have collapsed." Melawn clutched his chest, trying not to panic. "Many people are trapped or buried, but most of the leaders survived, including AnnaLee and Ellant." She turned to Melawn with a sad look. "There was no word about Thayne." Melawn tried to control his breathing.

"Fatalities?" Grace asked.

"Unknown number. At least 15."

"Oh, no." The council members gasped all around.

"More people are trapped and debris removal is slow. They still have access to their underwater spring. I've brought a sample. They're cut off from their food supply, so that's the focus of their digging."

Grace frowned. "They're not going after survivors first?"

"Council, my report is put together from lower-level people and guards. I wasn't admitted. The guards say the caves are individually vented, so they won't suffocate. The guards asked me to send help. We waited a day for an official message or a meeting but didn't get one."

The council members looked at each other, concerned. A man asked about the tunnel. "The tunnel is open on both sides, but the road is blocked on our side. Here's a sketch by our artist." She handed it to Melawn, who gave it to Grace, trying not to let her see his hand shake. The council conferred quietly for a moment.

"Road clearing will have to wait until spring. Melawn, help Etazann organize a food train over the mountain. And tell the Dragon's Den that Human life is the top priority. Take Tenshi with you."

"Should I ask for anything in return?" Etazann asked.

"No. This is not a negotiation. They are under our jurisdiction, whether they accept it or not."

Etazann nodded approvingly.

"Thank you Etazann. Get some food and make sure your team is settled. Then give the full details to Melawn." They were dismissed. As they headed to the support area, Melawn whispered to her, "Thayne? Any word?"

"No. I asked specifically. But DeeZann lives. I sent a message to Jadee already."

"Thank you." And he spent the night dreaming of cave-ins at the mining colony.

5-Power

81-Petals, incoming to Radium Junction

"Radium Junction beacon confirmed!"

She did it! My mom, Sequoia Melody Kelson Coralia, exited the Tyee a-rings at only .3JV and prejumped to Radium Junction!

Terina and the crew tumbled out of their cocoons and shook hands all around. They were even more excited than when Beezan did it, because this proved it wasn't a fluke. Her mom was thrilled and amazed and humble, even hugging Honor Beezan and saying, "I saw it. I get it." Ra'Tama was equally excited, in his reserved way, confident that he could do it too. *And I recorded it all! History again!*

It was only after all the celebrating that they realized Jarvie was very serious, hush-talking with the Captain. "What is it?" Beezan asked.

"Well, there is some confusion, but their population is around 2300," Jarvie said.

"Lord have mercy," Kelson said.

But the victory of the jump was with them and they rode

over the concern with confidence. "We can take them all," Iricana said, "but we'll be at *81*'s non-emergency limit."

"There's a ship beacon," Jarvie said, looking at Honor Beezan. "It's the *Wheel of Fire*."

Terina was puzzled. How did that relate to them? Beezan floated to a panel. "*Wheel*, this is *Drumheller*. Tiati, come in."

There was some delay and then a groggy voice. "It's 2:00 in the morning. This better be good."

A smile spread on Beezan's face that Terina had never seen. "Tiati! Good to hear your voice. Go to our secure channel." And he started to choke up.

There was a click and then, "*Bee?* God in heaven! That's twice you're back from the dead!" And you could hear Tiati trying not to cry. Beezan signaled for Iricana to take over while he recovered.

"Captain Tiati, this is Captain Iricana."

"Greetings Captain. God is most Glorious. But umm, you're the Captain?"

"We're actually in the *81-Petals*."

There was a long silence at the other end. Terina expected some funny comeback, but Tiati asked, "Where's the *Drumheller*? Is Beezan okay? Can I see him?"

"We'll go to visual soon. The *Drumheller* is stranded where we found the *81*."

"Bee, no worries. I'll help you get it back." Everyone smiled, even knowing it couldn't happen. "So wait. *81-Petals*? The crew too?"

"No. No crew, we'll explain later."

"So Captain, I can only take 500 more. How many can you take?"

"Between us, we can take them all."

"Yes! Truly, you are the answer to my prayers. But hey! Cap—Beezan, don't let that go to your head."

7-Power

Wheel of Fire, at Radium Junction Station

Tiati's locs curved around his brown face from a slight widow's peak. His eyebrows angled over his wide eyes and nose, barely noticeable over a blinding smile. Beezan floated aboard the *Wheel* into the drifting embrace of his old friend.

"Oh my God, it's been so long," Tiati said, nearly crushing Beezan. Neither of them could speak for a moment.

Finally, Beezan let go and wiped his eyes. "You're a married man now?" Beezan asked.

"Yes, come up and meet the family. And I hear you're a father."

"Jarvie. He's 16. Adopted."

"Well," another pat on the back, "count on you to skip the hard part."

Beezan laughed.

Beezan met Hana, as good-humored as her husband, and their three-month-old daughter, already smiling like her funny parents. It was only then that Beezan realized what a brave thing they were doing to stay at RJ, just to keep people calm, by keeping everyone thinking that they would have a ride. And finally, *81* had made it true.

Beezan shared lunch with them and had a tour of *Wheel*. He saw all the same issues with refugees that they had on *81* and they exchanged a few ideas. Finally, he and Tiati retired to the Command Bay alone, where Beezan told Tiati about the freejumping.

"You're messing with me."

"No joke. I swear. Have you noticed the ways are different?"

"People have been saying they're different for twenty years."

"Yes, but not before that. Look." Beezan plugged his s'link into Tiati's screen and showed him their logs, how quickly they had jumped, how close they had tipped in, how easy it had been.

Tiati studied them seriously. "Could you teach me?" And Beezan smiled.

"Did you think I came just to visit?"

81-Petals, at Radium Junction Station

"What?" Iricana gave Beezan the "you're complicating my life" look.

"I want to jump the *Wheel* with Tiati. Show him how it's done." Sky, who was included in this informal breakfast meeting, looked up at Beezan with interest, miffed since he'd gone to the *Wheel* without her. "Sequoia could jump the *81*."

"You don't have to prove anything."

"I want to teach him—teach everyone. All the pilots on both ships. Imagine how much faster we could get around. We could avoid the Chike."

"The freejumping takes its toll," she cautioned.

"Yes," Beezan agreed. "But it's temporary, just like regular jumping, and without all the laps in the chairs."

Iricana looked tempted. She glanced at Sky. "We'll be taking thousands of people."

"Sky go," Sky said matter-of-factly. And Iricana had a little stare down with her.

"Okay. You and Sky prejump the *Wheel*. But we go first."

· · ·

2-Speech Eve

Nile Village

After dinner, Melawn sat at his information table in the hallway of the temporary council building. He flexed his sore writing hand, only made worse by today's scrubjub assignment—four hours of chopping wood. At last, his Chike orientation had come in handy and he managed not to chop off his own leg. But the pounding had traveled to his head. So now he sat, huddled in his coat, miserable, but steadfastly maintaining his post.

"Melawn!" Grace came out of her office. "You are not on duty!"

"I—"

"No. Go. There's room in the new men's hall now. You work four hours in the morning. That's it."

"But—"

"But nothing. You are not my servant and I won't have it."

"I don't mind."

"I mind!" She scowled at him and then continued in a kinder voice. "There are plenty of spacers in the hall. Go make some new friends. Go."

"Yes, Grace," he submitted, gathering up his gear.

2-Speech

Back at his post, only a little bit early in the morning, Melawn recited some Hidden Words about being content with God until Etazann came clomping in. "I figured you'd be here at this hour. He's alive—your Thayne. Alive and kicking."

Melawn couldn't help it. He nearly collapsed on the table in relief. "Thank you. Thank you for the news."

Etazann shook her head in exasperation. "Well, he wasn't

sitting around suffering. He spent his time writing a secret message—that I'm supposed to deliver to the council without showing to anyone else." She handed Melawn a thick letter, sealed with yellow wax. "And here's the secret message from AnnaLee—not to be seen by anyone else." She handed him a folded letter, sealed in red. "And here's one from Ellant." A gray seal. "And a cart card for you."

Melawn smiled, thinking it was from Thayne, letting him know he was okay. "I don't know why you're pining for him," Etazann said, obviously fed up. "That place should be called the snake pit. We're doing all the digging while they're planning their next scheme!" She turned and clomped off.

Melawn, one hand still holding the secret letters, flipped open the cart card. It wasn't from Thayne. It was from Nkiroo, letting him know that Thayne and Tenshi and he were all okay. Melawn turned Thayne's packet around to look at it. No message for him. And then a cold chill went down his spine. He knew exactly what was in that packet. A part of him considered throwing it in the fire.

I'm not responsible for him, Melawn thought. *He is not my hero. He is no one's hero. I am content with God.* And he sat there until Grace came, and determinedly handed her all three letters.

So Thayne was alive. But the news did not make his head stop hurting or his heart lighter, especially when, for the first time, he heard raised voices in the council chamber.

3-Speech

Melawn found himself called to the council the next day, and they were in a fierce mood. They had not recessed since getting the Dragon's Den messages. He sat in a small sturdy chair facing all nine of them. He had brought his notebook, but quickly realized this was not an assignment. He set it down and gripped his hands together to stop shaking.

Grace stood and took some deep breaths before addressing him. "If you had known what was in that letter from Thayne—"

"I do know."

She was taken aback. "It was sealed."

"I know *him*. Inside that letter was an argument so conniving, so insidious, so subversive that it took a council 24 hours to see through it and reunify."

Grace paled. They all did. Then they all relaxed somewhat. Grace sat down. "He undermines this council. He undermines AnnaLee. He undermines Sector 1 Council! He is in need of strong guidance and supervision. He thinks he is some kind of . . ."

"Hero. A savior of humanity. And in some ways, he is."

Grace shook her head. "You're his follower."

"No."

"Nkiroo?"

"No."

"Tenshi?"

"She never was."

"What can we do to bring him in line?"

"Nothing."

The chairperson intervened. "What do you recommend?"

Melawn shrugged. "Let him have his little kingdom."

"And allow him to lead others astray?" the chairperson asked.

"Free will."

Although Grace seemed aggravated with Melawn personally, the chairperson was more detached. "If you could go back in time, and change anything regarding your interaction with Thayne, what would you do?"

Melawn was tired, cold, hungry, displaced and yet somehow reluctant to sever that last thread of loyalty to Thayne. *What's keeping me from freeing myself?*

"The council is asking," the chairperson said calmly.

"O SON OF MAN! Be thou content with Me and seek no other helper. For none but Me can ever suffice thee."[1] Slowly, Melawn sat up in the chair, repeating his contentment quote to himself. "I wish I'd never abandoned my parents for him." He blushed with shame to admit it. "And now that I want to be free, I'm stranded on the same planet. I am not . . . responsible . . . for him!" Melawn slumped in the chair.

Only Grace understood what it had taken for him to say that. "We've agreed to send you on the expedition," she said. Melawn looked up at her. "Thayne isn't going. And something is going on out there. We need a firsthand report we can trust. You and Tenshi will go with the Dragon's Den expedition. You'll be our eyes and ears."

Melawn nodded. The chairperson folded his hands in front of him. "You are correct. Thayne is not your responsibility. You have no obligation to him, ever. We are all responsible to God. You may go."

81-Petals, at Radium Junction Station

Beezan stayed on the *81-Petals* while people and cargo from RJ Station were being loaded. He'd been unassigned as second-in-command, which was a huge relief. The *thought* of being in charge of thousands of people. He shuddered. And Thunder was a great choice. But he'd still been invited to the opening of the Torus Tram. They departed from Arc 1 with the captain and engineering crew in the leading tram. There were eighteen cars, two for each arc. The trams only circled in one direction, from

Arc 1 to Arc 9 and then on to Arc 1 again. Today, they would stop at every arc and make some ceremonial exchanges.

Inside the tram, Beezan sat in a back seat, with Thunder beside him, sheltering him from the standing, cheering crowd. As the tram entered and exited the stations, Beezan watched the faces of the spectators flicker past, mixed with images of riders reflected off the windows. Mirages of real people. Just like strangers that he passed everywhere on the ship now, people with no names, no substance, just flickers.

4-Speech

81-Petals, in the Radium Junction a-rings, headed for Hamada

Terina sat in her jump chair, an hour in the rings now. *Destination: Hamada*, she reviewed her notes in her mind. 3045 people and 178 podpups on the *81-Petals*, with the *Wheel of Fire* behind. Her mom would be making the prejump, which is what they were calling jumping early from the rings. Aside from Ra'Tama, no other jump pilots had come aboard at any station. All had left Sector 8 except Tiati and his backup pilot.

Honor Beezan was on the *Wheel* with Tiati, trying to show the *Wheel* pilots how to prejump. And then what? Would they be split up to train others? Terina hoped not. She didn't want to miss out on this front row seat to history.

As chief passenger monitor, in charge of coordinating Passenger Lounges in all nine arcs, Katie had reported earlier, "Captain, everyone in jump chairs. 3014 are conscious for the jump. 178 pups are secure."

They'd only been in the rings an hour so Terina didn't expect anything yet, but quietly, her mom asked Ra'Tama, "Do you see it?"

"I was wondering," he answered. "But it's too soon."

"I wasn't looking," Jarvie admitted.

On the next lap, "Yes," both Jarvie and Ra'Tama said, amazed.

"Two more laps, to be sure," Sequoia said. "Say mark when you see it." Good, Terina thought. The bumps are painful and we've gotten spoiled.

"Mark!" They said together, and then were even more excited.

"Okay, the a-ring tunnel is a little in the way. We need those darn control panels. I'll have to adjust." Bump. "Next lap."

Terina tried to squeeze in one more prayer, but she was excited and distracted. Bump. Bump. Breathe. The bumps were not as close together as normal for a jump, as they hadn't been in the rings that long. Bump. "Mark!"

They thrusted out of the rings at an odd angle, as if to backtrack a tiny bit. Terina gripped the chair as they pulled several gees to the right. And then a major thrust into the path.

Wheel of Fire in the Radium Junction a-rings, headed for Hamada

"They're gone!" Tiati said.

"What? It's too soon," Beezan said, but he felt a little ripple.

"Ha! I know Sequoia. She'd have to jump sooner than you." Tiati laughed.

She *is* a long jumper, Beezan realized. And so is Tiati, despite his complete lack of decorum in the rings. Or anywhere. But he had a heart of fire. They had spent two days praying together and Beezan felt much more in tune with Tiati than Sequoia. "Can you see it?"

"Me?" Tiati asked, surprised. But then he went quiet. They

came around three more times, letting the pain of the bumps just roll past them. "Something," Tiati admitted.

Yes! Beezan could feel it now. "One more time, for certainty." Hamada. Last stop in Sector 8. Next lap.

Bump. Bump.

Emerge from behind the veil, by the leave of thy Lord, the All-Glorious, the Most Powerful.[2]

Bump. Bump. There. And copying Sequoia's move with the smaller *Wheel*, they were in the path. And Tiati was whooping like a wild man.

33 / IN TOO DEEP

81-Petals, incoming to Hamada System

Jarvie gripped the arms of his jump chair. They were in the path to Hamada, but struggling. The fireball blazed. As the path unraveled at the edges, Sequoia took them deeper to stay in. After so many easy jumps, Jarvie was unprepared and had a moment of panic. *Breathe, breathe.* The sentries descended on them. So many, he thought, as he slipped into unconsciousness.

He awoke with a headache, trying to focus on his screen. He couldn't read. "*81*, private."

"Private channel open."

"Report." He forced down a sip of water.

"Hamada beacon confirmed. Arrival in 6 days. Hamada Station status: need assistance. Secure from blue zones. Status of passengers incomplete."

Jarvie reeled from depression, wondering why he should even bother with his job. He tried to be stern with himself. Then he remembered Star, and focused on the pup to clear his head.

"Private channel off. Captain, Hamada beacon confirmed. ETA six days. Passenger monitor, please report."

A dazed Katie answered in a rough voice. "In Arc 1 alone, we have 3 red lights and 47 yellow. I'm not getting coherent reports from other arcs." A bad jump. They made it, but they went too deep. Probably because of the fireball. Even with thousands aboard, they had way too many yellow and red lights. "Sequoia?"

No answer. "Jarvie, she's got a yellow light," Katie told him. "Ra'Tama?"

"I'm here," Ra'Tama reported. "Jarvie, monitor please."

He'd forgotten totally. "Hamada Incoming Authority, this is *Drumheller*." He wiggled out of his brackets, unsealed his cocoon, and pulled off his helmet as he waited. Thousands of people were recovering from their first jump, and it was a bad one.

"*81*, where's the *Wheel*?"

"No beacon from *Wheel of Fire*."

The command crew met in the Conference Room as soon as they could walk. They forced themselves to eat and drink. Sequoia was in the Med Bay, but would be fine, physically. Mentally, she would be devastated, even though she had saved the ship, battling to keep it in the path despite the fireball.

Terina and Iricana checked figures on a map of the ship, Iricana reporting what they could confirm. "Total of 37 dead, and 3 podpups." Jarvie hugged Star to his chest. "There are 98 people in Med Bays."

"Is there any pattern to the deaths?" Ra'Tama asked quietly.

"*81*?" Iricana asked.

"Yes. Cause of death was cardiac arrest for all. All but one were over 80. None had an immediate family member with

them. Three had elderly podpups. All but one had not jumped for three years or had never jumped."

Jarvie despaired. The elderly may have been better off staying. Or they could have waited for people to befriend each other more. Or maybe they were just not so attached to the world and nothing would have made a difference.

"*81*," Iricana asked, "who was the one not over 80?"

"Yan Azure, Arc 8."

"*NO!*" Jarvie gasped. He clutched his chest and burst into tears. Only Star in his lap prevented him from banging his head on the table. *No!* Yan was too upset to jump and now he was gone. And now Jarvie could never make peace with him.

Thunder started a prayer for the departed as Terina tentatively patted Jarvie on the back. They sat in silence for a moment after. "There is one bit of good news," Iricana said quietly. "P&P at Hamada is 42 and 4. We'll be able to take them all."

There was a beep from Jarvie's s'link. "*Drumheller, Wheel.* Tiati here."

"Praise the Lord," Kelson whispered.

Iricana answered, "*Drumheller* here, Captain."

"*Drumheller*, we had a rough jump, but everyone made it through. We're a few days behind you though."

"*Wheel*," Iricana said, "we had a very bad jump with many casualties, none on the command crew. Sequoia is in the Med Bay. We can pick up everyone at Hamada. I recommend you proceed directly to the a-rings."

Wheel of Fire, headed for Hamada a-rings

Beezan shared Jarvie's sad story of Yan with Tiati in the

Wheel's Command Bay. Tiati shook his head in despair. "Poor Jarvie. Poor Sequoia. Poor Iricana. Hard times on that ship."

A diagram of Sector 8 floated on the main screen, showing all but Hamada deserted, and the *Wheel's* trajectory to the a-rings. "Abandoned after all," Beezan lamented. "After all those years we spent, trying to save these systems. All alone."

"All that struggle," Tiati agreed. "And for what?"

"Do you really think we need to abandon?" Beezan asked, hoping Tiati wouldn't think he was questioning the council.

"You didn't see the Chike. Hear them. Their ships were so advanced. They had their own gravity balls. Their disdain for us, it was so thick. You could hear it through the translators." Tiati shivered. "They took the councils God knows where. They're no one to trifle with. The councils were trying to save us so they made a deal. That they would go with the Chike if they couldn't clear the sector. They sacrificed themselves."

"How advanced could these Chike be if they're leaving people stranded in stations?"

"They say we're ignorant to live on the stations. They called them space prisons. As if we had a large selection of nice planets to pick from instead. So people think they must be terraformers. And where are they taking the councils?"

Beezan looked away. He fully intended to tell Tiati what he knew. But he forced himself to wait for permission from Iricana.

"And this quest that they're on," Tiati continued. "This hunt for the harbingers. It makes no sense. Why would they be looking for a Human?"

Hana knocked and Tiati waved her in, changing back to his joking self. "I don't know how Beezan survived without me all these years."

"It was crazy to fly solo for so many years, but neither of us would give up our ships," Beezan agreed. *It was so lonely,* Beezan thought. *I'm not sure I'll ever recover.*

Tiati reached out and gripped Beezan's arm. "Beezan my friend, come with us. Bring your 16-year-old. When we get the refugees settled, we'll go for the *Drumheller.*"

"They'll never let us."

"Well, maybe we won't then. But seriously, either way. *Drumheller,* or stay with us. Hana's got four sisters aboard."

"Don't scare him," Hana laughed.

Beezan was touched. "I can't desert my crew. We have a mission."

"Now or later. You think about it. My deck is always open."

And Tiati didn't pressure him, aside from a family dinner with the many sisters of Hana. They were lively, but sensible. But Sky did not approve, which was odd, as podpups were known to be little matchmakers.

81-Petals, incoming to Hamada Station

As the Captain's diplomat, Jarvie should have attended all the funerals, but he couldn't, he was so distraught over the one. Terina and Taj accompanied him to Yan's funeral in Arc 8.

He could see now that in his 12-year-old grief and anger he had never given Yan a chance. He'd pushed him away and then thrown him aside. Of course, he was full of regret now. But if he were to relive that moment, that point of running away or not, of getting Yan in trouble or finding a better way, would he do it again? Would he throw away his life with Beezan, or stick with Yan, with station life, with the Sundering and the sorrow? He could not bring himself to wish he had never run away. During the funeral, he didn't speak or even offer a prayer aloud for Yan. He didn't come to know Yan any better. He only came to know the truth of his own actions. *How do you ask for forgiveness for something you don't really regret?*

Taj and Terina took him back on the tram, sitting with other somber, tired, depressed people on various sad visits. *One more day of funerals.* It wasn't like the outer sectors had no experience with these things. He wished for Star on the ride back, but that pup could not be trusted to behave at a funeral.

They stopped by the new podpup nursery in Arc 1 to pick up their pups. Arc 1 had 17 pups assigned, but it looked like they had a lot of visitors. As soon as Jarvie came in, the pups detected his mood, and a wave of sympathy passed over him. They tumbled over to him, none faster than Star or Rocket.

Jarvie gave into it and sat down, letting them surround him. He picked up Star and sat there, just soaking in the affection. He was heartbroken and guilty about Yan, but the bad jump was fading. And a bold, almost Ramian-like plan came to him.

Jarvie buzzed at Ra'Tama's door, Star squiggling in his arms. He was nervous as he'd never been here—never been invited, never stopped by. The door slid open. Ra'Tama stood at the foot of the stairs, giving Jarvie a cautious, but not unfriendly look. Vante Kay gave a slight nod and disappeared through the adjoining door, closing it. Jarvie feared he was interrupting something, but of course, Star broke free and scampered down the stairs to look for Cookie.

"Please come in, Honor Jarvie."

Honor? Jarvie came down as calmly and quietly as possible, putting on his best pilot manners. "God is Most Glorious," he said formally to Ra'Tama, and "here." He handed over two podpup treats. "I thought—in case they need to bond over treats."

Ra'Tama smiled. Although quiet, he seemed pleased to see Jarvie. He walked over to the pups and gave the treats, "one for each."

"Good Ra'Tama," they both said.

"How about for us?" Ra'Tama asked.

"Oh, a treat, ahh . . ."

Ra'Tama laughed and gestured for Jarvie to sit at the table. He brought out a tin of candied pumpkin seeds and put a large scoopful in a bowl for Jarvie. "Wow, thank you!" Jarvie said, and laughed, knowing he sounded as enthusiastic as the pups.

They ate quietly for a bit, enjoying them. Then Jarvie deflated a bit from his bold plan. "Well, I had this wild idea, to ask you, but maybe it's not fair."

"Ask."

Jarvie took a breath. "You know, we're not going to Sandune, since Tiati said it was abandoned."

"Right. We're going to Redrock."

"Well. It's kind of a special jump to me. I thought maybe I could try it."

Ra'Tama's eyes went comically wide at the same moment he crunched a seed. They sat there frozen. Finally, Ra'Tama said, "I was told you are in training."

"Yes."

"And you have not even jumped a regular jump by yourself."

"True."

"And you haven't achieved . . . the calm."

"Not nearly," Jarvie admitted.

"And you most likely will not be a long jumper."

"I don't know, but I see the paths, same as you."

"Can you get into the path and keep us there, without—without going too deep?"

"I don't know. I don't know if anyone can anymore. I just want to try."

"Why now?"

Jarvie got the sense that Ra'Tama wasn't being defensive. He was asking mildly and trying to understand. "I know it's your turn. But I'd like to try while Beezan is on the *Wheel*. Without Beezan knowing. And it was my first jump with Beezan."

"Ahh." Ra'Tama sat back and thought a long time. Then he nodded. "I defer my turn to you, provided the Captain and Sequoia agree."

"Thank you!" Jarvie was both thrilled and a little scared. He resumed eating his seeds, but slower, so he could stay a little longer.

"Have you done your gym time today?" Ra'Tama asked.

"No. Not for days. And Katie is after me about it."

"I find myself behind schedule too. Would you like to go together?"

"That would be great!" Jarvie smiled. "Wait. Did Katie put you up to this?"

"No. I thought she told you to collect me and that's why you were here."

"Well. She thinks she has her schemes. But we have our own schemes." Although it was entirely possible that she had out-schemed both of them.

Ra'Tama took his two last seeds and gave one to each pup. He had a generosity of spirit that Jarvie admired. Different, quieter, than Canim, but something to aspire to. Jarvie swallowed hard, thinking of his lost family, his lost brother. Now he'd found a new family, and maybe a new brother. Or was all this just temporary, like his bond with far-off little Quay?

• • •

Sandstorm

Zahar sat by herself in the beautiful but dim little kitchen that Chike engineering built in their former auditorium. It was late and Caspia, Evan, and Quay had gone to bed.

The Chike provided everything they needed, except their people. She liked the others, and she was relieved to be away from Thayne, but she missed her big family. Quay's door slid open and he headed her way, but stopped. "Come," she said. "It's so quiet here."

"It's midnight."

She shrugged. Quay got some green Chike crackers and sat down, offering her some. "Oh, no, thanks. They taste like seaweed."

"That's why I like them. They remind me of my family."

"Seaweed reminds you?"

"My parents ate food like this. They grew up at sea."

"Like on an island?"

"No, on a sailing ship. That's where they met."

"Wow! Hard to imagine. Being on such big water."

"We're an ocean-going people. All our planets have oceans."

All . . . it boggled her mind. "The only oceans we've found were under a lot of ice."

"They really miss the sailing, but they went to space. He looked up sadly and said, "I'm sorry, I know you miss your family too."

"I miss the noise."

"Noise?"

"My parents and three little sisters, my aunts, uncles, cousins, visitors. Always cooking, singing, playing games, being silly. Helping each other. We all lived together in a three-family unit. Always something going on."

He smiled. "What station?"

"Oh, we lived planetside, in habs of course, on Canyon, one of the food baskets of the outer sectors. My people were farmers. Some might be on shift at the mass driver, in the greenhouses, or even on the orbiting platforms. Everything at Canyon is coordinated, mass driver launches, spaceport launches, the big lights in orbit, jumps. It was so exciting to go to the port and see the shuttles coming and going. I wanted to be part of that. So I went to monitor training." He nodded for her to go on as he crunched his green crackers.

"It was a good life."

"How did you end up on the *Cheetah*?"

She frowned. "It's classified. Not that it matters now. When I was training at the incoming authority station, a ship came in from Luminesse. Talk of aliens. I had to be quarantined. It was supposed to be temporary."

"I know that story," Quay said, sitting up, wide-eyed. "My friend Jarvie. So long ago. Small galaxy. And now you can't go home."

She leaned over the table to grab his wrist. "I'm not giving up! We're both going to get home!"

"I hope—"

The outer door slid open with no warning. *Are they listening to us?* Pascal stepped in. They hadn't seen zir in weeks, not since the mourning ritual. And now, here ze was, stalking in with no guards as if ze was their midnight snack buddy.

They scrambled to their feet. "Exempt," they said, giving small bows, Quay brushing cracker crumbs off his sleeping clothes.

Pascal's snout swung to the side. "This one has news."

"Should I wake the others?" Zahar asked.

"Wake them early tomorrow. The last harbinger has been found."

They gasped.

"Tomorrow," ze continued, "we begin the long voyage to the convocation."

"Yes, Exempt," Quay answered.

Ze nodded but continued to stare at them with one eye and then the other.

"Exempt," Zahar asked, "are you okay?"

Alarmed by the question, Quay said, "Meaning, Exempt, have we personally offended in some way?"

No, that is not what I'm meaning.

But Pascal answered calmly. "This one is . . . ready." And ze turned and left.

"Ready for what?" Quay asked. "To jump? To talk to us again?"

"To go home," Zahar answered.

9-Speech

81-Petals, incoming to Hamada Station

Terina arrived at yoga after Ra'Tama and Jarvie had already picked their spots in the gym. She had a little pang of worry that Jarvie wouldn't be her friend anymore, since Ra'Tama arrived. She realized she'd thought of Jarvie as a replacement brother since she was unlikely to ever see her own brother again. But Jarvie had lost his brother too, and she was no substitute. It would be good for Jarvie and Ra'Tama to be friends, so she decided to be okay about it. However, Jarvie greeted her as usual and they made space for her.

Ra'Tama even talked to her. "No Rocket?"

"Huh. That pup. He loves being in the nursery. I think it's good for him to run around. He actually sleeps at night."

"Oh, good for you, too," Jarvie laughed. They stopped talking as soon as Katie came in to lead the class. Terina couldn't help but notice how coordinated and graceful Ra'Tama was, as if he were past the gangly stage Jarvie now suffered.

They were first out the door after class, still in their exercise clothes. But as soon as they got to the rimway, they heard raised voices. Jarvie hurried that way, with Terina and Ra'Tama following. There were a lot of people out, most pressed together in a little group.

"Leave her alone!" was the first thing Terina clearly heard. Shockingly, it was her grandfather, but not in a tone of voice she had ever heard: firm, commanding, almost angry. "This is a ship!"

"This is Arc 1," Kay Ling added, as Terina and Ra'Tama approached in Jarvie's wake. *Mom!* Someone was harassing her mom, who was pressed against the rimway wall, surrounded. She was frozen, arms crossed in front of her and head down. Terina's grandfather and Kay Ling stood between her mom and the unruly crowd. And something in Kay Ling's expression made Terina wonder why anyone would mess with her.

A man, old enough to know better, stood belligerently close to Kay Ling. "It's a ship. So what? It's not illegal to ask questions." He actually reached over and tugged on her mom's pilot jacket. People gasped. "Like why isn't she retired? After killing all those people." People gasped again and some objected, telling him to chill and leave it.

Jarvie's eyes nearly popped when the man touched Sequoia's jacket, but suddenly Kay Ling had a vice grip on his arm. "She saved the ship! And thousands of us! She's a hero!"

"So why are people dead?"

Kelson, with a look of such piercing focus, like the most intimidating, fear-inducing professor, took a step toward him. "You're out of line." Terina thought he wanted to say something else, but realized that they couldn't tell people about the pulsing star or they would panic. They had no idea what

Sequoia had done for them. "You need to use your ship manners here, and that means leaving the pilots alone."

"We have a right to our questions, and since there's no ArcRep, I'm going to ask."

Jarvie towered over the crowd. "Enough!" he said, more mildly than Terina expected. "Enough. Disperse." A few people broke away, shaking their heads or muttering they were just trying to help.

Kay Ling released the man and he took a step back, but didn't leave. He turned to Jarvie. "Who are you to tell me where to go?" *Good God*, Terina thought. Everyone knew Jarvie, even if he wasn't in uniform.

"I'm the Captain's diplomat."

The man looked up and down at Jarvie. "You don't look very diplomatic!" That was just too much, even for the crowd.

"Who are you?" Ra'Tama asked in a voice like ice. Kay Ling immediately stepped between Ra'Tama and the man, leaving Jarvie to step in front of Sequoia.

"Name's Prendez. Arc 6. Tell it to your captain."

"Prendez from Arc 6," Ra'Tama continued, "you will return there immediately, or we will return you. And you will not enter Arc 1 again without the Captain's permission." Terina was stunned. Ra'Tama, so mild-mannered. His voice was still quiet, but there was the absolute expectation of obedience. *Of course, he's a ship Captain, not just some substitute brother.*

"Come on Prendez," some of his friends said and started to press him away. He slapped their hands off him.

"Murderer," he muttered as he turned to stalk off, but he caught her mom's eye and she leveled a stern, dark look at him that made him step a little quicker.

Jarvie signaled for people to move aside so Kelson could

escort her mom onto their cabin. It was just so shocking to see people behave like that. Not just ignorance of ship courtesy, but outright rudeness, like you'd read about in old books. Books she'd thought were fiction. But maybe that sort of behavior sometimes bubbled up from the past.

She shook herself and hurried after her mom, slipping into their cabin with her and her grandpa. "Mom, are you okay? He was so terrible! And I know they explained ship manners."

Her mom sat down on a small foldout bunk and Kelson sat by her and put an arm around her. Terina sat on her other side and hugged her. "Well, I thought I was fine. But I didn't count on having to deal with such a fool."

"The wise don't need advice and fools won't take it," Kelson chimed in.

Terina and her mom laughed briefly. Sometimes it was good to have a saying. "You really are a hero, Mom."

She smiled and hugged Terina. "But clearly," her mom said, "I can't jump." She stared down at her hands shaking in her lap. "People need some time. I need time. And it's too late to rendezvous with *Wheel* to get Beezan back. It's Ra'Tama's turn anyway."

18-Speech

81-Petals, heading to Hamada a-rings

"Jarvie?" Both Iricana and Terina's mom repeated when Ra'Tama suggested it during the Redrock pre-jump meeting.

"I would be backup, of course," Ra'Tama added.

"He's . . . well . . . he's, he's only 16," her mom objected.

"Everyone has to jump the first time," Ra'Tama said softly. "I was only 12."

Her mom frowned. Terina knew her mom had jumped when she was 9. It wasn't even supposed to be her jump.

"And Hamada to Redrock is probably the easiest jump in the outer sectors. It's a good first jump," Ra'Tama argued.

Terina's mom surprised her. She was more open to new ideas lately. More accepting of Beezan. Willing to consider Jarvie. "Well," her mom looked at Jarvie, "I know you can see the path, so I'm willing."

Iricana asked, "Wouldn't you rather wait until Beezan gets back?"

"No," Jarvie said. "I want to follow him."

1-Questions

The population of the *81-Petals* was now officially 3051, with the Hamada people aboard. *Voting Day!* Terina wrote in her journal. The captain had decided that electing ArcReps would help people channel their grievances in more appropriate ways than attacking pilots in the rimway.

After breakfast and Feast, Terina set up her gear in the Arc 1 auditorium. They had official broadcasts from every arc. All arcs were to hold their voting at the same time, each electing an Arc Committee of five that would then choose who would be Chairperson, Clerk, Treasurer, ArcRep, and TechRep. There were no nominations or declarations for office. Everyone 15 or over would write on actual paper five names of people in their arc they felt were qualified. It was hoped they would get a good variety of people who were not eager for power. The catch to this system was that if you were elected, you had to serve. Terina, too young to vote, was allowed to observe as a journalist.

Command crew, jump pilots, people under 15, agents, and a

few others, such as the red-banded, or people like Ulf, were not eligible.

They couldn't fit everyone in the auditorium, where the voting would take place, so the feed was going to four other large rooms, including the gym, where people sat on rows of colorful yoga mats.

Generally, 14-year-olds were posted as witnesses, but there weren't enough, so the captain appointed three people in each arc to sit at the balloting table and witness.

Her grandfather read descriptions of the five jobs and other members of the command crew read prayers. Everyone was perfectly silent. For the first time, Terina realized how loud the ship was, now that it was full, with all the fans and pipes working.

After ten minutes of silence, the first row of people approached the table, ran their p'link over the scanner to be counted, and dropped their ballot in the transparent box. Row by row, as quietly and reverently as possible, people filed past the box, dropping in their lists of five.

As the auditorium emptied, people from the other rooms lined the rimway to enter and vote. Everything was silent and orderly. All other rimway traffic was suspended. Although they were not eligible, the command crew and pilots were allowed to vote. So Jarvie cast two ballots, his own, and the only absentee ballot, printed out by *81-Petals* at Beezan's request.

Most of the people aboard had experienced a vote like this before, from their lives on large stations or ships. To the Earth-born, it was normal. But there were some, especially from Sector 8, that had lived their entire lives in such small populations that there was never a vote.

When the last Arc 1 vote was collected, the five tellers, three witnesses, and Terina remained inside and the doors were locked. Terina could see on the top screens the same scene playing out in each arc.

Although strict silence was no longer observed, the sacred and reverent nature of the vote prevailed for several hours as every ballot was tallied by hand.

"There is no tie," a teller announced, and everyone gave a sigh of relief. Five names were written on a card. All tellers and witnesses signed. The card was put in an envelope and sealed with a wax strip and then signed again by the head teller.

Terina looked up at the screens. Two arcs had to run tiebreakers, which they did over the p'links, but it would take another twenty minutes or so. Meanwhile, the captain came in and sat at the balloting table. Arc by arc, witnesses and head tellers arrived, handing over their envelopes. There was both patience and anticipation in the room.

Finally, hours after they began, the nine envelopes from nine arcs were stacked in front of the Captain. Terina almost laughed to herself. Everyone thought it took a long time. As a historian, she might be the only one aboard that knew how long elections took in the bad old days. Months of campaigning and advertising and lies and accusations, until the populace was so sick of it, they didn't even bother to vote. This was all done in one day.

Iricana keyed her microphone. "Community of *81-Petals*, the vote is complete. Please reassemble." There was another long pause as everyone sat in one of the designated rooms. After watching the screens, Iricana finally picked up the first envelope. The witnesses and teller stood behind her as she showed it and opened it and took out the card. "ArcCom 1: Danbi, Eli, Hiro, Kamaria, Maura." There were sighs of relief and the nodding of heads.

A witness stepped forward. "I move to confirm the vote."

A second witness stepped forward. "I second."

"All those in favor?" Iricana asked. This vote was by p'link and the tally rocketed up on the screen. In favor: 274. No negative votes were taken. The voting population of Arc 1 was 275. If the number passed 138, the vote passed. Only one person didn't vote in favor, either distracted or in dissent. But it didn't matter. "The vote carries. ArcCom 1, please retire to Consultation Hall."

The process was repeated for Arcs 2-9, with unfamiliar names, tellers, and witnesses. When it was done and the command crew met for dinner, the Captain was exhausted, but happy. "Finally," she said. "We're an official community."

Thunder patted her on the back, "And you're not the boss of everything anymore."

"Fine with me."

And Terina felt a difference, walking out in the now-busy rimway. There was a sense of group accomplishment, of organization and togetherness. They were now all *81-Petals*. Now all the little problems the command crew had to deal with, like people not getting along, or requests for repairs or coordination of service projects, would go through the ArcComs.

Best of all, this was a structure that most stationers understood. Despite their recent upheavals, people were more upbeat and hopeful. She was glad it was done before they jumped.

And by evening, there were nine additional newsfeeds on the *81-Petals*: ArcComNews 1-9. ArcCom 1 announced their roles: Danbi, a doctor from RJ, was the chairperson. Maura was the ArcRep, who would represent Arc 1 on a Captain's advisory committee of nine. Another RJ person, Eli, would be clerk. Technical rep would be Kamaria, the former RJ commander; and Hiro would be Treasurer, keeping donations to the councils and charity in order.

Terina met a shocked Maura in the rimway. "Good luck to you," she said, but Maura just shook her head in shock.

"ArcRep?" she muttered. "I don't mind the bossin', but they said I gotta be patient!"

3-Questions

81-Petals, in the Hamada a-rings, headed for Redrock

Jarvie sat nervously in Pilot 1, locking on his last bracket. Beside him, in Pilot 2, Ra'Tama ran through all the routine stuff, allowing Jarvie to stay in a meditative state.

He'd barely slept. The reality of actually being the jump pilot haunted him all night. It was one thing to see the path, but to actually be the one to get in the path, and drag a huge physical entity with you? His whole mind went into denial that anyone could do such a thing. *Clarity*, he kept reminding himself. *Calm. Confidence. Craz-no! Calm.* Everyone on the ship should be praying by now. He and Ra'Tama had started hours earlier, when the *Wheel* was jumping. And only 1 hour and 43 minutes after entering the rings, Tiati jumped. Ra'Tama and Jarvie felt the ripple as it went. Jarvie tried to imprint that feeling on his soul. *That's the way.*

A tiny, quick woman with reddish-brown skin and short, straight, black hair entered the Command Bay. She was one of the Tundra monitors. "Falcon, reporting as monitor, Captain."

"Welcome to the command crew, Falcon," Iricana replied. "Please take Monitor 1." Although Falcon was a station monitor, she'd previously been with ships, as evidenced by her seven ship pins. She snapped into the brackets with no trouble.

I'm already tired, Jarvie thought. *It takes so long to get 3050 people situated for jump.* "Twenty minutes until a-ring entry," Falcon reported. And a few minutes later: "All secure for jump. Sixteen conscious. All podpups secure."

"We're go for jump," Iricana said. "See you on the other

side." And as if she had not the slightest doubt in him, she took her jump drug.

They entered the a-rings at reasonable speed. They'd agreed that Ra'Tama would manage the rings, so Jarvie could concentrate. So really, he wasn't doing the whole jump. Jarvie's excitement drifted away as the laps built up and the pain increased.

Jarvie opened his mind cautiously, getting a feel for the crew, and was greatly relieved to sense a solidarity of purpose. Redrock. Sector 7. Redrock, the scene of his 17-week run with Beezan. One of his favorite places as a child. But thinking of his family now could be dangerous, so he gently pushed them out of his mind. He felt no pressure to jump early, only to get it right, even if they had to go the full time.

After three hours, he had to admit to himself, he saw the path. Ra'Tama barely cleared his throat. "Yes, I see it," Jarvie said.

"Countdown?" Ra'Tama suggested.

"Yes, please Falcon. Three laps, could you?" Jarvie asked. He took some deep breaths, and focused on some final prayers.

Without feet they tread the path of the spirit, and without wings they rise unto the exalted heights of divine unity. With every fleeting breath they cover the immensity of space, and at every moment traverse the kingdoms of the visible and the invisible.[1]

"To me," Jarvie whispered, taking the controls for the final two laps.

I desire that you may see the divine ships. These ships are the blessed sails who are traversing the sea of Divine mercy; their propellors are the powers of spiritual love and their captains are the inspiration of the Holy Spirit. No ship is ever wrecked in this sea; its waves are life-giving. Each one of the friends of God is like unto an ark of Salvation. Each ark saves

***many souls from the storms of troubles. The signs and traces of these sails are never-ending and eternal. The future centuries and cycles are like the sea on the surface of which these arks glide blissfully toward their spiritual destination.*[2]**

Next lap. Next lap. Into the path. Jarvie was shaking with terror. Had anyone ever ripped a ship apart? *No! Focus. There!*

Jarvie boosted out of the ring in the right direction. The path was clear, but he had to make several small burns, almost panicking that it was evading him. Just going the right direction wasn't enough. He had to get his mind and soul in the path, and take the ship with him.

His implants buzzed annoyingly, but as he centered on the path, the waves became longer and smoother. He pictured wrapping the ship around him like the shell of an ancient sea creature. And suddenly, surprisingly, they were in the path. *Yes!*

Now stay in. The fireball was pulsing in their direction, but not as intensely as the last jump. The pulses were near enough to scare them, but not actually running along their thread. Jarvie focused on the path, centered himself in it, and held on. He felt Ra'Tama with him, steady.

Sentries again! Thousands, pressing forward, like their last bad jump. But the annoying buzzing had given way to long waves of resonance, as if his mind or spirit had blissfully synced up with the path between the stars. He could feel up and down that wave. And the call of salvation, a mass ahead. And paths!—converging ahead in a mess.

His moment of bliss snapped back to fear. That was the star ahead, and he had to tip out. *Wait or go?* Not too far. He sensed a small mass and immediately tipped out. *Normal space, please please.* His stretched-out mind was still riding the wave. He pulled as if to tear it away and it finally yanked back into normal space.

Everything he thought he knew about pilots and jumping had been a mere glimpse of the terror it really was. His own mind was pulsing with a hundred paths. "Beacon?" he whispered and Falcon replied. "Redrock beacon confirmed." *Yes!* His mind struggled to stay in his head as he collapsed in his chair, delirious with relief.

8-Honor

Redrock Station

Jarvie stood as inconspicuously as his height and pilot status allowed at the back of the ops room on Redrock Station. He was happy to be allowed to wait here as Tiati, Beezan, Iricana, and Kelson met with the Redrock Council.

The huge screen in ops was filled with beacons: the a-rings, outposts, Second Station, ships, shuttles, docking rings, tagged asteroids, and repair tugs. Blue trajectories for incoming vessels arced toward Redrock Station, while curved yellow paths towards the a-rings marked outgoing ships. On the right, three ships were listed on the Incoming Ship Tracker. *Wheel of Fire* was on the docking ring, and *"Drumheller"* was in stationkeeping, too far for the casual observer to see clearly.

Monitors worked at their panels, talking calmly to pilots and captains. Jarvie took some deep breaths, as if he could inhale the ordered thrill of ships coming and going.

• • •

Jarvie had only had a moment to greet Beezan and Sky before they disappeared into the council chamber. He'd been introduced to Tiati and felt his warm friendliness. He was surprisingly sensitive to people after his first jump. He really hadn't expected anything, had sometimes even wondered why they coddled pilots so. But it was as if the emotions of people swirled around him. Intentions seemed more intense. Someone's looking his way was not a glance, but an inquisition. Why would connecting to galactic threads connect him more to people? And why would connections make him shyer? Or was it just his reaction? Tiati was as bold as a Ramian.

Iricana was handing over all the information from Veez to the council here instead of going to Mirage. Details about the colony, the Gens, finding the *81-Petals*, everything. She didn't want the *81* to be the only ship carrying it. But Jarvie remained outside the chambers, at the back of the ops room. After an hour or so, Jarvie was offered a chair and a snack, which he accepted gratefully. An hour later, he was gifted with Sky, too grumpy to continue in the meeting. "What's the matter?" he asked, pulling her into his lap.

"Talk." She was mollified by a bit of cookie, and then fell asleep while he patted her. Jarvie was half asleep too when they finally collected him, Iricana and Tiati holding actual binders they'd been given by the council. *Secret orders.*

Just outside the door, Tiati went to hug Beezan. "Well, my friend—" Alarms went off in the ops room. They crowded in, watching the screen.

"Chike ship inbound" was flashing at the top and a blinking white icon appeared on the screen, some 7-8 days out. There were gasps all around. "One. Only one," he heard people say. The door from the council chamber slid open. Jarvie jumped out of the way as council members rushed into the ops room.

"Get to your ships!" one said to them.

Beezan and Tiati hugged quickly, Beezan pushing Tiati gently by the arm, "Go!" Tiati took off running. Sky was whimpering, so Jarvie passed her back to Beezan. Iricana was recalling their two other teams that were on station, but they could not run with Kelson.

"I'll go ahead!" he said, and ran toward the hangar sections of Redrock Station. Jarvie had to cross through ten stacks to get to the hangar. So many locks.

No need to panic, he told himself. That Chike ship was days out. Of course, it would take them days to get anywhere, so maybe they should panic. And who knew how fast a Chike ship could go? Double panic.

Jarvie walked quickly through crowded areas, not wanting to cause a panic. People showed great deference to him, and not just because of the jacket. It was as if he were surrounded by a soft bubble of pilotness that gently pressed the crowd aside.

Running now. Double locks to the parking level, checking every door for the green good air light. Breathing too hard. Not exercising enough. Pounding footsteps behind him. Teeve and company. Jarvie held the door. "Cook's about five minutes behind," Teeve reported.

Jarvie nodded, gasping. Through that final lock, carefully following the pedestrian paths marked in green. Row 12. They found the beat-up *Pinecone*, a shuttle that looked like it belonged to *Drumheller*.

Aboard, Teeve's team stowed their mechanical supplies, passing them hand over hand rather than trying to squeeze past each other in the aisle. Jarvie could see and hear other people running to their shuttles. The cook and her team clamored in, passing their supplies as Teeve had. They filled in the back seats, leaving the ones by the door clear.

Finally, Beezan sprinted up the ramp, deposited Sky in her box and slid into the co-pilot chair. "To you?" Jarvie asked.

"No. Keep it."

Pleased but still panicked, Jarvie asked for a count. They'd come with 17, but seven were staying and Beezan was added. "We need 11 and 1."

Beezan popped back to the main cabin, helping Kelson into a seat. "You good?"

"Yes, son. Fine, fine." But Beezan handed Iricana a medkit and she strapped in next to Kelson. Beezan called for a countoff starting in the back with Teeve.

"Good," Beezan reported back to Jarvie, strapping in. "11 and 1." He reached for his panel. "Redrock Hangar 1, shuttle *Pinecone*, deparking. Request clearance for departure."

"*Pinecone,* you'll be fifth in line. Stand by."

Beezan took a few breaths as they were pulled down the ramp and reclamped to the circular platform that would take them to the launch lock. He glanced over to the concentrating Jarvie. Something was different. Had something happened on the *81*? Iricana would have told him. First Sky acting grumpy and now this. Beezan reached over and patted Jarvie on the shoulder and he jumped a mile. "Sorry!"

"Oh," Jarvie shivered. "It's okay. Sorry. Welcome back." Beezan heard Iricana ordering everyone on the *81* into their chairs. They were going to try to outrun the Chike. Something told him that was foolhardy. But then, she was the one flipping through the top secret binder.

One shuttle was still in front of them when their comm system made a strange loud crackle. The people in the cabin threw their hands over their ears as if they knew what was coming—a blaring announcement. Beezan tried to turn it down, but it was useless.

"Hear this! / Hark! / Attention! Lesser ones: Sector 1 migration / inbound evacuation / ingathering of this system will begin. You have 100 days. No outward travel will be permitted. All ships will be inspected / scanned / reviewed before jumping, beginning in 12 hours at the a-rings."

"It's the Chike!" Someone shouted to the bewildered *81* crew.

Inspections? No one mentioned that before.

"We call on all beholders / onlookers / witnesses to present yourselves! Your duty / calling / mission is upon you! All ships will comply! / obey! / submit!" A loud incomprehensible garble followed, which Beezan assumed was the same message in Chike, however useless.

Finally, it stopped. Jarvie hastily checked systems and trajectories while Beezan, heart pounding, tried to clear his head. Only gradually did he realize that Sky was whimpering even more than before, but he could not get her as they were boosting. "It's okay Sky," he called to her. "I'm right here. Going home now." But not really. Home was the *Drumheller*. And she just kept whining.

Moments later the Chike ship disappeared from the Ship Tracker. Beezan said nothing, half not wanting to bother Jarvie as he was piloting, and half distracted by Sky's continued crying. Usually so good, he wondered what was wrong with her.

Back on the *81-Petals*, Beezan rode the lift with Iricana and Jarvie. Sky's whining was giving him a headache, so he held her close in the podpup pocket while he held his head with his other hand, struggling to focus on what Iricana was saying.

"We'll be going to Harbor, while Tiati goes to Firelight, to see if there is a route open to Earth." He barely got to say goodbye to Tiati. And now he was gone. And something was funny with Jarvie.

Jarvie reached out to pat Sky and touched Beezan's arm. It was almost electric. Their eyes met. "You!" Beezan said, shocked. "You're a pilot! You've jumped!" He swung to Iricana with a surge of *how could you?*

But Jarvie answered. "I wanted to follow you."

"We thought it would be better if you didn't worry," Iricana added.

Worry? I would have been freaked out. But still—"Wait. You did it!"

"Yes. Way scarier than I thought it would be."

He reached out to hug Jarvie but another wave of pain came from Sky. "Ahhh."

The lift doors opened. "We better get you, both of you, to the Med Bay," Iricana said, as Jarvie guided him down the rimway. "What's wrong with her?"

"I don't know," Beezan answered. "It happened just as we left the station. It got worse when we got the Chike message."

9-Honor

81-Petals, headed for Redrock a-rings

The next day, Terina was helping in the Med Bay's new podpup zone when Honor Beezan came in to collect Sky. He looked stressed and worried, which could have been from sleeping overnight in 1.2 gee. Thank heavens Captain had backed off this morning to .98 gee. But they did need to get to the a-rings.

"She's fine," Dr. Katie told Beezan as soon as he came in.

"There's no physical reason for her agitation, although, clearly, she is unhappy about something. However," Katie steered Beezan closer to Terina and away from Sky's bed. "I thought you should know . . ."

"What?" Beezan gasped.

Katie patted his arm. "It's okay. It's just that we ran deep DNA scans, and discovered that Sky is different than all the other pups."

"Different? A disorder? Mutation?"

"She appears healthy, so either a mutation or just something about podpups we don't understand. We know so little about them."

Beezan glanced nervously at the aide, who was getting Sky ready. "But," Katie continued, "There is a theory." She glanced at Terina. "Have you ever heard of locusts?"

"Yes," Terina answered enthusiastically. "They were a kind of insect on Earth that would swarm. They would eat all the crops."

"Yes," Katie nodded. "They had two phases, a quiet, solitary one, and a swarming aggressive one. Also with bees. They might create a new queen and swarm, looking for a new hive."

"But, podpups aren't hive-like, are they?" Beezan asked.

"They were discovered in a hive-like arrangement of pods," Katie answered.

"Which they could not have built themselves," Beezan said.

"Right. Not podpups as we know them. And many people think it was a nursery. But we've seen thousands of podpups get old, and they never become . . . techno sentient."

Terina realized what Katie was getting at. "So you're saying it's not a matter of age. That it's a phase?"

Beezan shook his head. "We've been around pups for

hundreds of years. And the pods on Azure were hundreds of years old when they were discovered."

Katie shrugged. "I don't want you to worry about it. Just be there for her."

"But Sky *is* different. She's so serious," Beezan said, staring off into space.

Katie nodded. "Maybe a little different. But nothing to worry about. She's serious, but she shows no signs of running off with your p'link—like a two-year-old Human would."

The aide who was helping Sky glanced over, looking concerned, so Beezan rushed over and collected her. "What's wrong, Sky?"

"Poking." She glared at the aide. "Asking. *Looking*." She hid her head in Beezan's chest.

"It's okay. All done. Good Sky. Let's go find a treat." And he headed for the door. "Thank you," he whispered to Katie, and nodded to Terina.

Terina watched them go, wild thoughts running through her mind. "But every set of pups has a matriarch, like a queen. And Sky is that matriarch, even though she's so young," she said to Katie, who nodded. "And if they have another phase, what could it be?"

Katie watched the other pups rollicking in their zone. "I have no idea. Will they be as aggressive as they are harmless now? And what will it do to the Humans bonded to them?"

11-Honor

Dragon's Den and western coast

Spring had arrived, in all its poetic glory, and the promised expedition to the coast set off. Melawn and his co-adventurers walked only an hour or so, just far enough to catch up with the carts which had left in the morning.

Ellant, AnnaLee's right hand, the expedition leader, called a halt. They really didn't need a rest yet, but Melawn noted they had just descended a small ridge and were now out of sight of the Dragon's Den. Ellant motioned for them to gather around. When people were situated, he put two fingers in his mouth and whistled, causing everyone to wince.

From out of nowhere, two Zann appeared and lightly ran to stand beside Ellant. "These are my scouts," he said. "This is Tepperzann." He nodded towards the older of the two, a woman, who was very lean but sturdy. "And this is Fezann." Fezann was a boy, probably no more than 10, graceful and less stocky than most of the Zann. Both were fully loaded with packs, bows and quivers, and spears that doubled as walking sticks.

"As you know," Ellant continued, "we'll be taking an inland route, rather than the known coastal route. Fez and Tep have scouted ahead." He paused and looked at them all sternly. "As you also know, I'm in charge of this expedition. Not 'in charge' like a committee chairperson. In charge—"

He looked at Halim, one of the aids, who said, "In charge, like a captain."

"That's right. So whatever agendas you have from other people, or yourselves, they are secondary to obeying me."

"Yes, honor," the spacers answered automatically, but DeeZann looked up at Melawn and scowled. Ellant nodded once, turned, and headed on, with the rest of them in his wake.

The expedition consisted of several Zann beast handlers, cart drivers, cooks, and support people, together outnumbering the scientists. The support people were divided into two groups, alternating as advance team and rear team, to be available to serve the expedition at all times.

Ellant had two assistants, former command crew of the *Dragonfly*. Melawn knew that Halim, a tall, middle-aged man, was the former head pilot of the *Dragonfly Dream*, who still retained the detached demeanor of a pilot. The other aid was Zonta, a big restless woman who seemed friendly. Head mechanic, Melawn remembered from the crew list. There were six scientists, Tenshi, Melawn, and DeeZann, who was a map-maker as well as botanist. And Benjai, Yuki, and Gowanan from *Dragonfly*, but Melawn didn't know their specialties, and no one had bothered to mention them.

After enduring the journey of the flags, Melawn didn't know how they could cross inland, but DeeZann assured him it was not like the desert side. "These are the plains where we get the beasts. There's grass, and they love this scrub." She kicked a scraggly bush with her thick boot. "Don't touch it. I don't know how they eat it. The spines are very strong—but they make good fuel."

Melawn made a mental note not to volunteer to collect fire-wood. DeeZann continued, "There is a lot more wildlife than you'd think. Besides the usual snakes, birds, and lizards feeding off the various sand insects, there are also small mammals. They're cute."

"There are wild beasts out here?" Tenshi asked.

"Oh yes, but they won't come close to a noisy group like this."

"So the beasts congregate near the water?" Tenshi asked.

"Oh, no. They're not that easy to round up. They can go a

long way between water. But don't worry. The scouts will know where the water is."

"Do you know them?" Melawn asked.

"The scouts? I've seen them."

"Do they know you?"

"Oh no. I'm not a Zann as far as they're concerned."

"Oh," Melawn felt bad for another impolite question. "I'm sorry."

"I'm not. The baby they traded will be treated as a Zann, and fit in. And I'm treated as a villager. It's fair."

"Humph," Tenshi said. "Zann, villagers, spacers, Dragons. There are too many divisions. We're forgetting we're all Human."

12-Honor

81-Petals, at Redrock a-rings

The Chike reappeared at the Redrock a-rings, where the Human ships had just lined up to enter. Beezan, in Pilot 1, in his brackets and cocoon, held his breath as the Chike ship approached *Pi Surfer* for this new "inspection."

Plan A was for *Pi Surfer*, *Wheel*, and *81-Petals* to pass inspection and jump, using the a-rings. All 3044 souls on the *81* were in jump chairs, possibly for a very long time. Beezan felt bad for their discomfort and worry.

The Chike ship approached *Pi Surfer* with a warning that went out to all of them: "Lesser ones: instructions / orders. Do not maneuver / move. Do not come between the ship and the gravity ball. Do not release any objects, people, or ships, for your own safety / life."

"Redrock Outbound Authority monitor reports they have the Chike Exempt on the com with them," Falcon relayed.

"Is that normal?" Iricana asked.

"No," Falcon answered. "Nothing about this is normal, even for the Chike."

Beezan realized why Iricana had requested Falcon for monitor. She was familiar with recent events in the sectors. He wished he knew what the Chike were inspecting for, and why they didn't just ask. As he understood it, Humans had been more than cooperative. Slowly, the Chike ship circled *Pi Surfer*, always keeping its nose toward *Pi* and the gravity ball away.

"Anything on our sensors or receivers?" Iricana asked Thunder.

"No Captain."

"Umm,"

"Speak up Jarvie," Iricana said crisply.

"Captain, my implants are buzzing."

"Other pilots?" Iricana asked.

"No."

"No."

"Nothing." Beezan wasn't concerned about his implants. He was distracted as Sky was whining again. He was wondering if he should have her tranked, as bad as he would feel about it. He had to focus.

The Chike ship completed two circles and smoothly backed away. "*Pi* ship is clear to proceed / leave."

Thank heavens! They all breathed a sigh of relief. Beezan's heart went from pounding out of his chest to mildly-heavy hammering.

Wheel moved into position next as *Pi Surfer* proceeded slowly to the a-rings. No one would be able to enter until they were all finished. Beezan breathed a prayer for Tiati, Hana, and their child. *Please, please let them go.*

Another long 45 minutes later, *Wheel* was cleared. Beezan would have cheered if they were not next, but hopes were high.

As soon as the Chike ship approached though, Sky started whining louder. "It's stronger," Jarvie said. "Almost painful."

"Wh—" Iricana started to ask. "You have Ramian implants!"

Oh, no. "But Sky doesn't," Beezan objected, even as Sky started to cry outright.

"What if they're inspecting for Ramian tech?" Thunder asked.

"Maybe Sky got some Ramian micro or nanobots on her somehow?" Terina suggested.

"How could they detect that?" Katie commented from the Passenger Lounge. "We can't even detect it from here."

"Bee, Bee, help," Sky begged.

Beezan couldn't stand it. "Please, Captain. We have at least 45 minutes. Let me take her to Med Bay."

"Katie? Can you meet him there?"

"I think I should go too, Captain," Jarvie said, obviously in pain.

"Yes, you too! Terina, get Sky. Beezan, take Jarvie. Sequoia, take over as pilot. Keep restraints in mind at all times!"

Terina, with Sky, and Katie pulled way ahead of him on the way to Med Bay, as Beezan dragged Jarvie along by the arm. "Just like old times," Beezan said.

"Don't remind me."

The Med Bay was empty except for a slightly sedated Ulf firmly strapped in an exam bed. Falcon reported, "The Chike are going to scan again! If we fail that scan, they will board!"

"Oh no," Katie said. "It must be the alien tech in Jarvie's head."

"Maybe we should remove it," Iricana said over the comm.

"No." Katie shook her head fiercely. "It would kill him."

"Better than being taken by the Chike!" Falcon said.

"We don't know that," Iricana said. Beezan knew that

Falcon didn't know about the colony, but there was no indication that the Chike were killing the Humans they took.

Falcon persisted. "And they don't take pups either. He'd have to—"

"Falcon!" Iricana cut in. "Monitor, please."

Beezan froze, devastated at the thought that if he went with Jarvie, he'd have to leave Sky. He suddenly realized how attached he was, even to the point of wondering if he could live without her. Her crying alone was making him crazy.

"Let's put her in the scanner," Katie said. "It might block the signals."

"Do we have a Human one?" Jarvie asked, holding his head.

"Yes. Terina, put Sky in there," she pointed, "with some water."

Katie slid another big scanning tube out of the wall. "We'll have to prep you for high gee. Get in and strap."

Beezan was useless, feeling some kind of primal panic running through his veins, until Terina closed the lid of the small scanner, isolating Sky. Gasping with relief, he went and looked in the top glass. She was limp, floating. He quickly checked the vitals. *She's okay*, he told himself. *Okay. Exhausted.*

"*Pi* and *Wheel* are entering the a-rings without us," Falcon announced.

Plan B already. *Godspeed Tiati.*

Meanwhile, Katie had strapped Jarvie in the tube and duct-taped a hydration pack and his s'link on him. "I made the arm cuffs loose, so you can slide your hands in and out. This may take some time."

"Thank you, doctor." Katie pressed the button to slide Jarvie inside and sealed the scanner. Both she and Beezan peered into the scanning tube from the top. Jarvie looked relieved and gave them a thumbs-up.

"Chike shuttle is approaching," Sequoia reported.

"Open the hangar!" Beezan ordered, forgetting he wasn't the Captain.

Katie slid Jarvie's whole unit back into its storage bay, behind the wall. "Medical robot," Katie ordered. "Priority order. Reassemble into a taller config right here. Attach yourself to the wall to cover those cracks and access panels." Terina assembled a pile of blankets around Sky's container and strapped them down.

"Shuttle is not heading for the hangar," Sequoia reported. Beezan had a wild hope that they'd changed their mind, but no. "It's going to land on top! Brace yourselves!"

Beezan just had time to dive for restraint straps, as Terina and Katie strapped down to exam beds. And for the second time in his life, an insane species landed a shuttle on his ship. "They're on the hub!" Ra'Tama shouted, as they jerked sickeningly in their restraints, creating instant nausea and headaches. The mass adjusters automatically slid out to compensate, making Beezan cringe. There was confusion in the Command Bay as Thunder and Sequoia fought to stabilize the ship.

Falcon came on. "Redrock orders us to submit to personal inspection. Do not resist under any circumstances."

"Four suited figures have emerged from the shuttle and are crossing the hub," Sequoia reported.

"Opening the top airlock," Thunder said.

"Katie," Iricana came on, sounding desperate. "Can you remove those implants?"

"No Captain."

"Can anyone?"

"No Human can do it."

"It could be his life."

"He'll die today if we try."

"Don't!" Beezan said. "If they take him, I'll go too."

Tears streamed down Beezan's face as he thought of leaving Sky, leaving the sectors, leaving humanity. But he knew he would do it, and in that moment, he realized that Jarvie really was family.

"Oh, no," Thunder whispered.

"Big screen," Terina called out, so the people in Med Bay could see what was happening on the hub. And there, standing on the hub, facing down the four suited Chike, was robot #9.

"God in heaven," Iricana whispered. "I thought the microbots were destroyed."

"There must have been both micro and nano builders," Thunder speculated.

"*81*," Iricana asked, "do we have direct contact with Robot #9?"

"If you are referring to the unauthorized robot config on the hull, I have created an interface."

"Tell it to stand down!"

"It does not recognize my authority."

"It's part of *Drumheller*!" Beezan said. "Let me talk to it!"

"A moment," *81* said, and Katie and Terina looked at Beezan with alarm.

"Trouble," Thunder whispered. "It's nanobalizing parts of *81* to make itself bigger."

"I am nogotiating. I have convinced the robot config that nanobalizing this ship endangers the crew."

"Oh, no," Ulf mumbled from his bed.

"*81!*" Beezan shouted.

"I do not have micro or nanobots under my control at the site. All have been . . . hijacked."

And suddenly, a wave of bots tumbled over the surface of the hull and engulfed the Chike shuttle. The four Chike turned in alarm, ran a few steps toward the shuttle, and then backed away, gesturing angrily.

The Redrock monitor was panicking. "You must not resist! All our lives could—"

"Redrock!" Iricana answered. "The bots are not under our control. Warn the Chike! They are rogue bots—rogue programming. We thought we had destroyed them. They're from an old encounter and have been stewing about it for 500 years!"

"Robot #9! Drumheller!" Beezan pleaded. "I order you to leave the shuttle alone. I order you to hide on the *81-Petals*!"

"Our orders are to protect." There were gasps all around as #9 responded.

"Azann is gone. The protect order is done. I am Beezan, Captain of the *Drumheller*. I am in command now."

"We do not recognize Beezan. Our orders are to protect."

The bots were not destroying the Chike shuttle. They were transforming it, rebuilding it into something else.

"Do no harm! It's the highest order. You may not harm Humans! Stand down!" Beezan said desperately.

"The Chike are not Humans. Protect!"

Ulf stirred on his exam bed. "You can't win."

"The shuttle is launching!" Falcon said, as the now-Human-looking shuttle deftly lifted off the hull. "Brace!" Beezan's head slammed against the restraints as the mass adjusters did their thing again.

"The *Wheel* is away!" Ra'Tama reported. "Jumped at only .18 JV!"

"Redrock says the Chike accuse us of having alien technology allowing the *Wheel* to jump," Falcon reported. "Captain! If you do not surrender, they're saying our entire crew will be quarantined and taken by the Chike!"

"Let me talk to the Chike directly!" Iricana asked. The

channel clicked. "Beezan! Get to the Command Bay! You'll have to freejump us out of here."

A voice came from Redrock Outbound Authority. "*81-Petals*, I'm going to declare your ship rogue, to protect everyone else."

"Commander, I understand. For the record, please, we didn't mean to resist."

By the time Beezan got to the Command Bay, the fleeing shuttle had morphed into a sleek rocket. "Oh, my God. Have they made a weapon?" he asked.

"Maybe," Sequoia answered, "but if they're aiming at the Chike ship, they're going to miss and hit that little gravity ball behind it."

Beezan remembered how that exploding gravity ball went down before. "We need to move!" Beezan shouted. "Chike or not! Ra'Tama, close all doors and blast the thrusters to warn the Chike off. Redrock! If that little gravity ball is destroyed we'll all be in danger."

"WARN THE CHIKE!" Iricana repeated to Redrock.

"Secure, secure," Thunder was chanting into the all-ship, as they felt a jolt from the thrusters.

"We're secure, Captain," Katie reported from the Med Bay.

"The Chike jet-packed off the hull, Captain," Ra'Tama reported.

"Sequoia, take us in Harbor direction, 1.5 gee. Go!" Iricana ordered.

Beezan was pressed back in his seat, head pounding and stomach churning, as he finished resealing his cocoon. He didn't even have time to get his brackets on. *Stay conscious!* He was going to have to get them to Harbor.

"Are they following?" Iricana asked.

"No, Captain. Look," Thunder put a new feed up. The bot rocket didn't destroy the gravity ball, it was transforming that too. It was morphing into something else. Even the color was changing.

"1.8 gee, if we can."

Redrock was panicked. They'd declared the *81* rogue and disowned them completely. The crew watched transfixed as the gravity ball became a giant yellow spider, legs pumping in creepy slow motion.

Beezan was about to pass out. The pain in his head was like a knife halfway down his spine. He gasped for air. This was a big jump. No one else could make it without the a-rings. But they had to get away. For Sky. For Jarvie.

Harbor. He imagined everyone on the ship with him, leaving that horrid space spider behind. And then they were in the path, leaving Redrock to their fate.

To be continued...

AFTERWORD

If you enjoyed this book, please consider leaving a review wherever you bought the book.

Thank you so much!

Chapter 1: Robot #9

Date: 12-Honor-1084 BE

81-Petals, incoming to Harbor System

Jarvie's eyes flew open when they dropped into normal space. He knew they were at Harbor, but he'd forgotten he was in the scanning tube, and it was only lit by his s'link. Immediate claustrophobic panic set in. He pulled his hands from the restraints and pounded on the tube with his forearms. "Let me out! *81!* Let me out!"

"Remain calm."

"Terina!"

"Jarvie, are you okay?" she answered over his p'link.

"I'm trapped in here!"

"Stay put! We're burn—"

Falcon's voice cut in. "All crew! Remain secure. We are burning for OSRI—the Outer Sector Research Institute, orbiting the fourth planet."

He wasn't in as much pain as he expected. Jarvie realized he must have received some pain meds during the jump. He pressed his hands against the dim curved walls to stay calm. *Breathe. Listen.*

Katie: "Captain, 47 yellow lights. No red lights."

Kelson: "Praise the Lord."

Iricana: "Beezan?"

Katie: "Yellow. Also no light for Jarvie."

Terina: "I've got Jarvie on comm. He's conscious."

Falcon: "Captain, I have Harbor Inbound Authority for you."

Iricana: "H.I.A., *Drumheller*. We are incoming from Redrock. Urgent! Do you have Chike in system?"

H.I.A.: "Not unless you brought them with you."

Iricana: "They may be right behind us. I need an emergency secure link with the council and OSRI command."

H.I.A.: "Stand by."

H.I.A.: "*Drumheller*, please provide your departure clearance."

Iricana: "We're not aware of the requirement for any clearance."

H.I.A.: "You should have been provided a code when you entered the a-rings."

Iricana: "H.I.A., we made an emergency jump. We don't have a code."

H.I.A.: "Very well. Send your departure log."

Falcon: "Stand by."

Falcon: "Captain, there's a giant yellow spider on the departure log!"

Thunder: "And being declared rogue."

Iricana: "There's no hiding it. Send it. Tell them it might take some explaining."

Iricana: "Sequoia, run the spin-up."

There was a clamoring of voices, and of the sucking sound of helmets being pulled off. "What was that yellow gravity ball thing?" "What will happen to Redrock?" "How close behind us?" "How much time?" "20 hours to OSRI." "We won't make it if the Chike are after us."

81: **"Burns complete. Stand down from blue zones."**

Iricana: "Please. Thunder, can you get Beezan to the Med Bay?"

Thunder: "Yes, Captain."

Iricana: "We'll reconvene in the Consultation Hall in thirty minutes."

As soon as the spin-up was complete, Terina crawled out of her cocoon. Ducking down, she released Star and Rocket. "Come on!" The three of them took off down the rimway, Terina racing to help Jarvie, the pups in excited chase. She almost slipped past the Med Bay stairway in her socks, grabbing the holdbar and reeling up. She beat Katie and the other med personnel; the only person there was Ulf, still strapped in his exam bed.

Terina faced the medbot guarding Jarvie's hiding spot. "Medbot, move." A light blinked on. "Medbot, stand over there," she pointed. It didn't budge.

"It's not going to obey you," Ulf grumbled.

"Why? I tell it what to do all the time."

Ulf sighed. "The doctor gave it a priority order. It requires authorization from the same person, unless you have an override code."

"*81*, please tell the medbot to obey me," Terina requested.

"Stand by."

"*81*?" Ulf asked, confused. "As in *81-Petals*? I thought we were on the *Drumheller*? Am I hallucinating?"

"No. Look around!" Terina was getting frustrated. But she remembered that Ulf hadn't been in his right mind all this time and tried to be more compassionate. "Sorry. This is the *81-Petals.* The *Drumheller* is just a cover name for the Ship Tracker."

Ulf unbuckled and sat up, looking around in awe. "*81-Petals?* The most advanced AI in—"

"Make way!" Katie, Thunder, and a med crew came charging up the stairs with two stretchers. Terina rushed to the exam beds and pulled two more down. "Hang on Jarvie. You'll be out of there soon!"

Terina helped get Beezan settled and stood next to him as Roza, the Tundra medtech, did an initial reading. While Katie tended to the other patient, Thunder headed back to the Command Bay. "He's probably just wandering," Katie called over.

"Pulse is way up though," Roza said.

"Terina, please get Sky out of the podpup scanner," Katie said.

Terina unburied the podpup scanner and peered in. Sky's readings were good, except her pulse was also up. Carefully, Terina opened it and scooped her out. She tiptoed back to Beezan and nestled her in his arm. Beezan's pulse immediately started to go down. Roza smiled and said, "Podpup cure." And then they were bombarded by Star and Rocket wanting to jump up onto the bed. "And the podpup curse!"

"I'll take them out. Doctor?" Terina called over her shoulder to ask Katie to move the medbot, but it was already moved, and Ulf was helping Jarvie out.

"Thank you!" Jarvie said, actually hugging Ulf, to his surprise.

"Sorry Jarvie! I was getting there! I'll take care of these two and see you at the meeting."

"Meeting. Right," Jarvie staggered behind her.

After unloading the unruly pups, Terina got her uniform on and went back to the Med Bay to help before the meeting. While she waited for instructions from Katie, Ulf whispered to her, "Where are we?"

"Harbor." Terina edged closer to Ulf while keeping an eye on Honor Beezan and Sky.

"How did we get here?"

"Jumped from Redrock."

"Redrock? I don't remember."

"You've been . . . confused. Adisa and Sho have been here every day, working with you."

He frowned and blinked, as if to clear his mind. "Harbor, Redrock . . ."

"Hamada, RJ, Tyee, Tetra, Tanuki, Tundra." He flinched when she said Tundra. *So he does remember his attachment to the Tundra AI.*

"Seven jumps. So many. So you're using the *Drumheller* call sign to be incognito. But what if the *Drumheller* shows up?"

Beezan started to toss and turn, "*Drumheller?*" he mumbled.

"It won't," she said sadly and lowered her voice, glancing at Honor Beezan. "We had to leave it behind when we found the *81.* Way out there."

"Oh, I see," Ulf said, looking at Beezan with real compassion. "I understand." He nodded and got back on his bed.

Beezan was calm for the moment, so Terina hung around while Katie scanned Sky. "There's nothing," the doctor reported. "No alien tech, no microbots, nothing." Holding her hand on Sky's side and peering at her scanner, she added, "But her pulse is up. She's agitated or in pain, even though she's asleep."

"No. No. *Drumheller,*" Beezan mumbled. "Sky."

"He's agitated too," Terina said.

"Put Sky back with him," Katie whispered. "Then you can get to the meeting. Thanks for helping."

"Yes, doctor."

"Falcon to Med Bay."

"Katie here," she said quietly.

"Doctor, we're going to do another burn in about five hours. No chairs, but everyone will need to be secure. Just giving you a heads up so Med Bays won't be blasted with multiple announcements."

"Thank you." Katie glanced at her sleeping patients as Terina lingered by the stairs. "Why?"

"Because of the nanos," Falcon answered. "Harbor Inbound Authority declared a clean zone. We can't dock. We'll have to go into a wide orbit."

Katie frowned. "Understood. Thank you."

Terina came back over. "Does that mean we can't dock *anywhere?*"

"I—well, there must be a way to sort it out."

"There was a movie once," Terina told her. "About a ship infected with bad nanos. Did you see it?"

"No," Katie said. "What happened?"

"I don't know. Mom wouldn't let us watch."

"*Nanexile,*" Maura was saying, looking at her p'link, just as Terina got to the meeting.

That's it! she thought. *The name of the movie.*

"Should we remove it from the catalog?" Iricana asked the assembled command crew.

"Way too late," Maura answered. "It's already hit the junk news."

"Can someone give me a summary?" Iricana asked.

"I've seen it," Jarvie answered, and Iricana nodded at him to go on. "Well, it's science fiction. They had these really powerful nanos that could do anything. Some of the nanos went rogue and took over a big ship. So the ship got exiled. They couldn't dock anywhere. So they jumped—using freejumping, even though no one could freejump then. They went from system to system, looking for a new home. It became a generation ship and all this strange cultural stuff happened. But they never found a good, uninhabited, planet to settle on.

"So the ship starts to break down, because it's several thousand years old. The secret group of people, the only ones who know the truth about the ship, decide to program it to fly into a star.

"But some people find out and they rebel and steal a shuttle and land on this ocean planet that can't sustain Human life. But the nanos rebuild the whole planet for Humans, destroying the original marine civilization."

"And?" Kelson asked.

"That's the end."

"Genocide is the end?" Iricana asked.

"I think it was meant to be a cautionary tale," Jarvie shrugged. "But it's just a story. We don't have nanos like that."

Thunder spoke up in a grave voice, "We do now."

What You Win: Stories for the Whole Family

• How can Mica compete at the science fair when parents are helping the other kids?

• Niccolo doesn't want to play in the symphony this summer, but can he bring himself to blow the audition?

• How will Jenna and Abby ever become astronauts if they're stuck on the farm, and lost in the maize?

From silly to serious, here are sixteen hopeful stories about walking your own path, finding friends, and fighting everyday battles.

ACKNOWLEDGMENTS

Thank you to everyone who read books 1-2, who bought the books, who wrote reviews, and who liked them on Facebook. Every little thing has helped the Sundering Series on its journey in the self-publishing world.

Special thanks to Brian Burriston and Raeleigh Price for proofreading and encouragement.

Thanks to the Brilliant Star Magazine Crew, past and present, for your support and mentoring in the Bahá'í writing world: Amethel Parel-Sewell, Amy Renshaw, Susan Engle, Annie Reneau, C. Aaron Kreader, Heidi Parsons, Katie Bishop, Foad Ghorbani, Lisa Blecker, Darcy Greenwood, and Dr. Stephen Scotti.

To spaceship designer and artist Tom Edwards of TomEdwardsDesign, thank you so much for bringing the *Drumheller*, the *Cheetah*, the *Watcher*, and now the *Sandstorm* to life.

And to Jeff Price, Don Burriston, Shirlie Burriston, Jordan Price, and the rest of my family all over the world, thank you for all your support and encouragement over the years.

-DRP

ABOUT THE AUTHOR

A native of Earth, D Rae Price lives in the San Francisco Bay Area with her family. She has a bachelor's degree in astronomy, but spent her class time thinking up space adventures instead of thesis topics. In real life, she's looking forward to the Lucy mission flybys of Trojan asteroids and finding out more about the origins of our solar system.

For updates, please join my mailing list:
https://www.draepricebooks.com/contact

amazon.com/stores/D-Rae-Price/author/B09QLLDSCX
goodreads.com/drp99
facebook.com/DRaePriceBooks
instagram.com/draepricebooks
bsky.app/profile/draepricebooks.bsky.social
x.com/DRP191

NOTES

1. COMING APART

1. Bahá'u'lláh, Gleanings from the Writings of Bahá'u'lláh, pp. 46-47 www.bahai.org/r/896595428

2. NO HAVEN AT SEVEN

1. Baha'u'llah, Gleanings from the Writings of Baha'u'llah, p. 323 www.bahai.org/r/260091024
2. 'Abdu'l-Bahá, Paris Talks, p. 108 www.bahai.org/r/010271882

5. THE 81-PETALS

1. The Universal House of Justice, 3 November 1980 www.bahai.org/r/684355342

6. THE SPHERE OF DESTRUCTION

1. Bahá'u'lláh, Prayers and Meditations, p. 216 www.bahai.org/r/829431181
2. The Báb, Selections, p. 181 www.bahai.org/r/477196506

8. THE WATCHER

1. The Báb, Selections from the Writings of the Báb, p. 173 www.bahai.org/r/737252777
2. 'Abdu'l-Bahá, Paris Talks, p. 29 www.bahai.org/r/512608651

10. THE RED FLAG

1. "O GOD, my God! Thou seest me enraptured and attracted toward Thy glorious kingdom, enkindled with the fire of Thy love amongst mankind, a

herald of Thy kingdom in these vast and spacious lands, severed from aught else save Thee, relying on Thee, abandoning rest and comfort, remote from my native home, a wanderer in these regions, a stranger fallen upon the ground, humble before Thine exalted threshold, submissive toward the heaven of Thine omnipotent glory, supplicating Thee in the dead of night and at the break of dawn, entreating and invoking Thee at morn and at eventide to graciously aid me to serve Thy Cause, to spread abroad Thy teachings and to exalt Thy Word throughout the East and the West.

O Lord! Strengthen my back, enable me to serve Thee with the utmost endeavor, and leave me not to myself, lonely and helpless in these regions.

O Lord! Grant me communion with Thee in my loneliness, and be my companion in these foreign lands.

Verily, Thou art the Confirmer of whomsoever Thou willest in that which Thou desirest, and, verily, Thou art the All-Powerful, the Omnipotent."

—'Abdu'l-Bahá, Tablets of the Divine Plan, p. 46
www.bahai.org/r/851830797

18. FIRE IN THE PATH

1. Baha'u'llah, Tablets of Baha'u'llah, p. 67
www.bahai.org/r/327958234

21. HOPE AND SALVATION

1. Baha'u'llah, Gems of Divine Mysteries, p. 66
www.bahai.org/r/731075255

23. LIFE IN PARADISE

1. The Báb, Selections from the Writings of the Báb, p. 148
www.bahai.org/r/464816503

24. SWING JUMPS

1. 'Abdu'l-Bahá, The Promulgation of Universal Peace, p. 27
www.bahai.org/r/075454706
2. Baha'u'llah, Gleanings from the Writings of Baha'u'llah, p. 118
www.bahai.org/r/978731768
3. 'Abdu'l-Bahá, A Traveller's Narrative, p. 79
www.bahai.org/r/037150047

26. THE REALM OF HEAVEN

1. 'Abdu'l-Bahá, Selections, p. 202
   www.bahai.org/r/274256520

31. UPHEAVALS

1. 'On the appearance of fearful natural events call ye to mind the might and
   majesty of your Lord, He Who heareth and seeth all, and say "Dominion is
   God's, the Lord of the seen and the unseen, the Lord of creation."'
   —Baha'u'llah, The Kitáb-i-Aqdas, paragraph 111
   www.bahai.org/r/377376846

32. WHEEL OF FIRE

1. Bahá'u'lláh, The Arabic Hidden words, #17
   www.bahai.org/r/176729752
2. Baha'u'llah, Gleanings from the Writings of Baha'u'llah, p. 148
   www.bahai.org/r/495621509

34. TRAVERSING THE KINGDOMS

1. Baha'u'llah, The Kitáb-i-Íqán
   www.bahai.org/r/636051742
2. Words of 'Abdu'l-Bahá: Star of the West, Vol. 8, No. 8, p. 104, August 11, 1917
   https://bahai-library.com/pdf/sw/SW_Volume8.pdf